Confession duet

KD Robichaux

BEFORE THE LIE
TRUTH REVEALED

Before the Lie Production Crew

Editing by Hot Tree Editing
www.hottreeediting.com

Cover Design and
Formatting by Pink Ink Designs
www.pinkinkdesigns.com

Cover Photography by FuriousFotog
www.onefuriousfotog.com

Cover Model: Matthew Hosea

Note:
This story is not suitable for persons under the age of 18.

*Potential triggers lie within this book

BEFORE THE lie

CONFESSION DUET

KD Robichaux

Also by KD Robichaux

The Blogger Diaries Trilogy:
Wished for You
Wish He was You
Wish Come True
The Blogger Diaries Trilogy Boxed Set

Standalones:
No Trespassing

Anthologies:
Tempting Scrooge

The Confession Duet:
Before the Lie
Truth Revealed

BEFORE THE *lie*

BEFORE THE

BEFORE THE

BEFORE THE

RE THE

BEFORE THE *lie*

BEFORE THE *lie*

Prologue

A HAND CLAMPS OVER MY mouth, and his full weight presses against my face, shoving my head into the pillow.

I had been dead asleep, but I'm fully awake now, panic rising within me like lava to the surface, wanting to burst forth through a scream that has no way out.

I claw at his arm, twisting my hips beneath him, but it only seems to help him remove my leggings and underwear, as he yanks at them with his free hand.

So fucking strong. I can't push him off.

My legs. My legs are my biggest source of strength. If I can just....

Naked from the waist down, still pinned in place by the hand over my mouth, I bring my feet up and push my heels against his bare hips, kicking with all my might.

It does nothing.

He rotates his pelvis enough to dislodge my feet and works his body between my thighs. No matter how hard I try to keep them clamped together, I'm no match for the man on top of me.

I begin to cry, realizing this is going to happen. No matter how hard I fight, I will not be able to stop him.

I shouldn't be here.

I only stayed because of the story my husband told me, about his girlfriend in high school who died when she vomited in her sleep. I grew up sheltered, without any alcohol in the house. I drank nothing my whole life except for a sip of wine every Sunday at church during communion. So in my head, liquor was bad. It brought nothing but bad.

My friend had been drinking, and with that damn story in my head, I couldn't very well leave my friend alone. What if it happened to him?

So I stayed. So I could be there to wake him up if he got sick in his sleep.

And now, as he shoves himself inside me, ripping me open as I wail behind his hand...

I wish I'd just left him to die.

One

Vi

Three years earlier...

I'M HANGING ON BY THE TIPS of my fingers and my big toes, clinging with a strength no one really thinks I have until they see it with their own two eyes. I feel a single drop of sweat trickle its way from my hairline, down my temple and cheek, until it finally drops off my jaw. Breathing in deep through my nose, the familiar and comforting scent of rubber I've grown to love fills my lungs. I breathe it out through my mouth before sucking it in once more as I make my move. With a burst of energy shooting me skyward, I leap from my perch on the crimper rocks screwed to the 90-degree wall and dyno to the much larger handgrip three feet above my head, grabbing onto it with perfect timing before finding two more to rest my toes on once again.

The dyno. A move in rock climbing that takes an obscene

amount of practice. It's a leap of faith, basically. You jump, hoping your grip lands on its targeted rock with enough strength to catch yourself with one hand before you fall to your death, or in this case, to the regrind—ground up recycled tires—that cushion your landing.

The smell of rubber, sweat, and hand chalk permeates the rock gym I call my home away from home. I wake up early every morning to shower it out of my hair, where it's clung to me and followed me home, only for it to reattach itself that same afternoon. The eight hours of sleep I get each night, solid and restful from the physical exhaustion I earn every evening, followed by the seven hours I spend at my high school finishing up my senior year, are the only hours during the course of a day that I don't spend here, at Rock On rock gym. It's only six minutes away from school, and fifteen from home, and the only reason I leave at night is because they close and lock down the place at 9:00 p.m. So for six blissful hours each day—from the moment the last bell rings, until the owners of the gym, Mr. and Mrs. Burrell, flash the overhead fluorescent lights to signal closing time—I get to spend it in my happy place, the only place in the world where I actually feel accomplished, good at something. No... amazing, truly talented at something.

It was by pure coincidence we discovered my hidden talent. My first boyfriend, Jax, invited me to go rock climbing with him here for one of our first dates when we were freshmen. At first, I didn't want to go. I'm the least athletic person on the face of the planet. At that point in time, I couldn't touch my toes. PE was a joke. I purposely forgot my gym clothes most of the time so I could just do health assignments instead of participating in class, and when it was time for testing, I would walk the mile run.

I always felt awkward and gangly, with my long, skinny arms and legs, and I was embarrassed to do anything physical in front of my classmates.

So no, I didn't want to go with my super cute blond-haired, blue-eyed boyfriend to the place he spent so many hours at after school. I couldn't understand why he liked it either. He was kinda nerdy like me. But rather than loving books and English class like I did, he preferred computers, and his giant bass in band. After his mother called mine to confirm mutual permission for this date, even my mom tried to reason with me.

"Vi, baby, you might like it. You should try everything once. You never know. You gave up on piano lessons and ballet class, and you haven't signed up to do any more plays after the one you did in eighth grade. So at least go see what this rock climbing stuff is all about," she persisted.

In the end, it was Jax's sister, Maddy, who talked me into going. She loved it as much as he did, and she was my body type, long-limbed and bony, not an ounce of muscle on her scrawny yet tall frame. "I don't like sports," she confessed, "but I love climbing. No balls flying at your face. No running. Just you and the rocks, at your own pace and skill level."

So I gave in. There were no buses at our private school, so when my mom picked me up from school on that crisp winter day, we followed Jax's mom's car until we arrived at the brick building just a few minutes away. The sign at the top looked like a man hanging from the roof by his hand and a harness, the bold letters next to him spelling out *Rock On* with a picture of the well-known hand signal of a pinky and forefinger pointing upward. I grabbed my bag containing the stretch pants and T-shirt Maddy told me to bring to change into out of our school uniform of white polo shirt and khaki dress pants. The four of us—my mom, Jax, Maddy, and me—made our way in through the glass door, the bell attached to the top jamb ringing loudly to announce our presence. Jax waved at his mom as she drove out of the lot. Apparently, she just dropped them off every day, and picked them up at whatever time they set.

It was the smell that hit me first. It was overwhelming. It smelled like the place my parents always went when they had to get new tires, but it was mixed with body odor and something else I couldn't put my finger on. I could feel it in the air though, like the oxygen itself was coating my skin.

Then I took in the interior of the massive structure. It was like they had taken a gutted warehouse and then built random giant foot-thick, ceiling-high walls throughout the space, and then poked holes all over them. Half the holes I saw were covered with multi-colored handholds. Most of the walls stood straight up, but others were angled, and as I peeked around one of the huge straight ones, I saw that the outer edge of the building was lined with one continuous wall of various angles and depths, and it led to a cave, an *actual* cave. Even its ceiling was covered in colorful rocks.

We walked up to the front desk, which was really a long glass display case that showcased all sorts of equipment. I had no idea what any of it was used for. Behind the middle-aged woman greeting us with a friendly smile, there was a wall of shoeboxes, racks of T-shirts, harnesses, cute little colorful bags, and rope.

"Hey, kiddos. Y'all brought a new friend today, I see. How are you, sweetheart?" she asked, turning to me, and I gave her a nervous smile.

"I'm pretty good. Just a little scared," I admitted, and she waved one hand, pushing a clipboard toward my mom, while Jax and Maddy signed their names on another.

"Oh, there's nothing to be scared of. This is meant to be fun. And if you listen to your friends and follow their instructions, they'll teach you how to not hurt yourself," she told me, pointing a pen at my boyfriend and his sister. "Now, if you want to learn to belay, just come and let me know. It's ten dollars for the twenty-minute class and includes rental of one harness for the student." When I looked at her confused, she chuckled. "Getting ahead of myself, hun. That's only if you want to get on the ropes and climb up, not over."

"Think we're just going to boulder today, Mrs. Burrell," Jaxon told her, and to me, he clarified, "That's when you climb sideways, just a little bit up the wall. No ropes or anything. There's a line marking all the walls at eight feet. Not allowed to go up past that without being in a harness."

I nodded then watched my mom sign her name at the bottom of the waiver after filling out all our information. She handed the clipboard back to Mrs. Burrell then smiled at me, rubbing my back briefly when she saw the nerves clearly written all over my face. *Fun*, she mouthed, and I rolled my eyes before shaking my head.

"Come on, Vi! Let's go get changed," Maddy called, skipping toward a set of bathrooms in the corner, so I took hold of my bag and followed after her.

An hour later, with my rented climbing shoes on my feet and chalk bag tied around my waist, dangling over my butt like a tail, and after some simple instructions, like correct foot position—always with the inside of your foot facing the wall—all my nervousness had disappeared and was replaced by a sense of assuredness. Mrs. Burrell even came over to where my mom was sitting on the worn-out, chalk-covered couch in the center of the gym, and I overheard her say that I was a natural. I was damn near keeping up with Jax and Maddy, although they stopped frequently to teach me better techniques to make getting across the wall even simpler for me.

That was the whole thing. I discovered rock climbing didn't require that much strength if you had technique. And with my long reach and small body weight, bouldering was easy enough not to be discouraging, but challenging enough that I wanted to conquer it. Jax told me that climbing upward would be a different story. Technique would still be a big part of it, but I'd need to work on my strength just to be able to pull my body weight up to the next rock. Luckily, I had pretty strong legs from the years of ballet I had taken, but gave up on when I got too self-conscious to wear a leotard in front of people. So until I had more power in my upper body, I could use my legs to push myself up when I needed to.

By the end of the night, I was hooked, and seeing how much fun I had, my mom went ahead and paid for a monthlong membership after I promised I would make use of it. That monthly membership eventually turned into a yearly one, and here it was four years later.

Jaxon and I had broken up just a few months after I started climbing. We realized we were great friends, but there wasn't anything there as far as chemistry. Whatever chemistry could be had by fourteen-year-olds. We continued to climb together often, but where he was ambitious about climbing outdoors, I really had no desire to leave the gym. The rocks changed positions every couple of months, so the routes were always different. And

I still preferred bouldering to climbing, no hindrances of ropes and harnesses, just me, the walls, and my Prana chalk bag—a Christmas gift from my big brother. I loved it as much as if he handed me a Louis Vuitton.

The bells over the door jingle on the other side of the gym, pulling me out of my memories. I don't look over to see who it is, figuring it's just another one of the regulars who will come say hi to me after they sign in. Instead, I walk to the wall directly in front of that same old worn-out, chalk-covered couch my mom is sunk into, where she's reading the latest Nora Roberts book. Even after all this time, she refuses to just drop me off. She stays the whole time, six hours a day, my biggest fan and greatest cheerleader. She even learned to belay soon after I made climbing a hobby I was going to stick with. So whenever I'm going up on the ropes, she puts on her own harness, hooks herself to the line and carabiner attached to the floor. One end of the rope loops through an anchor in the top of the rock wall that threads through her belay device, and she'll wait for me to tie my own harness to the other end of the same rope. We've done it so many times now that we do it more through mindless muscle memory than anything else. I can't even count how many 8-knots I've tied in the last four years.

"Momma, mark me," I call over to her, and hand her a piece of sidewalk chalk when she walks over to where I stand in front of the wall.

"Any requests?" she asks, making her way to the far left end of the blue-painted wall, which already has tons of markings all over it from people making their own routes.

"Hmmm... I need to practice squatted positions, so make it a low route," I tell her, and she begins circling hand and foot holds until she's all the way to the right end of the wall.

"There you go, doll." She hands me back the chalk stick, and I put it in my chalk bag dangling over my butt, reaching in farther to coat one hand and then the other in the sweat-absorbing powder.

"Thanks, Mom. That middle part is going to be a bitch," I point out, biting the inside of my cheek and trying to figure out how I'm going to make it from one set of crimpers (tiny rocks you can only grasp with your fingertips) to another without any jugs or mini-jugs (larger rocks that are easy to grab with your whole hand) in between.

"You got it. Take your time," she encourages, and I blow out a breath, taking up my start position at the beginning of the route.

I've fallen six times trying to make it from the first set of crimpers to the next, and I'm about to make my seventh attempt, when I hear, "Spidergirl!" yelled from the front of the gym, breaking my concentration, and my left foot slips off its precarious perch on a chip the size of a quarter. I get my legs under me just in time to land in a squat rather than on my ass.

"Dammit," I hiss, but then out loud, I reply, "Yeah, Sierra?"

"We have two newbs. Will you give them their belay lessons, please? I'd do it, but I'm in the middle of feeding little man his dinner." Sierra is the owners' daughter-in-law. She runs the office in the evenings now, and instead of putting her new baby in day care, she just brings him along with her to work. I spend lots of my breaks holding the adorable little guy. I don't work here, but I'm a part of the climbing team, so we often give the belay lessons to people who sign up for them. An actual employee just has to give them a final test before the climber earns their certification.

"Coming!" I call, and start making my way to the front, clapping and rubbing my hands together to shake off the remaining chalk. I'm almost near the entrance, when the tingling in my nose starts, and as it creeps up the back of my eyes, I know it's going to be a doozy. I stop where I am, look up into the fluorescent lights, and let it rip. *"Achoo!"* I sneeze, my feet coming off the ground with its force as I cover my face with my hands.

"I'd give that one an eight out of ten," Sierra scores, a long-standing tradition the regulars have when we sneeze from all the chalk in the air.

But then I hear the sexiest deep voice add, "Bless you," and that's when I finally look up at the newbs.

With my hands still covering my face, I peek over my fingers and take in the two men standing at the glass display case that Sierra is currently behind, baby Alaric hidden beneath a nursing blanket with just his tiny feet poking out. One of the men is super tall, probably 6'5", with a military haircut and kind eyes. But my eyes only land on him briefly before they lock on the ones belonging to his friend.

My heart pounds in my chest and I can't seem to take in enough oxygen as I watch his dark brown eyes trail down my body. His gaze travels from the top of my high ponytail to the black toes of my climbing shoes then back up to meet my green eyes, still the only thing visible of my face behind my palms. He's not tall, especially compared to his friend, maybe just a couple inches taller than me, but his body, dressed in a black wife beater, basketball shorts, and tennis shoes, looks like it was chiseled by Michelangelo himself.

Tattoos cover his arms and the upper part of his chest I can see above the neck of his shirt, and his head is shaved. But with as much as there is to take in, it's those gorgeous chocolate eyes that hold my attention. They're sucking me in, and I can't for the life of me look away or even move.

It's not until Sierra chuckles "She says thank you" that I finally snap out of it.

"Umm... hold that thought," I say, and jog to the bathroom in the corner. I get some tissue and blow my nose, and then wash my hands at the sink, glancing at myself in the mirror.

Jesus, I look horrendous. I have white streaks of chalk from my scalp down to my knees, and the mascara I put on this morning before school seems to be everywhere but on my eyelashes from sweating. I wet a paper towel and clean up the black smudges, but as I take in my red tank top and black spandex shorts, I know there's really nothing else I can do for my appearance.

I have no idea what I'm so worried about. I've never cared before what other people thought of my looks while I'm here in my happy place. It's the one place I'm never self-conscious. In my head, it doesn't matter what I look like, because my confidence in my talent radiates outward and disguises the fact I look like I crawled out of a swamp.

But that guy out there... I have never before experienced what I felt under his gaze. What the hell was that? Part of me wants to hide in the bathroom until I can sneak out and escape past them, but another part wants to hurry up and dry my hands so I can get back out there to *him*. Knowing there would be no way to signal my mom sitting on the other side of the gym if I tried to make a run for it, I go with the second option, using a couple paper towels before tossing them in the trashcan and yanking open the bathroom door.

When I get back to everyone, the guys are sitting on a bench in the shop area, lacing up their rental shoes. I walk behind the counter and grab my harness from where I keep it in one of ten cubbies reserved for the competition climbing team, carrying it over to the shop.

The tall one finishes first and looks up at me where I stand a few feet away. "Damn, that thing is way cooler than the one I've got," he jokes, holding up the plain black rental harness.

I smile, and look down at my personal harness in my hand. Another gift from my older brother, Henry. He was so excited when he learned that his baby sister was really getting into a sport that he went all out and got me a chalk bag, harness, and top of the line climbing shoes so I could stop renting the ones here at Rock On. He told me, "Now that you have all your own gear, you're a *real* climber, and you can't just give up on it like you did everything else." I had rolled my eyes but attacked his cheek with a hundred kisses, thanking him profusely.

The gear didn't come cheap. The harness is thickly padded around the waist and legs, and is obscenely comfortable, even while hanging for long periods of time. It's black on the outside and neon purple on the inside, with the same purple color thread stitched throughout the black. My climbing shoes are pure black brushed leather, streamline and sleek, fitting my feet like a glove. They feel almost like a soft-sole moccasin, but they lace up the top like a tennis shoe and have thick and hard places along the toes and outside edges. The shoes bend with your feet, but also protect them when pressed into a rock. You don't wear socks with your climbing shoes, which equals the stench of "sweaty pedis" as Sierra calls them, hence the never-ending supply of Lysol on the counter near the shoe drop-off table.

"Don't worry. Yours will still keep you up on the rope. Your junk just won't be as comfortable," I reply to Tall Guy, and he laughs, holding out his hand.

"Glover. Nice to meet you...." he prompts.

"Glover? Oh, you're military, huh? That's your last name?" I ask, placing my hand in his. We get quite a few Army guys in here for PT, since our small town is right next to Ft. Vanter, but I've never really hung out with anyone in the military except for Henry, who is in the Navy, stationed in Charleston.

"Oh, yeah. Sorry. Haven't been out in the civilian world that much in the past year. I was just stationed here right out of boot camp. Haven't used my first name in a while. I'm Brian," he tells me, and I smile.

"Nice to meet you, Brian. I'm Vivian, but most people call me Vi." As I pull my hand from his, his friend comes to stand next to him, and I feel his presence like I've stuck my hand on a doorknob after skidding my socked feet over a carpeted floor. I look down, and sure enough, the blonde hairs on my arms are standing up.

"I'm Corbin," he says, and he holds out his hand.

I hesitate for a moment, scared of what my body's reaction might be if I touch him; it's already acting strange just being near him. But I don't want to seem rude, so I timidly rest my fingers against his palm, and then feel his close around them. My breath catches as my heart stops for a moment, then restarts as if I've been shocked back to life. I feel his warmth blanket every cell of my body, along with a sense of excitement coated in complete calm. "H... hi."

All I can do is stand there, my hand in his, and I stare into those intense, mesmerizing dark eyes, entranced by the feelings roiling through me. He seems to be just as hypnotized, his breath coming and going deeply through his flared nostrils.

"Sir," I hear Brian say, seemingly from far away. "Um, Specialist Lowe?"

"Just Corbin," he says, his lips barely moving, his eyes never wavering from mine.

"Okay then. Corbin, you um... Sorry, sir. But uh, you ready to climb?" Brian asks, and a spark of confusion pulls me out of my trance.

My brows lower and I glance up at Brian, who towers over us, then focus back on Corbin. "Sir?" I prompt, and his eyes flare and his hand tightens around mine briefly before letting go.

"Yeah, he's basically my boss. I'm a Private, or a 'cherry' as they keep calling me, and he's a Specialist, three ranks higher than me," Brian explains.

"Oh. Cool. So um, are y'all ready to learn how to belay?" I ask, taking a step back, trying to get a little farther away from the intensity of the man in front of me. This pulls a chuckle from Brian, and my face heats.

"Yeah, little lady. Teach us how to belay," he says, not bothering to hide the sarcasm in his voice.

It strikes a match inside me, slightly offending me, but instead of responding, I decide to save it for the rocks. They may see me as a 'little lady' now, but I'll show them.

BEFORE THE *lie*

Two

Vi

STANDING AT THE BEGINNERS' wall, which is covered in nothing but jug grips, I step into my harness and pull the waist-strap tight, waiting for them to put on their own. I can't help but let my eyes wander over Corbin as he adjusts his thigh straps, pulling at his shorts where they rode up his legs when he pulled his harness up. I assume Brian gets his on fine, but I wouldn't be able to swear on it, because my gaze is like metal, attaching itself to Corbin as if he were a magnet.

"Okay, so who wants to be the belayer, and who wants to be the climber first?" I ask, and Corbin answers, "I'll belay first," coming to stand close to me where I'm holding onto the anchor attached to the floor.

"All right, so this attaches to your harness... um... there," I begin, pointing at the belayer's loop at the front of his harness, feeling my cheeks heat once again. I don't understand what is with me around this guy. Usually, I just snap the carabiner onto the loop, without even thinking about how close it is to someone's... private area. But with him, instead, I hand over the metal shackle with its spring-loaded gate and allow him to hook it on himself. "And it anchors you to the floor. That way if someone much larger than you is climbing, you won't end up trading places in the air."

I move over to Brian, taking hold of one end of the doubled-over rope hanging from its anchor at the top of the rock wall. "Okay, climber." I glance up at Corbin to make sure he's watching, so he'll know what to do when it's his turn, finding his eyes burning into me before lowering them to the rope in my hands. I clear my throat, trying to free my airway, because suddenly it's hard to breathe. "Um... so the climber will take one end of the rope, and measure out enough length that it goes from your fist to your opposite shoulder. So do that," I instruct, and Brian's long wingspan measures out his rope. "Now you tie an 8-knot at that length."

"Oh, I got this," Brian says excitedly, and I watch closely as he ties the rope into a perfect 8-knot.

"Good, now, you thread it through the two horizontal loops that sandwich the vertical belayer's loop. Yep, just like that, and you're going to make your knot into a double by lacing the end of the rope through and following the line of your eight. Perfect. Wow, this is so much easier than teaching a civilian." I laugh, and then add, "Now just finish it off with a safety knot at the top, and you're done." He quickly ties the simple knot above the more intricate one, and his part is complete.

I take the two steps back over to Corbin, dragging the second half of the rope with me. "You have your belay device?" I ask, looking down at his hands.

"No," he replies, and the one word reverberates through me. As little as he's spoken, when he actually does, it's like it sends a shockwave through the air.

"Oh, sorry. Let me go grab one real quick." I jog away, feeling my high ponytail swish across the back of my shoulders. Sensing eyes on me, I glance over my shoulder, and sure enough, Corbin's are once again boring into me. But this time, they're on my ass. The realization makes my step falter, and I nearly trip, but luckily I'm close enough to the glass case that I catch myself with my palms to the edge.

He's checking me out? The thought makes me both giddy and nervous. I haven't had a boyfriend since Jax and I broke up our freshman year, and with graduation just a few months away, the comments of the assholes at school who have picked on me mercilessly for never dating come to the surface of my brain.

She's such a snob. She doesn't think anyone is good enough for her.

What a dork. She'd rather go to that stupid gym than come to the Fall Dance.

What guy would want a girl who spends all her time climbing on walls?

All she does is talk about that rock climbing crap.

My mom comforts me when their words finally penetrate the armor I've been able to build around myself with the confidence I've gained since finding my niche. She calls them jealous and immature. In reality, I know she's happy I've spent the last four years of my life in love with a sport instead of chasing after boys.

But the fact is, it's left me completely inexperienced with the opposite sex. Jax and I had kissed a few times, but never with tongue. So here I am, eighteen years old and soon to graduate high school, and I have never even French kissed before.

So catching Corbin looking at my butt in my spandex climbing shorts is brand new territory for me. Territory I don't even know how to explore, so I decide to tuck it into a hidden nook in my brain so I can try to forget about it until absolutely necessary.

Reaching into the display case, I grab a belay device and hurry back over to Corbin, finding it impossible to look him in the eyes. "Y'all probably already know this, but I have to do my spiel. This is a tubular belay device. It attaches to the belayer's harness in the front by a locking carabiner."

My hands tremble, but I'm determined to act like I normally would with any other person taking the belay lesson, so I rotate the metal lock on the clip, and hook it onto the loop at the front of his hips. Being this close, his soft shorts tucked close against his body because of the harness, it is impossible to miss the movement of his penis behind the black fabric. I jerk my hands away, my entire body growing flushed and my skin suddenly feeling too tight around my bones. Even my scalp feels hot and prickly.

I've read romance novels before. I'm actually a pretty big fan of paranormal love stories. I don't have much time for reading nowadays, but I've read enough that I get the gist of sex, as much as you can get without actually experiencing it yourself. I've read all about 'twitching members' and 'tight channels', so I know exactly what just happened in Corbin's shorts.

He's affected by me as well.

With wide eyes, I look up into Corbin's. His expression is

unreadable. No cocky smirk, no blush of embarrassment from his body's reaction to me. Whatever emotion he is feeling is completely concealed behind the wall of his heart-stopping, perfect face. So, I clear my throat again and stutter through the next part of their lesson.

"Um... o-okay. S-so next, you grab your rope and pinch it in half, then stick the pinched part through one side of the belay device, so when it comes through the metal, it makes a loop that you will hook onto the locking carabiner too." I watch as Corbin does as I instructed, and when he spins the lock back into place, he looks up at me, waiting for my next step.

"I'm going to hook into the rope next to you so you can watch how I do it," I tell them, making quick work of unhooking my personal belay device from the loop I keep it on at my hip, and then strapping into the rope next to them so I can demonstrate the proper movements. Normally, I would just stand behind the student, wrap my arms around theirs, and teach them that way. But the thought of doing that sends me into near panic.

"Before you can climb, the climber and the belayer must let each other know they're ready. The climber will ask, 'On belay?' and the belayer will answer with, 'Belay is on,' if they're all set up. The belayer will then ask the climber if they're ready to start climbing by asking, 'On rock?' and when the climber approaches the wall and is ready to begin, they will respond with, 'Rock on.'" Without thinking, I say the last part while giving the rock-n-roll hand signal, a little growl to my voice out of habit. This makes Brian laugh. When I realize what I did, my eyes lift to Corbin, and I see one side of his lips is lifted, his dark eyes twinkling. I've given these instructions so many times, usually to kids and their parents, and I'm so used to trying to make it fun and calm their nerves that I always say the last reply to the belayer that way. Seeing the guys' reaction to my dramatics, my embarrassment doesn't have a chance to form, so I chuckle along with Brian. "Okay, y'all's turn."

Brian clears his throat animatedly, and then holds his hand palm up in Corbin's direction, asking, "On belay, sir?"

Corbin shakes his shaved head and runs a palm down his face. "You're such an idiot. Belay is on, cherry." Brian laughs and moves up to the wall. "On rock?" Corbin asks him.

Brian places one hand on a grip, and then looks over at me, his other hand copying my rock-n-roll gesture, as he growls loudly, "Rock on!" making me laugh at his antics.

"Very good," I tell them. "And now you can climb. As he moves up the wall, the rope is going to get slacker. With your right hand, you are going to pull the slack out of the line through the belay device. Between his moves, you lock off the rope by just pulling it in your right hand down by your hip. If he warns you he is about to fall, or if he falls without warning, he's not going anywhere if you already have him locked off. The only time you are not in the locked off position is if you are pulling out his slack."

"Got it," Corbin replies, watching me demonstrate pulling my empty rope through the device and locking it off as I instructed.

"Did you get all that, Brian?" I ask, and he nods from his perch on the first set of beginner rocks.

"Awesome," Sierra says, coming up behind me, and I smile over at her. She stays with our little group while Brian goes up the wall then lets go, letting Corbin practice catching him a couple times before lowering him to the ground one final time. They switch places, Corbin becoming the climber and Brian the belayer, and ten minutes later, they receive their certification.

"I'm going to get back to my route. Nice meeting you guys. Have fun," I tell them, and with an awkward little wave, I go back to the wall in front of my mom who's sitting on the couch. She's still reading her book, completely unaware of the emotional rollercoaster I was just on.

I reach into my chalk bag and coat my hands, then take up my starting position at the left end of the route once again, completely aware of Brian and Corbin choosing the wall across from me. They must not notice, or maybe they don't care, that the wall they picked is marked Expert, as they begin strapping themselves into the ropes. I don't say anything though. They're grown men and will figure it out on their own. Even if it's the hard way.

Corbin

WHAT. THE. FUCK?

Her presence caught my attention before the loud sneeze lifted her small frame off the floor. I had felt the approach of something... someone... as if it were a physical thing. Like the scene in *Jurassic Park*, the water rippling in the glasses as the giant T-Rex grew closer and closer, shaking the ground with its advance. So when I looked over my shoulder where I was standing at the front counter, and my eyes landed on the girl making her way from the back of the gym, clapping her hands together and forming a small dust cloud as she walked, I was struck stupid. Her? She was the one causing this strange feeling inside me?

She didn't look a day over fifteen. Her long, dark ponytail swished behind her as she hurried toward us. When she circled around one of the walls, I took in her thin arms and legs, exposed thanks to the bright red tank top and skin-tight black spandex shorts she was wearing. Her black sports bra peeked out from beneath her shirt, but it didn't seem like she needed it. Her chest was small, in proportion with the rest of her. But God, she was stunningly beautiful, her face clear of makeup except for the smudge of black around her eyes, and the chalk smeared on her cheeks, forehead, and the tip of her nose.

And then she had sneezed, and my automatic reaction to say, "Bless you," brought her eyes to mine, and it felt like I was being electrocuted. I vaguely heard the lady behind the desk say something about her being an eight out of ten, but to me, she far surpassed a dime. She was utterly perfect.

I watched her jog away, the toned muscles of her ass working behind those tiny black shorts, before she disappeared through the door marked Women. I shook myself. I shouldn't be checking out a little teenager. I'm a damn twenty-year-old Specialist in the US Army, soon to be up for my next promotion. That's the last thing I should be doing.

With that thought in mind, I tried to hold myself in check while Glover joked around with her. Glover, the nineteen-year-old Private from Kentucky, was my new cherry. He arrived to my unit a little over two weeks ago, and the poor kid hadn't done anything off base or fun since he'd made it to Ft. Vanter. Part of the job, aside from making sure the people beneath my rank do the right shit and follow orders, is making sure they keep their head straight. Nothing could be more disastrous than a depressed soldier. So when I noticed Glover looking a little down in the chow hall this afternoon, I asked him if he wanted to check out this climbing place I'd seen an ad for in the paper. His eyes had lit up like a Christmas tree, and we made plans to come right after we got off work for the day.

I'd kept myself under control as she gave us the first of the required instruction before we could be tested and certified for belaying. But when her hands came so fucking near my cock to hook the locking carabiner onto my harness, I couldn't control its natural reaction as it swelled and practically reached for her. All I could do was keep my face stoic, as if nothing had happened, even as she looked up at me, her breathtaking green eyes startled, confirming she hadn't missed my dick twitch.

Then, I couldn't help but smile when her tiny fist had lifted, and her pointer and pinky fingers shot up, her sweet, feminine voice deepening to a far from intimidating growl as she taught us the verbal cues to start climbing, ending with, "Rock on." A tiny bit of her true personality had shone through her nervousness around me. And I could tell it was just around me. She didn't seem affected by Glover—yet I hadn't missed the flare of her nostrils and the brief narrowing of her eyes when he laughed after she asked if we were ready to learn how to belay.

That had pissed her off. Most people probably wouldn't have picked up on that, but it's my job to read people, notice the tiniest of changes in their demeanor. And if his condescending tone had pissed her off, then that meant she was probably pretty good at what she did, and knew it. That, and the fact the lady at the front desk called her Spidergirl.

Now, as I belay Glover—trying his best to make it up a wall

that looks nearly impossible, since it has so few rocks on it, and the rocks that *are* screwed in don't look big enough to hold up a toddler, much less a fucking 6'5" man like him—I watch her in action. I see exactly why Vi would have been offended by him laughing in her face. I can also see the reason she would own the nickname Spidergirl.

Staying down low on the wall, never standing up straight to reach a rock above her head, I see she's only using rocks that have been circled in chalk, so she must be practicing a certain route. She starts at the far left side of the wall and places the outside of her left foot onto the first bottom rock, puts all of her weight on it, and she squats to place both hands on a larger grip, her arms outstretched. Her right leg comes up straight in front of her, running parallel with the wall. She doesn't place her right foot on a rock; she just seems to press it against the textured wall itself.

Taking a deep breath, when she lets it out, she pulls herself forward, her left foot somehow spinning on its tiny rock so that it's now her big toe pressed into it. Now, with the front of her body flush with the wall, her right leg stretches far enough to reach the next circled rock and her right hand grasps another. Observing her from this distance, right now, she looks as if she's in a deep side-lunge, yet I know she's somehow balanced on just a sliver of a foothold, making it look effortless.

Bringing her left hand to grip onto the same rock as her right, her tight ass juts out for a moment as she switches which leg her weight is on, now in a lunge to the right. Slowly, she outstretches her arms again, leaning away from the wall instead of holding herself tightly to it. It's fascinating to watch. So slight, so frail, as if there is no strength in her lithe limbs, yet she moves across the wall so gracefully, almost like she's floating.

A couple moves later, she reaches the spot where she's fallen several times since she finished with our belay lesson. It had been her hissed, "Shit!" that brought my eyes to her after I'd hooked myself into the floor anchor ten minutes ago.

Until now, I had been unconsciously belaying Brian as I watched her, my eyes never leaving her, but still completely aware of my soldier up on the ropes. We learned and practiced rope work and rappelling until we could do it in complete darkness, using only the tension in the rope as a guide. So yes, although the idea of the young woman *teaching* us to belay was laughable, I hadn't, because I never show my cards in a game of poker. I never know who I'll come across that may be better at something than me, someone I can learn from, even if I have experience in it. Also, I never know when I might win in a fight by tricking the enemy into thinking I'm helpless. Maybe that's a fucked-up way of thinking, not being an open person, but with the life I've led, it's the only way I've survived.

As he calls, "Falling," down to me, I lock him off until he lets go of the wall, then lower him without ever looking away from Vi, silently rooting her on in my head to make it past the part where she keeps slipping off.

She reaches for the miniature grip, thinks better of it, sticking her right hand into her bag for a fresh coat of chalk, and then places her fingertips on the rock once more. I watch, completely entranced, as she gently lays her cheek against the wall and slowly, ever so carefully, lets go with her left hand, bringing it behind her back to cover it in more chalk as well. Focusing in on her legs and ass, I can see the sleek muscles beneath her smooth skin flex and release, minute adjustments she probably doesn't even realize she's making as she keeps her balance in a near split.

This time, I hold my breath, shushing Brian with a raised fist before he even says a word at my side. The tension crackles in the air as we watch her, waiting for her to make her move. And finally, in one fluid transition, her body contorts until her left foot is where her right just was. She's pinching the tiny rock in her left hand now, and without another foothold, she hooks the top of her right foot around the edge of the wall. One last movement of her hands to a much larger rock at the far end, and she's done it.

She leaps off the wall and twirls with a whoop, the woman on the couch I noticed when we first walked over standing to high-five her then rub her back. Vi's face beams, her smile so wide I can see almost every single one of her perfectly white, straight teeth. Gorgeous. Absolutely gorgeous in all her pride at finally beating her self-given challenge.

Suddenly, both women's eyes move in our direction as Brian starts clapping, yelling "Freakin' awesome!" from our position at the wall across from them. Vi laughs and gives him a small wave before her eyes come to me, where I'm still staring in utter fascination.

"You want to climb now, Lowe?" Brian asks, and I pull my gaze away from her to look up at where he towers over me.

"It's Corbin. We're off the clock, bud," I tell him, wanting it to sink in that I've brought him here to have fun. We aren't Specialist and Private right now. We're just two guys hanging out after work. He needs to let loose a little so the stress of our job doesn't get to him, the way it looked like it was beginning to this afternoon at lunch. "Yeah, I'll give it a shot," I add, unhooking the belay device from my harness and trading it for his end of the rope.

Once I'm all tied in, I start my climb. It's slow-going, as I look for rocks big enough to grip onto. When I saw the sign marking this wall Expert, I'd blown it off. How hard could it be? But now that I'm up here, trying to power through this route, I realize I made a big mistake.

My arms are trembling as I hang on to one of the largest rocks on the wall, which is only about the size of a golf ball, when suddenly I hear that sweet voice call up to me, "Lean away from the wall, Corbin," and I glance down to see Vi standing beside Brian. Her hands rest on her hips and she's tilting her head up to look at me.

"What?" Does she want me to come down?

"Lean away from the wall," she repeats. "You're trying to muscle your way up the wall, and you can't do that on this route. Grip that rock with one hand instead of both, and then slowly lean back, straightening out your arm."

I do what she tells me, gripping the small hold with my right hand before leaning back. I take the opportunity to shake out my left arm, dipping my hand into my chalk bag. "Now what?" I ask her, when my biceps aren't shaking and I have circulation back in both arms.

"Now find some rocks to get your feet up on... no, don't turn your feet in. Always climb with your toes pointing outward. Never use the outside unless you're in starting position or if it's completely necessary. There you go. Bring your feet up as far as you can get them. That way you can just stand up to the next set of rocks above your head. No need to wear those big muscles out if you don't really need to use them," she calls, and I can't help the smile that pulls at my lips.

She's so small, and young, and had been so nervous around me up front. But here, in her element, having just conquered a challenge she had been working on tirelessly, her confidence is shining through, and she's feeling brave enough to try and help me, even though my dumb ass thought I'd be able to simply He Man my way up an Expert-level wall.

I bring my feet up as she instructed, still holding on with just one hand. "Go slow. Don't stand up too—"

But her warning is too late. Standing up on the tiny rocks the toes of my climbing shoes press into, I do it too quickly and my knees hit the wood, causing my feet to slip off the rock chips. I fall only a foot before my harness catches me, the rope yanking the straps tight into the creases between my legs and crotch. Brian lowers me to the ground, and as soon as my feet touch the floor, I jerk on the rope to give me more slack and pull the harness out of my balls.

"Good try. You actually got farther than most newbs would get on an expert-level wall," Vi tells me, and it does a lot to soothe my bruised ego.

"How long have you been doing this?" I ask her, untying my knot.

"Every day for four years. I started when I was a freshman," she replies, taking the rope from me and lacing it through the front of her harness.

Freshman. Four years ago? But she looks so young. It could be because of her fresh face and her petite frame, but I didn't think she could be any more than fifteen. "How old are you?" I question before I can stop myself.

"I'm eighteen."

Fuck.

Three

Vi

IT DIDN'T ESCAPE ME THAT Corbin's quiet and standoffish demeanor changed almost the moment I told him I was eighteen. Or maybe it's because I had just tried to help him with his technique. I'm not sure, but for the last hour, Brian, Corbin, and I have been climbing together, me showing them different fun routes around the gym that were easier than the Expert wall, but still challenging enough for two big, strong soldiers.

It did amazing things for my confidence when I demonstrated a route for them, and they'd clap and whoop for me before trying it themselves. Corbin really listened to everything I tried to teach him, taking it in with a nodding head before putting my instruction into action. Brian was just a big goofball, but he was able to get through most of the routes with his wingspan alone.

The strange feeling I had being near Corbin never went away, but it was easier to ignore when I was joking around with them in between teaching them stuff on the rocks. During Brian's turns, Corbin would stand close to me, his huge tattooed arms crossed over his muscular chest, and every once in a while, his bicep would brush mine, sending tingles throughout my body.

In the middle of explaining something, if I happened to look him in the eyes instead of at the wall we were working on, it would steal my words. I could be in the middle of a sentence and lock gazes with him, and it was like someone pressed pause on my brain. It wasn't until either my mom or Brian snapped us out of it that we continued with the lesson.

By the end of the night, when Sierra flashed the overhead lights, my stomach was hurting from laughing, and I was exhausted from my heart beating like I was running a marathon just being close to Corbin. We all sat on the worn-out couch to take off our shoes, Brian making me laugh once more by taking a whiff of one of his and falling to the floor, pretending he was dead. As funny as he was, and cute in a boy-next-door sort of way, it was Corbin I was unequivocally attracted to. Hell, I had never been more attracted to anyone in my life. And it wasn't just his gorgeous face, chiseled body, or sexy bad-boy tattoos. It was something else altogether. Something I couldn't really name, because it was an emotional connection instead of just a physical attraction.

Whatever it was pulled me to him and made me not want to let go. As tired as I was, I didn't want to leave his presence. I didn't want this night to end. So it was with an internal sigh of relief that I gave Corbin my phone number when he asked me for it, so we could get together again to climb. Out in the parking lot, as I was getting into Mom's car, I heard Brian's, "Bye, Vi! Ha! That rhymes!" before he folded himself into Corbin's dark green Camaro, making me shake my head. Corbin grabbed a black ball cap off his front seat and placed it on his shaved head, squeezing the bill before he waved at me over the roof of his car, and I smiled before closing the door behind me.

Mom and I didn't talk much on the way home. She tried to ask about what I thought of the boys, but I gave her a quick, "They were fun," before going back to replaying the past few hours in my head.

So here I lie, in my lavender-covered, pillow-top twin bed, wide-awake three hours later, still thinking about dark chocolate eyes and tattoos I want to hear the stories behind. I wonder when Corbin will text me, to see when we can climb together again. I really need to go to sleep; I have to be up for school in just six hours. But I just can't shut my brain off.

A half hour of tossing and turning later, my phone chimes, making me jump. When I pick it up off my nightstand, there's a message from a number with a weird area code, and my heart thuds behind my ribs.

I enjoyed meeting and climbing with u. I'll come on Friday if u'll be there. —Corbin

I kick off my covers, reading the message over and over again. *What should I say? Oh God, don't be a dork. Don't sound overly excited that he texted, but don't sound like he's bothering you either.* Jesus, I have no idea what I'm doing.

Me 2. I'll be there!

There. Short and sweet.

A smile tugs at the corners of my lips when my phone chimes

again, and I read his message.

Corbin: Ur still up? I sent u that thinking u'd wake up to it in the morning. Or did I wake u?

Me: Can't sleep. No worries.

Corbin: Me neither... Confession time?

My heart skips. What could he possibly want to confess? How do I even reply to that?

Me: Ok...

A few minutes pass, and I wonder if I said the wrong thing. But then his reply comes through, and I see it just took him a while to type it all out.

Corbin: This evening just keeps playing in my head over and over again. I can't stop thinking about u, and it's kind of freaking me out a little bit. When we first met... nah, never mind. It sounds stupid, and I don't want u to think I'm crazy.

Me: No, tell me! I promise I won't think ur crazy. I can't sleep because I can't get u out of my head either. I mean, the whole night was fun, getting to climb with you guys, but... idk.

Corbin: Well, since u promised. It's like I felt u before I saw u. Something inside me sensed u were there before I laid eyes on u. And I'm not talking about that weird feeling u get like someone is watching u. I mean like, a part of me recognized u before we even met.

Wow. I don't even know how to respond. I know exactly what he's feeling, because I did too. But for him to just come right out and say it? I always thought men played games and pretended like they weren't interested for a while. Maybe that was just all in the movies.

Corbin: U there? I didn't scare u off, did I?

Me: I'm here, just kinda surprised.

Corbin: Surprised about what?

Me: I had the same feeling. I'm just surprised u so readily told me. Aren't guys supposed to play hard to get LOL

Corbin: Can I call u?

A squeak leaves my throat as my eyes widen at my phone. Texting is one thing. I can read what he messages me, and then have time to think about my reply, with the ability to delete it and try again if it doesn't sound right. A phone call though... there is no backspace button.

But that voice. That deep, sexy voice I'd gotten to hear all night, once he finally started speaking. I want to hear it again, so I reply a simple, *Yes.*

My phone rings, and even though I knew he was about to call, it still makes me jump. I press Answer, and hold the cell to my ear. "Hello?"

"Hey, Vi," he says, his voice low, and I hear movement.

"Hey," I reply dumbly, closing my eyes. God, I'm so terrible at this. I hear a door close on his end, and then footsteps echoing. "What are you doing?"

"I'm walking out of the barracks so I don't wake anyone up. I could use some fresh air anyways," he tells me.

"Oh." I pause, and then I have to ask, because I have no idea what he's talking about. "What is a barracks?"

He chuckles. "How long have you lived here? Barracks are like shitty apartments for the military. They're more like dorms, actually. Or what I picture dorms to be like. I wouldn't know, since I didn't go to college."

"Oh, okay. I was born and raised here. But I've never met anyone in the Army before," I explain, listening to another door close and then the sound of him groaning lightly, like he was sitting down.

"Where have you been?" he questions with a light laugh.

"Literally hiding under a rock."

He snorts. "Nice one. But really, you've never met anyone in the Army, even living here your whole life?"

"Nope. I mean... maybe that's the wrong word. I've *met* some at the gym, but never really talked to them aside from giving them their belay lesson. For the past four years, I've gone to school, the gym, home, and repeat," I say quietly, feeling kind of embarrassed at how boring my life is.

"Nothing wrong with dedication, baby girl," he soothes, and his term of endearment makes me smile.

"I guess once I found something I was actually good at, I just stuck with it. I'm loyal like that," I joke.

"Loyalty is good." The tone of his voice makes it seem that simple statement means a lot more to him than he's letting on. "Look, I'm going to cut to the chase, okay?"

I gulp, and then pray he can't hear it through the phone. "O-okay."

"I don't know what this feeling is between us. I've never felt anything like it before. This instant connection before even saying a word to each other. I put it out of my head at first, because I thought you were way too young, but when you told me you're eighteen, I stopped ignoring it, and tonight was one of the best nights I've had in a really long-ass time," he confides, and I realize I'm biting my lip, taking in everything he's saying.

"Me too. And not just a long-ass time. I'm more like... *ever*," I confess, and hear him chuckle.

"If that's been your routine for the past four years, then I believe it. But I'm also jumping the gun here. Do you have a boyfriend, Vi?" he asks, and I barely keep myself from laughing.

"N-no. I don't have a boyfriend," I reply, my voice full of amusement. "If I had a boyfriend, I wouldn't be talking to you at almost one in the morning about the crazy feelings you give me. I haven't had one in four years."

"Crazy feelings?"

"A boyfriend," I clarify.

"Oh." A pause. "And you're eighteen?"

"Yeees..." I drawl.

"So are you... are you a—" He clears his throat, and my face turns hot when I realize what he wanted to ask but stopped himself.

"Yeah," I whisper, and the answer hangs in the air. "So anyways, Friday? I'm there every day. Literally. Sometimes I'll skip Sundays to give my body a rest, but that's rare. I go from 3:00 p.m. when I get out of school until they close at nine." I squeeze my eyes closed at my idiotic rambling.

"Wow, six hours a day. No wonder you're so good. You definitely earned that Spidergirl nickname."

I feel myself glow under his compliment. I roll over on my side, pressing my phone between my ear and pillow. "Thanks. How long have you been in the Army? What do you do?"

"I've been in the Army for almost three years, enlisted when I was seventeen, and left for basic the day I turned eighteen. Got here to Ft. Vander about two years ago. And I'm a sniper," he replies.

"A sniper? Like in the movies?" I ask, intrigued.

"Yep, like in the movies." He chuckles.

"And you've been here for two years?" I breathe, closing my eyes.

46   KD ROBICHAUX

"Yeah, right here. In these same barracks."

"All this time, and I didn't even know." My voice holds disappointment. I feel like I've somehow been cheated out of time with him for some reason, which is silly.

"Don't sound so down, baby girl. Everything happens for a reason. We met when we were supposed to. Two years ago, I was still a little shithead, and you were only sixteen," he soothes.

"Still a little shithead?" I prompt, my eyebrows furrowing.

"Yeah. I'm from California. That's where all my family is. In high school, I thought I was a little badass and joined a gang, got in some trouble. Anyways, I got caught, and they gave me the option, either I could go to juvie, and when I turned eighteen I could go straight to jail, *or* I could join the military. I chose the military," he explains, and I suck in a breath.

"What did you do?" I ask, before I can think better of it.

"Ah, that's a story for a different day. I want you to fall for me before I go telling you my deep, dark secrets," he jokes in his deep, sexy voice, and I nearly swoon.

"Fair enough," I breathe.

"Well, I gotta get some sleep. I have to wake up in about three hours for PT, and I know you've got school in the morning. Can I text you tomorrow? Or today, rather. Past midnight, so technically it's Thursday, huh?"

"Of course. If I don't answer right away, I'm in class. It's not so bad having to wait 'til Friday to see you again, when we can technically say it's tomorrow," I say, and I close my eyes and smack my hand over them. Oh, my God, how freaking corny and girly was that?

But his response makes me feel a whole lot less like an idiot. "My thoughts exactly, baby girl. Sleep well."

"Night, Corbin," I whisper, and I hear the phone disconnect.

Corbin

I SIT AT MY DESK like a zombie, hating life and counting down the hours until I can go to sleep, wake up, and it be the day I get to see *her* again. After talking to Vi, I never did fall asleep last night, lying in bed, unable to get her off my mind. Before I could doze off, my alarm went off, at 4:00 a.m. and I had to get up for our daily physical training. Four words kept circling my mind like a mantra I couldn't shut up.

Vivian. Eighteen. Virgin. Mine.

Maybe it was her innocence that made her seem so young when I first met her. I've been with eighteen-year-olds before, both before and after I was that age. Fuck, I lost my own virginity to one when I was fourteen. But they were all already experienced, with an air of maturity surrounding them from the life milestone of sex alone. I wanted her before, but now... now I crave her.

Untouched. Unscarred. No baggage. No one for me to want to kill for having put their hands on what's mine.

And completely moldable.

I scold myself, thinking that way. But really. I could be myself with her, teach her the things I like, no matter how fucked up they are, and she would never know the difference. She wouldn't know that what I wanted... what I *needed*... wasn't the norm.

"For the past four years, I've gone to school, the gym, home, and repeat."

So sheltered. No room for intimate socializing and experimentation with a strict schedule like that. Always under adult supervision, no matter where she went.

"I'm loyal like that."

God, could she be more perfect? Loyalty. The number one thing on my list of requirements.

My deal-breaker. My hard-limit. If you couldn't be fucking loyal to me, then get the fuck away from me. I have zero tolerance for disloyalty. If you're with me, you're with me alone. You could be the most beautiful and most amazing woman on the face of the planet, but the second you break my trust, I don't give a fuck who you are; I'm done with you. I've been burned too many times giving people second chances to ever give another one for the rest of my life. Never again. But for her to use that word, the most important one to me, right there in our very first real conversation? It feels like a higher power is at work.

Combine that with the immediate connection we had before we even spoke, that pull toward each other, that overwhelming sense of needing to be near her, to keep my eyes on her, to touch her, even just by brushing my arm with hers... It felt like fate. I believe in what I told her. Everything happens for a reason.

I've lived here two years. For almost a year of that, I've known about that rock gym she's been going to every single day for almost half a decade, but I never took the time to go check it out. But then yesterday morning, I saw another ad for it in the paper someone had left on the table I sat at for lunch. And with it fresh in my mind, I'd noticed my cherry, Glover, staring into his bowl of canned fruit cocktail, looking like a puppy that had been abandoned. So I invited him to go with me. And there she was.

I can't take it anymore. I've tried to leave her alone, knowing she's at school, but I can't go another minute without texting her. I look out the window behind me to make sure no one is walking up the sidewalk from the parking lot, and seeing the coast is clear, I snatch my phone out of my metal desk drawer and type out a message, pressing send.

Hope u got more sleep than I did. I never fell asleep last night. Awake going on 33 hrs now.

I drop my phone face-up into the drawer in front of me, keeping it cracked open enough so I can look down and see when it lights up, since I have to have it on silent. I'm actually not supposed to have my phone at all while I'm at my desk, but fuck it. There was no way I was going to miss a call or text if Vi decided to send me one. God, so wrapped up in her, and we only met yesterday.

My fingers tap against the top of my desk, and I play a game of solitaire on the ancient computer in front of me. My eyes constantly glance down to see if she responded. I light up my screen a few times to make sure I didn't miss anything while I was looking away, but nothing. When I can feel my sanity starting to slip, my phone finally lights up with Vivian's name.

I feel like a kid on Christmas morning as I open up the message, and I shake my head at myself. The fuck is wrong with me? But I can't help the smile that spreads across my face as I read her text.

I ended up taking a bath to relax, and then finally got about 3 hrs of sleep.

My dick hardens immediately, thinking of her, naked in a bathtub, unable to sleep because she can't stop thinking of me. I reply quickly, hoping she hasn't left her phone yet.

Are u trying to torture me at work?

My smile widens at her response.

Huh? What do u mean? I just got to Chemistry. Cool teacher, so we can text all we want.

God, so innocent. I check the time, seeing that everyone will still be at lunch for another twenty minutes unless they decide to leave early.

Just thinking about u taking a bath, baby girl.

She takes a couple minutes to respond, and when she does, it makes me chuckle.

Oh.

But then I frown when I realize she still doesn't get what I was trying to say, and growl at her follow-up text.

Thinking of me naked is torture? I don't look that bad, do I?

I close my eyes and take a deep breath, letting it out slowly to calm myself before I write her back.

Vivian, I will tell u this 1 time, and 1 time only. Save this message to reread as u see fit if u have to, because this is the only time I will type out these words. U are fucking perfect. There is not a single thing about ur body that I would change. Never doubt I wouldn't kill to see and touch every inch of ur perfection. No, thinking of u naked isn't torture because u look bad. It's torture, because I have the most painful hard-on right now, thinking of u naked, and there's nothing I can do about it.

I try to relax, reminding myself she's inexperienced with the opposite sex, and even less experienced with someone like me. Her short reply comes a few minutes later.

Oh. I'm sorry.

I groan. So. Fucking. Perfect. No excuses. No defensiveness. No arguing. Just an apology. The only thing that could've made it better was if she had said it wouldn't happen again, topped off with a "Sir." God, when she called me that, her tiny hand gripped in mine when we first introduced ourselves, I could barely contain myself. My hand had tightened around hers, ready to yank her to me, so I quickly let go.

I can't wait to see you tomorrow. I'm going to try to get off early so I can get there around the same time you do. Give us more time together.

Her response comes quickly, eager to latch onto my change in subject.

I can't wait either! Will Brian be coming too? We'll have to play takeaway.

The only thing I want to take away is everyone and everything separating us, including her clothes. But not wanting to scare her, my reply is much more G-rated.

Looking forward to u teaching me takeaway. IDK if Glover will come. He told me this morning that he's sore as fuck.

I actually laugh out loud at her incoming text. Knowing she's so tiny makes it even funnier, coming from her.

What a wimp. Tell him to quit being a baby.

My watch beeps, letting me know it's a new hour, which means people will soon be walking in the door.

I'll do that. I gotta get back to work for now, but I'll talk to u later, ok?

I don't get to see if she replies, because the door next to me opens and I swiftly hide my phone in the drawer, shutting it silently.

Three hours later, I'm in my barracks room, lying in my single bed. My roommate was deployed two months ago for an eighteen-month stint in Afghanistan, so I have the place all to myself. As you enter, my bed is in the corner, pushed up against the left wall next to the door. I look around, seeing only the backsides of two floor-to-ceiling wardrobes, one at the foot of my bed, and one to my right, making an opening just big enough to get into the enclosed haven I've created with the furniture, and just wide enough to peek out through to watch the TV sitting on a dresser across the room.

My eyes move to the ceiling, counting the tiny holes in the tiles. As exhausted as I am from not sleeping last night, I still can't shut my brain off, even now, when I can finally pass the fuck out. The image of a small, almost frail girl with long dark hair, green eyes, and a smile that lights up an entire room won't clear itself from the backs of my eyelids.

God, the things I could do to her. The positions I could put her in. It would be effortless. And now, knowing that if I were to take her, I would be her first... it's not even the virgin-aspect that's so fucking hot about it. It's the fact that I would be the one to set the baseline, the standard, for anyone after me. She would always remember me, as her first. She would always compare everyone else to me. The thought makes me both hard and want to punch something, just thinking about anyone else having her. Because another thought hits me.

If I were to have her, and things worked out between us, I would get to live my life knowing I was the only man to ever be inside her.

Before I realize what I'm doing, I take my throbbing cock in my hand, stroking it from tip to root then back up again, already feeling wetness at the head. I didn't allow myself to jack off last night, no matter how badly I'd needed to come. I refused to let myself give in, knowing it was Vi who controlled my thoughts and need, and not me. She'd taken over without my permission, without even trying, just by simply... existing. And to both my relief and distress, I come within seconds.

I clean myself off and lie there for a few minutes, willing myself to go to sleep, but as I realize the sweet bliss of unconsciousness is still not coming, it makes me angry, and my anger brings me to my feet, where I pull on some basketball shorts and a fresh wife beater before lacing up my sneakers.

I grab my keys, glancing at my watch—6:37 p.m. Without thinking, I hop in my Camaro and head off base. Ten minutes later, I pull in and park, slamming the door behind me. I barrel through the glass entrance, making the bells above the door clang violently, and it does wonders to calm the raging bull inside me, the girl currently halfway up the rope two walls over being the red matador's cape.

My loud entrance startles her, and she loses her footing for a moment, but quickly recovers before looking through the space between her lifted right arm and her body to see who had come in, her face annoyed. When she sees it's me, her features soften before breaking out in a wide smile.

And just like that, all frustration leaves me and I'm left with a sense of completeness just being in the same room as her. "Evening, Spidergirl," I call up to her.

"Howdy, soldier," she giggles. "Be right down." Instead of letting go of her grips though, she resumes her focus, and I watch, fascinated, as she finishes her route to the top, making the Expert level wall look effortless in her grace. "Falling," she calls to her mom, who begins letting out slack, allowing her daughter to lower.

On her descent, making my heart stop for a moment, Vi lets go of the rope with her hands and lies back, her body completely horizontal except for her dangling legs as she shakes out her arms. Sensing her nearness to the ground, she grasps the rope in one hand and pulls herself back up just as her feet touch the floor, and then unties her harness before slipping that down her long, bare legs.

She hands it to her mom, kissing her cheek and whispering something I can't hear before finally coming to me. "What are you doing here? It's not Friday yet." She smiles shyly.

"Honestly, I have no idea. I went to bed as soon as I got off work at five, couldn't sleep, and next thing I knew, I was here," I confess, taking hold of one of her chalky hands and pulling her to me before enveloping her in my arms. God, she fits me so perfectly.

I've never been self-conscious of my shorter stature, but I've been told it could possibly be a contributor to my personality, a 'Napoleon Complex' someone once called it. They said my drive, my domineering and aggressive behavior, was an unconscious compensation for my height. I told them to fuck off.

I've dated women in all shapes and heights, ones who towered over me and ones who couldn't even reach my chin wearing heels. I didn't really have a preference. Until now. Vi, who had been stiff when I first pulled her into my embrace, is now completely melted against me, her face going into my neck and breathing me in deeply. When I loosen my arms, she stands back, able to look me in the eye, being as she's only an inch or two shorter than me.

"Are you going to climb?" She glances at the oversized clock on the wall behind the counter. "We still have two hours before closing time."

"Might as well," I reply, swiping the tip of my finger down the bridge of her nose, where she had a streak of chalk. I'm surprised at my own touchy-feely behavior, not usually one for intimate gestures not meant specifically as an act of foreplay, but the pretty blush that fills her cheeks followed by another shy smile makes it worth my confusion.

And the next two hours are filled with these small, stolen touches, becoming an internal game of how many times I can draw out that sweet look on her face.

BEFORE THE *li*
EFORE THE *lie*
BEFORE THE *lie*
RE THE *lie*
lie

Four

Vi

I SLEPT LIKE THE DEAD LAST night, after the excitement of Corbin showing up at the gym unexpectedly. We spent the two hours working mostly on bouldering techniques on the forty-five-degree-angled wall. No ropes or harnesses, just me teaching him different ways to handle a route when gravity was fighting against you. With the pit of regrind beneath us, there was no worry of getting hurt. Just frustration when we'd lose our grip or footing and would fall into the ground-up tires. He had the advantage of massive upper body strength, so he could virtually monkey-bar his way across the wall if he needed to, but that meant he would wear out faster than me, who used less strength and smarter moves to beat a route.

I'd gotten so used to praise for my climbing abilities. I never really knew how to respond to people's admiration, and usually just said thank you and waved off their compliments. But for some reason, under Corbin's impressed and admiring eyes, it meant more to me than anyone else before.

Climbing was always something I did for myself. It made *me* feel good doing something I was talented at. I joined the competitive team, not for the competition itself, but just to test myself. Could I keep up with all of these veteran climbers, who traveled from out of state to gather here and see just who among them were the best of the best? I wasn't in it to win any trophies or titles. I just wanted to see how good at this sport I actually was, seeing how I only did it for fun. When I found out I scored better than my coach, that was pretty mind-boggling. But even that moment didn't compare to the silent but intense way Corbin followed me with his eyes, seemingly spellbound. It also made me feel pretty great knowing that I impressed *him*—a big, strong, badass soldier.

The day has gone by torturously slow. Every time I glance at the clock on the classroom wall, thinking it's almost time for the bell to ring, it's only been a few short minutes. I haven't been able to concentrate worth a crap, but thankfully, being a senior, and with SATs already out of the way, there isn't much to worry about.

Graduation is next month, and it can't come fast enough. I'm going to the community college starting in the fall. I'm not really sure what I want to major in, but I have a lot of time to figure that out while I take care of all my core classes first. I've never really aspired to be anything. When I was little, when people asked me what I wanted to be when I grew up, I always said I wanted to be my mom. To me, nothing could be greater than spending all day

BEFORE THE LIE 59

taking care of your babies, who love you as much as I love my momma. Being a mom seemed to make her so happy, and that was the most important thing to me—not being rich or famous, or whatever.

Finally, the last bell rings, and I hurry to my locker to grab my stuff before running outside. Mom is usually one of the first cars in the pick-up line, since she knows I like to get to Rock On as early as possible. I hop into her car, throw my bag on the floorboard, and click my seat belt in place, pulling down the visor to look in the mirror.

When I pull my makeup bag out of the front pocket of my backpack, my mom turns to look at me oddly. "What in the world are you doing?" she asks, eyebrows pulled down low.

"What do you mean?" I play dumb, swiping mascara onto my lashes when she stops at a light.

"Why the hell are you putting on makeup when you're about to be at the gym for six hours? Better yet, why are you putting on makeup at all? You never wear makeup. Something that's made your daddy very happy for the past four years." She accelerates gently when the light turns green, allowing me to finish up the other eye before putting the mascara away and grabbing my concealer.

"Nothing. I just... I noticed I looked a little pasty in the bathroom at school today, so I'm just putting on a little something so I don't look sickly," I tell her.

"Uh huh. And it has nothing to do with that adorable little soldier boy who came back to see you yesterday?" She smirks, raising a brow.

"Adorable little soldier boy, Mom? Really? He's a badass Army man," I duck her question.

"He's adorable. I want to put him in my pocket and carry him around with me so I can pull him out every once in a while, to pet his cute little bald head," she says in a baby voice, making my eyes widen in horror. She laughs when she sees my face. "He's twenty, doll. He's almost half the age of your big brother. It's all right if I call him adorable."

"Just swear not to do it to his face," I beg, pinkening my cheekbones with a dab of blush.

"I can't make any promises," she teases, mischief in her bright blue eyes when I glance her way, making me groan.

As she pulls into the gym's lot and parks, I hop out with my bag, but then duck back into the car to hiss, "Behave," when I see Corbin standing propped against his Camaro on the other row of parking spaces.

Mom glances in her rearview mirror at him and grins. "Cute little guy," she says, giggling when my eyes narrow at her before I shut the door, standing up straight to smile at Corbin over the roof of Mom's Cavalier as he approaches.

"You got off early." I smile as he comes around, immediately pulling me into a hug, and I'm instantly filled with the sense of coming home after a long time away. My face automatically goes into the crook of his neck and I breathe him in. His scent is intoxicating. I can tell he's wearing a familiar cologne, but mixed with his chemistry, it's combined to make a unique scent that does *un*familiar things to my body.

"I snuck out. I worked through my lunch hour, so all my shit is done for the day, but I bolted before they could give me anything else to do. But now I'm starving," he adds.

"I only had fries for lunch," I confess, getting pushed away from his body to the sight of his furrowed brows over concerned dark eyes. "I was too excited to see you and it gave me a nervous belly. I could totally eat now, though."

"I could go grab y'all something if you like," Mom offers, having overheard us as she came around the front of her car.

"I'll buy if you fly, ma'am," Corbin tells her, and she smiles at him.

"Deal, but only if you stop calling me ma'am. It's either Eva or Mom, and usually Vi's friends go with the latter." She holds out her hand when he pulls out cash from his wallet. "What do y'all want?"

"Chinese," Corbin replies, at the same time I yip, "Kyoto's!" and we turn to look at each other. I grin as his face softens. "Jinx," he says, his eyes twinkling.

"Not exactly, but I'll still count it," Mom inserts, pulling our attention back to her. "Kyoto's it is. Chicken rice bowl with white sauce for you, doll?"

"Yes, please," I answer, wanting my usual.

"I'll take the same but add beef too, please. And there should be enough there to cover whatever you want too," Corbin tells her, and to my utter dismay, she reaches out and rubs the top of his shiny head.

"See, Vi? Adorable." She winks at me before circling back to get into her car, my mouth hanging open and my cheeks burning as I turn to look at Corbin, who is grinning.

"Your mom thinks I'm adorable," he whispers, as she backs out of her spot.

"I am so freaking sorry. She's getting crazier with age," I breathe, but he chuckles.

"No, this is good. She thinks I'm adorable. Everyone knows the first step is to win over the mother," he tells me, and I tilt my head.

"The first step in what?" I inquire.

"In getting the girl." And with that, he grasps my hand and tugs me toward the entrance of the gym, with me smiling like a fool while trying to hide it with my long hair.

I grab the pen off the desk and sign my name on the clipboard before handing it to Corbin, hurrying off to the bathroom to change out of my school uniform. I shove my clothes into my bag, grabbing my hairbrush out of the front pocket. I pull my hair into its customary high ponytail, taking more time than usual to make sure it's actually straight and smooth on top of my head. "Well, this is about as good as it's gonna get," I tell my reflection, quoting Mia from *The Princess Diaries,* and then I grab my bag and head out the door to put it all in my cubby.

"So what do you want to do first?" I ask Corbin, tying my chalk bag around my hips. When he doesn't answer, I look up at him, and find his eyes narrowed on me. "What?" I grow self-conscious, wondering if I have something hanging out of my nose.

"You look different," he says, taking a step closer.

"Um... I bathed? You haven't seen me not covered in chalk before," I tell him, playing dumb.

He takes another step forward, his head tilted a little, as his eyes burn into me, making me squirm. "You doll yourself up for me, baby girl?" he asks, his voice low.

My eyes widen before I look away, unable to meet his, as I lie, "What? No! You've just never seen me before I start climbing for the day is all."

When I finally look him in those gorgeous chocolaty pools, he smirks. "Okay, Vi," he says softly, "but just for future reference,

I think you're absolutely perfect, covered in chalk, unbathed, messy hair... just the way you are, sweetheart. So in case you ever feel you need to doll yourself up to impress me, just know you don't have to. I'm already impressed."

I feel my face soften, and all I can do is nod.

"But to answer your original question, how about you finally teach me this 'Takeaway' game you told me about?" he suggests, and I jump on it like a lifeline.

"Okay! I love Takeaway!" I grab his arm and drag him over to one of the moderate-level walls, and then pull out my stick of chalk from inside my chalk bag. "So here's what you do. Whoever starts will take their turn making their way across the wall. When they make it to the end, they get to 'take away' one of the rocks by circling it with the chalk. The next person goes, and they aren't allowed to use any of the circled holds. It starts out super easy, but eventually...." I grin, seeing he's got the gist. "If one of the climbers falls, the other climber has to make it in order to be named the winner. If both fall, you each get to try again... *until there is only one*," I say the last part in my best action-movie trailer voice.

He laughs, shaking his head at me. "Sweet. Okay, baby girl. Ladies first." He gestures to the wall and I put the stick of chalk in his hand, turning to start the game.

I make it across in three moves, choosing to use the big, easy jugs while I can. I take the chalk, circling one of the huge handholds in the center, and Corbin takes his place at the start.

I stand back and admire him from behind, loving the way his muscles ripple beneath all those tattoos. I wonder why he's got so many already, seeing as he's only twenty. Did he really get two sleeves and a chest piece all within just two years?

His wife beater fits him like a second skin, showing off the muscles in his back working as he makes his way across the wall. When he finishes and turns to take the chalk from me, he catches me checking out his ass, and my face heats. He doesn't say anything though, just smirks as he chooses the rock he wants to take away.

"Your turn," he tells me, and I swiftly boulder from one end to the other, avoiding the rocks we circled. This time I choose to take away a foothold, bending down almost to the floor to circle one of the rocks. When I turn around to face him, his eyes are on my lower half. I squeak then giggle, swatting at his arm. "What? You're allowed to check out my ass, but I'm not allowed to look at yours?" he teases.

I scoff. "Hey, you checked out mine on day one, thank you very much!"

"Ah, you caught that, did you? I was wondering what you'd tripped over. Guess it was nothing." He chuckles, and I point at the wall.

"Go!" I try to sound stern, but I can't help but laugh.

The game continues, the option of grips and footholds slowly dwindling until there are barely enough to get across. It's Corbin's turn when my mom returns with our food, and she sets it on the picnic table next to the wall we're playing on, sitting down to watch the final couple rounds of our game.

He makes it the two moves to the middle, squatting down low, since we've taken away anything higher, and then leans away from the wall, trying to see where the next handhold is to his right. It's way out of reach, and I smile to myself, realizing he hasn't noticed the mini-jug above, right below the eight-foot bouldering line drawn across the wall, marking the height you're allowed to climb without being on a rope. I don't say anything though. Oh no, I want my bragging rights if I can beat the big, bad soldier.

He readies himself, his muscles bunching, preparing to spring. And when he does, I'm surprised he's able to grasp the rock in his hand, but he misses the foothold and lands on the floor. "Ah shit," he growls, but then laughs, looking up at me. "Your turn, baby girl. I don't see how you're gonna make it though. You're good, but I don't know if you're *that* good. I will bow down if you do."

Won't that be a sight to see, I smirk to myself, reaching into my chalk bag to get a fresh coat on my hands.

I get in the ready position, taking a deep breath, knowing this is the moment of truth. This is the feeling I live for. People underestimate me. They look at me and they just see a slight, plain Jane, thinking nothing of me. This... this is what I love. Getting to show people I'm so much more, at least on the rocks.

I swiftly make it the two moves to the middle, and then rechalk my hands, my heart pounding. But where Corbin had only squatted down enough to bring his body level with grips, I crouch much lower, until my arms are out straight above my head and my ass is nearly on the floor, my feet pressing into the tiny chips screwed into the wall.

"What is she doing?" I hear Corbin mumble to my mom, but I don't hear her answer, tuning everything out but me and the wall.

My eyes glance way up and to the right, seeing the faded olive-green mini-jug I'm aiming for. My heart races as the rest of the world seems to slow down, my focus turning internal, zeroing in on the small but powerful muscles in my legs, the mighty strength in my delicate-looking fingers. *I can do this.*

And with one last pull of air in through my nose, at the moment I force it out through my lips, it seems to send me skyward like a rocket as I lunge for the rock, all of my muscles working together. In one fast, powerful jump up from the low position, I spring like a Jack-in-the-Box as I nail my target, sticking the dyno perfectly with my right hand.

I hear my mom's loud yip along with Corbin's, "What the fuck?!" as my left foot comes to rest on the rock my right hand had left open. I chalk up my left hand before switching my grip on the mini-jug to do the same to my right, and then finish out the route in two more quick moves. I jump from the wall and twirl, my ponytail swinging out from my head and coming to rest on my chest as I land, grinning from ear to ear as I see his shocked face.

Next thing I know, his hard body is pressed to mine as he lifts me in the air, spinning me around and making me laugh. "What the hell was that?" he exclaims. "That was fucking awesome! You gotta teach me! Teach me your ways, great and powerful Spidergirl."

When he sets me on my feet, I take a step back, lift a brow, and point to the ground in front of his rented climbing shoes. "I do believe you said you would bow down if I made it," I say haughtily, but then giggle, not expecting him to actually do it. But to my utter surprise, and Mom's fit of laughter, Corbin drops to his knees, raises his delicious, bulging, tattoo-covered arms above his head, then bows face-to-floor, chanting "We're not worthy," mimicking Garth on *Wayne's World*. It sets off my own full-body laugh, seeing the mostly serious, sinfully sexy man before me being a goofball for once.

When he stands, a heart-stopping smile across his gorgeous face, he brushes his hands together sending chalk into the air. But then suddenly, his eyes narrow, and his smile fades, and I think something is wrong, until...

"*Achoo!*" He sneezes right as he covers it with his wife beater, the lower half of his face disappearing into the neckline of his shirt.

"Weaksauce. I give it a five out of ten," I say, and then spin on my heel, starting toward the bathrooms to go wash my hands.

Suddenly, Corbin is beside me, and asks, "What is that all about? The scoring thing?"

"Oh, they've done it since before I started coming here. I guess the owner is an atheist or something and got tired of hearing 'bless you' a million times a day, so he started scoring people's sneezes as a joke. I've only been around one perfect ten before. My teammate Joshua came to practice when he had a sinus infection, and when he sneezed, the biggest, greenest snot bubble ballooned out of his nose in front of everybody. It was disgusting and fascinating at the same time," I reply, and he chuckles at my shudder.

We each go into our designated bathroom to wash our hands, and then meet back at the picnic table, where Mom has spread out all our dinner for us. I take a seat on the bench where she's set my bowl of rice covered in hibachi chicken with four lidded containers of white sauce. Corbin sits next to me, and he looks at the thick condiment questioningly as I empty the first one onto my chicken.

"What is that stuff?" he asks, grabbing a fork and tearing it free of the clear plastic wrapper.

"White sauce," I say, licking the remnants from the inside of the little bowl, unconsciously letting out a small moan.

"White sauce?" he repeats, his brow arching and a smirk forming on his lips.

"Mmmmm. Mmm-hmm. I could do shots of this stuff. I think they also call it yum-yum sauce in other places," I tell him, dumping a second container on top of the chicken.

"You'd like shots of yum-yum sauce... in your mouth," he states, and coughs when I nod.

"It's so delicious. Have you never tried it before?" I ask, before licking that one clean too.

"Nope, can't say I've taken white sauce to the face before," he says, his voice tight, as if trying not to laugh.

Suddenly, my hand stops midair as I'm about to dump a third one onto my dinner, and when it clicks in my head why he sounds like that, my face jerks toward him, my mouth and eyes wide open, and my cheeks flaming red. And that's when he and my mother both burst into laughter.

Five

Corbin

THERE IS NOTHING MORE fulfilling than toying with Vi's innocence. Growing up where and the way I did, and then being in the military, around a bunch of testosterone-filled, dirty-minded soldiers 24/7, the sexual innuendos never end. But then there's Vi, so sheltered, so focused on her sport, and her almost anti-social teenaged years, which would normally have been spent with friends and dealing with hormones. She takes everything anyone says at face value. It reminds me of Drax the Destroyer in *Guardians of the Galaxy*, the way he only understands things literally, unable to grasp the concept of metaphors.

But she finally caught on to my gutter-minded references to her yum-yum sauce, and thank God her mom has a great sense of humor, as she damn near fell off her bench, laughing on the other side of the picnic table. And the look on Vi's face—priceless.

We finish eating, and I grab the plastic bag all the food came in and collect our trash, tossing it in the giant trashcan in the very center of the gym. As Eva takes a seat in her usual spot on the couch, Vi gets into starting position on a route she told me she needed to practice, so I plop next to her mom, sending up a huge cloud of chalk and making her laugh.

When it settles, I take a deep breath, calming my nerves so I can do what I told myself I'd do all day at work. No way I'm pussing-out now. *Win the mom, win the girl.* "I have a question for you," I begin, leaning forward and resting my forearms on my knees, clasping my hands together.

"Shoot, honey," she tells me, and gives me her undivided attention.

"Maybe it's old fashioned of me, but as I get to know Vi... she's not like anyone I've ever met before. And I wanted to ask your permission to take her out on a date. I mean, I don't know if her—would you call it *sheltered?*—personality was your parenting style, or if it's just who she is. And I don't mean that in a disrespectful way at all," I add, holding my hand up to assure her. "In fact, I applaud you if it was your doing, because come on. She's eighteen, smart, beautiful, and talented, and somehow hasn't dated in four years."

We both glance over to the wall as we hear Vi hiss, "Shit!" and watch as she stands up from where she fell, brushes off her ass, and then starts at the beginning of the route once again.

"At first, it was a blessing," Eva says quietly. "And Lord knows her father still thinks it is. And in many ways, yes, I still believe it is too. She never stuck with anything when she was younger.

Always so self-conscious. She gave up dancing, because she was too embarrassed to wear the costumes. She gave up piano, because she'd get frustrated when she couldn't follow along with the sheet music the very first time she tried. This is the first and only thing she's put effort into. I think it was because she was naturally gifted in the very beginning, and then she worked at getting even better at it. It wasn't something she initially sucked at, and then had to work hard to *become* talented at it. Call it a character flaw."

She shrugs, and I nod, beginning to understand where she's going with this. "But then she became almost obsessed. Not in a bad way necessarily. I suppose anyone who is really good at something they love could be described as *obsessed*, when they eat, sleep, and breathe that hobby. Yet this isn't a very social sport. Football, basketball, cheerleading... all of those kinds of sports, you're on a team. You have to work together in order to win. This... this, it's just you and the rocks. You shut everything and everyone else out, and you put all of your focus into yourself and keeping your body on the wall, not falling." She looks at me with an almost sad smile.

"I mean, she's on the 'climbing team,'" she continues, gesturing with air quotes. "But really, all they do is warm up and condition together, and then the coach will either teach her a new technique or fix the way a climber is doing something, but there's really nothing social about it."

She sighs. "I guess what I'm trying to say is no, it wasn't me. Yeah, I wanted her in an extracurricular activity to take up some of her time after school to keep her out of trouble, but the way it's taken over her life"—she shakes her head—"that was all her. But to answer your request, yes, *please*, by all means take her on a date. I've never seen her act the way she does around you. She's never really been excited to spend time with another person before. And most importantly, I've never seen her smile so much. You are the only *person* who's ever made her eyes light up the way they do when she beats a hard route." She grins, and it's contagious.

"Wow. That was a lot easier than I thought it would be," I chuckled. "Confession time? I was seriously psyching myself up to asking you all day. I didn't think you'd want your daughter going out with a guy like me." My forearms still resting on my knees, I ungrasp my hands, palms up, and use my eyes to indicate all my tattoos before looking back at her.

"One, you're a Specialist in the army at just twenty years old. That means you don't joke around when it comes to your job. You probably haven't done anything stupid to make you lose rank." She lifts her brows to confirm, and I nod. "Two, the way you were with your lower-ranking soldier. You took great care in making sure he knew y'all were here to have fun. You had him call you by your name, made him your equal for a little while."

One corner of my lips pulls up as that observation reminds me of something. "I had a Master Sergeant once who told me, 'Lowe, when you take off your dog tags at the end of the day, you should take off the soldier mentality along with them.' It kinda just stuck with me, so I try to pass down that bit of advice when I can," I tell her.

"That's very good advice. My husband—Vi's dad—and I have been married since I was 19, many, many moons ago. He's retired Navy. You can still see the military in him, in his neatness and the way he can't stand clutter. The way he eats fast, little things like that. But he was also very good at 'taking off the mentality' as you put it, and I think that's why we've lasted this long," she confides, and it makes me smile.

I really enjoy talking with Eva. She's not like most moms I've met in the past of girls I was interested in. She's never once looked at me disapprovingly, which is a nice change, and she talks to me like the grown man I am, instead of down at me.

"So why is it that you always stay? I see other parents just drop off their kids, much younger than Vi. But you've been here with her all three times I've come. Just curious," I ask.

"Vi's big brother is much older than her. And we tried for a really long time to have another baby, but they just never came. We finally threw in the towel and stopped hoping it was going to work, and since I had some health issues, we didn't feel it was safe for me to do any type of fertility treatments. But then, about three months before Marshall's retirement date from the Navy, lo and behold, I was pregnant. At almost forty years old, with Henry—Vi's brother—about to go to boot camp for the Navy himself, I finally conceived. Not only that, it was a baby girl. I grew up with all brothers, and then I had Henry, so all I wanted in the whole world was a little girl. And there she is," Eva says, holding out her hand toward her gorgeous daughter and smiling, as we hear Vi growl, *"Mother of Gooooooood,"* as she tries desperately to stretch and reach a foothold with her right foot, the tip of her toe barely missing it, with her body turned almost completely sideways on the wall.

"So, one, I just love spending as much time with her as I can get. She was a dream come true for me, and I treat her as the gift she is. There's no way I could just drop her off anywhere and leave her by herself. And two, she's always been so tiny. I mean, look at me." She lifts her arms, indicating how rail-thin she is too. "She takes after me. She can eat a meal the size of a horse—and let me tell you, ever since she started climbing, the girl puts away some damn food with all the energy she burns, so fair warning for your wallet when you take her out. But there isn't anything wrong with her, just a crazy high metabolism. Yet being that little and practically defenseless, I've never been able to let her go off on her own. Because it would be *on her own*. She doesn't really have any girlfriends. The little assholes at school picked on her so bad she never opened up to anyone to make an ally."

"Who the fu—"

"Corbin!" Vi calls, cutting off the fury filling me that someone, anyone, would be giving her shit. "Will you come spot me for a second?" Her voice is strained as she keeps her body flush with the wall.

I jump up and rush to her, shaking off my anger. "What do you want me to do?"

"Just put your hand flat on my back. I've got to see if I'm even tall enough to reach this bitch," she breathes, and I do as she requests, taking some of the strain off her arms as they struggle to keep her close to the rocks.

My hand still pressed there, I take a step back, enough to see if her toe is within reach of the foothold. "You're still about an inch off, baby girl."

"Son of a bitch," she gripes, relaxing into my palm and placing her feet on the ground before standing upright. Her hands shoot to her hips, and I hear her frustrated growl.

I can't help but smile at the pensive look on her face as she tries to figure out how she's going to conquer this route. I have no idea how she'll be able to fix something like not being long enough to reach a rock, but knowing her abilities, I don't doubt she will. She bites her lip as her eyes dart between the holds, and it makes my dick twitch in my shorts.

Not wanting to get a hard-on in basketball shorts in the bright gym, her mom right there watching us, I place my hand on her cheek and turn her to look at me for a moment. "You've got this, baby girl," I tell her, kissing her forehead, and then make my way back to the couch. I sit down gently so I don't send up a chalk cloud, and when I look up at Vi, her wide eyes are on me, mouth slightly open. The look on her face is hard to read, but then she smiles shyly when our eyes meet, and she turns back to the wall.

"Yep," Eva says from beside me, and I look at her. "I'm calling it right now. You're my future son-in-law." She nods once, picks up her book, and flips to her bookmarked page, not saying another word.

As surprising as her words are, what shocks me more is the fact I don't hate the idea. I always told myself I didn't want to be in a relationship, being in the military. Much less married. All you hear are horror stories, soldiers going off to war and receiving Dear John letters, or significant others cheating and rumors getting back through the grapevine.

Nothing good ever comes from being in a serious relationship when you get deployed. Not only all the infidelity bullshit, but also the state of mind it puts you in. When you have someone back home, it can make you depressed and unfocused, so that's why I decided a long time ago that I would be married to my job instead. I haven't had an actual girlfriend since I dropped out of high school and got my GED to go ahead and join the Army.

But after spending the last three days with Vi, and our immediate and unwavering connection....

I sit back, prop my elbow on the arm of the couch, and toy with my bottom lip with the tips of my thumb and pointer finger as I watch Vi work out the route in her head. Then she gets back into starting position once again. This time, when she arrives at the place that's been giving her problems, she doesn't try to reach so far with her foot first. She pulls herself up, both hands on one tiny rock before extending to the next handhold with her right arm. As she grasps it, she's able to swing her entire body to the foothold she had previously been unable to get to, and then completes the route.

Hopping down off the last rock, instead of her customary twirl, she collapses to the ground and sprawls out. I jump up, my heart sinking to my stomach, and run to her, but as I look down, I see her face is covered in a wide grin as her chest pumps with exertion, her arms stretching out above her head. I step over her, putting one foot on the ground on either side of her chest, and cross my arms over mine, glaring down at her. "You just scared the piss out of me," I grumble.

"Sorry," she giggles, her eyes twinkling from the fluorescent light shining down on her from the ceiling.

"I think you should make up for it by going out with me," I state, smirking when her heaving breaths stutter for a moment.

Her eyes widen, her grin relaxes, and she turns her head to glance at her mom, who I see nods her head in approval, before Vi looks back up at me. "O-okay," she replies, and I hold my hand out for her to grasp.

She places her delicate hand in mine, and I pull her up effortlessly to stand, then jerk her forward, wrapping my arm around her lower back to hold her to me. "A kiss to seal the deal?" I prompt jokingly, and she gulps. But to my surprise, she leans up and places a soft, quick kiss to my cheek, and it does more to my heart than the heaviest make-out session I've ever had in my life.

I look over at Eva, with the biggest smile I've had on my face in a long-ass time. "Tomorrow night good, Mom?" I ask her, and lay my cheek against the top of Vi's head as I feel her rest her forehead on my collarbone. The act is so small, but knowing it's Vi—my guarded, innocent, sweet girl, who I now understand doesn't open up to anyone—it makes me feel like the king of the world that she's allowing herself this tiny bit of intimacy.

Voice choked up, Eva replies, "Sounds good to me. Vivian?"

I feel Vi nod against me, and I rub her back gently, hearing her almost purr before she stands to her full height, smiles, and then asks, "So. You ready to climb?"

I chuckle, but allow her to change the subject, knowing I got more out of her than I had expected. "Definitely. How about another game of takeaway? I got to try to win, since you beat me."

And just like that, self-assured Vi returns. "Bring it, soldier boy."

BEFORE THE *li*

EFORE THE *lie*

BEFORE THE *lie*

RE THE *lie*

BEFORE THE *lie*

Six

Vi

NERVOUS DOESN'T EVEN BEGIN to describe what's going on inside me as I wait for Corbin to pick me up. We decided last night on the phone that we'd go see a movie and out to eat. There's not much else to do in our small town next to the base, so we're sticking to the classic first date.

Mom took me shopping this morning, when I started freaking out that all I had were school uniforms and athletic clothes. I think she was more excited than I was for our girly excursion, and ended up buying me way more than just an outfit for tonight. I am now the proud owner of three pairs of skinny jeans, two pairs of denim bellbottoms, about ten new cute tops, and five dresses. Also, a ton of new shoes for every possible occasion, and one thing I've never had a reason to own in my life, but saw and actually drooled over it when we were passing by it in the window, a purse. But not just any purse. It's a lavender solid leather Coach bag that has silver details.

I stroke the leather in my lap as I sit at the small desk in my room before tossing in my lip-gloss, smiling as I remember what Mom said. *"You never ask for anything. You didn't go to prom. I have an envelope tucked away full of money I stashed for things you never ended up wanting to do. If you want the bag, it's yours, doll."* I had squealed and hugged her ferociously before we both danced into the store.

I hear the doorbell ring and glance at the time on my cell—5:42 p.m. He's eighteen minutes early. I'm kind of grateful though. I've been ready for half an hour, and my anxiety has been growing ever since. I toss my bag onto my shoulder, and check myself in the mirror. My white V-cut super-soft T-shirt looks crisp and clean paired with my dark-wash skinny jeans and brown sandals. My long, dark hair is down my back and straightened—something I never take the time to do normally—and it surprises me how long it's gotten, since it usually stays in a bun or ponytail on top of my head. I put on a little blush, some mascara, and lip-gloss, but I don't know how to do much else, so I left it at that instead of attempting and failing anything fancier. With a deep breath in and out, I square my shoulders, feeling more confident in the way I look than I think I have my whole life, and head downstairs.

When I get to the bottom, I see my dad has the door open and is shaking a hand attached to a tattooed wrist, and my heart flips.

"Nice to meet you too, Corbin. My wife speaks very highly of you," Dad says, and opens the door wider, allowing Corbin to step all the way in. When the door shuts, there he is, in all his heart-stopping, drool-inducing glory.

I've never seen him in anything but workout clothes before. Tonight, he's wearing thick-soled brown boots, dark jeans, and a black T-shirt that looks like the seams may burst open it's stretched so tight across his massive biceps. When I look up into his face, he's placing a black ball cap on his head with one hand, and then lifts the other to the bill to squish it, making it frame his forehead. It's a habit I've noticed him do the couple times he's put it on as he leaves the gym.

I smile at him, feeling my face heat as he licks his lips, taking me in much the same way I did him. And we just stand there staring at each other silently until my dad comes back into the foyer, snapping us out of it, when I hadn't even noticed he'd gone outside in the first place.

"All right, Specialist Corbin Lowe, ma man. I took a picture of your license plate, and I now know your full name. If you don't bring my daughter home by a decent hour, I will hunt you down," Dad tells him, clapping Corbin on the shoulder. "Have fun, princess," he directs at me, before heading into the kitchen just as Mom is coming out, wiping her hands on a dishtowel.

"Ignore him, honey," she says, giving Corbin a brief one-armed hug before turning to me. "Oh, Vi, my baby girl. You look beautiful!" She walks over to me, slides open the zipper of my new purse, and I see her tuck a couple of folded bills inside. As she hugs me, she whispers, "A girl should always have cash to get herself home, just in case, baby," before kissing my cheek. "Now y'all have a good time."

I walk over to the open door and feel Corbin's hand come up to rest on my lower back. "Movie starts at 6:30, and we're going to dinner right after. I'll have her back no later than midnight," he tells her, before mouthing to me, *Princess*, and I use the back of my hand to slap him in the gut. Yet I discover there is no gut at all, just rock-hard abs, and he doesn't even flinch, giving me a smirk instead.

"Bye, Mom," I say, and we head out the door. Corbin opens the passenger door of his Camaro for me, and I slide into the black leather bucket seat. As he closes it behind me, I tuck my bag under my legs and put on my seat belt. The interior is completely spotless and empty, except for the small American flag hanging from the rearview mirror.

As he gets in on the driver's side, he starts the car and pulls out of our driveway. Once he's out of my neighborhood and on the main road, he shifts gears and hits the gas, my body suddenly pressing into the seat.

"Like that, do you, baby girl?" he asks, and I realize I have the biggest smile on my face.

"Oh yeah. My brother has a Mustang and takes me on rides when he's home. It's the only time I get to go fast. I'm a roller coaster junkie too," I confess, and laugh as he revs his engine, shifts gears, and speeds through a yellow light.

Soon, though, he slows back down to the speed limit. "As much as I'd like to go all *Fast and Furious* for you, I'd rather not get a speeding ticket on our first date. Your dad would probably never let me have a second one," he says, and I giggle.

"True story."

"Where do you go to ride roller coasters?" he questions, stopping at a red light before turning right.

"I've been to Disney World, Busch Gardens, and King's Dominion, but the closest one is Six Flags. I've been to it several times, since it's only about four hours away."

"I can't remember the last time I went to an amusement park," he confides, and I look over at him with wide eyes.

"Really? Oh, my gosh, we'll have to go soon." The words escape my mouth without thinking, and I feel my face heat. "I mean, if you want to," I add quietly.

He glances at me, hearing the abrupt change in my tone, and reaches over, resting his hot palm on my thigh. "I'd fucking love to take you to ride roller coasters. When we going?"

I grin. "Well, I graduate in about two months. Two weeks before the rest of the school lets out. Probably be a good time to go, before the summer rush. Fewer lines," I suggest.

"Sounds perfect to me, baby girl." He turns up the radio suddenly. "Oh, I love this song. Good shit." I listen to the lyrics, and look at him questioningly before he begins to sing, "*Did you do too many drugs? I did too many drugs. Did you do too many drugs too? Baby.*" He tickles my knee on the last drawled out word, making me laugh.

"What the heck is this?" I ask.

"'American Music' by the Violent Femmes," he replies, then taps along as he belts out the rest of the song.

When it ends, I smile over at him. "That must be some kind of California music or something. I've never heard of them before."

"Yeah, I used to smoke weed and listen to them and Pink Floyd all the time back in the day," he says so nonchalantly that my exasperated look catches him off guard. "What?"

"You smoked weed?"

"Who hasn't?" He shrugs, giving me a sexy smirk.

"Um, me. I've never even smoked a cigarette. Much less something illegal."

"Somehow, that doesn't surprise me, baby girl." He squeezes

my leg.

"What's it like?" I ask quietly, turning to face him as much as I can in the bucket seat.

"What, weed? It's really not as big of a deal as people make it out to be. For me, it was just super relaxing. I'd smoke, and then just lie in bed and listen to music. It helped me turn my brain off so I could sleep. I had a lot of bad shit going on around me back then, and it was my escape," he explains.

"What kind of bad shit?" I pry.

He glances over, lifting an eyebrow at me. "Promise not to run?"

Like that would happen, I think. Seeing the kind of man he is now, I'd never hold his past against him. "Promise."

"Well, I told you I was in a gang before I was given the choice of jail or joining the military. But we're not talking about some stupid little no-name group of kids that just call themselves a gang. I was part of one of the big ones out in Cali. I had it tattooed... here," he tells me, pointing at a place on his arm before holding it over for me to see, but all I see is the beautiful Americana sleeve. "Feel it."

I run my fingertips over his bicep, and sure enough, the skin there feels raised in places, as if it's scarred beneath all the ink. "What was it?" I ask, wrapping my hand around his arm as he rests his elbow on the console, proud of myself for bravely keeping up the contact.

"It was the gang's symbols, but in order to join the military, I had to get rid of it. Fastest way to do that, and what many people do, was to take a rock and scrub it out."

"Ouch, didn't that hurt?" I flinch.

"Hell yeah, it hurt, but I wasn't about to waste the money

and take the time to do that laser bullshit. I had a lot of tattoos already by the time I was seventeen, so after it healed, I got it covered up."

"How did you have tattoos already? You have to be eighteen, right?" I probe, feeling like I'm interrogating him, but I can't get enough of how open he's being. He's so interesting, and I want to know everything about him.

"Maybe to get one legally. But I had a buddy who was a tattoo artist, and he did them at his house. I got my first one when I was fifteen. I had all sorts of them by the time I was eighteen. I wasn't happy with the way it was looking, getting patchwork tattoos. I felt like a car with a bunch of mismatched bumper stickers. So when I got here, with one of the best tattoo shops in the US right outside the base's gate, I decided to go in and turn them into sleeves," he explains, and I look down at his arm again.

Sure enough, looking closely, I can see hidden pictures within the overall traditional Americana style artwork. "We'll have to play seek-and-find story time when I can actually see better, instead of in a dark car."

We pull into the parking lot of the movie theater and he chuckles. "I'll tell you all about them, baby girl. Might take a while, because each one has its own meaning. I never got anything that wasn't symbolic to me in some way."

He pulls into a spot and puts the car in park. "What about you? You want any tattoos?" he asks.

"I love tattoos. But as far as I understand, they're really expensive. And since I don't have a job...." I shrug. "No way my parents would give me money for a tattoo. So that will have to wait until I can afford them on my own."

He opens his door and hops out, coming around and opening

mine, where I struggle to get out of the slick and deep leather bucket seat. He holds out his hand to me and chuckles, pulling me up before closing the door. "What are you doing after graduation?" he asks, taking my hand like we've done it every day our whole lives. It's that way for me too. It feels so natural holding hands with him, even though it's something I've never done with anyone before.

"I'm going to the community college in the fall. I was thinking about working at Rock On over the summer during the day. I've actually done that before, worked there during my summer breaks. I mean, I'd be there anyways. Might as well get paid for it too," I reply.

We approach the window of the box office and he buys our two tickets, and I thank him before he takes my hand once again, leading me into the lobby. "What are you going to school for?"

"I don't know yet. I figure I have plenty of time to decide while I get my core classes out of the way first," I admit, as we get in line for the concession counter.

"What, you don't know what you want to be when you grow up?" He smiles.

"No, not really. To be perfectly honest, I've never had any big dreams of becoming something professional. I'm not really good at anything besides climbing. I always just wanted to be my mom." I blush, looking away, embarrassed I don't have a more interesting answer.

"Your mom? Like, you want to be a homemaker?" he asks.

"Yeah. I mean, some people think that's an easy job, but it's really not. It's a lot of work running a household. And she not only keeps it running, but she's amazing at everything that goes into it. We have delicious home-cooked meals every night. She cleans, bakes, grocery shops every week, decorates the house for every season and holiday, all sorts of stuff. And that's with grown children. I can't imagine how busy she was with babies. But she always does everything happily, with a big smile on her face. It all brings her so much joy just taking care of her family."

He tugs on the hand he's holding, bringing my body flush with his, and I lift my eyes to meet his. "There is nothing to be ashamed of about wanting to be a homemaker. Look at *you*, and from the little bit I've heard you two say about your brother, it sounds like he turned out great as well. Maybe if I'd had that, I wouldn't have been such a little shithead when I was younger. That's a very admirable job, Vi," he assures me, and I melt against him. "I just don't see how you planned on seeing that dream out, keeping to yourself and never dating." He chuckles, winking at me.

"No one ever made me stop and take a second look before you," I breathe, getting lost in his amazing dark chocolate eyes.

He smiles, and his eyes lower to my mouth when I unconsciously bite my bottom lip. The next thing I know, his soft, full lips are against mine, and a jolt runs through my whole body. As his hand comes up to rest against the side of my neck and I feel him trace my jawline with his thumb, everything and everyone begin to disappear.

The bright lights and menu above the concession stand are the first to dim, as I take in the heat of his body pressed to mine. The sound of the popping machine and the people talking around us in line are the next to fade, as I enjoy Corbin's steady inhale and exhale through his nose, and then the barely audible growl he lets loose as he wraps his arm around my lower back. Finally, the strong smell of buttery popcorn and sugary sweet candy in the air dissolves, as all I breathe in is the delicious and intoxicating scent of the man before me.

The entire world has completely evaporated as time stands still, and all that's left are the two of us in our sweet embrace. It's not an inappropriate public display of affection, nothing overly passionate for anyone around us to lewdly observe, but heart-stopping just the same. And it seems to end just as quickly as it began when Corbin gently pulls away.

I blink up at him. "I thought the first kiss normally comes at the end of the date," I whisper.

His face serious, he presses his forehead to mine, and replies, "You'll learn not much about me is normal. I just hope none of it scares you away."

I smile, trying to brighten his suddenly somber tone. "Maybe if we mix your un-normalness with my boringness, we'll even each other out."

"Vi, there is nothing boring about you, baby girl. You just needed someone to bring you out of your shell," he says, tucking my hair behind my ear.

"Are you calling me a hermit crab?" I giggle, as we make our way to the front of the line.

"Hottest hermit crab I've ever seen." He chuckles, and looks up at the menu board. "Do you know what you want?"

"Chocolate-covered almonds and Sprite, please," I answer, a little stunned. No one's ever called me hot before, at least not right to my face like that.

"Chocolate-covered almonds, a large Sprite, and a large popcorn please," Corbin orders, and pulls out his wallet to pay.

"Ew, popcorn is gross," I mumble teasingly.

He gives me a horrified look. "What? I don't know if this is going to work. Who doesn't like popcorn?"

I laugh, smacking his arm. "Again, me, that's who. It always gets stuck in my teeth."

We grab our snacks, and then find two seats in the back of the theater, where he places the giant drink in the cup holder between us.

"You said you didn't have what I do. So what *did* you have, if your mom wasn't home with you like mine?" I ask curiously.

"My mom and dad divorced when I was little, and I lived with my mom in California, while my dad lived in the Midwest. She had an office job that paid really well, but it had long hours. She didn't like leaving me alone, so I had a babysitter that would come over and hang out with me until bedtime, and then Mom would get home sometime after that. It was all well and good until I got a new babysitter when I was fourteen, and I was kind of pissed that she still thought I needed to be looked after. I mean, I was fourteen, not a child anymore. But then the babysitter showed up, an eighteen-year-old college student, and that was the end of my bitching," he tells me, and a feeling I can only describe as jealousy fills me.

"Pray tell," I prompt, because apparently I want to torture myself.

"Well, she was this hot older chick, and although I was only fourteen, I've always looked older. I took wrestling in school, and was a third degree black belt in Kenpō, so I had quite the body, even back then. I lost my virginity to her soon after—"

"Your eighteen-year-old babysitter slept with a fourteen-year-old?" I gasp, completely flabbergasted. "Isn't that illegal? Plus, um... she was in college, you said. So why the hell would she want to sleep with a kid when she had people her own age?"

"One, it's only illegal if you get caught, and two, I didn't look much younger than I do now, so I'm sure she wasn't thinking about my age at the time. We were just two people alone in my house who knew my mom wouldn't be home until late," he explains.

I look at him, imagining myself in his babysitter's position if I would've cared how old he was, and I guess I can see why it didn't matter to her. He's freakin' perfect. "I suppose."

"But it all went downhill from there. She's the one who introduced me to drugs. It started out as just weed, but then she started bringing over things like Ecstasy and all sorts of shit. She snuck me out to a party, and introduced me to her friends who were in the gang, and one thing led to another." He takes a sip of drink before eating a handful of popcorn.

"And your mom had no idea?" I ask.

"Nope, not until I was sixteen and she happened to see one of my tattoos. But by then, I was already so submersed into all the bad shit that I didn't really care about her feelings. Maybe if she'd caught me before then…. But I don't waste time on 'what ifs'. Because if my life hadn't been that way, I would never have joined the military and I wouldn't be the person I am today. It's not my mom's fault. I don't blame her for never noticing. She was just a trusting person who believed her son when I told her I really liked my babysitter and how all we did was my homework and watch TV until I went to bed. Also in her defense, I got really good at lying and hiding shit. A person becomes very crafty when they become an addict."

Just then the lights lower in the theater, effectively cutting off our conversation. I open my box of candy, and pop two in my mouth. As we watch the previews, I glance over at Corbin, the lights and shadows playing over his handsome features, and I can't help but think how grateful I am that his babysitter was such a bad influence, because I probably wouldn't have met him otherwise. I reach over and grab a handful of his popcorn, not being able to resist the smell any longer, and toss it in my mouth.

He looks over at me, eyebrows furrowed. "I thought popcorn was gross?"

"But it just smells so good. I can't stand the way it makes my teeth feel though," I tell him, swiping my tongue across my teeth, unintentionally drawing his eyes to my mouth. "Plus, it tastes really good when you mix the salty popcorn with the sweet chocolate."

"Really? Let me see," he whispers, and moves forward to kiss me, but before his tongue can dip into my mouth, my head jerks back as an explosion goes off on the big screen, startling me as the surround sound makes it seem like we're under attack. Seeing that it's just part of the trailer for an upcoming action movie, I giggle and shake my head.

"Here," I murmur, and pour out a couple of my chocolate-covered almonds into my hand before holding them out to him. But instead of letting me drop them into his hand, he dips his face and eats them directly out from between my fingers, the feel of his lips on my sensitive fingertips sending a surge of tingles to my core.

I watch as he eats another handful of popcorn, his face becoming thoughtful. He leans toward me to whisper in my ear, "You're right. That's delicious, but I would've rather tasted it on you."

My face falls, but I try to be as open as he's been with me. "I... I've never done that before, Corbin." He pulls back and looks me in the eye, but my gaze drops to his chest. "Just... don't get frustrated with me, okay? I know I'm not some super cool chick who has all this experience that'll rock your world like your babysitter did. So just please... try not to get mad at me when I don't know how to do something, all right?"

Suddenly, the drink is removed and the armrest is lifted from between us. He sets his popcorn in the chair next to him, and next thing I know, I'm in Corbin's lap and he's cradling my face with his hand.

"One thing I can promise you, Vi. I will never get frustrated or be mad at your innocence. We will take this thing as slow as you need. I'm normally not a patient man, but if it means getting to taste you and have you all to myself, I'd wait forever," he says so sincerely I feel tears prickle the backs of my eyes. He pulls my face down to his for a soft, tender kiss, and then he lifts me back into my seat, grabs his bag of popcorn, placing it between his knees, and turns his attention back to the screen. I blink a few times, wondering how the hell I'd gotten so lucky to find someone who actually *gets* me. And with that thought in mind, I bravely reach over with my right hand and lace my fingers with his left, feeling his grip tighten as he rests our joined hands on his thigh.

After I finish up my candy, I spend the last thirty minutes with my head on Corbin's shoulder, feeling more at peace snuggled against him than I ever have.

Corbin

My ass is completely numb, my arm is asleep, and I'm pretty sure my fingers are about to fall off from lack of circulation, but I'll be damned if I move even a centimeter. I don't want to risk Vi's head leaving my shoulder or her hand pulling out of mine. Especially since she's the one who initiated both.

I've never been one for holding hands, and I damn sure haven't ever been known for being a cuddler. But having Vi so close, snuggled into my side, her tiny body fitting against mine so perfectly, I could sit here forever.

But the movie ends, and as soon as the credits start rolling, Vi lifts her head and reaches across me for the drink, and I feel the loss like she's cut off one of my limbs.

"I'm starving. Where we going for dinner?" she asks, standing up and stretching her arms above her head, which lifts her shirt and bares a sliver of the perfect, creamy skin of her stomach, making me instantly hard.

I exhale slowly and stand, waiting to adjust myself until she turns away from me to lead the way out of our row of seats. "How about Olive Garden? It's just right up the street," I suggest.

"Ooh, sounds good," she replies, holding the railing to make her way down the steps ahead of me.

"I love their breadsticks," I say, watching her ass sway with her every step.

"Psh. No. If it's breadsticks you want, then you need to try Fazoli's."

"No way. No one has better bread sticks than Olive Garden." I shake my head.

She turns around on the bottom step to face me, looking up at me with a challenge in her eyes. My dick throbs behind my waistband, where I've got it tucked. "Trust me. Fazoli's has the most delicious, hot, buttery, garlicky breadsticks ever. Olive Garden's don't hold a candle."

"Wanna make a bet?" I ask, a smirk pulling up my lips.

She straightens and tosses her hair over her shoulder. "What kind of bet?"

"I don't know yet. Let me think about it on our way there."

As I get into the driver's seat of my Camaro after closing Vi's door, I realize something. "Vi, I noticed your mom's car in your driveway, and what I assumed was your dad's truck, but no other vehicle. Do you not have a car?"

"Why have a car if I don't have a license?" She shrugs.

"You don't have your driver's license?" I ask, my face obviously showing my shock, because she giggles and touches the crease between my eyebrows. "But you're eighteen."

"I mean, I went through Driver's Ed and got my permit and stuff, but driving terrifies me. The thought of having to be in control of anything, even a vehicle...." She shakes her head. "In my class, I was okay, because my teacher had his own set of pedals and a steering wheel on his side of the car, so I knew if I were to screw up, he could take over and get us out of danger. But in a normal car.... Scares the shit out of me."

I try to ignore the images that her hating to be in control of anything brings to mind, and I refrain from telling her I'd happily take control of whatever she'd like. But her being too scared to drive pushes past all that. "Baby girl, you need to get your license. You don't want to be dependent on everyone else to get you anywhere you need to go. It's just lack of confidence.

I think with enough practice, your fear of driving would lessen."

"I don't really need it though. I only go to school and to Rock On. Plus, cars and insurance and all that is expensive," she justifies.

"Yeah, but soon, you'll be going to college, and then working at the gym. You don't want your mom to have to keep taking you everywhere, do you?" I ask gently.

"I guess not. I haven't really thought about it," she replies honestly, wringing her hands in her lap.

"I've got it." I reach over and place my hand between hers, lacing my fingers through hers to stop her nervous fidgeting. "If I don't like Fazoli's breadsticks better than Olive Garden's, then you have to practice driving with me. If I do, then you don't have to."

"That's not fair," she whines. "You'll say you don't like their breadsticks better just to make me drive."

I smirk. "That's true, even though I doubt anyone is going to be able to top my love of Olive Garden's breadsticks. I mean, come on. Their initials are OG. They're the OG of Italian food, straight up gangsta," I reply, gaining the laugh I was hoping for. "Then just let me teach you to drive. I promise I won't let anything happen to you."

She lets out a growl of frustration, looks over at me with the most adorable scowl I've ever seen, and then looks down. "Oh hell no! You have a stick shift. No way," she says, shaking her head.

"I'll take you in your mom's car then. It's an automatic, right?" I prompt, knowing her mom has a little four-cylinder Chevy Cavalier.

"Ugh. Fine. If you can convince my mother—the woman who

won't let anyone drive her car—to let you take me to practice driving, then yes, Corbin. I'll learn," she says with such self-assurance that it makes me believe there's no way in hell I'll be able to talk her mom into letting me use her car. But after our conversation at the gym, I'm confident I'll be able to sweet-talk Eva out of her keys.

"Deal. Now where is this place? I'm hungry."

"WOULD YOU LIKE another breadstick?" the waitress asks, the wicker basket full of the carb-loaded little pieces of heaven hanging on her arm, her tongs at the ready to give me another two after the dozen I've already eaten.

"Last round and that's it for me. I'm stuffed," I reply, looking over at Vi, her expression of triumph still in place since my first bite of the best damn breadsticks I've ever tasted in my life. The waitress leaves, and I lean forward so only Vi can hear me. "If you don't wipe that smirk off your face, baby girl, I'm going to bend you over my lap and spank your sexy little ass."

Her jaw drops and her cheeks turn an attractive shade of pink in the dimly lit restaurant. Her eyes dart to the couple at the next table over, and she leans forward, over her plate of half-eaten spaghetti. "I'd like to see you try, soldier. I've never been spanked in my life," she tells me haughtily, and my dick instantly hardens. She's grown bolder over dinner, talking to me openly as she's answered every question I've asked about herself. I think it's because I've been open and honest with her as well, sharing everything about my past without trying to hide anything.

"It won't happen the first time I make you mine, Vi, but you can bet that sweet ass I'll be turning it red someday soon."

Her mouth opens and closes like a fish before she sits back in her seat and takes a sip of her drink. "I skipped a night of climbing to get threatened with spankings," she pouts.

"Trust me. When it happens, you'll be begging for more. And by that time, rocks will no longer be your favorite thing to climb," I assure her, and sit back to watch what I said click into place. Yup, there it goes. And as usual, when one of my sexual innuendos finally meets its mark in her mind, her eyes widen, her face pinkens, and her mouth falls open once more. One of my favorite expressions I can get her to make.

She clears her throat and tries to change the subject, but I'm having too much fun making her squirm to let her escape my dirty mind. "What's your favorite movie?" she asks.

"*Harry Potter*. And after we watch it, I'll *avada kedavra* that pussy," I reply, and she gasps.

"You did not just say you'd use the death spell on my *lady bits,*" she hisses the last bit, and I can't help but chuckle.

"What's yours?" I counter, taking a bite of my fresh breadstick, which I begrudgingly admitted were the best ones I'd ever eaten as soon as I took a bite of the first one that came with my chicken fettuccini alfredo.

"*My Big Fat Greek Wedding,*" she answers, and I nod.

"Love that movie. I have it on DVD."

"Really?" Her eyes brighten. "Okay, you win some cool points back. What's your favorite color?"

"Pink... like your pu—"

"Corbin!" she cuts me off, covering her eyes with her hands. "I know pink is not your favorite color, dammit."

I throw my head back and laugh, and when I look at her once again, she's uncovered her eyes and is watching me with a sweet smile on her face, as if she's enjoying my laughter. "Orange. My favorite color is orange."

"Seriously? I don't think I've ever heard anyone say orange is their favorite before." She tilts her head to the side.

"It's a bright, happy color. I've just always liked it for some reason. I bet I can guess yours," I say, and she sits up straight.

"Shoot."

"Purple."

"How'd you know?" she questions, her brows lowering but a smile on her lips.

"Your harness and your bag. The harness is important to you, a piece of crucial gear for your favorite activity, and it has purple details. Your bag isn't a cheap one. So one would assume you wouldn't get it in a color that isn't one you really love."

"Nice. Yes, purple is my favorite. I'd wear a lot more of it if I didn't have a school uniform. My whole room is done in different shades," she tells me.

"Even your bed?" I ask, an evil little grin spreading across my face.

"Yeees, even my bed." She rolls her eyes.

"Ah, so now I can better picture you when I'm lying in my bed talking to you on the phone every night."

Her smile returns. "What does yours look like?"

"I'll show you mine if you show me yours, baby girl," I tease, laughing at how easy it is to make her squirm. When she growls, I give in. "Okay, okay. Mine has an outdoor scene on it. It's a buck in the middle of the woods. I have a thing for stuff like that, and Native American artwork. I'm half Cherokee, and I love hunting, so it fits me."

"Cherokee. That must be where you get your gorgeous dark eyes from. Which half?" she asks, and my chest puffs up a little that she likes my eyes. Even though I've heard it countless times before, it actually means something coming from her.

"My dad's side. My mom is Irish." I glance down at my G-Shock watch, seeing it's only 9:38 p.m. "Well we have lots of time before I promised to have you home. Anything you want to go do?"

"I can't think of anything. I'm usually in bed by now, right after getting home from climbing," she replies with a shrug.

"I could take you to an empty parking lot and teach you how to drive stick," I suggest.

"Hell no," she squeaks, but then looks at me with a straight face. "If you promise not to bug me about learning manual transmission, I'll seriously consider saying yes to the driving practices in my mom's car. I'm sure if I asked her nicely, she'd say yes. Especially if you were the one going with me and not her."

"Deal. I had already planned on sweet talking her into it anyways." I grin, and she throws her napkin at me. "When's your birthday?" I inquire.

"September 3rd. Yours?"

"August 26th."

"You'll be 21, yeah?" she confirms, and I nod. "What do you want to do for your birthday? Any big plans to go out and get white girl wasted?"

"Nah, I don't drink anymore. Did enough of that when I was way younger. Doesn't seem like it'll be very cool after I can do it legally," I joke.

"Really? I've never heard of anyone not wanting to drink on their twenty-first birthday."

"Confession time?" I wait for her nod. "I had a pretty fucking tragic experience when I was a teenager that turned me off drinking for the rest of my life." I shift in my seat, clearing my throat. I've never told anyone this story before, because I try not to ever think about it. "I had a girlfriend. She was a total sweetheart. She was the only person who ever got me to pay attention to anything besides the gang I was in. One night, there was a little fair in town, and we used our fake IDs to drink while we were there. We went on all the rides, the typical shit, like The Zipper and Rock-n-Roll Express, all those spinny type of rides. We went back to her house, where I spent the night. Her parents weren't home. We passed out, totally drunk, and exhausted from all the fun we had at the fair. And when I woke up the next morning... well, she didn't."

Vi gasps, covering her mouth. "Oh my God, Corbin. What happened?"

"She had vomited in her sleep and suffocated. We were so drunk that her throwing up didn't wake either of us up. The only thing I can be grateful for was she didn't suffer. She died in her sleep. That day, I swore I would never drink again. If not for myself, then for the safety of my friends. I'll stay sober to take care of them, so if that ever happens to any of them, I'll be there to wake them up."

"I'm so sorry," she tells me quietly. After a beat, she offers me a bit about herself. "My parents don't drink. My dad was a sailor for twenty-two years and never drank a sip of anything other than wine at church every Sunday. We've never had it in our house, so I've never had a drink before. Add that to the long list of things I've never done."

"Trust me, it ain't all that great. Now weed, on the other hand. That's a whole different story." I grin, trying to get back to the jovial conversation we had before.

"I'll take your word for it." She smiles. "You ready to go?" she asks, scooting back from the table.

"Ready to go, but not ready to leave you. We'll figure it out." I stand and take her hand in a loose hold, running my thumb across her palm. I discovered, while sitting in the theater and holding her hand, that though small and delicate, she has some pretty impressive callouses across the top of her palm, right below the webs of her fingers. I actually love that she has that tiny bit of toughness to an otherwise soft and fragile exterior. It's much like her interior as well. She's innocent and sweet, but God knows the walls she's built around herself are as strong as a fortress.

The dynamic between us is completely opposite of what I'm used to. It's usually me hiding, closing myself off, not letting anyone know the real me. It's always the other person trying to pry bits and pieces of my true self out of me. But for some reason, with Vi, I'm an open book. I spill everything freely. All she has to do is ask, and the truth is hers for the taking. And it's been so long since I've given a shit about another person enough to want to get to know them that me pulling answers from Vi feels like a new experience in itself. But it's a challenge I readily accept. With her, I can't just order her to tell me things or do something, like I would with one of my soldiers. I have to treat her equal to me. Give and take. It's confusing the fuck out of the Dominant part of me, but oddly exciting to the man.

"Is there a park around here somewhere?" I ask, making a

left onto the main road that leads to her neighborhood.

"A park? It's probably closed this late, but yeah. Right up here," she tells me, pointing me in the right direction. We pass the fire station, and behind it, I see a couple of baseball fields, a basketball court, and finally an open area with a playground, a large swing set, and a merry-go-round.

I pull into the parking lot and turn off the ignition. There isn't much light out here, just a couple of floodlights that illuminate a piece of the playground and one of the baseball fields.

"It's closed, Corbin. That sign when we entered said park hours were from 5:00 a.m. to 7:00 p.m. It's almost ten," Vi says, looking around the abandoned area.

"Is there a locked gate keeping us out, baby girl?" I prompt, and she looks over at me, brows furrowed.

"Clearly, there's not a fence around it," she replies, gesturing out the windshield.

"Then it's all good. Live a little," I tease, unbuckling both our seatbelts. "If a cop shows up, we just didn't notice the sign when we came in, and we go on our merry way." I open my door and hop out, going around the car. I literally have to drag her out of the vehicle, but as soon as she's in a standing position, I reach beneath the backs of her thighs and swiftly lift her into my arms, and she immediately stops her playful struggle. Her arms come up to lock around my neck, and she melts against me. It's a curiously abrupt change in her demeanor, but I'll take it nonetheless.

I kick her door closed and carry her over to the merry-go-round, sitting down on the edge with her in my lap, and it brings me back to the movie theater, when I'd pulled her into my lap to assure her I wouldn't get upset with her inexperience. There's something about this position, her small body cocooned within the strength of my arms, that puts her completely at ease, the most relaxed and at peace I've ever seen my beautiful Vi. The ever-present worried look in her eyes, which is only ever replaced by an expression of complete concentration when she's climbing, disappears, and words can't describe what it does to me that I can give her that sense of comfort just by holding her.

She sinks against me, her head resting on my shoulder, the heat of her pressed against my chest soothing something inside me I didn't know was there. Suddenly, it isn't thoughts of dominating her, teaching her the things *I* needed to satisfy my urges that play on repeat inside my mind. No. Instead, in their place is an overwhelming need to protect her, to remove the weight of the walls she's built around herself and place them on my shoulders, just so she won't have to bear the weight on her own. For the first time in my life, I want to be someone's savior; I want to be the person *she* turns to, to make things better for *her,* without anything in return but the satisfaction that I made everything all right in her world.

It's a strange feeling, because God knows I'm a selfish bastard. It's why I get uncomfortable when random people tell me, "Thank you for your service." They thank me like I do my job for them, when really, I do it for myself, for my family, for *our* freedom.

But Vi brings out a facet of myself I didn't know existed, one that is a fierce protector who wants to snap and snarl at anything that would dare do anything to harm what's mine.

Mine, it growls, as I turn my face and bury my nose at the top of her head, inhaling the scent there.

"Is it always this way?" she asks suddenly, and I feel her arms come loose from around my neck, but her fingers begin to play at the back of my head, lightly stroking along the stubbly hair that's probably tickling her fingertips.

Such a vague question, but somehow, I know exactly what she means. "No, baby girl. It's never been this way for me before," I confess, laying my cheek on top of her head.

"It's like I've known you forever. You don't feel like a stranger—well, not a *stranger*, but someone pretty new—to me. Almost like I might've known you in another life or something. Does that sound weird?" She tilts her head back and I lift mine, looking down into her gorgeous green eyes, which are imploring me to soothe away her doubts.

"Before I met you, I would've said yes, because I wouldn't have understood what you're feeling. But, Vi, it's the same one I'm having right now. I know exactly what you mean. And as weird as it may be to someone who hasn't felt it before, how scary it is to be falling for someone so quickly"—I shake my head—"I'm not going to fight it. It was fighting and stupid shit that landed me in juvie. I fight every day in the military. When I get deployed, it's a war over there too. But you? I'll fight *for* you, but that's the only battle you ever have to worry about when it comes to us."

She blinks up at me, a sweet smile lifting the corners of her lips. "So what does that make us?"

"It makes you mine. And I'm yours, baby girl," I whisper, bending down to kiss her softly.

"Does that mean I'm your girlfriend?" she breathes against my lips.

I lift my hand to her jaw then slide it down to let it rest against her sternum, watching as she closes her eyes and presses herself into my palm, seemingly unaware that she's doing it. My cock hardens painfully behind the zipper of my jeans, and she must feel it, because she squirms in my lap.

A growl escapes me before I can stop it, and my nostrils flare, but when I get myself under control, forcing myself not to spin around, lay her flat in the middle of the merry-go-round, and take her right here in this empty park, my voice is steady. "You're so much more to me than what that word implies. But for all intents and purposes, yes. I'm not even going to ask, because you have no choice." I grin, so it seems like I'm joking, but I'm really not. I wasn't kidding when I told her I'd fight for her, and I wouldn't take no for an answer.

Thankfully, this isn't a battle I have to worry about, because her face alights with the most beautiful smile I've ever seen and she laughs before nodding. "Fair enough," she says, and lifts her chin for another kiss. I give her what she wants, but when I try to deepen the kiss, tracing my tongue along the seam of her lips, she ducks her head, burying her face in my neck.

"Don't run away, little mouse," I murmur against her ear, and she nuzzles further into me. "What are you afraid of?"

"That I'll be terrible at it," she replies softly.

"And if you are, I'll teach you, and we can practice all you want until you get it just right," I rumble, feeling her shake her head in the crook of my neck.

"Is this your character flaw coming out to play?" I ask.

"Huh?" Her hot breath puffs against my flesh.

"Your mom told me you don't like to try anything new because you're afraid to fail right off the bat. You won't allow yourself to even attempt something, not knowing whether you'll be a pro at it from the start or not," I tell her, and she mumbles under her breath, *"I'm gonna kill her."*

"It's okay, Vi. No one's going to laugh at you. No one is going to make fun of you. I'm sure as hell not, and I'm the only one you're going to be kissing. So let me teach you," I implore, my hand moving around to the back of her neck then up into her hair before fisting it between my fingers. I use my grip to gently tug her head back, forcing her to look up at me instead of allowing her to hide any longer. "Can I teach you?"

She doesn't reply, but her chest rises and falls rapidly with every panted breath she takes. I lower my mouth to just above hers and hover there, the tension building as the seconds tick by without her answer. I tell myself I will not do it without her permission. I will give her sweet pecks pressed to her lips, and that's it, until she actually tells me she's ready to go any further.

She still doesn't say anything, so I decide to make a confession, hoping to shock her into answering. "You know, that's my favorite part about you. Physically, that is. You couldn't stop me, even if you wanted to. I could control you," I whisper slowly, allowing every ounce of my desire for her to fill my voice.

She gulps, and her perfectly white two front teeth clamp down on that luscious, pouty bottom lip of hers, making my cock throb beneath her ass. I feel her tremble, and it takes everything in me not to say fuck it and show her exactly what I want to do to her without waiting for her consent. Yet, I wait, showing more self-control than I ever thought possible.

"I *could*," I repeat, "but... I want you to want me bad enough to ask for it. I won't make you beg for me. At least not yet." I do nothing to hide the mischievous glint in my eyes as I stare down into hers, which I see are glazed with want, but still enough fear that she just... won't... answer.

Suddenly, she stands, and I release my grip on her hair before

I accidentally hurt her. I watch as she flees, but she doesn't go far. Just to the swing set on the other side of the playground, where she picks the one directly in the center and sits, using her feet to walk herself as far back as the chains allow before lifting her legs in the air. I watch her swing herself for a few moments, letting her have her space.

When she comes to a stop, she clasps her hands together, her arms circling the outside of the chains, and she leans way back, looking up into the cloudless sky. I stand and make my way over to her, sitting down in the swing next to hers, and mimic her position.

We're quiet for a long time, just enjoying the silence. It's not an uncomfortable silence, which is surprising, seeing how she just ran from me. But eventually, I speak up, if nothing but to get to know her more by opening up myself. "When I first moved here, the first thing I noticed was all the stars. We arrived in the middle of the night, and as soon as I stepped off the bus, I looked up, and the whole sky was filled with them. In the city I'm from in California, there's so much smog you can't see the stars." I look over at her and see her eyes are on me instead of the sky. "I mean, you can see a few of the brightest ones, but nothing like this."

"I guess since I grew up here and they've always been there, I never take the time to appreciate them," she murmurs, glancing up once more. "That, and I don't spend a lot of time outside."

"You don't go real rock climbing?" I ask.

"I've never been, no." She shakes her head.

"Isn't that the point of climbing in a gym, to learn so you can eventually go climb a mountain or something?"

"Not for me. I really have no desire to outdoor climb. The

thought actually scares me," she admits.

I spin my swing around to face her, the chains crossing in front of me. "Have you ever considered, baby girl, that what you think you're feeling as fear is actually just excitement? Adrenaline?"

She looks at me, her eyebrows lowering. "What do you mean?"

"I'm seeing a pattern with you. You think you fear trying new things, when in all actuality it's probably the same feeling everyone gets before they take a leap of faith. I get that feeling every time I try something I've never done before. Learning to rappel, the first time I shot my rifle, the first time I jumped out of an airplane. But now, it's like a habit. Where most people would take that leap, no matter how small, knowing it's a learning experience, you just can't seem to make yourself jump. Is it all a fear of failure, or is it something else?" I press quietly.

"You jump out of airplanes?" she asks, instead of answering, and I sigh, shaking my head.

"Yeah, Vi. I jump out of airplanes. I'm a paratrooper," I mumble.

"I thought you were a sniper." She tilts her head.

"You really know nothing about the Army, do you?" I ask, chuckling, and she shakes her head. "I'm in an airborne infantry division, which means I'm a paratrooper. I jump out of airplanes to get into otherwise denied areas during an operation. Then, once I'm in, I'm a sniper. I don't run in guns ablazin'. Alone, with a partner, or with a small team, we set ourselves up in a concealed position. Our slogan is *One Shot One Kill*. Only the best marksmen can have my job. I'm highly trained in many more areas than the regular Joe. I've always been good at shooting, ever since I was a kid and my dad took me hunting, but it wasn't until I was in the Army that I learned just how good I could be.

All that bullshit my teachers used to tell me in school about if I just applied myself, I could do great things... I finally did that once I saw what a natural talent I had at making a bullet hit its target. Every. Single. Time."

"That was me with climbing. Once I saw I had a natural gift for it, that's when I really got into it. It was the trying it for the first time that was the hard part," she confides, and then softly, she asks, "Have you... have you ever had to shoot anyone?"

I look her in the eyes. "No. Not yet. I've never been deployed. But when I go, I will. It's my job. It's what I've been trained to do. Do I feel what you're feeling every time you're faced with something you've never tried before? You bet. Anxiety, excitement, and maybe a little bit of actual fear. But I know when I get over there, it'll be either kill or be killed. If I don't do my job to the best of my ability, I won't make it home. So I have to suck up those feelings, store them away, and do what I'm over there to do."

Finally, I'm rewarded for my complete honesty, because she opens up at last. "Apparently, I'm an easy target," she whispers, looking down into her lap. "For some reason, bullies single me out the minute they meet me, and they're ruthless. I hate confrontation. When someone picks on me, I seize up. I think I might've been a possum in another life, because when confronted, I basically play dead. Words won't come out. My brain doesn't make up any witty comebacks in my defense. Nothing. I freeze. I can't even run away from it. I just have to stand there and take their wrath. Cruelty I did nothing to deserve."

A single tear slides down her cheek, and I see red, wanting to tear apart every asshole who's ever said an unkind word to this amazing girl before me. But I swallow it back, wanting to hear what she has to say. "What could they possibly pick on you for?" I murmur, trying to keep the growl out of my voice.

She scoffs. "It would be easier to name the things they don't tease." She wipes at her face with the back of her hand then grips the chain of her swing once again. "I'm skinny. Always have been, and looking at my mom, I probably always will be. No matter how much I eat. So they spread rumors I was anorexic. The one time I tried to defend myself, pointing out how much I eat, for everyone to see right there in the lunchroom at school, they said I must be bulimic then. 'Don't sit near Vi. She probably smells like barf, since she throws up her food.'"

She sniffs, and the sound breaks my heart. "When all the other girls my age started hitting puberty and growing boobs, mine never came. I got a poem in my locker disguised as a love letter one day. I had been so happy that a boy was actually nice to me. I had a secret admirer? Like... you have no idea how absolutely thrilled I was someone had written me a note. I didn't even care who it might've been from. Sad, I know. But then I opened it up, and it wasn't very loving at all. 'Roses are red. Violets are black. Why is your chest as flat as your back?'"

She laughs, but it's not a happy sound. "To make it worse, the boys who had sent it to me were standing across the hall watching me while I read it. And when they saw how much it hurt me, did they apologize? Hell no. They pointed and laughed at me, then snatched the paper out of my hand to gloat to anyone who walked by. So proud of themselves."

She shakes her head and looks up at me, her eyes brimming with tears. "You know, I was actually pretty good at dancing. I had been doing it for several years. Tap, ballet, and jazz classes twice a week. I grew up with a lot of the kids. No one in the class was from my school, so it was my escape, to be around people my age who weren't complete jerks to me. I loved it there." She looks back down into her lap. "But then these new kids signed up. A set of twins, a boy and a girl. They were really good, having moved here from another state, where they danced since they were little too. The girl was really nice, but the boy... it's like he had that same radar in him, the one that singled me out as an easy target. Not only did he pick on me for the usual—how skinny I was, how flat-chested—but he also went after my actual abilities. If it took me longer to learn choreography, if I messed up a step during a routine, if I stumbled during warm-up, anything. He zeroed in on me and gave me hell, like I was the *only* one who ever messed up."

"Where was your teacher during all this? What did your mom do?" I growl, unable to contain it any longer, balling my fists as I picture throttling the little shit who tortured Vi into thinking she was anything less than perfect.

"Oh, he got into trouble every time he did it. Time out, scolding, that sort of thing. And to me, my teacher would just say that boys are mean to girls when they like them. But that never made me feel any better. And my mom raised hell at my school when I'd come home crying, but then I just got picked on for being a baby who ran home and tattled to my mommy, so I stopped telling her," she says, making my gut twist when I realize she started taking the blows all on her own, hiding it from her mom.

I've taken as much as I can stand, giving her space to open up and tell me about the part of herself she keeps hidden. I reach over, grab the chain of her swing, and pull her to me, sitting her—seat and all— in my lap as I wrap my arms around her middle. "I can promise you one thing, baby girl. No one will ever say another unkind thing to you without having to deal with me. If anyone ever says a hateful word to you again, you tell me. And you will never have to worry about them giving you shit for it afterward either, because it'll be hard for them to tease you with their tongue ripped out of their head." She makes a sound, half giggle and half surprised squeak, as if she thinks what I said is funny, but can't figure out if I'm exaggerating. I'm not. "Promise you'll tell me, Vi," I demand.

She blinks up at me, clearing her vision. "I promise, Corbin," she whispers, and I lean down, pressing my lips gently to hers, not attempting to take the kiss further. Now is not the time to push her. I'll give her time to come to me when she's ready to take our physical relationship to the next level. From the sound of it, she's had enough assholes pushing her around to last her a lifetime. The last thing she needs is me coercing her into doing something she's not ready for.

"Knowing you've got me by your side, no matter what, you think you might be able to let go of some of your fears?" I breathe against her lips, pressing my forehead to hers.

After a brief pause, in which I can tell she truly thinks about her answer, she whispers, "Yeah. I think I can."

Warmth spreads throughout my chest. Feeling the weight of the moment, I try to lighten the mood, the seriousness of the past few minutes too heavy to end our first date on. "I'm glad. Your first driving lesson is tomorrow then... my beautiful girlfriend." I grin, seeing her face scrunch up as I pull back to look at her.

"Ugh. Fine. You can ask Mom if we can use her car when you take me home, *boyfriend*," she concedes.

"Good girl," I tell her, giving her a light swat on the ass as I slide her off my lap and let her swing away. I stand and hold out my hand to her, and when she takes it, I pull her out of the seat. "Let's get you home."

"But it's still early," she says quietly, and I love the disappointment I hear there, knowing she doesn't want this night to end either.

"I know. But think of the brownie points I'll earn with your dad for bringing you home way before curfew. Plus, I'm going to come over bright and early tomorrow. After you get comfortable, you can drive us to Rock On, and we can make up for some of the hours you missed climbing today while you were being threatened with spankings."

BEFORE THE *li*

EFORE THE *lie*

BEFORE THE *lie*

RE THE *lie*

lie

Seven

Vi

MY HEART POUNDS INSIDE my chest, and I place my trembling hand on the shifter, pressing the brake with my foot so I can move it into drive.

"Nice and easy, baby girl. We're just gonna do a couple of laps around the school," Corbin tells me, and I lift my foot off the brake and move it over to the gas. The car begins to roll forward without me pressing the pedal, and I wonder for a minute if it would be acceptable just to let the car drift around the building going three miles per hour. "Give her a little gas," he orders, cutting off that hopeful train of thought.

I can't believe Mom agreed to let us use her car, no questions asked. After a sweet kiss on my doorstep, I'd opened my front door last night just as Mom was coming out of the kitchen, and seeing Corbin there on the porch, she'd come over to tell him goodnight. He asked her simply, "Would it be all right if we used your car so I can take Vi to practice driving tomorrow? I'd happily let her use mine, but I have a manual, and she told me no."

"No problem, sweetheart," she told him, and after thanking her, he turned to me with a smirk and a wink before telling me goodnight, kissing me on the cheek, and heading out to his car. If he weren't so freakin' sexy, my palm would've itched to smack him.

So here we are now, in the parking lot of the high school near my neighborhood—what would be my home school if I didn't go to a private one. It's Sunday, so it's completely deserted.

I press the gas gently and get the car going a little faster. It's been two and a half years since I took Driver's Ed, and the same length of time since I sat in a driver's seat. I had no desire to be in control of a moving vehicle, the responsibility feeling way too overwhelming. But Corbin was right. I can't depend on other people to get me where I need to go for the rest of my life. And with him by my side, I feel a little bit of his strength and a whole lot of his protectiveness seeping into me as I begin my second lap around the school.

"Okay, great. Now, you ready to take it on the road? We can just drive around your neighborhood if you want. Nothing crazy yet," he suggests, and I take a deep breath and nod.

I stop fully and look both ways at the parking lot's exit, and seeing no one coming, I pull out onto the empty road, traveling only a few yards before putting my left turn signal on and turning into my neighborhood. I get up to the speed limit, 25 miles per hour, and follow each of his instructions, when he tells me to take a left at the next stop sign, or a right in the fork. I do a

U-turn in a cul-de-sac, and we practice parking, backing up, and three-point turns.

After another fifteen minutes of this, with my confidence building higher and higher with his words of encouragement and praise, he tells me, "It's almost time for the gym to open. Your mom has my car if she needs to go anywhere today, and she said it was okay with her if you felt comfortable enough to drive hers to Rock On. She'll meet us there later to switch cars."

"Couldn't you just take me home?" I ask, trying to stall before making my final decision on whether or not I have the balls to drive across town for the first time.

"Not tonight, baby girl. The gym is much closer to the base than your house, and I've got to be up before the sun tomorrow for PT. Not unless you want to quit climbing early this evening," he offers, but I shake my head.

"No. That's okay. I want to climb as much as I can tonight, since I didn't go at all yesterday," I reply, my grip tightening on the steering wheel.

"I figured as much. Okay. You've got this, Vi. Just go the speed limit, if not slower if you're scared. But I've got you. Not going to let anything happen to us. We'll take the back roads your mom told me about, so you won't even have to get out on the busy main streets if you don't want to," he assures, and I nod.

After twenty minutes, five minutes longer than it normally takes to get to the gym from my house, I pull into the parking lot of Rock On, my blood pumping with my racing pulse as if I just won a national climbing competition. I ease into a parking spot, put the car in park, and turn to Corbin, my whole body trembling with unspent adrenaline.

My eyes lift to meet his proud ones sparkling down at me,

and the look is my undoing, as I tell him, "I need something, Corbin."

"What do you need, baby girl?" he asks, his eyebrows lowering in confusion.

"I... I don't like this jittery feeling. I need it out of me," I tell him, my voice a little shaky as I try to figure out a way to convey what my body is demanding.

"Do you feel like you're going to have a panic attack? What is it, Vi? You need some air? Let's get you out of the ca—"

"No!" I shout, wincing at my volume in the enclosed space, repeating "No," in a much quieter voice. "I... I'm already past that wanting to run feeling, and at the part where I'm ready to be a little reckless and just say eff it and try something new for the first time. The fight feeling instead of the flight, yeah?" I implore him with my eyes, begging him to get what I'm saying. "Th-that stuff you were saying last night...."

Suddenly, understanding blankets his face, and his eyes go soft. "I got you, baby," he murmurs, unhooking his seatbelt before reaching across the console to do the same to mine.

My eyes never leave his as I feel the tight belt disappear from across my body, until I feel his hot, strong hand wrap around the back of my neck and he pulls me to him. And the next thing I feel is his breath against my lips, as he whispers, "I fell asleep when I got home from our date, thinking about this very moment, Vi. Then, my night was filled with dreams of kissing you, of getting to taste my girl for the first time. Of being the very first man to ever *get* to taste you. I want your first *real* kiss to be one you remember until your dying day."

My world tilts on its axis, and I feel dizzy listening to his intense words, my adrenaline pumping and my pulse pounding, so with my eyes still closed, I reach up to grip his muscled forearm to ground myself. "Corbin, please. Dyno," I beg, hoping he gets me.

Finally, with a growl that reverberates from his chest and shoots straight to my core, he takes my lips possessively with his. After a moment, I gasp as he bites down on my bottom lip, his tongue dipping in, and I taste Corbin for the very first time, savoring it as he seemed to do in his dream.

With a whimper, I tentatively flick the underside of his tongue with mine, and he lets loose another growl, tilting our heads to deepen the kiss. I'm enveloped in an all-consuming bubble of sensuality, memorizing everything from the sound of his quiet groan, to the heat of his mouth against mine, to the taste of... him. Just Corbin.

I feel him subtly guiding my movements, as if leading me in an erotic dance of tongues and panted breath. And now that I've finally taken this leap of faith, I never want this feeling of flight to stop. I soar higher and higher with every stroke, every flex of his strong fingers around my nape, every moan that escapes, until I feel like I've flown so high I've reached the sun. My body is ablaze as I give myself over to Corbin, showing him I'm putting all my trust in him and that I want him to teach me everything he's willing to.

We devour each other for what feels like forever yet no time at all, and when we finally pull back from each other, we're both out of breath and flushed. As I meet his eyes, they swarm with all the emotions I feel inside myself, and it's a comfort that our kiss affected him just as much as it did me.

He pulls me back toward him, but only to rest his forehead against mine, as he whispers, "Never letting you go now, baby girl. That kiss just sealed our fate. You're mine."

The little hairs on my arms stand up as my skin prickles before a feeling of warmth washes over me. All I can do is nod, as I pray that he always feels this way about me, because it's exactly what I feel for him.

Eight

Corbin

THE NEXT MONTH AND A half passes in a blur. Every moment I'm not at work or sleeping is spent with Vi. From the second I get off work in the evenings until the rock gym closes at night, we spend it climbing, Vi teaching me techniques that have improved my skills tenfold, while I return the favor with strength training. It's amazing what it's done for her self-confidence, both seeing me as her student get better and better at my climbing, and also as her teacher, who has made her work hard and gotten her to the point where she can now do ten pull-ups, when before she could only do one.

I've been lucky enough to have weekends off for a while now, and they've been spent together, going to countless movies, trying out every restaurant in town, and venturing a little ways to go to the history museum an hour away. It's been blissful, nothing standing in our way as we learn everything about each other. She comes to life under my touch. She's still too shy to initiate anything intimate between us, but I have no problem taking control and giving her what I know she wants but is too submissive to ask for. Nothing past the best kisses I've ever had in my entire life, but she's worth the wait.

Our... courtship, I guess you would call it, has been so different from any relationship I had in the past. Almost as if we're living in a different era. We've taken our time reaching each milestone, making each one special, instead of rushing to get to the immediate gratification of going all the way. The first hug, the first date, the first peck, the first passion-filled kiss with tongue... every marker has been distinct, had its own story, its own memory to look back on and cherish separately from all the rest. For once in my life, I feel like I'm doing something right, outside my job.

Our two personalities seem to have been made for each other. I can read her like a book, knowing what she needs from me when she can't seem to figure out what it is she actually wants. It keeps the dominant inside me satisfied having so much power over her needs, being able to please her without her having to say a word. He puffs up his chest and struts, feeling like her savior, her knight in shining armor, after a lifetime of feeling like a worthless asshole who couldn't do anything right. It soothes my soul, much like her sweetness. The way she looks at me, like I hung the moon and every single one of those stars we saw in the perfectly clear sky that night in the park, it makes me want to be the man she sees me as.

I've heard lots of those inspirational quotes on relationships, but never paid much attention to them until now. "Be the man your dog thinks you are." "Be with the person who gives you the same feeling you get when you see your food coming at a restaurant." Or the one that really hits home when it comes to Vi and me, "A perfect relationship is just two imperfect people who refuse to give up on each other." God knows we both have our flaws, but we seem to fit each other like jigsaw puzzle pieces, filling in the gaps of each other. Her softness cushions my roughness. My overabundance of fearlessness spills into her over-cautiousness, making her braver. At the same time, it pulls me back, making me take a second to think about the consequences of actions I wouldn't have taken the time to worry about before. Two imperfect people, with too little of some characteristics and too much of others, but then we come together and we are a perfect balance.

As I said, bliss. But I got some news today that didn't make me very happy, yet I suppose it'll be our first lesson in the military life causing disappointment in our relationship. I just hope Vi doesn't take it too rough.

When she finishes her route inside the cave we've been climbing in for the last hour, I take hold of her hand and pull her down next to me in the regrind I've been sitting in while I watched her boulder. "Gotta talk to you, baby girl," I murmur, wrapping my arm around her hips to pull her side flush with mine.

"What is it?" Her eyes immediately fill with worry, and I hate that I am the one who put it there.

I reach up and tuck the fallen strands of her hair behind her ear. "I just found out my unit will be going into the field for training for three weeks. The bad news is while I'm out there,

there is no communication. No phones, no email, nothing," I tell her, and she visibly wilts at this information. "Also, worse news, it takes place during your graduation as well. I'm so fucking sorry I have to miss that, Vi. I know you wanted me to be there, but there's nothing I can do."

She looks down in her lap and nods. After a moment, she asks quietly, "That was the bad news, so what's the good news?"

"Well, the good news is that at some point during the three weeks, I'll get a few days completely off in the middle of the week. I'll have to do twenty-four hours of straight guard duty at the barracks one day, but then I'll get time off to do whatever the hell we want, and I'll take you wherever your heart desires to make up for missing your walk across the stage." I squeeze her hip, and her eyes lift to mine.

"Can we go to Six Flags?" She tilts her head, her face full of hope that I'll say yes, and I grin.

"Anywhere in the world, and you want to go to an amusement park?" I chuckle.

"I told you I love roller coasters," she says with a shrug.

"Then that's what we'll do." I lean over and kiss her, making her smile and some of the disappointment leaves her face as she glances away.

"That's actually way less terrible than what I thought you were going to say," she confesses, and my brows lower.

"What did you think I wanted to talk about?" I question.

She sighs. "I always have this tiny voice in the back of my head that says any day now you're going to realize I'm nothing special and—"

"Not another word, Vi," I growl, taking her jaw in my hand and forcing her eyes to meet mine once more. "Nothing pisses me off faster than when I hear you putting yourself down." Her face falls, but I don't back down. She needs to hear this. "*You* are amazing. *You* are the one who is too good for *me*. You make me want to be a better man, one who deserves you. So never let me hear you say you're nothing special, because there's no one else who could've gotten me to learn patience. Or self-control. Or how to care about anyone other than myself." My grip tightens, wanting to make sure she pays close attention to what I'm about to say, because it's the most important thing that will ever come out of my mouth. "Just stay loyal to me, my beautiful Vi, and you will never have to worry about that stupid-ass voice in the back of your head being right. Got it?"

She bites her bottom lip and her eyes go soft, and I can't tell if she actually realizes when she says it, but she whispers, "Yes, sir," and my cock swells inside my basketball shorts. I drag her into my lap, sitting her soft ass directly onto my erection to soothe some of the throbbing as it's sandwiched between my body and hers.

I tug her face down to mine with a hand tangled at the back of her hair, and kiss the breath out of her. And I don't let up until we're interrupted by Sierra calling, "Get a room, you two!" from the mouth of the cave.

I allow Vi to slide off my lap, and I adjust myself, bringing her eyes to my painfully hard cock. She unconsciously licks her lips, red and swollen from my assault, and I growl deep from within my chest. "You keep looking at it like that, baby girl, and you're going to make me eat my words about having patience and self-control." I watch her eyes widen when she sees me grasp my shaft, giving it a brief squeeze to ease some of the ache. She lets out a soft gasp, my size and shape no longer left to the imagination, clearly visible through the soft fabric of my shorts, and I groan, the sound pained, even to my own ears.

Her eyes meet mine, worry filling them yet again. "Does it hurt, Corbin?" she whispers, and the concern in her voice puts another stitch in my previously ripped soul. God, with as much *bad* as I have done in my life, how the hell did I manage to find and fall for someone so undeniably *good*?

"It could feel better, baby girl. But I'll survive." I give her a soft smile before leaning over to steal a gentle kiss from her pouted lips, and then get to my feet, adjusting my hard-on to sit behind the waistband of my shorts. Her eyes flare then dart away when she catches a glimpse of the swollen head before I cover it with my black T-shirt, and I can't help but smirk, knowing mine is the first cock she ever had a peek at in the flesh.

Face red and a voice breathy, she tells me it's my turn to try out the ceiling route. Without a word, deciding not to tease her, I get into starting position.

Vi

IT'S BEEN TWO WEEKS since Corbin went into the field. I've tried to keep myself busy, sticking with the routine I had the four years before he came into my life. But now that he's in it, I can't help the emptiness I feel without him there.

I used to be completely content, spending hours climbing by myself, with no one there to hang out with except my mom. But now... now I find myself constantly listening out for the jingle of the bell above the door, when before I barely paid attention to it. Now, I brace myself for an excited whoop and to be spun in the air by massive and protective arms whenever I finish a super hard route, when before, just my satisfaction of knowing I did it was enough.

It's a double-edged sword. But as lonely as I feel right now without him with me, I wouldn't want to go back to the way it was before. I might have been content in my self-imposed solitude, but I didn't know happiness until I met Corbin.

I had no clue when his break would be during the three-week training, in which he explained was out in the wilderness of Ft. Vanter. He just said he'd call as soon as he got his hands on a phone to let me know he was in from the field to pull his 24-hour guard duty, and then after that, I'd have him all to myself for a couple of days before he went back out to finish training.

A part of me had expected his call to come a lot sooner than this. And that evil little voice in the back of my head kept trying to whisper that maybe he just didn't want to see me, so he hadn't called like he promised. But I always push it back, choosing to trust Corbin, to believe what he said when he told me that as long as I stay loyal to him, then he'd never have a reason to leave. I scoff every time I think about it. I would never in a million years cheat on anyone, and the thought of ever doing that to Corbin, the only man who has ever made me *feel* anything, is completely ridiculous. So I guess he's stuck with me.

Graduation was last night. I actually hadn't been too upset that Corbin missed it, because I didn't want him to be there to see I had no friends to hug after we threw our caps in the air, or feel sorry for me when no one clapped. My brother had driven up from Charleston for the day to see me walk. I had dreaded crossing the stage, expecting to hear nothing but crickets chirping after the principal called my name, but with Mom, Dad, and Henry in the crowd, they made as much ruckus as even the most popular graduates' families, making me laugh as I got back to my seat.

Tonight, I lay restless in my bed, unable to fall asleep, so I chose an old favorite off my small bookshelf and began to read about sexy shifters and their loveable heroines.

My eyelids are finally beginning to get heavy, and I'm just about to bookmark my page as I read the last one in the chapter, when my cell suddenly rings, making me jump and drop the paperback right on my face.

"Shit!" I hiss, and then realize I hit the green answer button with my arm in my fight with the book. "He-hello?" I sit up in bed, rubbing the bridge of my nose.

"Baby girl, you okay?" Corbin's voice comes through my phone, and immediately the bit of pain I felt disappears as a feeling of pure joy washes through me.

"Corbin!" I squeal, hopping up on my bed.

"Vi, you all right?" he asks, and I hear a door slam closed in the background.

"Yeah! Your call just startled me. I was reading and dropped my book on my face." I laugh. "Did you just get in? I've missed you so much!" My heart pounds with my excitement, and any tiredness I felt before has completely vanished.

"God, I've missed you too, baby. I just got to the barracks. I have half a mind to come see y—"

"Do it!" I cut in, the words flying out of my mouth without my permission, and I bite my lip, snorting. "Sorry. I was literally drifting off to sleep, but then the phone scared me and now I'm

BEFORE THE LIE   129

all jittery."

"You were just now falling asleep? It's like one in the morning," he points out, and I hear him climbing stairs.

I plop down on the bed, pulling my covers over my naked legs. "I haven't been able to fall asleep very well since you've been out there," I admit quietly.

"Aw, Vi...." There's a pause, and then I make out the sound of a door opening and closing before I hear his voice much more clearly, as he stops moving. "If you truly want me to, I will drive over there to see you. God knows I'd give anything just to hold you for even a moment. My 24-hour shift starts in two hours. And then after I get some sleep when it's over, you and I are going to Six Flags. Just say the word, baby girl, and I'm there in thirty."

As much as I want to be selfish and tell him to come see me, even for a brief moment, just knowing he kept his word and called me the second he got in is enough to soothe me until I see him after his guard duty. "No, Corbin. That's okay. Get you a nap in before your shift starts. I'm so glad you're back. I've missed you *terribly*," I sob the last word, the roller coaster of emotions in the past few minutes crashing down on me, making me feel weepy. I also just got off my period, so that could be a factor in why I suddenly feel like crying I'm so happy he's home.

"You sure you're okay, Vi?" he questions, his voice soft and concerned.

"I'm sure. I promise. I'm just being a girl." I laugh, waving away his worry, even though he can't see the gesture. "It really is so wonderful to hear your voice." My own comes out dreamy as I lie back down, turning over on my side.

"Yours too, baby. I can't wait to see you. Just one more day and a handful of hours, all right? And I'll be the only one here, guarding my empty building tomorrow, so I'll be able to text you all day. Then I'm all yours for two days."

I hear shuffling, as if he's removing his clothes then getting into bed, and heat fills my chest then spreads lower, thinking about the part of his body I'd caught a glimpse of in the climbing cave. "O-okay," I reply, my voice coming out husky.

"Vi?"

"Yeah?" I breathe, my eyes closing, imaging what Corbin would look like right now, undressed and lying in his bed as he talks to me.

"What are you thinking about that's got your voice sounding like that?" he inquires, his own voice going low and deep.

"I... I... I'm just wondering what you look like right now, is all," I confess, my face heating to match the fire spreading toward the place between my legs. I cross my thighs, trying to tamp out the inferno starting to blaze there.

I hear him exhale a moment, before he replies in his sexy, gruff voice, "I just took off my boots and my BDUs. I've been in the field for two weeks without an actual shower, but me and the boys jumped into the lake today, so I'm a lot cleaner than I was." He groans, and I hear movement, as if he's getting comfortable in his bed. "My whole body is sore from all the training we've done, and I've got a few scrapes and bruises from being out in the woods, but otherwise, I look just the same as I did the last time you saw me. Just... naked."

As he says the last word, my core clenches, imagining him lying there in his bed, a blanket with an outdoor scene beneath him, the glorious parts of his body I've already seen—those beautifully muscled arms, the top of his tattooed chest, his strong calves, the bulging head of his erection—perfectly clear in my mind's eye, while my imagination fills in the rest I haven't. "Oh...." I breathe.

"What about you? What are you wearing?"

God, the tone of his voice is like an injection of liquid fire into my veins as it makes a roadmap beneath every inch of my skin.

I glance down, feeling suddenly naked, even though I'm in what I normally wear to bed. I can't help but giggle. "My favorite lavender long night shirt and undies. Sorry, nothing special. Only thing sexy about it is the Victoria's Secret label." I roll my eyes. *Could you be any more of a turn-off, Vi?*

He groans, a delicious sound from deep within his chest, and my cheeks flush. "No, baby girl. Sexy as fuck. Sweet and innocent, like you," he whispers, and his breath comes out in a shudder.

Is he...?

"Corbin?"

"Yeah, baby?" His voice sounds distant.

"You... you falling asleep?" I ask, because there's no way I could bring myself to ask if he's doing what I *really* think he's doing.

"Far from it," he exhales.

I hold my breath, listening intently, trying to let the sounds on the other end of the line paint a picture inside my head. I imagine his perfect face, eyes closed, his lips parted, and then his chest rising and falling with every pant I hear. "Do you want me to let you go?" I offer quietly, feeling like a voyeur, as if I'm intruding on a very personal act. The feeling isn't quite uncomfortable, but almost. Like I'm peeking in on something I know I shouldn't, but I just can't look away.

"No," he growls, and it sounds more like a command to stay

on the phone rather than an answer to my question.

"Well... what do you want to talk ab—"

"Are you wet for me, Vi?" he groans, and my heart thuds in my chest.

"Wh-what?" I squirm beneath my covers, feeling exposed and vulnerable.

"I'm so hard right now, baby girl, thinking about finally seeing you, kissing you, wrapping you up in my arms. God, I can almost imagine the smell of you. Tell me, Vi, are you as wet as I am hard?" The question comes out as a demand, and my natural reaction is to give him what he wants. It's always my response to him, wanting to give him exactly what he asks of me, no questions asked.

"I... I don't know," I reply honestly. My thighs squeeze together, trying to relieve some of the growing ache there, the feeling still new, having only experienced it since I met Corbin, yet I have no clue what to do about it.

"Touch yourself, baby. Tell me exactly what you feel," he commands, and my hand grips the soft fabric of my T-shirt's hem.

"Corbin, I... I don't know how to do that," I confess softly, feeling awkward but completely turned on.

"Vi," he groans. "Are you telling me you've never gotten yourself off before?"

"Of course I haven't," I whine. "I only started feeling any type of... anything down there when I met you. So why would I have ever... touched it?"

"Oh, fuck," he growls, and I bite my lip, thinking I'm somehow in trouble, which I know is ridiculous. After a few moments of listening to his ragged breath, I hear movement before he settles back down. "Like a fucking schoolboy. Swear to Christ."

"What's wrong?" I ask, confused.

"Your untouched little pussy, baby girl," he tells me, and I suck in a sharp breath, my entire body flushing at the vulgar word. "You made me come just thinking about the fact that it's never been touched, not even by you. I had wanted to hear you make yourself come, but knowing you've never done that is somehow even hotter."

I don't know what to say. I want him to stop talking, to stop making me feel this way, but at the same time I don't. I feel special instead of like an inexperienced freak. Desired. *Alive.*

"I can't wait to make you mine, baby girl. I'll wait forever for you, but God... I can't wait to feel you. To make you feel good. To bring you pleasure you've never experienced before," he says quietly. Thankfully, he continues, saving me from having to stutter out a response. "But I'm going to pass out until my shift now. I'll text you soon."

"Okay, Corbin," I whisper. "Goodnight."

"Night." And the line goes silent.

I SPEND THE ENTIRE next day at Rock On, trying to pass the time by climbing while texting with Corbin between routes. We spend his lunch hour talking on the phone, excited about tomorrow. We plan on him picking me up bright and early to make the four-hour drive there. I tell him he should sleep in after his long shift, but he swears that five hours will be plenty, so to be ready around eight.

I'm eating the Whopper Mom brought me for lunch, when Sierra plops down on the picnic bench opposite me, stealing a French fry. "So... when do you want to start working?" she asks, popping the fry in her mouth.

"Maybe after school lets out. The week Climbing Camp starts?" I suggest. "I want a week or two just to feel what it's like being out of high school."

"Uh huh... more like you want a week or two to be at your boyfriend's beck and call," she teases, and I toss a fry at her face. She catches it and eats that one too. "I'm just playing. Speaking out of pure jealousy. Your man is freaking eye candy. You two must go at it like bunnies constantly."

My face heats and I look over at my mom, who's absorbed in her book on the couch about twenty feet away. Balling up the wrapper that had been around my burger, I avoid responding.

"Oh... em gee. Vi," she hisses.

"What?" I hiss back.

"You're as easy to read as a large-print book. Have y'all not done it yet?"

"Uh..."

"Vivian. Marie. Brown. How in the hell have you been able to keep your hands off of *that?*" she whisper-yells, leaning over the table. "You've been inseparable for almost three months!"

"Well, seeing how I've kept my hands off everyone, including myself, it hasn't been that hard," I tell her quietly, and watch her face turn completely shocked. "Yeah, apparently that's super crazy to people. Corbin had an equivalent response."

"You told your boyfriend that you've never masturbated before? God, to be a fly on the wall to see his reaction." She shakes her head.

"How the hell did we get on this subject? Why are we talking about my sex life? This is so not appropriate coworker conversation," I say haughtily, cleaning up the bits of lettuce that had fallen off my lunch.

"Oh, shut up. We're much more than coworkers, and you know it," she tells me, throwing a French fry at me this time.

I look up into her pretty face, tilting my head. I hadn't actually thought about it before, since I've never seen Sierra outside of Rock On before, but now that she's pointed it out, I guess she is my one and only real friend. Conversation has always come easy with her. She's always been incredibly nice to me, not a mean bone in her tall and curvy body. We've spent what adds up to be countless hours together over the years, just chatting and hanging out in the gym during my rest breaks. I don't know why I never considered it before. Maybe because she's a few years older than me, or the fact she's married with a baby, at a much different stage in her life than I was, so I just never thought of her as anything more than an acquaintance.

"Geez, Vi. I knew you were super devoted to your sport, but wow. How have you made it this long without ever double-clicking the mouse?"

"Huh?" My eyebrows scrunch.

"You know... tiptoeing through the two lips. Buffin' the muffin. A little ménage à moi." At my confused face, she finally hisses, "How the hell have you never fingerbanged yourself, woman? You're eighteen!"

I shrug, feeling surprisingly comfortable confiding in her, now that I've come to the realization I actually have a girlfriend to talk about this stuff with. "I never had a need for it. I never wanted anyone before I met Corbin. I was always so focused on climbing I never really paid attention to anything that would've made me... get an urge," I whisper the last bit, even though there are no climbers near our table.

"Hmm." She leans back, reaching out and pulling the bag of fries with her, and starts to munch on them while she ponders something. "But you said you told Corbin about it. I assume you're still a virgin then. Because now that I think about it, God knows you don't spend enough time away from this place to even sneak in a quickie."

"Yes, I'm still a virgin. But...."

"But what?" she prompts.

I tilt toward her, my eyes squinting in concentration as I try to put into words what I haven't spoken aloud. "I... I think I'm ready *not* to be," I murmur, and her face splits into a beautiful smile.

"Well, you couldn't have picked a better guy to lose it to. The way he looks at you... gosh." She giggles, shaking her head.

"What do you mean?"

"Aww. Sweet Vi. You really have no idea, do you?" At my disgruntled face, she chuckles and continues. "When that man looks at you... it's like that emoji, the smiley face with hearts for eyes. Just like that. He's totally head over heels for you. No question."

I bite my lip for a moment. "I mean... I hoped what I saw wasn't just my imagination. But... really? That's what you see too?"

"Oh. Girl. Absolutely. And the way he wards off other guys with just that super sexy scary look. He's totally marked you as his territory," she says, waving her hand in the air nonchalantly.

"What are you talking about?" I ask, genuinely having no clue what she's referring to.

"Dude. For real? I'm going to start calling you Cher, because you are totes clueless. When you're up on the wall, and people come over to watch you, you do realize that you've got most of those guys bonered-up, right?" I cock an eyebrow, and she rolls her eyes. "There is not a guy who comes in here who doesn't want to bang you against one of these rock-covered walls. They get one look at your tiny self going all Spidergirl, and their tongues practically roll right out of their heads. But ever since you and Corbin got together, one glance from him, and they all back away, exposing their vulnerable necks to him or some shit. He's definitely an alpha. *Ah-ooooo*," she howls, and I can't help but laugh.

"But like I said, if you feel you're ready, there's no way it would be anything but perfect. He takes such care with you *now*. I can't even imagine how good he'd be to you intimately. Plus, I saw you two making out in the cave. Y'all's nookie is going to be hot as fuck, giiiirl. Yaaas, honey!" she whisper-sings to me as she stands, throwing the empty fry bag into the brown paper bag all my food came in. She swishes her hips as she makes her way around to my side of the table, then leans down to my ear. "If you need to talk about anything, I'm always here, girlfriend. Muah!" She plants a hard kiss to the side of my head, and then prances to the front of the gym.

I smile, warm all over from the sweet feeling of having a real friend.

BEFORE THE lie
EFORE THE lie
BEFORE THE lie
RE THE lie
EFORE THE lie

Nine

Vi

THIS MORNING'S REUNION with Corbin was almost painful. As he stepped out of his Camaro in my driveway, I slammed into him so hard that even he stumbled back a step as I wrapped my entire body, arms and legs, around him like a spider monkey.

"There's my girl," he whispered in my ear, his arms wrapping around me to squeeze me to him. "God, I've missed you, baby."

I pulled back just enough to look into his eyes, so happy to see him in the flesh, and he reached up with one hand to pull my face down to his, kissing me right there in the driveway.

We spent the day riding rollercoasters and eating giant turkey legs, but most enjoyable of all, just holding hands as we walked through the amusement park and flirting playfully while we stood in line for rides. Being the middle of the week, we basically had the place to ourselves except for a couple school field trips taking place there, so we were able to ride everything we wanted multiple times, and left before the sun went down.

Halfway home, Corbin clears his throat and adjusts in his leather seat as he drives. "So... we got done a lot earlier than expected. Do you want to do something when we get back?" he asks.

"Sure, like what?" I turn sideways in my seat, my left leg coming up beneath my right, and admire his profile. The masculine ridge of his brow countering the almost feminine pout of his full lips, his straight nose, and his killer jawline, which is now dark with a five o'clock shadow. I can barely look at him he's so handsome when he's clean shaven, but when he's got that bit of facial hair at the end of the day, and even more on the weekends when he doesn't have to work, jeez, he's irresistible—if I would ever gain the courage to tell him I'm ready....

"Well, there aren't any movies out I want to see at the theater. Do you want to rent one and take it to my room?" he suggests, and my head tilts.

"Like... at the barracks?" I question. When he gives me an, "Mmm-hmm," I add, "I thought chicks weren't allowed in the barracks."

"No, chicks in *high school* aren't allowed in the barracks. But as of this past weekend, you are officially a high school graduate now, baby girl." He smiles lightly and glances in the rearview mirror before eyeing me for a moment. "It doesn't matter to me what we do. I'm just not ready for this day to end. If you don't want to—"

"No!" I cut him off. "I do. You just caught me a little off guard is all. I'd love to go see where you live."

He chuckles. "It's nothing to see. But it is somewhere quiet and private we can go to just be by ourselves. I like having you all to myself."

My heart drops into my stomach and is swarmed by butterflies at the thought of being alone with Corbin... just the two of us... in his room... on his bed.... I glance outside, seeing on a sign we're sixty-three miles from Ft. Vanter. A little over an hour before we get home—no, not home. *Corbin's* room. Why couldn't he have asked me this when we were closer? When I had less time to sit and dwell on what could happen while we're alone... just the two of us... in his room... on his be—

"Vi?" His deep voice reverberates through the interior of his Camaro. "No pressure, baby," he tells me, staring into my eyes before facing forward once again.

The tension in me releases somewhat. God, could he be any more perfect? It's like he's tuned in to me, sensing everything inside me, even when I know I do a damn good job of hiding it. But at the same time, he still hasn't read my mind, broadcasting telepathically that I want him. Or maybe he's receiving my mixed signals. My emotions are everywhere. I want desperately for him to take me, to make love to me, to make me his in every way. But the thought of it actually happening scares the shit out of me.

I wish he would take control, ignore my nerves he's picking up on, and just rip off the Band-Aid, so to speak. I'm entirely too intimidated and inexperienced to voice or even passive-aggressively show that I'm ready to have sex for the first time, to give him my virginity. All he'd have to do is make the first move, give me any opening, and I would make it clear to him that I'm all for it. Just kiss me deeply, and I would pour myself into the kiss and not let go until he understood. It's just the lead-up that's terrifying.

"What movie do you want to watch?" he asks me, obviously trying to bring me out of my stupor, and I shake myself, realizing I had been staring straight through him.

"A comedy. Definitely a comedy," I reply.

"What, you don't want to watch a scary movie, where you'll have to cling to me to keep you safe from the boogie man?" he teases, tickling up my leg, making me squeal.

"I don't do scary movies. My brother traumatized me when I was little." I pout. "He was supposed to take me to see a Disney movie, but we went into *Gothica* instead. At first, I thought it was cool I was going to see a grown-up movie with my big brother, but an hour in, he thought it would be funny to grab me right at the crescendo of a scary part, and it frightened me so bad I screamed and peed, right there in the chair. I avoid horror movies at all costs now."

The confession is worth every ounce of embarrassment, as Corbin throws back his head and lets out one of his rare belly laughs. I feel it to the very depths of my soul. It doesn't happen often, so when I can make him laugh like that, when he lets his guard down and shows every bit of his amusement, I feel so accomplished and happy that I can make him feel that way for a few moments. It's not often my serious soldier gets to be carefree, so when I get to witness these fleeting seconds, I take a mental picture of the look on his face, and try to record the sound of his laugh to play back later, because God only knows when he could be sent somewhere.

These weeks he's spent training in the field have been hard enough. I don't know what I'll do with myself if and when he ever gets deployed. So I try to capture the tiny dimple that forms on one side of his lips when he smiles this big. The gasp of breath he takes between bouts of laughter. The tiny line that forms between his eyebrows, and the even smaller ones at the corners of his sparkling brown eyes.

When he finally catches his breath, he looks over at me, and heat joins the sparkles in his gaze. "If you keep looking at me like that, baby girl, I'm going to have to pull this car over and have my way with you," he growls, his sight zeroing in on my mouth, where I was unconsciously biting my bottom lip as I watched him.

"Please do," I breathe, and then my eyes widen when I realize I said it out loud.

He lifts his eyes to mine and his brow furrows. Time seems to stand still as he stares at me with that intense stare. I feel as if he is looking into my very soul, reading into my two slipped words. *Yes*, I implore, *I mean it.*

"Are you ready, baby girl?" he asks, his eyes never wavering from mine.

The tension grows even more potent, and it forces me to glance toward the road. I'm fascinated the car stays perfectly centered between the lines of the open road, even as I feel his intense look boring into the side of my face. I take a deep breath in through my nose, let it out slowly through my mouth, inhale once more before I turn back to him, wet my lips with the tip of my tongue... and dyno.

"I am."

Corbin

I WATCHED CAREFULLY as Vi gained her courage, much like she does before a tricky move on the rocks, and when she turned to me and said those two words, *I am*, her voice was steady, strong, and determined.

I'd used self-control I didn't know I possessed, when it came to her. Although I usually never had to try to pursue a woman for very long in order to take her to bed—if at all, seeing how I got hit on the majority of the time, not the other way around—I hadn't tried to get her to move any faster than her own pace. I waited for clues, letting me know she wanted me to kiss her, when with anyone else I would've done it whenever *I* wanted.

The only things she seems courageous enough to do herself are placing her tiny hand in mine to hold while we walk, or sit in movie theaters, playful swats while we joke around, and the occasional hug that she initiates. But every kiss to date has been me giving it to her, not her taking. Part of me wonders if she is that naturally submissive, while the rest of me believes it's just fear from being so inexperienced. Yet the way she just answered my question left no room for doubt that she wants me, and I'm not about to give her a chance to change her mind.

Pressing down on the gas, my speed goes from a steady cruise of fifty-five miles per hour up to ninety, and I hear her sweet giggle from beside me. She loves going fast in my Camaro. And I know she loves watching me shift gears by the way she always bites her lip while her eyes follow my right hand on the stick. I don't often get to race around with her in our small town, but out here, on the deserted back road we took to get to and from the amusement park four hours away, I open it up and give her a thrill.

I hear her gasp, but I don't take my eyes off the road. "Corbin! You're going a hundred!" she squeaks.

"Hundred and eight, actually," I correct, and feel her swat my arm.

"Slow down! You're going to get a ticket."

"Radar detector says otherwise, baby. Hasn't beeped in the last three hours. Now, grab my stick."

"*Excuse* me?" she scoffs, and I laugh.

"The stick shift, perv."

"Why?" she asks suspiciously.

I grab her hand and put it on the black knob of the gear shifter, then cover it with my palm. "Ready?"

"For what? What are you doing?" she asks, her voice panicked.

"Down to fourth," I say, and we downshift into the lower gear, slowing down a little. "Third." Our hands move again, and the car slows even further. "Second." The trees outside stop whizzing past as our speed lowers until I finish with, "First," before bringing the Camaro to a stop in the middle of the abandoned street. "Neutral," I tell her, centering the stick and wiggling it a little.

"Oh, my God, Corbin. What if someone comes up behind us? They're going to nail us right in the ass!" she squawks, spinning to look out the back windshield.

"I'm going to nail you right in the ass if you don't chill and listen for a sec," I threaten, and her eyes come to me.

My right hand still on hers, I take it off the shifter and yank her across the center console, tangling my fingers in the back of her hair with my left. Her other hand comes to press into my chest for balance as I pull her face to mine and crush my lips to hers. I let my need for her show in this kiss. This isn't one of the sweet, innocent pecks she's used to. No. And it's more heated than any of the times we've made out since that first time I taught her how to French kiss.

Feeling her hand move up my chest, I breathe her in as she sighs, enjoying the combination of her watermelon-flavored drink mixed with something uniquely Vivian, and savor the touch of her fingers against my skin as she wraps them around the back of my neck, holding me to her. *Yes. God, yes.* This is what I've been waiting for. For months, all I've wanted was for her to show me she wants me just as badly as I want her, and finally, with her grip locked on, I now know for certain my girl will be all mine.

Just not right this second.

I let go of her hair and pull away slowly, so she doesn't feel rejected, and smile down into her beautiful face when I see her eyes are still closed, her breath coming out in short pants. "You ready, baby girl?" She nods, never lifting her lids, so I place her hand back on the stick shift, and tell her gently, "Then get us home."

She scoots back into her seat, lets out a deep breath, and finally opens her eyes, blinking a couple times to get her bearings. "Okay," she replies with another small nod.

"Over and up to first," I instruct, helping her with the first gear as I work the pedals to get us going. "Down to second." This time, she does it on her own, and when I coach, "Third," and she pushes it straight up flawlessly, I remove my hand and stretch my arm out to rest behind her shoulders.

I can't help the sense of pride I feel when I rev the engine, push in the clutch, and she moves the gear into fourth without my direction, and then finishes off with fifth the same way. She looks over at me with a beaming smile, obviously proud of herself too. "I'll have you driving stick in no time." A sound escapes her that's a cross between a hiccup, a giggle, and a snort, and I look at her in surprise. "Was... was your mind just in the gutter, baby girl?" I ask. "The one time I wasn't making a sexual innuendo...." I grin.

"You're rubbing off on me, I guess." She giggles sweetly.

"Not yet, but I will be."

BEFORE THE *li*
EFORE THE *lie*
BEFORE THE *lie*
RE THE *lie*
lie

Ten

Vi

AFTER SHOWING THE GUARD at the gate our IDs, soon, we pulled into a parking lot between two huge, rectangular, four-story, plain beige buildings. The area was almost eerily silent. There were a ton of cars parked, but there wasn't a soul in sight.

"Where is everybody?" I whisper, the feel of the place making me want to be quiet and not disturb the silence.

"Half are deployed, and a lot are still out in the field for training. Only three of us come in at a time to guard the building, each taking a one-day shift and two days off, before we go back out in the woods," he explains.

As we walk in through the heavy-looking door, we pass an old metal desk that has a half-eaten meal in the center, but no one there to eat it. "This is where you spent all day yesterday?" I ask, and he nods, grabs my hand, and starts up the stairs. "No wonder you were bored out of your mind."

He doesn't reply, just continues to guide me up the four flights of stairs until we come out another metal door into a long, creepy hallway, a numbered, beige door breaking up the painted off-white cinderblock walls every eight feet or so. The lights must be motion-activated, because another buzzes on in the ceiling as we walk farther down the hall, and as I look behind me, I see the one closest to the stairwell door we exited through flicker back off. I hold Corbin's hand tighter in my right, and reach across my body to squeeze his bicep with my left, making him chuckle.

"Not gonna let anything get you, baby girl. These barracks are just old and decrepit, built in the 1950s," he soothes.

"All I'm hearing is 'This place is haunted as shit, and super old, so lots of years for ghosts to take up residence,'" I mumble, bring my side flush with his as he lets go of my hand and wraps his muscular arm around my back. I feel his fingers dig lightly into my ribs near my breast, and it sets off tingles throughout my body, doing an awesome job of distracting me from the scary setting we're in. And finally, he stops at a door, one that looks like all the other beige doors we've passed, only this one has a set of black numbers in the center: 308.

He takes his key out of his pocket, unlocks the door, and shoves it open, holding it for me to step through. When he lets go, it shuts on its own with a loud, echoing bang, making me jump. I try to shake off my nerves as I take in his home for the past two years. To the left, there is a giant wooden piece of furniture with a set of double doors. I don't know the proper name for it, but it's like an external closet. A wardrobe, I guess. It's kind of what I pictured when I read the Narnia books several years ago. Just past it, I can see about two feet of a bed covered in a fluffy blanket with an outdoor scene on it, and then another wardrobe at the foot of the bed. It makes me smile as I peek in.

"I used to do this with my bed," I tell him. "My mom would get frustrated with me, because I'd sneak off with all her pushpins out of her craft room and use them to attach sheets to the ceiling, like a canopy around my bed. It didn't work too well though, and they'd all end up falling after a couple hours. She finally got me one of those pretty sheer mosquito nets that hang down over the bed. I don't know. I just liked being in an enclosed space, kinda like little boys like to build forts, I guess."

The right side of his mouth tugs upward. "Totally get it, baby girl. It's the only way I can sleep. I feel too exposed otherwise. Also, it's for privacy. My roommate is deployed right now, but when he's here, he's a fucking chatty Kathy and wouldn't leave me alone before I arranged it like this," he explains, and I look farther into the room. Sure enough, past the second wardrobe is a twin-size bed along the back wall. Above it, I assume there is a window, but it is covered in a thick, black piece of fabric. In the center of it is an American flag attached with safety pins at the corners, and I can't help but smile. I love how proud and patriotic my soldier is. Looking to the right, there is a large dresser, with a good-sized TV on top with a DVD player next to it, and then yet another beige door.

"Is that the bathroom?" I ask, and he snorts.

"I wish. No. That's the next room over. We have latrines here," he says, and at my confused look, he adds, "Big shared bathroom down the hall. Kind of like in a locker room."

"Well crap," I grumble.

"What's up?"

"I definitely have to pee after all that watermelon Arizona drink and four hours in a car," I confess, fidgeting on my feet.

"There's nobody here. I'll take you down there." He opens the door, but I hesitate. "You coming?"

"I'm imagining a long wall of urinals and me trying to pee standing up."

"Soldiers still gotta take shits, Vi. There are two stalls with doors," he tells me, and I scrunch up my face, making him grin.

We only have to walk about ten feet down the creepy hallway before we reach the latrine, and I keep my eyes averted and head straight for the two stalls in the corner. Even though it's completely deserted, I still feel like I shouldn't be in here, since this is a place only men use during what would normally be private moments for civilians, using the bathroom and showering. I finish my business and quickly wash my hands at one of the faucets above the trough-style sink lining one of the walls. There's a metal shelf the length of it above the faucets for the men to place their toiletries while they shave and brush their teeth, or whatever else men do in the mirror.

As I step out into the hallway, I'm suddenly grabbed roughly from behind, and as I go to scream, panic flaring inside me, a hand clamps over my mouth. It's not until I smell Corbin's familiar, intoxicating scent, and then feel the fingers of his other hand begin to tickle my sides that I start to laugh, swinging my elbow behind me to get him back.

My back flush with his front, the heat of him sinks into my chilled bones, and as I laugh hysterically, wiggling against him, I'm no longer afraid of the unnerving old building. I stop fighting and let my body become dead-weight, and he stops his tickle torture and wraps his tattoo-covered arm around my narrow body beneath my breasts, holding me to him. He removes his hand from my mouth and uses it to pull my hair back so he can see the side of my face.

"Sorry, baby girl. I couldn't help it," he chuckles. "I wanted so bad to do that when we first got here, but I didn't want you to pee on me. Couldn't resist, knowing you had a freshly emptied bladder."

"You're a dick," I gasp, trying to catch my breath, but giggling still.

He laughs heartily then spins me around, making me squeak as he picks me up in his arms bridal-style and carries me back to his room and through the door, not stopping until he tosses me through the narrow opening onto his bed. "What do you want to watch?" he asks.

"What do you have?" I counter.

"As far as comedies," he begins, opening the top drawer of the dresser in the corner, "I have *Night at the Roxbury, A Knight's Tale, My Big Fat—*"

"*—Greek Wedding?* Yes! My favorite!" I exclaim, and he puts it into the DVD player, using the remote to turn on the TV as he walks back toward me. He tosses it onto the mattress next to me, and I watch, my eyes widening, as he grasps hold of the bottom of his T-shirt before pulling it off over his head in one quick motion. I gulp, taking in the perfection of his bare torso and arms.

He has a body the likes I've never seen on a real-life person. Maybe in fitness magazines, music videos, and action movies, but never up close, within reach. Sinewy forearms, bulging biceps, up to obscenely wide shoulders, fist-sized traps on either side of his strong neck, down to his pecs, wide and hard, but not overly big and puffed up like I've seen on some body builders. They're proportioned to the rest of him, the perfect canvas for his vibrant chest piece, the vivid green-and-red snake battling the black eagle, the beak of its white head about to take a chomp out of the long, slithering body.

My eyes trail downward, over the six perfectly symmetrical protruding abs, a deep trench between the two columns leading my gaze even farther south, to the V-shaped muscles above his hips. *Jesus, is he even real?*

He takes a pace forward, and I fight the urge to move back on the bed, instead holding my seated position on the edge as he uses his knee to separate both of mine and steps between my now spread legs. My heart thumps, and I stare straight ahead into that flawless tattoo, unable to look up to meet his eyes. My hands tremble where they clench the edge of the mattress, and I can't seem to inhale.

His hand comes up beneath my chin, and as he lifts it, my lids close on their own. My stomach clenches as I feel him press closer, his body coming into contact with my most intimate place, and I finally suck in a breath just as his mouth presses to mine. His palm lowers to the base of my throat, and it's a much lower part of my body that clenches this time, as his hand rests there, firm and hot, sending a thrill down my spine. Using pressure against my sternum, he lays me back on the bed, his lips never leaving mine as his tongue slips between them, and his other hand comes down at the side of my head to brace him. Just like the kiss in his car, I melt into him, following his lead and losing myself as his tongue dances with mine. Without a spoken word, he teaches me ways to draw out the most pleasure, and unconsciously my hips begin to move against him, my core suddenly needing... something. I don't know what.

The hand at my throat starts to move downward, his fingers spreading wide as he slides over the center of my chest and stomach until he reaches the hem of my shirt. He tugs it up, and I swallow but bravely help him pull it off me, finally breaking our kiss. I hold my breath as he looks down at the lacy light gray bralette that covers my small breasts, watching his face heat and his eyes turn stormy. But the gentleness of his touch that follows doesn't match the aggression I sense just beneath the surface, and I can tell he's holding himself in check so as to not scare me.

With the tips of his fingers of his right hand, he traces the edge of the lace over the gentle swell of my breast, and as they reach the clasp at the center of the flimsy cups, he unhooks it effortlessly, letting them fall open and to the sides of my body. I feel lightheaded, realizing I haven't exchanged the oxygen out of my lungs in a while, and I see his eyes follow the movement as my chest expands then relaxes. The dark chocolate pools staring so intently at me make me squirm, and to make it stop, I reach up to grab the back of Corbin's neck, trying to force him down to kiss me again. But he doesn't budge. The only thing that moves is his gaze as he raises it to meet mine.

"So fucking perfect, baby girl," he growls, and my gut tightens.

"N-no one's ever seen me naked before, Corbin. You're making me nervous just staring at me like that," I whisper.

"I could just stare at you for the rest of the night, Vi. You're so goddamn beautiful." He lowers his face to the center of my chest then trails his nose across my skin, making it prickle and hardening my nipples. When he exchanges the soft touch with the roughness of his stubbled cheek, I shudder, my arms coming up to encircle his shoulders, my hands clasping behind his shaved head. When he finally takes one nipple into his mouth, I let out a loud moan, the sound surprising me, and I clamp down on my bottom lip in embarrassment.

He must hear the abrupt way I cut off the noise, because he stops what he was doing, leans up over my face, and uses his thumb to pull my lip free. "Don't ever silence yourself when I'm giving you pleasure. There's no sexier sound than one that comes out of you, letting me know I'm making you feel good." The tone of his voice sounds like both a command and a reassurance, and all I can do is nod.

Before I know what's happening, his strong arm shoves between my lower back and the mattress, I'm moving, and my head is suddenly lying on his pillow, his scent filling my lungs as he lowers himself on his elbows, one on either side of my head, as his body comes to lie between my legs. The weight of him on top of me is both comforting and thrilling, and I fight the urge to move beneath him like a cat seeking attention. His face lowers to my neck, kissing up to my ear until he takes the lobe between his teeth, making me whimper.

My hands come up to grasp at his back as he drives me into a frenzy, his mouth doing magical things as he trails his tongue back down to my breast, the one that hadn't received his earlier attention. This time, I don't stop myself as the moan escapes me, and I'm rewarded with a thrust of his hips against my pulsating center.

He travels farther down, and when he reaches the top of my jeans, I tell myself to keep breathing as he undoes the button and zipper, leaning back on his knees to pull them down and off, leaving me in nothing but the light gray lace panties that match my bralette. Instead of focusing on his eyes, devouring me like I'm a buffet and he hasn't eaten in days, I decide to take in his glorious body, in perfect view as he rests his ass back on his heels between my thighs. For the first time in my life, I feel sexy, desirable, because if a man who looks the way Corbin does is gazing at me like he's contemplating which part to consume first, then I'm not going to worry about my body anymore.

So it's with this thought in mind that when he takes hold of the lace at my hips and sweeps it down my legs then onto the floor, I try not to react. I feel my knees involuntarily begin to close, wanting to protect the place between them, but Corbin stops their movement with palms to my inner thighs, making them move in the opposite direction as he opens me up farther than I was to begin with. I close my eyes as he lowers himself there, feeling his massive, hard shoulders against the soft part at the backs of my thighs.

"Breathe, baby girl," he says against the inside of my legs, as he begins to kiss his way downward.

I inhale, grasping at the sheets beneath me, not knowing what to do as he gets closer and closer to the place that needs his touch so badly. And without further torture, the anticipation nearly killing me, I feel the first lap of his tongue against my flesh and shudder, my whole body trying to close in on itself, but Corbin wraps his hands around the base of my thighs, where they connect to the rest of me, keeping my hips steady as he begins to devour me. There's no other way to describe what he's doing, as he doesn't just flick his tongue against my clit. No, he covers and consumes me with his whole mouth, the sounds almost obscene but undeniably sexy as he eats me.

There would have been no way to hold back my cries of

pleasure, even if I wanted to. Never have I felt anything like what he's doing to me. Is this why it was so shocking to Corbin and Sierra when they found out I've never masturbated? Is this what it felt like just by touching down there? Surely not. I have a feeling nothing I could do to myself would ever feel as all-consuming as this. I feel every stroke of his talented tongue from the roots of my hair down to the tips of my toes, which curl then flex, as I'm unable to keep myself still.

And suddenly, something starts to build inside me. As if I've begun running up a hill, climbing my way to the top. It's almost frightening in its intensity, and I'm not sure what I'll find once I make it to the peak. But as his grip tightens on my legs when I squirm, and his mouth keeps up its relentless rhythm, the runner inside me gets an unexpected burst of energy and starts sprinting toward her finish line.

Abruptly, every muscle in my body seizes, tightening to an almost painful degree, and my breath catches in my chest as a sudden explosion goes off inside me and I call out his name on a sob. I fold in on myself, trying to curl into a fetal position around Corbin's upper body before my limbs and everything inside me goes lax, feeling like I've turned into liquid as he takes one final lap from bottom to top. A shudder runs through me as he presses a kiss to my clit, and then he crawls up my body, hovering over me as I pant, my heart feeling like it's beating so hard it's going to levitate right out of my chest while the rest of me melts into the mattress beneath me.

But before I can even come down from my high, I feel Corbin between my legs, and I open my eyes to glance down and see his hand disappear at the apex of my thighs just as I feel his finger enter me. My back bows off the bed at the pleasurable intrusion, bringing me up against the hard muscles of his torso. Then his lips cover mine before his tongue dips between them, mimicking what his finger is doing inside me. I moan into his mouth, tasting my own flavor for the first time, finding it oddly sexy. Soon, I'm almost uncomfortably full as a second finger joins the first, so I concentrate on what his mouth is doing to mine, whimpering as he presses them deep then sweeps them across my inner walls.

"I've gotta get you ready for me, baby girl. Just relax. Let me make you feel good," he breathes against my lips. "So fucking tight, but you're so wet for me. God, you're going to feel like a fist around my cock."

His words make me clamp around his fingers, and we both groan. He leans down, his face going into the side of my neck, and suddenly a sense of calm washes over me, being completely surrounded by Corbin. With his tongue tracing up the column to my ear, while his hand that's not working magic inside my soaking-wet heat braces him on the other side of my head, I'm enveloped by an art-covered wall of muscle. My inner muscles relax as I breathe in his familiar, comforting scent as his teeth send tingles through my extremities when they clamp down on my earlobe. I shiver and feel my nipples tighten against his rock-hard chest, my hips beginning to move against his knuckles.

My breathing becomes heavy again, and just as that feeling starts to build inside me once more, he pulls his fingers away, and my eyes shoot open in confusion. But then I look down, seeing him use the wetness on his hand to spread over the head of his erection. My heart thumps, knowing what this means, and I'm both nervous yet anxious for it to happen.

"Stay relaxed, baby girl," he whispers in my ear, the heat of his breath making goose bumps prickle across my skin, but I consciously try to do what he instructs.

I watch as he uses his hand to line up the bulbous head with my center before taking one of my hands in his grip, bring it above my head before doing the same with the other. His elbows then press into the mattress at the sides of my head for balance, and I relax even further as he cages me in, my small breasts pressed against his chest as my arms are stretched up the pillow. He laces his fingers together with mine, as he tells me clearly, "I'm clean. Got tested the week I met you, and there's been no one since. I've never been with anyone without a condom before, but I'll be damned if anything is between us when I take you for the first time. Do you trust me?"

Without hesitation, I nod, and my fingers squeeze between his as I feel him slowly start to ease inside me.

"Breathe, Vi. Don't hold it in, my love," he commands gently, and his use of the word steals all the oxygen out of my lungs before I inhale once again as he sinks deeper. "Look at me. I want to see those beautiful eyes while I finally make you mine."

When my eyes meet his, they feel like they lock into place, and I'm unable to look away, even as they fill with tears as my core starts to burn. It's not the pleasant heat that had blazed there before, when the new sensation of need had sparked. No. It's the fiery sensation of tearing as he presses ahead, breaking through the bit of flesh that is the only thing separating us from becoming one entity.

But even as I whimper at the pain, my gaze stays locked on his, and I focus on the look of pleasure and concentration in those chocolaty depths. And when he's completely seated inside me, the weight of him fitting perfectly between my thighs, only then does he lean down to kiss me ever so gently, staying perfectly still to allow the hurt to dissipate. He trails kisses over my jaw and up to my ear, flicking his tongue across a sensitive spot just below it, then he whispers, "You tell me when to move, baby girl. I'd stay like this all night, so fucking happy just to finally be inside you. I won't move an inch. Won't cause you any more pain, only pleasure from here on out."

His words cause me to flex around his steel shaft, and an amazing sensation shoots from my center outward, making me gasp. He lifts himself to look into my face once again, and his eyes go soft, seeing nothing but desire written there. I nod, unable to speak, but he understands me nonetheless.

He begins to move, and everything around us fades to black as every one of my senses zero in on where Corbin's and my body are joined. My hands relax and flex in his, and I struggle to tug them free, having an urgent need to curl myself around him as he thrusts. He gives in, letting go, and I immediately wrap my arms around his torso, grasping onto the deep trench of muscle at the center of his back. It brings our bodies flush together, and his face goes back into my neck where he breathes me in deeply then lets out a sexy groan that has me shuddering beneath him.

"Never felt anything so perfect, Vi," he whispers. "Made for me." He stops his rhythm and sinks all the way in for a moment, grinding his hips. "I can feel where you end. The head of my cock is kissing it. Right... there." He presses even deeper, and I moan, feeling him against what must be my cervix. My nails sink into his back and he sucks in air, thrusting hard and making me cry out. "God, baby girl. You're going to have to retract those claws, because you're not ready for what that does to me." His eyes gleam with something I don't understand. I relax my hands, moving them beneath his arms to wrap up and grip onto his shoulders instead.

He returns to his smooth, rhythmic pulses, his body moving in a sensual dance above me. I wish there was a mirror anchored to the ceiling, that way I could watch from a distance what he looks like as he brings me pleasure I never knew existed. So closely pressed against me, I feel every one of his muscles working, but I bet the actual sight of seeing them ripple as his body rolls and thrusts would be glorious and overwhelmingly erotic.

Suddenly, his legs are no longer stretched out behind him, where I'd previously had my ankles wrapped around his calves. Instead, he brings the massive trunks beneath him to rest on his knees as he wraps his arm around my lower back, elevating my hips. This new angle causes him to rub something inside me that has me moaning in pleasure, my legs clamping around his hips as his tempo begins to speed up.

But as good as it feels now, the pain completely gone except for when he goes just a little too deep, that building feeling doesn't return, no matter how hard I concentrate. My eyes closed, my brow furrowed, my front teeth clamping down on my bottom lips, I start to get frustrated that the runner inside me hasn't begun to make her journey up the hill.

Being so in tune with me, Corbin's arm tightens around my body, and his bicep squeezes my upper back, lifting me up to him so tight I can feel our hearts beating against each other. "Relax, baby girl. It probably won't happen this time. A virgin never comes her first time. But I swear I'm going to take care of you. Not going to last much longer. You just feel too perfect." He groans into my neck as he circles his hips, and I do as he says, relaxing and enjoying the sensations he's setting off inside me instead of chasing the orgasm I thought was supposed to come.

In all the romances novels I read, the virgin heroine always came after the hero broke her 'maidenhead.' But his words make me feel better, understanding nothing is wrong with me, and I melt into him as his thrusts become more powerful.

With my breath coming out in forced gusts that match his every plunge, his muscles suddenly tighten, and he squeezes my small body to him so close that for a moment I can't tell where I end and he begins before he swiftly pulls out, spilling his hot liquid onto my stomach.

Keeping his hips elevated, as not to smear his cum between us, he lowers my upper body back to the pillow, kissing me gently as we both catch our breath. I look up into his eyes, seeing a look that matches what he called me when he first entered me, but I don't say anything, even though I feel exactly what his expression is telling me without words. He smiles down at me, his perfect, straight white teeth flashing, making my heart skip, and then he glances down our bodies before looking up at me once more.

"Don't look, baby girl," he orders quietly. Normally, if anyone else would tell me that, my automatic reaction would be to do the exact opposite. But being Corbin, and the way I naturally want to do exactly as he says, my eyes stay locked on his. They twinkle, looking happier and more carefree than I've ever seen him, and it makes my soul twirl that I did that to him. "I'm going to go get you a wet washcloth to clean up my mess. It looks like I *avada kedavra*'d your pussy." He chuckles.

"What?" I gasp, and just as I start to glance down at myself, he catches my chin and locks a more serious look with mine.

"Don't. Look," he commands. "It's not a big deal, Vi. Just a little blood and a shit load of cum. I'll be right back." He kisses me once more before backing up off the bed, wrapping a towel around his hips that had been laying across his dresser. He disappears behind the wardrobe, and I hear the door open and shut. I lie there, and force myself to obey his order, taking comfort from the fact he had been so nonchalant about it.

He returns moments later, and as I reach out for the slightly steaming washcloth in his hand, he bats it away, shaking his head. "It's my job to take care of you, my love," he murmurs, and everything inside me goes soft as he begins to carefully clean between my legs. When he's finished there, he wipes away the liquid on my stomach before folding the mess up inside the cloth then sets it somewhere out of sight.

When he comes back, I expect him to lie down next to me, but instead, he positions himself between my legs once more, placing my calves over his shoulders. I tug the pillow above me to beneath my head and peek down at him as he trails gentle kisses down my still-trembling thigh. He must feel my eyes on him, because his lift and lock on mine, his intense stare sending a chill down my spine as he continues his path to my center.

When he reaches his target, he hovers there, his breath the only thing he touches me with, but as sensitive as I am right now, I feel it as clearly as if he were stroking me with his tongue. His gaze too penetrating, my lids close and I turn my face away, becoming suddenly embarrassed as he watches his effect on me. But he growls, and somehow I know it's his unspoken order to return my eyes to him.

"Good girl," he murmurs, his hot breath on my core making me moan as much as his praise. And what he says next, turns my world upside down. "I love you, Vi. Have since before I even actually saw you. That feeling I told you about, the one I had when you were walking up to the front of the gym to give me the belay lesson that first day? I swear, baby girl. That was my soul finding its mate. It was so shocking, because I truly didn't think I even had a soul, knowing all the bad shit I've done in my life. And I don't deserve you. I *know* I don't fucking deserve someone so sweet, and beautiful, and *good*. But I promise, I'll spend every day for the rest of my life trying to be a man worthy of you."

With tears in my eyes, and before I can respond, without warning, his scorching mouth covers me, and all thoughts of replying to his heartfelt confession twirls to the back of my mind. Instead of being too overwhelming as I thought it would be, being so sensitive, the heat of his mouth is actually soothing, and my tense muscles relax as he does exactly what he promised before he orgasmed—takes care of me like no one ever has.

BEFORE THE li
EFORE THE lie
BEFORE THE lie
RE THE lie
lie

Eleven

Corbin

TIME.

It used to move so slowly.

I can remember when I was a kid, being bored out of my mind at home. Trying to pass the time by playing video games or outside with friends in my neighborhood in California.

School days moved at a snail's pace, each period seeming to last for hours, my nonexistent attention span making the time spent in a classroom a slow form of torture.

Or a few years later, after my babysitter introduced me to her friend, who eventually oversaw my initiation into the gang. Time had virtually stood still between the second I lifted my booted foot above the back of a rival gang member's head, and then the next, as it connected with his skull, breaking his jaw where his teeth were clamped down on the sidewalk's cement curb.

The fifteen-minute drive in the back of the police car after I got caught stealing from the liquor store when I was seventeen felt more like a year, not knowing what my future held.

Boot camp. God. From the second I sat in the barber chair for them to shave off all my hair that first time, until I stepped off the bus in Ft. Vanter after it was complete, it was the slowest point in my life. After living as what I thought was a hard-ass in an unstoppable gang that didn't have to follow rules, basic training was a whole new world. One full of drill sergeants who made it their life goal to break me. And they eventually did. Those ten weeks felt like a decade.

But on this night, as I look down at the ring inside the velvet box in my hand, I think back to the first time I made love to Vi, now seven months ago. Time has absolutely flown by. That's not to say there haven't been times when the hours, days, and weeks didn't crawl by, like when I was in the field just a few months into our relationship, or the three weeks I spent at Non-Commissioned Officer school, before I earned my rank as a sergeant back in July. But it seems like just yesterday I took her virginity on the same night I gave her my confession. I love her. I've never loved anyone before, but I know without a shadow of a doubt that I love Vivian.

And God does that girl love the shit out of me. She still looks at me like I hung all those damn stars. She still responds to my touch like it's the very first time. And for once in my life, I truly trust someone to the depths of my soul.

There is a part of me I haven't fully shown her yet. The part that still wants to protect her and keep her safe, but at the same time use her small, almost fragile body in ways that would scare someone as sweet and innocent as her. I fantasize about adding pain to her pleasure, dominating her in ways other than with my commands, which she still follows without batting a lash. I don't think she even realizes she's following an order when I give her one. My control over her is a subtle thing, one we've never talked about, having always just been there. And since everything I've always told her to do has been for nothing other than bringing her more pleasure, or keeping her safe, or improving something in her life—like when I taught her to drive, then eventually took her to get her license, before surprising her with a Chevy Malibu for her birthday two months ago—she's never had a reason to bring it up.

But it feels so good being a man who Vi deserves, a fierce yet affectionate protector for my doting and faithful lover, that I haven't minded putting that part of me aside. Keeping her is worth more than fulfilling my darker needs.

At last, her family arrives, the bell above the door jingling as it always has. Vi looks over her shoulder for a moment from where she was marking rocks with her stick of chalk, a route she's dying to try that her boss was telling her the climbing coach couldn't even beat, and I hide the ring box back in my shorts' pocket.

A look of confusion registers on her face when her mom and dad walk into the rock gym, and it quickly turns into surprise when her brother comes in behind them. "Henry?" she cries, and takes off running across the gym. I watch, a smile splitting my face when I see her launch herself at him before he catches her. "What are you doing here?" Her voice is shrill in her excitement, and it carries throughout the entire building.

I see Sierra pop her head out of the office. She looks at Vi before her eyes come to meet mine, and I give her a slight nod, giving her the signal. A grin covers her face before she disappears again, and just as Henry stops next to me on the couch, carrying Vi as he followed their parents, I stand, and all the lights in the gym go out.

"What the...?" Vi whispers, and she reaches out to grasp hold of my forearm, sensing exactly where I am without having to see me. I pull the blindfold out of my pocket then trail the hand of the arm opposite of the one she's holding, up from her hand, all the way to her shoulder, feeling her skin prickle. When I reach her neck, I pull her closer to me before lifting both my hands to place the blindfold over her head then down to cover her eyes. "Corbin, what's going on?"

Vi doesn't see it, but Sierra flips the switch that turns on all the newly hung blacklights around the gym. Vi had a genius idea about a month ago to install them and coat the walls with invisible paint that only shows up under a blacklight. Now, Rock On offers birthday parties and lock-ins, where you can climb on the glowing walls. She got the idea after I took her cosmic bowling, told Sierra about it, and the owners approved. They even offered her a cut of every birthday party and lock-in sold.

I take her hands in mine and look at her family, all three of them giving me an encouraging nod, her mom's hands coming up to cover her mouth, as tears flood her eyes. Sierra comes to stand next to them, the biggest grin on her face. She and Vi have become close over the past several months, and I'm so happy that my girl has such a great friend. She'll need all the support she can get, for when I go to Ranger school next cycle, and when I get deployed.

Taking a deep breath, I give her the short but meaningful speech I've been rehearsing in my head since last week, when

I asked her dad's permission to ask Vi to marry me. "Vivian, something inside me recognized you before I ever laid eyes on you, and as I told you that day I confessed I'd fallen in love with you, I believe it was my soul finding its other half. From that very second, I went with my gut. For once in my life, I listened to my heart. And now, I'm using my brain, because for the first time in all twenty-one years I've been on this earth, my head is screwed on right, and it's all because of you. And what all four of those parts are telling me to do is to snatch you up before anyone else can try to steal you away from me, before you realize you are way too good for me." I lean close to her ear, whispering for only her to hear, "Keyword, *try*. Because I'd kill any motherfucker who ever attempted."

When I pull back, she's biting her lip, her natural reaction any time I say something that turns her on, and I thank God she finds my possessiveness sexy, because that's one part of me I'll never be able to push aside. I get down on one knee and let go of her hands to take the ring box out of my pocket, opening it up. Then I reach up and tug down her blindfold.

When she opens her eyes, she looks up first, her mouth falling open as she reads what's painted on the wall behind me. The very one she had been marking with her chalk not five minutes ago and had no idea it had been repainted. Glowing there in bright purple—a nice touch suggested by Sierra, knowing it's Vi's favorite color—the wall now reads, *Will you marry me, Spidergirl?*

She then looks down at me, seeing the ring I'm holding up to her, and her hands shoot up to cover her gaping mouth, a younger version of her mom standing in the exact same pose behind her. And then she launches herself at me, able to knock me backward in my unbalanced position on one knee, and lands on top of me. We land with an *oomph,* and as everyone laughs, she sobs a, "Yes!" before kissing me.

And with a grin, I let myself soak in the moment, her family and best friend cheering behind us, as I realize... after almost a year together, *she* finally kissed *me.*

The End of Our Story...

Before the Lie

Epilogue

The Lie
2 years later...

THE PHONE RINGS AND MY heart thumps painfully, seeing the unknown number. Three days have passed since I last spoke to my husband, the love of my life. He's been deployed to Afghanistan for four months now. He calls me when he can, normally every three days, when we'll sit and talk to each other for the allotted twenty minutes, usually just repeating over and over how much we love and miss each other, and how we can't wait for the deployment to end so he can come home and make love to me, hold me, see me in person instead of just pictures.

"H-hello?" I breathe, my hand trembling as it holds my cell to my ear, and I close my eyes as Corbin's deep voice comes through the line.

"Hi, baby girl. You okay?" he asks, hearing my stutter instead of my usual chipper greeting of 'Hey, honey!'

I take a deep breath, ready to spew the lies I've rehearsed over and over in my head, feeling in my heart it's the best decision. If Corbin knew the truth... God. He'd lose it—his composure, his sanity... his freedom. He'd go to jail for the rest of his life for going after the man who has ruined mine, my chance at living a happily ever after. Or he'd lose his life if my attacker was somehow miraculously able to get a one-up on Corbin. There's no other way. I have to lie.

"No, baby. I'm not okay," I answer, my voice weak, quivering.

"What's happened? Is your mom all right? Babe, talk to me," he urges, panic starting to fill his normally strong, unwavering timbre.

"Something... something happened at Sierra's neighbor's party. I—"

"What party?" he interrupts, and I close my eyes.

"Sierra's neighbor had a going away party. They're deploying with her husband, who's already over there. She invited me to go with her, wanting to get me out of the house," I explain. The one truth in this dreaded conversation.

"Okay, what happened?" he repeats.

"We were all drinking. I had too many to drive home, so I stayed with Sierra and her roommate. I... I did something *horrible*," my voice cracks on the last word. It wasn't me who'd done the most vile act anyone could possibly do to a person besides murder them. A sob escapes my throat before I can stop it.

"Baby... what are you saying? What did you do?" he prompts,

confusion clear in his tone.

He's the man of my dreams. My soul mate. There's no way he would think I'd cheat on him, so he won't read between the lines himself. I have to actually say the untruthful words. I have to let them come out of my mouth, even though I would never do that to anyone. Especially not to the man who is the center of my universe. But I have to make him believe it.

Why not just keep it a secret? a voice inside my head suggests. The same suggestion it's offered up countless times over the last seventy-two hours. But I can't. There's no way I'd be able to make love to my husband, knowing someone else had been inside me—however unwanted—without him being aware of it. The guilt would eat me alive. No, this would be best. I'd tell him I'd made a mistake, he'd forgive me, and then he could just move past it. It would only be my burden to bear, no extra weight on his shoulders. He has enough to deal with, over there fighting for his country.

"I was drunk. I... I slept with someone." There. The lie is out. An equal mix of relief and shame sweeps over me, making me dizzy, so I sit down on the edge of our bed. Opening my eyes to look at the picture of us on our nightstand, the image goes blurry as tears fill them to the brim.

He doesn't say anything at first, but I can hear his breathing become rapid. My tears overflow and spill down my cheeks. Dear God, what have I done? I've hurt him. I've hurt the man I promised to protect and love for the rest of my life. I feel my heart break as he gulps audibly on the other end of the line. If he's anything like me, he's feeling sick to his stomach, swallowing back the bile that wants to spew from its depths.

"Ba—" I start, but I think better of it. I'm sure he doesn't want me calling him any terms of endearment. "Corbin. Say something."

It's then that I recall the one thing he always told me. From day one. Even reiterating it in our wedding vows. *Just stay loyal, and I'll always be yours, baby girl.* And even though I should have seen it coming, when he finally speaks, I shatter.

"I'll have the divorce papers sent to you."

And the phone goes dead.

You can join my reader group,
KD-Rob's Mob, here:
https://www.facebook.com/groups/361767417319236/

Note from the Author:

When I sat down to write Truth Revealed, I didn't know where to begin. I knew it was going to be a second-chance romance, but there was so much to Corbin and Vi's start that I didn't believe flashbacks within the one book would do it justice. Therefore, I decided to tell their first story through a novella... but then that novella turned into a full-length novel, and so now we have *Before the Lie*.

Truth Revealed is the tale that actually originally popped into my head. Yet it wasn't until I began to plot out how their second chance at love would go that I realized nothing would make sense unless I told everyone about their beautiful then tragic beginnings. Although painful to write for personal reasons, I'm hoping that in knowing their story, Part 2 in the Confession Duet will be all the sweeter in its vengeance.

One last thing I should mention: Although Matthew inspired Corbin's looks and a lot of his personality, he allowed me to make up stories about his tattoos. And just so we're clear, sweet yet badass Turd was never in a gang in California, nor did he join the military because he was given the choice between it or jail. #merica

Acknowledgements

Matthew Hosea, thank you for helping me with so much of the hero in this book, and for being the—really, really ridiculously good-looking—face of Corbin. Thank you for your infallible support when I got scared to put this story down on paper. It's heavy and scary, but as always, you lent me your strength and courage to put it out there. I don't know what I would do without your belief in me. Love you, Turd. #nerdandturd

My Hot Tree girls, Bec, Barb, Mandy, and Tina, thank y'all for all the work you did on BTL. It was rough for me to write outside my romantic comedy voice, and your notes and tweaks helped me so much. And Sierra, for your unique way of making me feel like I am somebody special. Y'all's tears made my soul happy. *evil grin

Finally, DB. Thank you for reading, even though you claim you don't know how. You'll always be a hero in my eyes.

TRUTH *revealed*

CONFESSION DUET

KD Robichaux

Truth Revealed Production Crew

Editing by Hot Tree Editing
www.hottreeediting.com

Cover Design andFormatting by Pink Ink Designs
www.pinkinkdesigns.com

Cover Photography by FuriousFotog
www.onefuriousfotog.com

Cover Model: Matthew Hosea

Note:This story is not suitable for persons under the age of 18.*Potential triggers lie within this book

Also by KD Robichaux

The Blogger Diaries Trilogy:
Wished for You
Wish He was You
Wish Come True
The Blogger Diaries Trilogy Boxed Set

Standalones:
No Trespassing

Anthologies:
Tempting Scrooge

The Confession Duet:
Before the Lie
Truth Revealed

Warning

This story contains:
Triggers
A woman's recollection of being raped
Stalking
A damaged submissive heroine
and a possessive alpha
Dom who would do *anything* to heal her

Note from the Author

In this story, Vi learns how a BDSM relationship could be healing after experiencing her sexual assault. The information my character, Dr. Walker, gives to her during her therapy sessions is real documented cases from survivors who found a D/s relationship therapeutic.

This is not to say it would work for everyone.

If you are a survivor of a sexual assault, please do not attempt the things in this story without consulting a professional first. What worked for Vi could cause a trigger effect on someone else.

Just know I've done my research, not only on the internet, but also by talking to an actual therapist very familiar with alternative lifestyles.

TRUTH revealed

TRUTH revealed

TRUTH revealed

TH revealed

TRUTH revealed

Dedication

To all the survivors out there.

"I imagine healing
will be slow
and deliberate.
I imagine healing
will be whatever
I want it to be."

~J.R. Rogue

TRUTH *revealed*

TRUTH *revealed*

TRUTH *revealed*

revealed

revealed

TRUTH *revealed*

TRUTH *revealed*

TRUTH *revealed*

TH *revealed*

revealed

One

Corbin

BLACK HOODIE PULLED UP OVER my shaved head, I keep my face lowered but my eyes raised, following thirty feet behind her. Either she feels me watching her, or she's paranoid about where she's headed. I shadow her often, and usually without her hurried footsteps or quick glances over her shoulder, so I'm gonna go with the latter.

Where are you scampering to, sweet Vivian?

My obsession. My guilty pleasure. I'm a glutton for punishment. She breathed life into my soul nearly thirteen years ago, only to suffocate it until it was dead three years later. A decade. Ten whole years I've been keeping tabs on my ex-wife. The hobby causes a mixture of emotions. It's thrilling yet soothing. I fucking know it's wrong. But for some reason, even after she admittedly broke my trust and cheated on me, I still feel protective of her.

I've background checked every person she's spent time with. She's had relationships here and there. Only a few have turned intimate. Soon after, and without any of my doing, those relationships ended. She was the one who always broke up with them. I've studied her expressions closely when she thinks she's alone, trying to figure out what she's thinking. The only conclusion I can come up with to explain her sudden ending of her relationships after the first time they have sex is because of me. I once told her I would ruin her for all other men. Looks like I kept my word.

Unlike her.

Loyalty. That's all I'd fucking asked for. My one deal breaker. I'd gone back and forth in my head before I sent her the divorce papers, wondering if I could forgive her, work through her adultery. But in the end, I stuck to my guns. My lawyer took care of everything. I never even had to speak to her again after that last phone call.

"I... I slept with someone."

With those words, she'd not only broken my heart but killed a part of me. The human part of me. The part that cared about people's feelings and worried about others' wellbeing.

Vi turns right at the end of the block, and as I near the edge of the building, I peek around it, seeing she's continuing her trek at her hurried pace. I follow, staying out of her direct line of sight if she were to turn around, always keeping a few bodies between us for her eyes to land on first instead of my dark figure.

It's early evening; the sun's barely visible above the horizon in the distance. It's the time just before the streetlights turn on. This is out of the norm for her. Completely out of her routine. *Where are you going, little mouse?*

For the next seven years after we divorced, I spent my time "being all I could be." I made my way up the ranks, winning marksmanship competitions in Ft. Benning, earned my Ranger tab, blah, blah, *blah*. And then, three years ago, I was deployed to Afghanistan. In the middle of a firefight, I was shot twice, once in the back and once in the leg, while I helped my men onto a chopper getting everyone out safe. The one in my back is still there. Apparently it was safer to let it become a permanent part of me than to try to dig it out that close to my spine.

They gave me a bunch of awards for getting shot. How weird is that? I was fine. I wanted to stay with my men and fight. But they sent me home. Kicked me out of the army with honor. But, ya know, at least my Purple Hearts—yep, plural, since they'd given me one after a previous deployment, when I was stabbed in the arm during a raid—and my Medal of Honor are real pretty.

But throughout all this, I've kept tabs on Vi, kept an eye on her every step of her journey. From finishing college after she finally settled on journalism, to quitting her job at Rock On Rock Gym, then starting out as the lowest person on the totem pole at the newspaper. There she made her way up through the ranks for several years until she earned her own column, before she suddenly quit.

For weeks, I watched out my window as she only came out of her apartment to make a grocery run before locking herself back in for five days at a time. It made me anxious, almost itchy, when I didn't see her multiple times a day anymore. She no longer left early in the morning for a workout at the climbing gym before her eight-hour day at the paper, which was broken up only by wherever she decided to have lunch that day. Nor did she go out for after-work drinks with her coworkers.

So I started following her everywhere. Maybe I wouldn't have done this for so long and so obsessively if I hadn't kept her from being mugged. Just thinking about that night pisses me the fuck off, so I shove it to the back of my mind.

Those brief moments I could see her had been enough for me between mercenary missions—or security jobs, as we call them out in the open. But when the third month of her only coming out to make a quick trip to the grocery store came to pass, I became fed up. What was she up to?

You couldn't have paid me to believe the answer to that question.

I pulled a B and E and installed a program on her computer to track all her activity before slipping out undetected—but not before stalling at the coatrack by her door and burying my face in one of her sweaters. Fuck, she still smelled the same, like warm vanilla and gardenias.

After opening my MacBook Pro, with a few keystrokes my computer's background changed from my normal plain, solid black, to one of Vi and Sierra smiling at the bottom of a rock wall while holding up peace signs. I was in her computer, seeing it as she would. I glanced to the right of the screen, seeing column after column of word documents. Clicking on the top left one, my brows lowered in confusion.

Her Savage Master
a BDSM Romance
by
VB Lowe

I closed the doc and opened the one beneath it.

Her Master's Revenge
a BDSM Romance
by
VB Lowe

I sat forward in my office chair, heart pounding as I closed that one and opened another.

Taming Her Master
a BDSM Romance
by
VB Lowe

File after file, story after story, written by VB Lowe. Vivian Brown Lowe. Not only was my sweet Vi writing BDSM stories, but she was doing it under a pen name created from her old married name—*my* last name. When we'd divorced ten years ago, she'd gone back to her maiden name. What could all this mean?

I opened up Safari and searched VB Lowe, throwing myself in my seat as if I'd been knocked backward when the results popped up. *New York Times* Bestselling Author VB Lowe. Authorvblowe. com. Wikipedia. Amazon page. Goodreads page. Facebook page. Twitter. Instagram. The search results went on and on.

I clicked on her Amazon page. Every title on her desktop screen was listed with a book cover next to it, each with a dark theme and red font, and every single one with a hot couple in various sexual poses in different states of undress. All with an average rating of at least four stars.

This? *This* was what my sweet, innocent, virginal Vi had been doing, locked inside her apartment?

I checked the publishing dates of her books, seeing the first one had been published over a year ago. She must have been writing while she was still with the newspaper, and when she became a success, decided to quit and write full time. The perfect job for my reclusive, loner ex-wife.

Seeing her cross the street at the next intersection snaps me out of the memory. As I speed up my pace so I don't lose track of her, I catch a glimpse of her dark curls disappearing into a building with an unmarked door.

An unmarked door I'm *very* familiar with.

And rage fills me as I realize...

My Vivian just walked into *my* BDSM club.

Two

Vi

WHAT THE HELL AM *I* DOING? I think, as I shakily hand the bouncer my driver's license after giving him the password he demanded when I walked in. Checking my name to make sure it matches the one on his list, he eyes me then hands the card back, opening the door behind his tall, solid body. He doesn't say a word, and I timidly step forward. As I cross the threshold, the door closes behind me, and I'm engulfed in darkness except for the tiny red lights along the floor that lead up a set of stairs.

My heart pounds, my anxiety through the roof. My contact, known only to me as Seven, gave me all the instructions I needed to get inside to meet him here. I had found him over a year ago when I was researching BDSM for my books. Without hesitation, he kindly and openly answered all my questions and volunteered information I didn't even know I was looking for. His stories and experiences were inspiring, and I found myself writing novel after novel, hitting best-seller lists with each new story I released.

I've never met Seven in person before. We've Facetimed, but he wore a black mask that covered his entire face. He kept his voice low, and I don't think I'd be able to recognize it if I had to pick it out of a group.

After over a year of learning the lifestyle and writing my series, it never dawned on me to meet him until he brought it up in our last conversation on Messenger. I haven't been out with anyone, friends nor family, in three months. These stories and this world have consumed my entire being, calling to a part of me I didn't know existed. He invited me to come so I can watch scenes play out in person instead of just the videos he's sent me, with the participants' permission, of course. They were all thrilled when I included their nicknames in the acknowledgments of my books.

So here I am. At the top of the steps, I look around, taking in Club Alias in its dim lighting. The main room is a large, circular, open area. A dance floor is in its center, and there are two bars on either side. Leather booths surround the dance floor, creating a short wall around it. Behind the booths, I see the outer wall has open doorways leading into separated alcoves. These are the playrooms. There are no doors. Seven told me this is a safety precaution. No one is locked behind closed doors where they can't call for help if needed.

The process of getting a membership here is extensive. Only the most trustworthy clients are allowed. Yearly memberships are a hefty sum of money too. The logic behind it is that only people willing to pay that kind of cash would be dedicated to keeping Club Alias the high-class and safe environment it's known to be.

Seven told me to meet him at the bar at 7:00 p.m. I pull my phone out of my purse and check the time; it's 6:38. Early for any type of nightclub, especially for one such as this, I assume. There's no one on the dance floor and only one couple in a booth over to the left. I could use a drink to calm my nerves. I don't drink much or very often. Usually only a glass or two of wine every once in a while, but now is definitely one of the times I could use a little liquid courage. So taking a deep breath, I make my way forward until I reach the bar on the right and take a seat on one of the barstools.

A woman in a tight red corset and a black thong behind the bar makes her way over to me, her eyes downcast behind a lace half mask. "What would you like, madam?" she asks, keeping her eyes lowered and her face blank.

"Ummm, do you have any type of wine or just mixed drinks?" I question, not seeing anything but liquor behind the bar.

She lifts her gaze to mine, a bright smile lighting her face. "Ah, you must be a new sub. Yes, we have wine. Would you like sweet or dry?"

"Sweet, please. And no, I'm not a sub," I reply, and she quickly lowers her eyes once more, her face looking almost panicked.

"Oh, I'm sorry, madam. I meant no disrespect. I assumed you were a submissive because of your question instead of a command." Her voice almost trembles.

I quickly try to calm her. "I'm neither. I mean, I'm not a Domme or a sub. I'm here to do research for my books. I'm meeting Seven here... at seven." I can't help but snigger.

She gasps, gives a little hop, and clasps her hands together. "You're VB Lowe? Oh my goodness, I'm so excited to meet you! I'm Dixie. You put me in the acknowledgments of your last book!"

A smile splits my face at recognizing Dixie from her videos before I feel heat rise in my face. I keep my real identity off the internet. There are no pictures of me on any of my accounts, and I don't do book signings. I ship autographed books to my readers through my website, but there is no real information about who I am anywhere. My author bio is more fictional than the stories I tell. Dixie is officially the first person who has ever met me as an author, and I tell her so.

"I've never told anyone who I am. You're the first to put my pen name to a face," I say shyly, tucking my hair behind my ear.

"Are you fucking serious right now? Shut up! Can I hug you? Like, don't think I'm a stalker fan or something, but I have *all* your books. I fucking *love* you!" she squeals, and I nervously glance at the couple in the booth on the opposite side of the dance floor, seeing their curious expressions. "Sorry," Dixie whisper-hisses, covering her mouth and hunching down, as if to hide behind the bar.

I laugh, shaking my head. "I've never gotten to hug any of my readers before, even though several have told me they wish they could. So yeah. I'll take one."

She hops again before making her way out from behind the bar and over to me. I spin on my barstool and barely have time to stand before she throws her arms around my neck and squeezes me to her. She jumps up and down and squeals, her excitement infectious. When she pulls away, I'm grinning from ear to ear.

"It's so nice to meet you. Thank you for sending me the video of your bullwhip scene. That was incredible to watch," I tell her.

It had been fascinating to watch her complete trust in her Dom. She hadn't moved a muscle as his bullwhip whizzed through the air before making a loud crack against her skin, the area turning a pretty shade of pink. She'd moaned in pleasure. I can remember clearly the sound of wanton lust as if I were hearing it through headphones as we speak.

"You're more than welcome. Reading it after you put it into written form was so fucking hot," she says. We then hear a door close somewhere as it echoes throughout the empty club, sending her to scurry back behind the bar. She hurries to fix my glass of wine, setting it in front of me before taking her place where she was when I first sat down, her eyes casting downward once again.

Her immediate change in attitude and demeanor sends nervous butterflies into flight inside my belly. I sit back down on my barstool and glance at the time on my phone.

It's 7:00 p.m.

Corbin

"THE FUCK IS SHE doing here, Seth?" I roar, my fist coming down on his desk inside his office of Club Alias, our mercenary team's headquarters. To everyone not privy to the BDSM club upstairs, it looks like a mere security services office on the bottom floor.

The club was Seth's idea. He wanted a stable job outside of our missions, since living on split commission checks made him nervous. We never knew when a job would come in, and he wanted the security of knowing he had a backup. It rubbed off on the rest of the team, so the four of us invested in the club, which is now a great success.

"What the fuck, man? Who are you talking about?" Seth asks, leaning back in his chair and pushing his glasses up the bridge of his nose. I point at Vi on a security monitor behind his desk as she makes her way toward the bar, my nostrils flaring. "Oh, that's VB. She's an author here to do research for her books. I've been chatting with her for over a year, bro. No big," he says casually, waving his hand in the air before wiggling his mouse to bring his computer back to life on his desk.

I hear a menacing growl fill the room before I realize the sound is coming out of me, and Seth's eyes meet mine. "Corb, what's up?"

"That's my goddamn ex-wife, *bro*," I sneer, and watch as his eyes grow wide behind his lenses.

"Corbin, I swear to God, I had no idea who she was. She keeps her identity on lockdown. You've never shown me a picture of Vivian, so I had no idea that was—"

"VB *Lowe,* Seth. Vivian Lowe. Are you fucking kidding me with this?" I growl.

"Dude, it never even crossed my mind. She just contacted the club one evening, asking if there was anyone who could answer some questions about the lifestyle for her books. I thought it was pretty cool she wanted to get facts straight instead of making up her own shit, so I've been helping her," he explains. "I even made sure to keep my own identity hidden, because she said she was local, and I didn't want to risk running into her around town."

"Well what the fuck is she doing here tonight then?" I seethe, leaning across his desk and bracing myself on my fists.

He visibly gulps. "I invited her to come watch some scenes live. I've been sending her videos, always with my mask on, but I thought it would be cool for her to come and see it for herself. We're sort of like... friends," he tells me cautiously.

"What kind of *friends?*" I hiss, nausea and fury making the hairs on the back of my neck stand on end.

"Nothing like you're thinkin', man. She just asks questions about BDSM, and I answer them. I've sent her videos of scenes here in the club, and we've Facetimed a couple of times. I wore a mask during those too," he conveys, and I feel my temperature skyrocket.

"You Facetimed... with my wife?" I lunge at him, but he rolls backward in his office chair just in the nick of time before my hand can clamp around his throat.

"One, your *ex*-wife. And two, *I had no idea it was her, Corb!* And nothing went on during our video chats. Just more of me answering her questions!" he yells while I pant through my rage.

"And she has no idea what you look like?" I snap.

"No! She never saw anything of my face, and I always wore my normal Dom attire. Standard long-sleeved black shirt and jeans. She wouldn't have seen my tats."

An idea pops into my head, scattering most of my wrath. "Give me your mask. I'm taking over from here on out," I order, and his eyes narrow.

"What are you going to do?" he asks, sounding almost protective of Vi. It both pisses me the fuck off and cools me down. Seth is a good guy. Even though he runs a BDSM club and kills people for money, he's still a good man with a good heart. I believe everything he's telling me, although none of it makes me very goddamn happy.

I take a deep breath and force myself to calm. "I'll be her contact from now on. I'll be answering her questions and giving her this evening's tour. Got it?"

He pushes his glasses up his nose once more, visibly deliberating over what I'm saying. And when he speaks, it takes some of the wind out of my sails. "Corb, she's... something ain't right with her, man. Something is broken inside that girl. There's... there's a sadness to her, and she's sweet. It's kind of shocking that she writes the stories she does for a living. It doesn't match *her* at all."

I internalize his words to chew on later. But for now, I don't show any weakness when it comes to Vivian Brown. "Don't let her fool you, Seth. That woman ripped my fucking heart out. Now give me your mask."

Three

Vi

A COUPLE OF MINUTES PASS AFTER the door slammed shut and reverberated through the empty club, giving my nerves just enough time to ease before a strange feeling comes over me. I shiver, looking down at my arms crossed in front of me on the bar, noticing the little hairs are standing up on top of goose flesh.

My heart thumps inside my chest and pulses inside my ears. Everything inside me is telling me to turn around and run. After taking a sip of my wine, I reach for my purse and start to stand to do just that, but when I spin around on my barstool, I gasp and drop my bag to the ground, coming face-to-face with a black leather mask.

My hand shoots to my chest as if to keep my heart from leaping out of my ribcage. My eyes instinctively drop from the dark ones staring into me from the two small slits in the mask, and when they do, I take in the body covered in a long-sleeved black shirt and dark jeans, the same outfit I've seen Seven wearing in all his videos, pictures, and even when we Facetimed. I let out a nervous laugh, realizing it's my friend—or the closest thing I've had to one for the past year.

"Seven," I breathe, "sorry, you startled me. You're freaking stealthy." I get down on my knees, gathering up everything that had scattered out of my purse, stuff it back in the bag, and zip it closed. It's then I realize the position I'm in. Seven hadn't stooped to help me. He's still standing tall, feet shoulder-width apart, arms hanging at his sides, but his hands are in fists.

Still on my knees, I realize my face is level with the zipper of his pants... and what's behind it, so I force myself to look farther up his body, taking in the bulging biceps stretching the sleeves of his black shirt within an inch of their lives, and then up to the traps sitting like bookends on either side of his neck. He's a lot more muscular in person than he looked on my computer. But cameras have a funny way of skewing one's perception. I also thought he'd be taller. From down here, though, as I finally look into those dark, almost menacing eyes behind that scary mask, he looks like he's a giant executioner, ready to carry out an order of "Off with her head!"

I glance away once more, my eyes landing on his black boots, and my heart pangs.

"Spit on it, baby girl," Corbin told me, and I looked at him, horrified. "No, really. Spit on it. Why do you think it's called a spit shine?" He chuckled at the look on my face, the sound filling my soul with happiness.

"Just, like... hock a loogie on your boot? That just seems so...

unpatriotic. Like stomping on a flag," I said, and he threw his head back and laughed heartily.

"Like this, babe." He took his uniform boot from my hand where I had been scrubbing it with shoe polish but unable to make it gleam the way he did. I watched as he gathered saliva in his mouth before spitting it onto the toe of the shoe, and then he took the cloth from my hand and began to make tiny, quick circles against the leather. After a few moments, the black hide began to shine.

"Holy shit," I squeaked. "Who knew?" I smiled when his chocolaty eyes met mine and he grinned.

"I've got something else you can spit shine, baby girl."

A hand reaching down in front of my face brings me out of the memory, and I blink back tears. I tuck my hair behind my ear and take his hand, and he pulls me to my feet effortlessly.

"Thanks," I breathe. "I, uh...." I look around, not knowing what to say or do. Seven still hasn't said a word, and I feel a lot more awkward in his presence than I thought I would. He's always been so kind and friendly when we chat.

Finally, he speaks, and his low tone sends a shiver up my spine. "You were having a drink." A statement, not a question.

"Um, yeah." I glance back at my wine glass still sitting on the bar.

"Would you like to finish it while we wait for more people to show up? I can answer any questions you have," he offers.

"Yes. Yes, that sounds good. Thanks, Seven." I sit back on the barstool and set my purse in the one it had originally occupied before my klutzy moment, and he takes a seat next to me. I take a sip of wine, letting the sweet, cool liquid soothe my suddenly parched throat. I hadn't expected my reaction to meeting him in person to be like this. I mean, sure, he was sexy as hell in his videos while doing different demonstrations, but I didn't feel a pull toward him like I do right now. Maybe it's just being in his actual, physical presence. I couldn't feel it through a camera. I hadn't felt a pull like this since—

"How is the wine, V?" Seven asks, tugging me away from my dangerous line of thinking, but not quite forcefully enough for me to move on. I never let myself linger on thoughts of *him*.

I don't know why I've suddenly thought of him twice in the last few minutes. Once I'd made it forty-eight hours without having a single memory of my ex-husband pop into my head. Once. But when I realized I hadn't thought of Corbin Lowe for two days straight, it was like overwhelming guilt flooded every cell of my body, and I spent the next week in a depression, where all I could think about was him. It took my psychiatrist prescribing Xanax to pull me out of it. She had since retired, and I hadn't found another therapist. Luckily I hadn't really needed one in the past year, ever since I discovered the world of BDSM and started writing my novels. I always felt guilty talking to her anyway, because I never gave her the full truth.

"V?" Seven prompts, grasping my chin and lifting my eyes to meet his. "The wine. How is it?"

I clear my throat and pull my face away, unused to people touching me. "It's good. Thanks. Um... so this is your club. It's a lot bigger than what the videos made it seem. I like the atmosphere. It's a lot... cozier than I expected."

"We wanted it to be welcoming as well as sexy. We'd been to some... not so clean establishments, and wanted to make sure to provide our clients with only the best experiences." His voice is low, like it always is during our chats, but in person, it has a much more pleasing tone than through my computer's speakers. It spreads over me like soothing aloe on sunburned skin, instantly cooling and refreshing. "To get the look and feel of the place right, we did our research, touring many clubs, both low-class and high-class, throughout the States, so we'd know not only what to do, but also for sure what *not* to do."

I could probably listen to him read a phone book and be completely entertained for hours. His voice does something to me, healing something inside my chest while making me ache in a much different place. His deep timbre makes my core clench, and I want him to keep talking, so I ask him, "What are some things you found that you made sure not to include in Club Alias? I could have my characters find themselves in a not-so-swanky place." I quickly reach into my purse and pull out my small notepad and lucky pen one my favorite authors sent me along with her signed books. I always used it to jot down ideas that popped into my head for my stories.

"There was one place in Vegas we went to. When you walked in, the atmosphere just felt... dirty. And not the good kind. Not the naughty, sexy kind. But the 'I feel like I'm going to catch something if I sit on that couch' kind," he says with humor, and I laugh. The noise is foreign even to my own ears. It's been a long time since I've let out such a girlish sound.

I clear my throat once again, jotting down a note about what he said. "Anything else about that place?"

"Yeah. A few things. It was brightly lit. It was gaudy and looked like they bought everything during a Valentine's Day clearance sale. Reds and mismatched pinks everywhere, from the bed coverings to the couches and benches, pillows, rugs. Even the walls were painted hot pink. It looked cheap, like the cheesy lingerie you find at Wal-Mart during the holidays. I mean, it was Vegas. There wasn't a membership. It was geared more toward vacationers who wanted to take a walk on the wild side, be voyeurs, and have sex in front of other people. It wasn't really for people who lived the lifestyle," he explains, and I nod.

"I see. But your club, it's members only, correct?"

"Supposed to be," he tells me, and the way he says it makes me think he's talking about me being here, which doesn't make sense. He's the one who invited me here. He must see the uncomfortable look on my face, because he adds, "But sometimes we allow special guests. If we know someone from out of town who is in the lifestyle and would otherwise be members here if they lived nearby, then they can pay for a pass. Also, once every three months, we open the doors for new members. It's only during this time that we go through the application process, since it's so extensive. It's would be too time-consuming and difficult to leave that open all the time. It takes the whole team to establish whether a person is a good fit or not."

"Team?" I prompt, my head tilting to the side as I bite my lip.

He shifts in his seat, looking away from me for a moment to take a breath before exhaling. When he faces me once more, his tone is darker, less forthcoming than he was just moments ago. "Yes. There is a team of us. Each one has a different job to take care of behind the scenes."

It seems I've touched upon a subject he's not comfortable sharing about, so I move on. "Okay, so what are some of the things you *did* want to include in Club Alias that you discovered elsewhere?"

"There was a club in California we went to, and we liked the setup. The main room was a circle, like this one, so if you stood in the center, you could see into every playroom. What we did differently is add the booths to give the illusion of privacy without adding doors. You have to be on the other side of the booths to see into the playrooms, instead of being able to from the dance floor," he tells me, nudging his hooded head toward the empty space between us and the bar on the other side of the room.

When I glance to where he indicated, I see a few more people have taken up some of the booths around the dance floor. I hadn't even noticed, completely enthralled with what Seven was saying. God, he hadn't affected me this way during our FaceTime calls. Nor while I was watching the many demonstration videos he sent me, and I had seen him do everything from a simple flogging to gagging and roughly fucking women against St. Andrew's Crosses. Yes, I'd been turned on. The same as I would be while watching pornography. But it was nothing compared to the rapt attention Seven stole from me with his physical presence.

"Umm... w-what—" I bite my lip and take a breath, trying to calm the hurricane of feelings swirling inside me. "—what is the application process?" I finally get out, looking back down at my notepad to nervously start doodling along the perforated edge. The question is more out of my own curiosity than it is to go in one of my books.

The air around me grows thicker as Seven leans closer to me, and suddenly, I can't breathe. I feel more than see his dark eyes take in every inch of my face, as if he's reading each micro-expression like a large-print book. Somehow I know he sees right through my question, yet he answers anyway. "First, one may only start the application process by knowing an established member, someone who will vouch for the person's character. That member is their sponsor who is responsible for them during the six-month probationary period. That just gets them in the front door. Next, there is a background check, for obvious reasons. Then, since we are in the world of sadism and masochism, they must see our psychologist for no less than a month, one session per week, to ensure we aren't letting in someone with ill intentions. After one month, if our psychologist approves, then they are allowed into the club as a prospect. If he isn't sure after the four sessions, he may continue sessions until he makes a decision. Usually, though, he can tell within the first month whether or not a person is hiding anything. It may seem over the top, but safety is our first and foremost priority."

I've completely forgotten my notepad as I take in his every word. The way he's responding to my question, it sounds more like he's giving me instructions, telling me what *I* should do, rather than just explaining rules a person would need to follow in order to get in.

I tuck my hair behind my ear and glance away from the mask. His voice makes me want to see the man speaking to me, find out what face belongs to the low timbre. But I know the rules. It was one of the first I ever asked Seven, when he'd sent me photos of the men all wearing leather masks that covered their whole face, the kind one pulls over his entire head like a hood. Most of the women seemed to prefer smaller, daintier masks, just surrounding their eyes. A few women didn't wear masks at all. Seven had explained the expense of club membership, and the type of people who could afford such a hefty sum were the same people who wouldn't want anyone to know their identity outside a BDSM club: doctors, lawyers, some of the high-ranking military. He also told me the women who weren't wearing masks were openly in the lifestyle, so they didn't feel the need to keep their identities hidden.

I'm pulled from my thoughts as Seven gently taps upward beneath my chin, effectively gaining my eyes. He must have noticed my automatic reaction to pull away last time he touched me, and tried a different approach. His notice and care to not make me uncomfortable did even more to warm me toward him.

"Anything else you'd like to ask? A lot more people will be coming in soon, so now will most likely be your last chance for the night, before the demonstrations begin in the playrooms. There's no talking allowed once a scene begins," he explains.

I think for a moment, and finally come up with one last thing, wanting to clarify his last response. "The timeline of membership, just so I... ya know, get it right in my story. Say the next opportunity to join is...?" I draw out the last word, prompting him to fill in the rest.

He pauses for a few seconds. Deciding whether to tell me the truth? "In three days, actually."

My eyebrow quirks. "In three days. Okay, so a member says 'Hey, I have this person I will vouch for who wants to join.' The person shows up and fills out an application, and...?"

"And after leaving their $1000 deposit, we run the background check. If it comes back all clear, then we set up their first appointment with our psychologist," he finishes.

"Who they see once a week for a month. And *then* they're a full-blown member?" I ask.

"No. There's a six-month probationary period. During that six months, depending on their level of experience, they have to go through our program. There are tests they can take—placement tests, if you will—in order to skip ahead in the program, but we are very strict about who can use and do what inside the club. For example, we aren't going to let anyone who has never picked up a bullwhip use one on another person. They must be thoroughly and properly trained to use any equipment or tools," he explains.

"How do you keep up with who can do what?" I ask, trying to wrap my head around it.

"Each playroom has it's own theme, scene, equipment, etc., and each one has a card reader by the doorway. Every Dominant member has a badge they scan in order to enter the room. If they have passed the test for the equipment inside that room, the light turns green, and if not, red. We have security to ensure people go only where they're supposed to. If they break any type of rule during their probationary period, they're out."

"Submissives don't have badges?" My brow furrows.

"A submissive wouldn't be using the equipment. If a couple comes who are switches, then both parties must have badges. But someone who identifies only as a submissive, who would not be implementing any of the devices, does not need to go through that training process. They do, however, have the option to go through a different training program, one that teaches them the... art of submission, if you will," he almost purrs, and images fast-forward through my mind of me as a student of submission, with Seven as my teacher.

My nipples tighten behind the soft fabric of my T-shirt. I cross and uncross my dark gray legging-covered legs, trying to soothe the throbbing that's suddenly started there. I take a sip of my wine, my mouth parched. When I gain some composure, which isn't easy under the weighted stare Seven is watching me with, only one word is able to sneak past my lips on an exhale. "Interesting."

They're mostly hidden, but the look in his eyes gives me the impression he's smirking, even though I can't see his mouth. The leather of his mask doesn't cover it, but the way he has the fabric adjusted, his lips sit in the shadow cast from the piece over his nose. With the dim lighting in the club, it's impossible for me to make out the shape of his lips.

A small green light above one of the doorways behind Seven comes on, and he follows my eyes, looking over his shoulder. "Ah, little one. Looks like a demonstration is about to begin. Shall we?"

His endearment warms my insides, catching me off-guard. Usually I hate when people call me anything but my name, but for some reason, his has a different effect on me.

I take a deep breath and shake off the feeling. "Let's do this."

TRUTH *revealed*

RUTH *revealed*

TRUTH *revealed*

TH *revealed*

revealed

Four

Vi

TWO DAYS HAVE PASSED since my night at Club Alias. Tomorrow, if Seven answered honestly, would be the one day in three months someone could apply for a membership. I've mulled over it constantly, hardly able to concentrate on my word count, thinking about the way he seemed to be telling me what to do instead of just answering a random question.

I sign on to my Facebook and send Seven a message.

Me: I was wondering...

Seven: Yes?

Me: We've known each other for a little over a year now.

Seven: -_-

Me: Sorry. I don't really know how to ask this.

Seven: You've never had trouble asking questions before. What's up?

Me: Well, you said a person who wants to apply for membership must know someone who is already a member, and they have to vouch for them.

Seven: Correct.

Me: Well... you're kinda the only person I know who is a member.

There's a long pause before the three dots begin to dance on the screen, indicating he's typing his reply. I hold my breath, waiting to see what he says.

Seven: Are you saying you want to apply, V? I'd be your sponsor in a heartbeat. But, I've made you aware of the fees, and also the process.

I bite my lip, second-guessing my decision. The fee isn't the problem. Hitting all those best-seller lists, I sold countless books, and all the royalties sit in my savings account. I still live in the same small town I grew up in outside Ft. Vanter, which still doesn't have much to do, nothing really to spend my money on. I'm a recluse, so I don't waste my wealth traveling anywhere. I mostly use it to spoil my parents and big brother.

The only thing holding me back is the therapist situation. I'm not much of a talker, especially about the deep subjects a psychologist would want to touch on while considering me as a prospect in a BDSM club. I don't know why I am the way I am, have the cravings I crave. One would think, because of what happened to me, I would never want someone controlling me, taking away my free will ever again.

I've always thought it might do me some good to talk about these things with a professional, but if I think about it too deeply, actually opening up and revealing all, I start to panic, anxiety overtaking me until I can't even breathe. My old therapist, I told her I had been sexually assaulted, but I never mentioned I was married before. I never said Corbin's name once. She didn't even know he existed. When she prescribed me the pills when I had my breakdown, I told her it was the anniversary of my assault. But what Seven had said at the club *"He can tell within the first month whether or not a person is hiding anything,"* it made me think if I went through with this, I wouldn't be able to keep that part of my life to myself.

But the prospect of finally gaining some release.... God, even the thought of experiencing some of what my fictional subs felt during a scene, being able to let go of all control, handing over all that power to someone I truly trust and know will not hurt me, it's enough to make my final decision.

Me: Yes, I want to apply.

Corbin

"Sooo... THERE'S A situation."

I glance up from my computer, my gaze landing on Seth's fidgeting form in the doorway to my office inside the club. I sit back in my leather chair, taking a deep breath to prepare myself. This "situation" could only be about one person, because Seth is *not* a fidgeter.

"I'm just going to come out and say it. But you're not allowed to try to throttle me again." He looks at me expectantly, and I nod once. "V is applying for a club membership. She contacted me on Messenger and asked if I would be her sponsor."

With my feet planted on the floor beneath my desk, I swing my office chair back and forth a few times, trying to assess my feelings. If I were honest with myself, I would admit that when I was answering Vi's questions, I was really giving her all the information she needed in order to join the club herself, exact step-by-step directions.

"Okay. Here's what's going to happen," I say with finality. There will be no room for discussion. "I'm going to make another Facebook account with your name. I will send her a friend request from it, stating that the other account got reported and I'm in Facebook jail. From here on out, you have no communication with her. Use the Post Privacy setting to block her from seeing new posts."

He looks up to the ceiling and blows out a lungful of air before meeting my eyes once again. "Agreed. But just..." He runs his hand down his face in frustration, clearly loyal to his comrade, but also wanting to be loyal to his friendship with Vi. I lift an eyebrow, waiting for him to continue. "Just don't use this as an opportunity to seek revenge for what she did a decade ago. I'm telling you, she's got something going on with her. Thinking about what you told me long ago, about how she cheated on you while you were deployed and y'all got divorced... she doesn't match the girl I've known for the past year."

"Yeah, well, she had me fooled too," I reply bitterly.

"Corb, people make mistak—"

"I will not use this as an opportunity for revenge. You have my word. But no one touches her but me." I cut him off.

He sighs. "Okay, bro." He turns in the doorway, getting ready to leave, but says over his shoulder, "You might want to make that new profile now. She's waiting on a response about Walker."

"On it." I sit up in my chair and wiggle my mouse to wake the computer back up. "What was her last question exactly, so I can reply accordingly?"

"I believe it was 'So how do I get an appointment with the shrink so he can tell me I'm just the right amount of fucked-up to hang with the cool kids?'" He lets out a chuckle, and my eye twitches at his obvious fondness for my wife.

Ex-wife.

"Got it," I growl, and he takes that as his cue to exit.

I make quick work of creating a new profile, saving a few pictures off Seth's real profile for his Seven persona, and uploading them to my fake one. I feel no guilt for deceiving Vivian, but I also have no ill intentions. Honestly, I don't know why I'm doing all this. I guess just the thought of anyone else teaching her about our lifestyle—the very lifestyle I had suppressed for *her* when we were together—makes me crazy.

When everything is in place, I find Vi's profile in Seth's list of friends and send her a request. In no time, she accepts, and a chat window appears at the bottom of my screen before I even have a chance to message her myself.

> VB: New account?
> Me: Yeah, someone must've got the red-ass and reported one of my pics. That account is in FB jail for a month -_-
> VB: Well that sucks.
> Me: It's ok. Perfect excuse to take a break from social media, but I didn't want to leave you hanging.
> VB: I appreciate it. Soooo...
> Me: One sec, and let me look at the schedule.

I'm surprised to find my heart is thumping inside my chest, the same way it was a couple of days ago when I was actually in Vi's presence. It'd taken me a few minutes to even speak when I first approached her. And when she turned around, dropped her purse, and kneeled before me to pick everything up off the ground, my mind had gone blank. When I slip into my mask, one similar to but not exactly matching Seth's, I become Sarge, and everything but my Dominant persona disappears. And with her on her knees, unconsciously bowing her head to look away from my eyes, my cock had instantly hardened at the perfection of the situation. She had accidentally greeted me the way a sub would properly greet her Dom before a scene.

I log in to Walker's scheduling program and see he has a session available for tomorrow.

> Me: I know it's short notice, but maybe since you work from home, this will work. Doc has an appointment available tomorrow morning at 10 if you want it.
> VB: I'll take it.
> Me: OK. I'll put you in.

I'm finishing out a mission tonight, one the team and I have been working on for nearly four months. Thank God for that, or I would've been useless the next month, while monitoring Vi's therapy sessions.

> VB: Thanks, Seven. When should I come by to fill out the application and leave my deposit?
> Me: If you want to just do that at the appointment tomorrow, I will give Doc everything you need. I won't be at the club tonight.
> VB: Oh... all right.

It would be impossible to tell over the typed-out message, but the way I just read that in my head, it's as if she's disappointed. Because she's unable to see Seth... or me? I shake off the thought, telling myself to interrogate Seth later.

> Me: Talk to you later, baby girl.

I stop, staring at my screen, my fingers hovering over the Enter button. Acid rises in my throat. The endearment flowed out so easily, without any thought behind it, as if no time has passed at all. I caught myself before I sent it, and knowing it would be a bad idea to give even the smallest hint of who I really am, I tap Delete until the last two words in the message disappear.

> Me: Talk to you later, V :)

And I close out my browser.

I SIT IN THE shadows next to the hot tub, not ten feet away from the Olympic-sized indoor pool. It's pitch-black outside, and the only lights on in the building come from inside the pool and the glowing Exit sign above the door in the back, near the locker room. Bleachers line the two longer walls of the rectangular-shaped area, and the only thing between me and the enemy is the diving board structure.

Brock Williams, the Ivy League student known previously by all his classmates as the head of the swim team, had gotten drunk one night and raped and murdered an unconscious girl at a frat party. Being the rich little prick he is, with the help of Daddy's money and the best lawyers they could buy, the fuckstick spent only three months in jail.

How, you might ask? *"There's no way of knowing if the girl wasn't already dead when he had sexually assaulted her."* Yep, the lawyers had ingeniously convinced Brock that it would be much better to be labeled a necrophiliac than a rapist-slash-murderer. And since Brock had no prior record and was twenty years old, the judge went along with it. Yes, the victim's blood alcohol level was astronomical, but witnesses said they saw her—albeit drunkenly—pushing away the jock earlier in the night. The more they testified, the clearer it became—to everyone but the jury, apparently—that Brock had finally taken advantage of the girl when she'd passed out in a room at the frat house. Whether her death was an accident or not became a moot point when the defendant showed absolutely no remorse for any of his actions. What put the final nail in his coffin, was when he was released from jail, his final words to the press were "Three months in there was a steep rate for fifteen minutes of action."

The victim's parents, not only heartbroken from losing their only daughter, were now outraged. Her murderer had essentially just said their baby was no better than an expensive prostitute. And that's when Imperium Security stepped in. Her father was all too willing to hand over the reins of taking care of the smug little shit, as well as half our fee for doing all the dirty work.

So for the past four months since he's been out of jail, we've been laying low, watching, taking note of his every move, waiting for him to establish a routine. For the past six weeks, he's been coming to the pool after hours five days a week to train, even though the National Swimming Association banned him for life. Turns out one of his old frat buddies' parents owns the place, and gave him a key so he could come swim in peace—as if the fucker deserves it.

Seeing the two hours he always spends in the pool is almost up, I center myself, visualizing one last time all I need to do in order to make his demise look like an accident.

Mere minutes later, as I exit the building, I only look back once to see Brock's body floating near the edge of the pool, redness emerging from the top of his skull as if he'd miscalculated his strokes and ran into the cement himself.

I send a text, *Done*, and before I even make it to my truck half a mile from the scene of Brocky-poo's little accident, I receive a notification that the other half of our fee has been paid.

Imperium Security Job #27: Closed.

Five

Vi

I WOKE UP THIS MORNING TO a message from Seven, giving me the address of Dr. Lee Walker's practice. I'd gotten up, showered, and readied myself for the day, but skipped my usual breakfast of a bowl of oatmeal and a mug of sugar disguised as coffee. My gut was nervous enough. No need to add caffeine to the mix. The results wouldn't have been pretty.

So here I sit, in a waiting room like all other waiting rooms, nervously glancing at my phone every few seconds until it's time for my appointment. I'd filled out the normal patient information paperwork when I first arrived here, figuring Dr. Walker has the application for club membership inside his actual office. It makes me wonder if his receptionists know he's part of a team who runs a BDSM club.

Finally the door opens, and a short, plump, middle-aged man

in business casual steps out and I get to my feet. Just as I'm about to reach my hand out to shake his and introduce myself, he turns in the doorway, saying goodbye to a person coming up behind him. When he moves out of the way and swiftly leaves out the front, my eyes return to the figure now taking up the entire door of the office. They travel from the nice brown leather shoes, up the long legs encased in khaki slacks, higher over the perfectly fitted crisp white button-up, and land on brilliant blue eyes. Taking in the rest of his face, I note the well-groomed beard, and the purposely-disheveled dark hair atop a head that nearly reaches the top of the doorframe.

"Ms. Lowe?"

The name coming from him jerks me out of my ogling. "Brown. Vivian Brown. Lowe is just my pen name. Sorry, Seven set the appointment up for me, and he only knows me by that name."

He gives me an unreadable look, but says, "Ah, I understand. Right this way, please." He gestures inside his office, and I wonder how he expects me to enter with him taking up the whole doorway. He then moves out of the way so I can get inside, pulling the door shut behind him as I take a seat on the brown leather sofa. I glance around quickly, taking in the masculine but comfortable room. There is an entire wall of floor-to-ceiling bookcases over to my left, and in front of it is a massive wooden desk with a cushioned rolling chair behind it. It sits atop an ornate rug, but the rest of the flooring is dark gray wood-grain laminate.

Dr. Walker takes a seat in the matching brown chair in front of me, grabbing a clipboard off a small, round, glass side table next to him before handing it to me. "Seven dropped these off for you last night. You can fill them out before you leave the office, but if you look at the one I've put on top there, I need you to go ahead and sign that, if you will. They didn't give it to you at the front, because it's only for my Alias clients—which they know nothing about, by the way. So please, do not feel uncomfortable when you come, because they do not know you are any different from any of my other patients."

I smile slightly. "I had actually been wondering that."

"Everyone does," he states, returning my smile. "That is a consent form. Normally, there is doctor/patient confidentiality. What this paper states is there is still that confidentiality, but you give me permission to share my findings with the rest of the Alias team. They have all signed a NDA, a non-disclosure agreement, also known as a secrecy agreement. So basically they've all been sworn to secrecy when it comes to anything that goes on in these therapy sessions."

I squirm in my seat. It was one thing to come into this thinking I'd have to divulge everything to one person. But allowing him to tell a group of people my deepest, darkest secrets....

"You have to remember, everyone who is a member of the club has to go through this process. The four people, including me, who are privy to your background, go through this with every member. They've heard every story under the sun. There's nothing you could say that would shock them, make them judge you, or cause them to treat you any differently," he assures, and I relax into the soft leather. "There are two reasons we do the therapy sessions before membership is offered. The first, as I'm sure Seven told you, is to make sure a prospect has no bad intentions."

"I'm sorry to cut in, but how exactly do you figure all that out?" I can't help it. My author brain loves to absorb information to potentially use it in a book.

"Seven told me you write BDSM romance novels, is that right?" he asks, and I nod. "So you more than likely know what sadism and masochism is. Sadism is the tendency to derive pleasure, especially sexual gratification, from inflicting pain, suffering, or humiliation on others. A masochist is a person on the other end. They derive the pleasure from being humiliated, hurt, or controlled. Ah... and there it is."

My eyes focus on his, and my brow furrows. "There's what?"

"You, my dear, are a masochist. A natural submissive. I can decipher the smallest of micro-expressions, but with you, your emotions play over your face like a pantomime. The thought of being sadistic, inflicting pain on others, visibly turned you off. That's not in you. But the moment I said the word *controlled*, your lids nearly closed at the thought, your breath caught, and your legs rubbed together." He smirks as I look down at my knees, which I had unconsciously and tightly clamped together. "Now, say you were a sadist. It would be my job to make sure you weren't someone who would go too far when inflicting pain. Someone who would want to actually harm another person, instead of giving them mutual sexual pleasure."

"I see." I tuck my hair behind my ear. "And the second reason you do the therapy sessions?"

"To understand how to heal," he replies, and I tilt my head in confusion. "Normally, there is a reason one gravitates toward BDSM. It doesn't just one day sound fun to be flogged or gagged. It had to come from something, no matter how small. For some, it's as simple as they have a very high-powered position in their career, so when they come into the club, they like to hand over the power and be controlled. Or maybe the opposite: the executive assistant who has to wait on her boss hand and foot all day likes to come and feel what it's like to be completely in control, to be the one giving out the orders and receiving someone's willing submission. But then there are the more complicated cases. The ones we have to take care of. The ones where something happened to them and caused them to have these needs. Unwillingly."

The last word hangs in the air like a physical thing, and I wish I could swat it away like an annoying gnat. Am I really that easily readable? But the more he's talked, the more I want in. I'm not special here. Everyone in Club Alias has their own stories, their own reasons to be there. They've probably heard my type of story over and over again and won't bat an eyelash. So I take the pen attached to the clipboard and sign on the line at the bottom of the page, giving permission for Dr. Walker to share with his team.

"Very good," he says, and I set the clipboard down in my lap. He glances down at his watch. "We have thirty minutes left in your session. Shall we begin?"

I take a deep breath then nod. "All right, doc. Shrink me."

The next half hour is spent telling him my life story from the very beginning. We only make it up until I reached high school before time runs out. We haven't even reached the juicy part of my life yet, and he's already got some theories.

"Even before you hit your teenage years, you were leaning toward a more submissive nature. You had an eagerness to please. You had a good childhood, with a strong male for a father, but also a very doting and loving mother. Instead of taking advantage of her spoiling ways, you went another route. You seemed to want to earn the love she gave you, impress her by doing well in school and trying out the different extracurricular activities she wanted to put you in, even if they didn't interest you. I'm eager for our next session because I have a feeling there is way more to your story than that though," he summarizes, and as we stand, he reaches out his giant paw of a hand for me to shake, and I place mine against his palm. He's gentle when he closes his fingers around me, and the contact is brief. Can he sense I'm not used to people touching me?

"I look forward to seeing you next time, Vivian. Have a good week," he tells me, and I smile weakly.

Although it seemed oddly easy to ramble on about myself with Dr. Walker, we hadn't reached the part of my life that haunts me. That would most likely come during our next session. Would the words spill out of me so easily then? Could I close my eyes and pretend I was telling him about a character in one of my books? Or better yet, could I write it all out as one of my romance novels and hand it to him, demanding, "Here. Read this."? Now that I think about it, I bet that would be therapeutic in itself, typing out my story and calling it fiction, writing the ending different from reality, the way I would want my life to play out.

Before I leave, he has me stop at the reception desk to make my appointment for next week. I also fill out the application for membership at Club Alias, checking the boxes for "Submissive," and "Yes" when it asked if I would like to participate in the optional training program. When it asked if I had a preference on who would be my teacher, I wrote in Seven's name. There's no way in hell I would let anyone else.

Six

Corbin

I'VE WATCHED THE VIDEO OF VI's first session with Doc over and over again for the past week. We'd dated for nearly a year before we were married for two, so there's really nothing during this session I didn't already know about her. Doc's insightfulness spelled out in layman's terms what I had felt about her when we were getting to know each other. I had sensed that natural submissiveness in her, and always thought it was one of the things that drew me to her.

Hearing her talk about her mom and dad brought back so many memories. I had been damn close to my ex-mother-in-law, and realizing I never spoke to her after Vi and I separated makes me feel like an asshole. I know she loved me too, and I never really thought about how she would've felt losing me as part of her family.

I close out the video file and push back from my desk. I move into the bedroom of my condo to change into my workout gear, glancing out my window to see the lamp is on in Vi's room across the street. I can just make out her silhouette behind her sheer gray curtains as she sits at her desk, most likely typing away on one of her books.

We live in the part we call downtown in our small city. The section of town with the library, courthouse, police station, etc. Vi's building is one of the oldest in the city. It actually used to be the nurses' quarters for the hospital, back in the '50s. They had turned them into spacious luxury apartments, keeping all the original hardwood flooring and fixtures. You could smell the years when you entered the building.

My complex is brand new, built the year I got out of the army. An apartment was available in her building, but one, I didn't want to risk running into her, and two, I could keep a better eye on her from over here. In the past few years, she has never once had anyone over but her family. Not even Sierra, because her husband had been stationed in Hawaii five years ago, taking her and their son with him.

I had been pretty fucking lucky when I was booted out of the army. Not even a day after I received my papers stating I was now a civilian, Doc had contacted me, stating he had been following my career since I won the National Marksman competition. He said he had put me on the back burner of his mind, assuming I would be a lifer in the military, but when I had been discharged, he took the opportunity to swoop in and give me a proposition.

He and two other men at the time, Seth and Brian—as in Brian Glover, my former private who had served his four-year enlistment and got out—had established Imperium Security. But it was no normal security service they provided. They were mercenaries, contract killers with a conscience. They only took on cases where the enemy deserved their permanent punishment, those fucktards who had escaped justice by using money and red tape. And since all I knew for the past decade and a half was *one shot, one kill*, having spent all that time in the army as a sniper, the job was something I slid into like I was slathered in KY.

My phone vibrates in my pocket, alerting me to a text.

Dr. Neil Walker, M.D., M.F.T., Ph.D.
Appointment Reminder:
Vivian Brown
Tomorrow at 10:00 a.m.
Send YES to confirm.

I glance up at the window again, watching through the sheer curtain as Vi moves across her room to where she keeps her phone plugged in on her nightstand. A few seconds later, my phone buzzes once again.

Dr. Lee Walker, M.D., M.F.T., Ph.D.
Thank you for your confirmation.
We look forward to seeing you at your appointment.

My heart speeds up, knowing that tomorrow Doc and Vi will pick up where they'd left off during their last appointment. She'd been just about to start talking about her freshman year of high school, when Lee had cut her off, telling her their time was up. I'd slammed my fists down on my desk so forcefully my laptop had bounced between them the first time I'd watched it. Twenty views later, and it still pisses me off when it ends. But tomorrow, we'll see what she has to say about her teenage years, the years in which she met and married me.

TRUTH *revealed*

TRUTH *revealed*

TRUTH *revealed*

revealed

TRUTH *revealed*

Seven

Vi

MY COLORFUL AZTEC-PRINT legging-covered knee bounces in nervousness as I sit across from Dr. Walker. I've gone through what I'll say during this session in my head over and over again. He'll want me to continue with my life story. Would I give him the modified version, the same version I gave my last therapist? Or would I just give him the God's honest truth?

I had concluded I need to tell him the whole story. I've held onto my secret for the past ten years, and at thirty-one years old, I'm tired of carrying around its weight. It may be nice to let someone else help me carry the burden. And since it's clear there's no chance I can hide anything from him anyway, I may as well not make him drag it out of me. It will still be painful, but far less this way.

"So, Vivian, when we ended our session last time, you had just finished telling me about your middle school years. You had dropped out of your ballet and piano classes, after your mom told you she knew you were only taking them to make her happy. So that brings us to your freshman year of high school," Dr. Walker summarizes, then gestures with his pen for me to pick up from there.

I adjust myself on the leather couch, sliding my feet out of my flip-flops and drawing my legs up beneath me. This is a long story, so I may as well get comfortable.

"So... yeah. Freshman year. A fresh beginning at a new school, right? Ya'd think. But alas, the little fuckers who went to my private middle school followed me right into the brand-new private high school. And it didn't take long for the new kids who'd signed up to catch on to the way my old classmates treated me. They joined in on the continued teasing... all except for Jaxon." I smile at the thought of my old friend, my very first boyfriend. "He was a beautiful boy. He was tall, and blond, and tan, with the most amazing big blue eyes I'd ever seen. He didn't understand everyone's relentless teasing about me being skinny, because his little sister was super thin too. He began sitting next to me in our classes, sticking up for me when people would be assholes. And that made me open up to him, and we soon started dating.

"He introduced me to rock climbing. I hadn't wanted to go at first, but Mom talked me into it, just to see what it was about. I went, just because I wanted to hang out with Jaxon outside of school. I had no idea I would end up being a natural at it, and then become completely obsessed with the sport," I say, smiling as I stare off in the direction of Dr. Walker's bookcase.

"You were good at it?" he prompts, jotting something on his notepad.

"Damn good at it. Let's just say it was something my mom didn't have to talk me into going back and trying again. I basically lived there for the next four years. But as much as I loved it, it gave all my classmates something else to tease me mercilessly about," I tell him, my voice dropping.

"Why is that?" he asks, his brow furrowing.

"Well, not too long after I got into rock climbing, Jaxon and I broke up, realizing we were better off as friends. No matter how many times both of us tried to tell people it was a mutual split, they still made up rumors that he had dumped me because I was some stuck-up bitch since I never talked to anyone, or because 'What guy would want to date a girl who spends so much time at a gym, climbing on walls?' So I never even tried to make any friends. I just had to grin and bear it every day during school hours before the last bell rang and I could go to Rock On."

"Rock On? That's the climbing place just down the road, right? I've been meaning to try it out, but haven't made the time," he adds. He did this in our last session too, putting in tidbits to make it feel like we're having a conversation instead of it being an interrogation. It definitely helps me open up to him.

I perk up, my face forming a wide smile. "Oh, God. Yes! You have to go! You won't regret it at all. It's so much fun. You get a full-body workout without having to just lift stupid dumbbells. I miss it a lot. I don't go very often anymore."

"Why is that?" he repeats in his shrink voice.

"I just got busy, I guess. Five years ago, my one and only best friend, Sierra, moved to Hawaii. Her husband is in the army. His family owns the rock gym. I kept going for a few more years after she left, just for a couple hours in the morning before work, but then I started writing. Once my books took off and I quit my job at the paper, climbing wasn't part of my routine anymore. What they don't tell you when you start working from home is that you actually end up working *way* more. I write from sunup to sundown, because I don't have set hours to do my 'job.'"

"This is very true. Plus, stopping your only form of physical activity and leading a sedentary life as an author can lead to you having more of your anxiety issues. We'll have to revisit this in a later session. But for right now, I want you to continue with your timeline. What happened after you and Jaxon broke up? Tell me about your next relationship," he prompts innocently enough, and my gut drops to the springs of the couch.

I swallow hard, my face turning hot, and my heart begins to pound. Spots form in front of my eyes. I can see Dr. Walker's form, but not his actual features, and I think I may throw up.

Next thing I know, he's crouched in front of me with a cup of water, but it's not until his hand lifts my chin to meet his piercing blue eyes that I can take a deep breath—a gasp at being touched. "Vi? In through your nose and out through your mouth. Come on. There you go," he soothes. "Take a sip of water. You're pale as a ghost."

"I'm... I'm so sorry," I wheeze, taking the cup from his hand and swallowing some of the cool drink.

"Don't be sorry. Looks like we've touched on something that needs to be discussed," he states, and I almost whimper. The turn in conversation had been a sucker punch. One second we were talking about rock climbing, and the next, there *it* was. The subject I had been dreading talking about since I agreed to do the therapy sessions.

Without my permission, tears fall from my eyes and down my cheeks, and still crouched before me, he reaches over to the end table and grabs me some tissues.

"Y-you have to understand, I... I haven't told anyone about this time in my life. I've g-gone to therapy before, Dr. Walker, and I managed to keep this part of me hidden. It... it's the most painful thing I've ever been through," I sob, wiping my face as he gets up to sit next to me on the couch.

"I understand, Vivian. Before we continue, I know you have space issues. Would you rather me take my normal seat, or here, closer. Which would you prefer?" he asks in a completely professional tone. There's no innuendo, only sincere concern in his voice.

"Here, please. This is gonna be tough." I let out a half laugh holding no humor whatsoever. It's more like a gush of nervousness expelling from my body.

"Okay. Take your time and tell me. What was your next relationship like after Jaxon? Your original response only makes me assume it was abusive, perhaps? So take all the time you need," he says, but my head is already shaking as I look up at him next to me through watery eyes.

"Oh, God, no. Not at all." My lip trembles and my nose stings. "My next relationship was with the love of my life. I found my soul mate, Dr. Walker. He was my everything. And I had to give him up."

His brow furrows, and he jolts back a bit in surprise. "Ah, well then. Please continue," he says, standing momentarily to grab his notepad and pen before sitting back down beside me. He props his ankle up on his knee and turns to face me as he rests his elbow on the back of the couch.

"God, where do I even begin?" I sigh, glancing up at the ceiling before closing my eyes, and Corbin's perfect face plays across the back of my eyelids like a movie screen. Tears still trickle out of the corners and a sad smile tugs at my lips. "It was my senior year," I breathe, starting from the very beginning. "I was at Rock On, and I was up on the wall. Heard the bells chime over the doors, but thought nothing of it until Sierra called me over to do a belay lesson. Before I even approached the front, I had... a feeling. Thinking about it now, it wasn't too different than when I feel a panic attack coming on, but... in a good way. Like something big was about to happen. And there he was. Our eyes locked, and I couldn't breathe. He was... he was my world. Corbin Lowe."

I feel Dr. Walker shift in his seat, but I hold my position, unwilling to allow my ex-husband's face to leave my mind's eye. Those dark chocolate eyes, and that smile that never failed to warm my soul. "Tell me about Corbin, Vivian. Lowe—you still use it as your pen name?"

"I do. When I was trying to come up with my author name, I did some research. A lot of people said to use a name you'd love to have. A lot of people came out with a pen name using Grey, for Christian Grey of course, fantasizing they were his Ana, I guess. Others said they used the last name of some of their movie star crushes. But me... there was only one last name I fantasized about having, and it was one that had been mine. I *was* Mrs. Corbin Lowe years ago, and I still would be if I'd been given a choice." My head finally drops, and my tears fall onto the backs of my hands in my lap.

"I don't want to miss anything, so let's go back to the beginning again. Start from when you first met at Rock On," he instructs, and after a deep breath, I nod, and tell him the story of my great love affair.

Corbin

"*OH, GOD, NO. Not at all.*" From the angle of camera one, I see Vi's face crumple as she speaks. "*My next relationship was with the love of my life. I found my soul mate, Dr. Walker. He was my everything. And I had to give him up.*"

My gut clenches, watching her pain come through my computer screen. It's almost palpable. She talks about me with such fondness. So why the fuck did she cheat on me if I was the love of her life? Why would she break the one rule I had? Just stay fucking loyal. That's all I asked.

"*...and after a few months, I gave him my virginity,*" she tells Doc, and I listen to his question and her response for what has to be the hundredth time since her second session ended almost a week ago.

"*What was that like? Was there much pain? Any issue surrounding the milestone? Did you feel pressured? This is very important since we're trying to find the source of your desire for the BDSM lifestyle.*" Doc scribbles something on his notepad, and my eyes follow Vi's face as she leans her head back on the couch cushion.

"*Never has there been a more perfect first time between two people. I've tried, God knows I've tried writing love scenes in my books that could compare to the first time Corbin made love to me. But nothing ever seems to hold a candle. It was truly magical. To answer your questions, there was a little pain, but not much. He was an unselfish lover, who always made sure I was ready. He never rushed me. He took care of me. Made me feel like a queen he was worshipping. And I never felt pressured. In fact, I can remember wishing he would make the move to finally seal the deal."* She chuckles lightly, and I realize my face has softened, as it does every time I get to this part in the video. *"But I know it was just his way of making sure I was ready. He wanted me to make the first move, so he knew it was all my idea. And when I finally grew the balls to tell him I wanted him, I couldn't imagine it having ever been better for another person."*

I always wondered what she thought about her first time. If she had regretted it in any way. I had taken her virginity in my barracks room. It wasn't some fancy hotel after I'd wined and dined her. No. It was after a day spent at an amusement park riding roller coasters together, and I had taken her back to my decrepit old building on base, where I made love to her surrounded by ugly army-issued furniture with a movie playing in the background.

But the way she tells the story to Doc, it sounds like a love scene in a movie, one any woman on the face of the planet would fantasize about.

"...and after we married, he never changed. I had worried about that. Once he put a ring on my finger, would he stop being so doting? Would he stop trying to be the man of my dreams? But he never did. He was always my same Corbin, who put me on a pedestal and treated me like a goddess. He was my protector, my lover, and then finally, the day we had dreaded for almost two years came. He got orders to deploy to

Afghanistan." I watch as she uses her tissue to swipe at her nose before Doc interrupts what she was going to say next.

"*Our time is up for today, Vivian. But we made some really great strides. I think next time, we'll really get to the heart of everything. But I can tell you one thing. I think you will fit into Club Alias as a submissive beautifully. And Seven is definitely a good match as your trainer.*" Doc glares in the direction of the camera for a moment, and I know that last line was meant for me. What he meant by it, I'm not exactly sure, but I plan to find out as I close my laptop and head out my door for our meeting tonight before Vi's next session tomorrow.

I reach the glass door with our security service logo on the front, glancing to the right, at the unmarked door Vi had entered the club through. In just a couple more weeks, I would be meeting her inside, training her on how to be a proper submissive. Something I had fantasized about during our years together but never brought up. I had given up that part of myself, hiding it from her innocence, not wanting to scare her away.

I still can't wrap my head around the fact that she got into this on her own. What could've possibly happened between our divorce and now that I wouldn't have picked up on while watching her? Or was it simply the books she read? She'd always loved reading "vampire porn" as I called it. Had she just started reading BDSM books and become interested? Maybe it was something as simple as that, and it just so happened to call to the submissive side of her I was always drawn to. I guess I'll find out in her last two sessions with Doc.

As if thinking of him conjured the man himself, I step back as the door opens from the inside, and I see Doc standing before me. "Evening, Corb," he greets, and I give him a chin lift. "We have a lot to discuss." His tone sounds almost scolding.

"Sorry, bro. Not a switch bone in my body. So any idea you have of bending me over your knee, giving me a spanking, and telling me I've been a very bad boy needs to find its way out of your brain," I growl, walking past him as I enter our building.

"What the hell are you thinking?" he snaps, and I roll my eyes as I stride to the back and open the door that connects to a hallway leading to the club.

"And here we go," I grumble, as he continues chewing me out, all the while following me up the set of stairs that leads to our individual offices.

"You told me years ago you divorced your wife because she was a cheating whore who slept with someone while you were deployed. You painted her into this... this terrible person, this Black Widow adulteress. And then it turns out she is Seth's friend, so you take his mask, pretend you're him, and now she's applying to be in a BDSM club that you own, all while thinking you're Seth. This is fucked up, Corb. And we do some pretty fucked-up shit. So if I think this is fucked up, then you know it's so far *beyond* fucked up it's... it's—"

"FUBAR?" I supply, and he sighs.

"This isn't right, Corb. You're better than this. That woman... she's not anything like what you made us believe." He shakes his head.

That statement pisses me right the fuck off. "I didn't make you believe anything. I told you what happened. I told you that while I was deployed, my wife, the woman I gave up a huge part of who I am for, slept with another man. She had me in the palm of her hand. She made me trust her, made me believe I had nothing to worry about. And she. Fucking. Betrayed. *Me.* Whatever else you added to the story is on you. But the truth itself should be enough."

He walks over to the leather couch up against the wall and sinks onto it, resting his elbows on his knees and his head in his hands. "Look. I understand she hurt you all those years ago. She broke your goddamn heart. I get it. But I'm telling you right now, that woman still worships the ground you walk on. She called you her soul mate, the love of her life—"

"Yeah, I heard her. I watched the fucking footage a thousand goddamn times," I interject, plopping down into my office chair angrily.

The office grows quiet, so quiet my ears begin to buzz. When Doc speaks again, he's using his shrink voice. "Corbin, why are you doing this? All judgment and what's right or wrong aside. Why are you doing this? Why pretend to be Seven? Why use your Jedi mind trick to get her to apply for membership in our club? Why do any of this?"

His tone calms the rabid wolf inside me. I've always opened up to Doc about everything. He's one of my best friends, more like a brother, and I know he only wants the best for me. So I take my time to form an answer, instead of just spouting off to make him leave me alone.

I lean back in my chair and lift my hands to run over my shaved head, and then hunch forward to place my elbows on my desk, blowing out a breath. "I've always been a Dominant. Since the night I lost my virginity, it's just always been something inside me. Shit, maybe even before that. I always had to be in control. I've told you all this crap before, Doc. Napoleon Complex, or whatever the fuck they wanted to call it when I was young. It's always been there. And then Vi came along. And she was so sweet, so goddamn innocent. I didn't want that dark part of me to touch her light. I didn't want to risk dimming her in any way. Instead, I wanted her light to rub off on me.

"And it was easy. It was so fucking easy to just put that Dominant part of myself on the back burner, way, way far away from her, so it never dulled her. I mean, it still came out in other, much more subtle ways. In my protectiveness, and yes, in bed. I was never her Dom, nor her my submissive, but there were still hints of it. The way she always wanted me to be in control, and the way I took over, gladly. The roughness I tried to hold back, but she would do little things to egg me on." I pause, trying to gather my thoughts to see just where I'm going with this.

"But then you saw her here," he prompts, and I meet his eyes.

"I've watched her for a decade. I've kept tabs on her, making sure she was okay, even after all this time. I hated her, all while I continued to love her. God only knows what your psychology has to say about that shit," I murmur, scrubbing my face with my hands.

"My psychology says that you feel like you made a mistake. You had told yourself that her cheating on you was a deal breaker. No matter how much you loved her, you forced yourself to believe that if she were to do that one terrible thing, no matter what, you would leave her. No trying to work things out. Not trying to forgive her. That was it. And after all this time, you regret sticking to your guns," he replies, and I can't really argue with him there.

"When I followed her that day and I saw her come into our club, our motherfucking BDSM club," I scoff, "I cannot even begin to explain the emotions I went through. I don't think half of them even have a name. She had been my woman. Mine. I had wanted to share this side with her so badly but didn't because I didn't want to tarnish her. She was so perfect, so shiny and clean. I didn't want to dirty her with all this. And then there she was, ten years later, walking in here all on her own. Under no one's influence. It was something she wanted to do."

"Yes, she did," he agrees with a nod.

"Why, Doc? Why did she want to come here? Why did she suddenly start writing books about the very lifestyle I tried to hide from her?" My voice is almost pleading.

"I don't know yet, Corb. But I have a feeling we'll know sooner rather than later."

TRUTH *revealed*

RUTH *revealed*

TRUTH *revealed*

TH *revealed*

revealed

Eight

Vi

THIS TIME, IT'S MY RED WITH yellow roses legging-covered knee that bounces nervously as Dr. Walker takes his seat across from me after shutting the door behind us. And this time, I speak up before we get started for the day.

"Dr. Walker, if your plan is to pick up where we left off in my life's time line... I should warn you..." My voice cracks and I have to clear my throat. "...I've never once told another person on this entire planet what I'm prepared to share with you today. And after seeing what happened when I told you about the happiest time in my life, I can only imagine what will happen telling you about the worst."

"What do you need, Vivian? What do you think will make this easier for you?" he asks, and his tone is soothing, caring, not patronizing in the least.

"Would you mind sitting with me again? I know it might be silly, but you seem less threatening when you're closer, rather than over there being able to scrutinize me. Which seems backward, and—"

"Vivian," he interrupts, as he gets up from his chair and folds his ridiculously tall frame onto the couch cushion beside me. "Always, *always* tell me if there is something I can do to make our sessions less stressful for you. Understand?" His voice is commanding yet gentle, and I nod, a promise to do as he says.

He glances at his notes, flips to a clean page, and then meets my eyes. "When we left off, your ex-husband had just gotten deployed. When you're ready, continue there."

I look down into my lap, and a feeling of being uncomfortably exposed overwhelms me. Will I be able to do this? I came here, determined to tell him the truth, to reveal all my secrets. Will I be able to force the words out?

I slide my feet out of my flip-flops, pull them up onto the leather couch, and spin in place, leaning my back up against the armrest of the couch, so Dr. Walker and I are now facing each other. My folded legs create a wall between us as I peek at him over the tops of my knees, and then I focus my attention on one of the yellow roses on my leggings. That rose, the one on my right knee, slightly off-centered, framed by its red background. I'll tell that rose my story.

When I begin to speak, my voice is low, monotone. "My best friend, Sierra, and her husband lived in a townhouse-style apartment. They had a roommate—Alan. It was a three-bedroom apartment. The third one was Sierra and Todd's son's room. I was friends with Alan. I spent a lot of time getting to know him because I hung out with Sierra there at the apartment. When we found out we both needed a credit in the same class at our community college, we took it the same semester, so we could help each other study. Corbin was deployed, so I used the opportunity to take as many semester hours as humanly possible, to get as many out of the way while he was gone as I could. It helped keep me busy, less time to sit around and miss him."

A blanket of sadness folds around me, remembering how badly I missed Corbin while he was gone. It was like a piece of me was gone too, as if he'd reached in, stolen my heart, and taken it with him. I was miserable without him, and add that to the worry I felt constantly with my soul mate overseas, fighting a war I really didn't know anything about or why we were even over there to begin with....

"Todd's best friend lived in the same apartment complex, and he was getting deployed the following day. So, they were throwing him a goodbye party. Sierra invited me, wanting to get me out of the house. At this time, I lived in a little one-bedroom apartment across town, closer to my parents. I didn't really know anyone who would be there. Todd and his best friend were in a different platoon than Corbin, so it was a totally different crowd. But Sierra would be there, of course, and so would Alan. So I went."

I lean backward slightly over the armrest, cracking my back. It's something I do in my office chair when I'm writing, when I'm about to tell a part of the story that will devastate the reader. But instead of having a keyboard to place my fingers on, I slide them into my hair at my temples until my hands rest firmly against my scalp, and I brace my elbows on top of my knees. I lose focus on the one yellow rose and stare through the gap between my thighs, zeroing in on the piping of the leather cushion I'm sitting on, how it has a three-inch space between it and the piping of the cushion Dr. Walker occupies. I talk to that cavity, hoping my words will somehow fall between the couch cushions, never to be found again, so I'll forget it ever happened.

"Corbin had once told me this story... the saddest story I'd ever heard. He and a girlfriend from high school went to a fair, and they'd gotten super drunk using fake IDs. They'd gone back to her house and passed out. When he woke up the next morning, she had thrown up in her sleep and suffocated on her vomit. She was dead, right there in the bed with him. Seeing how I grew up with no alcohol in my parents' house, I had never been around people drinking before. This story... it scared me. The impression it made on me... at the time, it made me think that even a sip of beer would intoxicate a person, and they wouldn't be safe alone," I explain, glancing up into Dr. Walker's eyes long enough to see he's watching me closely, before my eyes move back to the crevice.

"Sierra and Todd's son, Alaric, was with Todd's parents for the night, and they were taking full advantage of the night out. Alan had a ton to drink too, and he was ready to go home before Sierra and Todd were. I didn't drink—back then, at least—so I was sober, witnessing all their laughter, their stumbling around, their slurred words. I saw Alan heading for the door to leave Todd's friend's apartment, so I told Sierra I was going to make sure he got home okay. I don't even know if she registered my words as she and Todd were doing shots when I hollered to her over the music. But I hurried after Alan, wanting to be there to help him down the flights of concrete steps."

I close my eyes and rub my forehead. I... I don't—

"Vivian, take a breath." Dr. Walker's commanding voice cuts

through my panic, and I realize I'm crying, tears spilling down my cheeks rapidly, and my whole body is trembling. My head shakes vigorously as I open my eyes to meet his, trying to convey I can't. I can't do as he said and take a breath. My lungs aren't working. My brain's signal for them to inhale is being rerouted. My hand shoots out toward him, reaching for him in my terror that I feel like I'm suffocating. *Help me,* my eyes plead, and that's when he moves.

In one fluid motion, he reaches out and grabs me by the tops of my arms, spins his body to sit forward on the couch, and pulls me across his lap. The moment my stomach flattens against his thighs, his huge, strong hand slaps my right ass cheek, and I gasp, pulling in a lungful of sweet, cool air. My entire being melts across the couch and his legs as I pant. I can feel my heart beating as it thuds against the cushion on the opposite side of Dr. Walker.

A sense of calm I haven't felt in a decade washes over me, and when my breathing evens out, he scoops me up and sets me back in my place. He picks up his notepad and pen off the floor, where he must've thrown them before he grabbed me, and his face shows absolutely no emotion as he jots something down. When he looks back up at me, I feel he's waiting for me to continue my story, as if nothing had just transpired between us. I'm grateful for this, because my head would swim if I had to digest what just happened.

My voice returns to its quiet monotone. "I walked with Alan down the stairs, across the long yard between the complexes, which separated the apartments from the townhouses, and got him up the staircase that led to the bedrooms at their place. I got him into his bed and had only planned to stay in his room long enough for him to fall asleep. Then I was going to move the baby monitor into his room and sleep in Alaric's with the receiver. The entire time, all I could think about was the story Corbin told me. His girlfriend choking on her vomit in her sleep, so drunk her heaving never woke her up. That's what was in my head when I lay down on top of the covers next to my friend, waiting for him to fall asleep peacefully. That's what was going through my mind as I closed my eyes, just for a minute, because it seemed like it was taking forever for Alan to stop fidgeting beneath his comforter."

I take a deep breath as my heart pounds once more, but when I close my eyes, I allow myself to remember the feel of Dr. Walker's stinging smack across my ass, and the calmness I felt afterward spreads through my veins. When I open them again, I meet his concentrated stare and finally reveal the truth.

"The next thing I knew, Alan was on top of me. He had his hand over my mouth and he was bearing down on that hand with his full weight, pressing my head into the pillow. I came fully awake then, realizing I had accidentally fallen asleep in his bed, never making it to Alaric's room. I clawed at him, fighting with all my might twisting underneath him, but the way he had his hand clamped over my mouth, it felt like my neck was going to snap. Plus, my movements only seemed to help him get me out of my pants."

Even though my eyes are still on Dr. Walker, I don't see him. My brain isn't absorbing the handsome, bearded face before me. No. In my mind's eye, all I see is Alan's black hair falling over his tan forehead, and the crazed look in his almost-black eyes, his pupils overtaking his irises. His mouth was slack, his breathing steady, as if my flailing and fighting with all my strength was nothing for him, just a tiny bug beneath his giant boot.

"I can remember thinking about my legs. My legs were super strong, my biggest strength, from years of working out at the rock gym. If I could just get them between us, I could kick him off me and run. So even though I was naked from the waist down, still pinned in place by the death grip he had over my mouth, I managed to bring my feet up and push my heels against his already bare hips. He must've taken off his jeans before he attacked me. I kicked him with every ounce of strength I had in me. But it did absolutely nothing. And then he—"

I choke on the sentence, unable to finish. All that comes out is a sound somewhere between a gulp and a sob. I stare into my lap, trying to gather the strength to tell the rest of the story, but the only thing that leaves any part of me are the tears falling from my eyes.

Suddenly, a giant mitt of a hand enters my field of vision, palm facing up, and it stays there. A silent invitation for loaned strength. And timidly, I finally place my much smaller, trembling hand in Dr. Walker's. The contact opens the floodgates, and every second of gut-wrenching, body-wracking, pain-filled wailing I had held in for the past ten years takes the opportunity to escape. He doesn't move to hug me, which I'm grateful for. The physical connection we have is more than enough, more than I've been able to stomach in the past decade.

"Let it out, Vivian. Let it all out," Dr. Walker murmurs encouragingly, and damn it, I do.

I don't know how long I sit there, crying, sobbing, and whimpering. I lose count of how many tissues I go through, as he goes from handing me individual sheets to just handing over the box. I'm sure if I were to take a moment to look in the small trash can next to the couch, it would almost be overflowing with the drenched, balled-up white pieces of waste.

When I've exhausted myself to the point where all I can do is sniffle, my eyes feeling like a bucket of sand has been poured into their sockets, that's when Dr. Walker asks me to do one of the hardest things I've ever had to pull up my big girl panties and do. "All right, Vivian. Finish your sentence. And then he... what?"

I close my swollen eyes, and on a weary exhale, I finally confess my deepest, darkest secret. "And then he raped me."

UTH reveal
reveal
UTH reveal
UTH rev

Nine

Corbin

"**A**LL RIGHT, MOTHERFUCKER. I'M HERE. You want to tell me why I was denied access to the goddamn session video when I tried logging in?"

It had taken every ounce of my self-control to not throw my fucking laptop across the room when my username and password wouldn't let me into the footage. Fifteen minutes after Vi's session ended, I received a message from Doc telling me to meet him at the club. So here I am, after storming into his office like a raging bull.

Doc sits at his desk, his face solemn. It's not until Seth speaks that I even realize he's sitting on the leather couch against the wall. "Corbin, we... we didn't think it'd be a good idea for you to watch the video alone."

"What the fuck is that supposed to mean?" My heart pounds angrily against my ribs, like a prisoner behind bars.

Doc stands, gesturing to his office chair as he moves away from it. "Have a seat."

I glare at him for a moment before circling his desk to take his place. Just then, Glover's tall frame comes through the door, and suddenly I'm in a sea of giants. He comes to stand next to Doc, feet shoulder-width apart, and he crosses his arms over his chest. Gone is the bright-eyed and bushy-tailed young cherry from nearly a decade and a half ago, and in his place is a hardened grown man who had seen a lot, both on the battlefield and during his time as a mercenary.

"Well, the whole team is here. You want to tell me what's going on?" I growl, hating the way my three best friends are looking at me. Their faces are a mix of worry, anger, and... is that a hint of pity? Fuck this. "Somebody better fucking speak up, or I'm gonna start throwing shit."

"Vi's last session was... revealing, to say the least. Not at all what we were expecting. Seth and Brian have not seen the video, but I have given them a full debriefing. Corb, before you press Play, just know we are all here for you," Doc says in his shrink voice, and I suddenly feel nauseous. What? Did she go into so much detail of her affair that they thought I wouldn't be able to handle it? That I'd go off the deep end after hearing the who, what, when, where, and how of her cheating on me while I was deployed?

If they only knew how many different scenarios I'd come up with in the past ten years of her fucking another man, they wouldn't have bothered calling in the troops.

Without wasting another minute, I click on the triangle across the video to make it start playing. And as always, the moment I see Vi's beautiful face, the bees in my stomach take flight, buzzing and stinging my insides. Even so obviously nervous, her little knee bouncing a mile a minute, there is no denying she is still the most perfect woman I've ever laid eyes on. I hate that I still find her so attractive. The ugly thing she had done to me should've masked those gorgeous, delicately feminine features, but they never did.

"Dr. Walker," she begins, "if your plan is to pick up where we left off in my life's time line, I should warn you..." She visibly chokes on her words and clears her throat. "I've never once told another person on this entire planet what I'm prepared to share with you today. And after seeing what happened when I told you about the happiest time in my life, I can only imagine what will happen telling you about the worst."

My brow furrows. Except me. "Never once told another person on the planet," except me, right? She must mean she never told anyone else about her affair, after she'd confessed it to me over the phone while I was in Afghanistan. I don't have time to think much more about her opening, before heat rises up the back of my neck as I watch her ask Doc to sit with her, him complying and taking up the cushion next to her small frame. He dwarfs her, making her look childlike, especially as she slips off her shoes and curls in on herself, turning to face him on the couch after I hear Doc tell her to start this week's session with where they'd ended last week, with me deploying.

When she starts speaking, her voice is devoid of all emotion. "My best friend, Sierra, and her husband lived in a townhouse-style apartment. They had a roommate—Alan."

Alan. Is that who she slept with? Did the motherfucking homewrecker finally have a name?

"...I was friends with Alan. I spent a lot of time getting to *know him, because I hung out with Sierra there at the apartment. When we found out we both needed a credit in the same class at our community college, we took it the same semester, so we could help each other study."*

Ah, I remember Alan now. She talked about him every once in a while, when I'd call home every few days from overseas. She had painted him to be a completely unthreatening nerd-type, someone she crammed for tests with, always at Sierra's house, and never alone with him. So I guess that was a goddamn lie.

"Corbin was deployed, so I used the opportunity to take as many semester hours as humanly possible, to get as many out of the way while he was gone as I could. It helped keep me busy, less time to sit around and miss him."

The look of pain on her face is unmistakable. At least she really did miss me while I was gone, even if she did pass the time by fucking another man.

"...Sierra invited me, wanting to get me out of the house. At this time, I lived in a little one-bedroom apartment across town, closer to my parents. I didn't really know anyone that would be there. Todd and his best friend were in a different platoon than Corbin, so it was a totally different crowd. But Sierra would be there, of course, and so would Alan. So I went."

I scoff. Yeah, her little fuckboy would be at the going-away party, so why not?

She leans backward over the armrest, cracking her back the way I've seen her do while she's writing. Normally, she'd then stretch her arms high above her head, arching her back before rolling her head in a circle, as if getting rid of a crick in her neck, and then she'd set to typing like a woman possessed. But this time, she just continues her recollection, speaking to Doc almost robotically.

"Corbin had once told me this story... the saddest story I'd ever heard. He and a girlfriend from high school went to a fair, and they had gotten super drunk using fake IDs."

My brow furrows once again as she tells Doc, almost word for word, the story I had told Vi on our first date. Shit, I hadn't even thought about the night of that tragic event since I had told Vi. And here she was, stuck on it after all these years?

"This story... it scared me. The impression it made on me... at the time, it made me think that even a sip of beer would intoxicate a person, and they wouldn't be safe alone."

Her face conveys the fear she's speaking of, and I almost feel guilty for telling her that part of my past if it traumatized her this much.

"...I saw Alan heading for the door to leave Todd's friend's apartment, so I told Sierra I was going to make sure he got home okay. I don't even know if she registered my words as she and Todd were doing shots when I hollered to her over the music. But I hurried after Alan, wanting to be there to help him down the flights of concrete steps."

Yes, chase after your secret lover, I think. *Wouldn't want him to fall and break his dick, since you needed it to kill time until I got home.*

I'm stewing in my bitterness, acid sitting heavy in my throat, when Doc's voice suddenly comes through the computer's speakers.

"Vivian, take a breath."

My eyes narrow, watching closely as Vi goes from unemotional to full-on panic mode, bursting into tears and visibly trembling, even from the distance of the camera aimed at the couch. Her hand shoots toward Doc, as if she's drowning beneath the water's surface, flailing to grasp hold of anything to pull her to safety.

And what I witness next makes me see red.

Doc tosses his notepad and pen to the ground before swinging his arms toward Vi. He takes hold of her biceps, his hands looking so huge around her thin arms it looks like he could snap her without applying any force, and then pulls her tiny body across his lap.

The second I see and hear his palm connect with her ass, without even thinking, I lunge across Doc's desk, my fist a hairbreadth away from connecting with his face, before I'm tackled to the ground. The wind is knocked out of me, and it takes me a moment to realize both Brian and Seth are on top of me. And then, like a wild animal, I fight back.

By the time I exhaust every ounce of my energy, my knuckles are throbbing and my head feels like it's going to explode. But the way the two larger men are panting and cussing, at least I know a couple of my punches landed.

I glare up from the floor at Doc, who towers over our piled bodies. "You put your fucking hands on my goddamn woman!" I snarl.

"Corbin," he starts in his calm shrink voice, "she was having a severe panic attack. By now, you know we've already determined she's a natural submissive. I did the first thing I thought of to bring her out of her panicked state before she passed out. If you would just get up and watch the video, you will see—"

"Fuck you!" I yell, launching upward at the fucker who had dared to touch my sweet Vi, much less spanked her ass.

"Corbin." His voice is sterner this time. "Get up and watch the video."

My eyes shoot daggers up at him, but it's Seth's voice that breaks through the ringing in my ears. "Bro, just watch the fucking video. You need to hear what she says." His tone holds warning, and a sense of foreboding washes over me, making my anger sizzle as if it were doused.

After a minute, I sigh and then jerk against their hands holding me restrained. "Fine. Get the fuck off me."

Brian stands first, placing himself between me and Doc like a human shield. Seth stands quickly, jumping back like I'm a firecracker he just lit. But even in my fuming rage, I get up calmly then walk back around the desk. I rewind the video, then fast forward it just a second after Doc's hand landed on my ex-wife's perfect ass, so I don't have to hear the sound of the slap again.

I watch as she goes limp across his lap, her body going from painfully rigid to melted butter within one breath. And I'm begrudgingly thankful when I see not even five seconds later, Doc sitting her back upright in her spot on the couch. His face holds no emotion—not the satisfied smirk of a Dominant, nor even a look of concern a doctor gives his patient. He simply picks up his notepad and waits for her to continue.

Vi's voice goes back to that eerily robotic monotone. "I walked with Alan down the stairs, across the long yard between the complexes, which separated the apartments from the townhouses, and got him up the staircase that led to the bedrooms at their place. I got him into his bed and had only planned to stay in his room long enough for him to fall asleep. Then I was going to move the baby monitor into his room and sleep in Alaric's with the receiver."

My heart slowly sinks into my gut. Why would she be planning to sleep in a different room if she'd been fucking him? What, she could have sex with him, but she thought sleeping next to him was going too far? I bite my lip as she continues.

"The entire time, all I could think about was the story Corbin told me. His girlfriend choking on her vomit in her sleep, so drunk her heaving never woke her up. That's what was in my head when I lay down on top of the covers next to my friend, waiting for him to fall asleep peacefully. That's what was going through my mind as I closed my eyes, just for a minute, because it seemed like it was taking forever for Alan to stop fidgeting beneath his comforter."

As my heart takes up residence somewhere in my intestines, my breathing starts to pick up.

"The next thing I knew, Alan was on top of me. He had his hand over my mouth and he was bearing down on that hand with his full weight, pressing my head into the pillow."

No. *Nononononononono....*

"I came fully awake then, realizing I had accidentally fallen asleep in his bed, never making it to Alaric's room. I clawed at him, fighting with all my might twisting underneath him, but the way he had his hand clamped over my mouth, it felt like my neck was going to snap. Plus, my movements only seemed to help him get me out of my pants."

Oh, Jesus fuck, no. My hands shoot to the armrests of the office chair, and I hear the wood pop in my grip.

"I can remember thinking about my legs. My legs were super strong, my biggest strength, from years of working out at the rock gym. If I could just get them between us, I could kick him off me and run. So even though I was naked from the

waist down, still pinned in place by the death grip he had over my mouth, I managed to bring my feet up and push my heels against his already bare hips."

My eyes shut of their own accord, the picture she's painting vividly playing out in my mind. My sweet, tiny, innocent Vi, beneath not only a man, but one whose strength was enhanced by the alcohol he'd drank that night, which made him reckless and uncaring if he hurt my fragile wife.

I want to cover my ears and rock back and forth, anything to cover up what I know must be coming next, but I can't. If my angel had gone through this, then I need to hear it. I need to experience her pain through her retelling of that night. A night I'm starting to realize went down *nothing* like she had said all those years ago.

"He must've taken off his jeans before he attacked me. I kicked him with every ounce of strength I had in me. But it did absolutely nothing. And then he—"

Her words stop abruptly, and I force my eyes open to see what's happening in the video. She's fighting with herself, appearing like she's trying to make the words come out, but they just won't.

I want to jump into the screen and wrap her in my arms, tell her she doesn't have to say any more, and that everything will be all right now. I've got her. But instead, I see Doc hold his hand out to her. She eyes it warily, and it makes me think about the way she jerked away from my touch the night she came to Club Alias. And it all makes sense now, why she appeared shocked, maybe even a little repulsed by the physical contact.

But then finally, she slowly, delicately places her tiny hand in

Doc's huge one, and as if the contact electrocutes her, she jerks, and then she crumbles.

She cries so long and hard that my heart crawls out of its hiding place in my gut and up into my throat where it lodges itself, causing me to be unable to swallow. An unfamiliar stinging starts at the backs of my eyes and in my nose, and I find myself having to fight back the tears filling my eyes.

"Let it out, Vivian. Let it all out," Doc tells her, but I don't want her to. I have never experienced such unbelievable pain in my life, more devastating even than when she had obviously lied and told me she cheated on me. Then, she was the enemy; she was the one who had hurt me. But now... now, knowing the truth, that this had happened to my baby girl....

But I don't look away. I don't fast forward the video. I sit through every second of her heart-wrenching sobs, until she finally exhausts herself, and Doc prompts her, *"All right, Vivian. Finish your sentence. And then he... what?"*

I watch her close her beautiful green eyes, and then finally, after a sigh that seems to leave only enough oxygen for her to respond, she says the words I already know are coming and will change my life forever.

"And then he raped me."

I can't.

I see there are twenty-two minutes left in the video, but I can't take any more. At least not right now. So I pause it and just stare at the computer screen.

I don't know what to do.

I don't know what to say.

I don't know what to think.

My... my beautiful wife.

I had been the only person who ever touched her. She had been completely innocent before I made her mine. And then someone took her sweetness, her caring and nurturing personality, and they'd used it against her. My baby girl, so naïve, didn't want to leave some drunk motherfucker alone, because of a story I'd told her. And he fucking—

No.

I can't think about that right now. If I think about that... no, I just can't.

Why? Why had she lied to me? Why had she told me she'd slept with someone?

And now that I think about what she'd told me all those years ago—*"We were all drinking. I had too many to drive home, so I stayed with Sierra and her roommate. I... I did something horrible"*—I should've known something was up. *"I was drunk. I... I slept with someone."* I had been so shocked by the words that came out of her mouth that I didn't take the time to think about their deception. It didn't click in my head that Vi didn't drink. It never dawned on me that even on her twenty-first birthday, she had a virgin strawberry daiquiri, so why would she all of a sudden be drinking at a party?

The mouse in my hand cracks, but I'm so internally distraught right now that I barely register the sharp plastic stabbing into my hand. What I do register is the video begins to play once more, and all the questions running through my mind are answered.

"...and then Corbin called a couple of days later. He was always so protective of me, so possessive, but in a good way. But... he had a darker side. I could see tiny hints of it, a facial expression here or a snide comment passed off as a joke there. I could see that if he were pushed, that dark side he hid so well

would surface, and he could probably do some pretty serious damage—to whatever person set him off, or to himself. It was the damage to himself that I was worried about, and that's what made me lie to him.

"I knew... knew as clearly as if I had a fucking psychic glimpse into the future that if I told Corbin I had been raped, he would murder Alan. I knew it in my very soul. If I told him the truth, there would've been no stopping him from actually beating my rapist to death. And then Corbin would've been sent to prison. Or, in an alternate scenario, Corbin could get hurt. If he was so upset when he went after Alan, not thinking straight, then it was possible that Alan could get a one-up on my husband. I couldn't risk that. I had to keep Corbin safe. I had to keep him from getting hurt, or being sent to jail for the rest of his life. So... I lied."

I run my hands over my shaved head and close my eyes. She was absolutely right. If she'd told me she had been raped, the very second I returned home from Afghanistan wouldn't have been spent on the airfield's tarmac hugging and kissing my beautiful wife who held a Welcome Home sign. Oh no. It would've been me gunning for the motherfucker who had taken my sweet girl's light.

All this time... all this fucking time....

Ten years I've spent both loving and hating Vivian. Watching her from a distance, scrutinizing her every move. And the whole time she dealt with this truth on her own. This fucking tragic... awful thing had happened to such an angel, and what had she done? Only thought of me. Wanted to protect me. Wanted to keep me safe, out of jail.

"What did you tell him when he called, Vivian? And what

did he say?" Doc asks. I hear he's trying to keep his voice in its normal calm tenor, but I can tell he's shocked by this turn of events.

Vi looks into her lap, where her hands are wringing. *"There's no way I could pretend nothing had happened. I wouldn't be able to keep this secret to myself, not from Corbin. He was my soul mate. Plus, even the thought of him coming home and sleeping with me, not knowing another man had been inside me, made me feel guilty as hell. He used to tell me constantly how much he loved that he was the only one who'd ever touched me."* She smiles and glances up at Doc. *"Corbin was my first real kiss. I gave him my virginity when I was eighteen. He was my first and only love."* Her eyes move back to her fidgeting fingers. *"The only thing he ever asked of me was that I stay loyal. I would always scoff and roll my eyes at him. As if I'd ever want anyone else. Oh my gosh, Dr. Walker. You have no idea."* She sighs almost dreamily. *"He was so freaking gorgeous. The most handsome man I'd ever seen. Still to this day, I've never laid eyes on another man who would even hold a candle to Corbin Lowe."* She side-eyes Doc, and murmurs, *"No offense."*

Doc forces *out* a chuckle. *"None taken."*

"Just... it's needless to say that I would've never willingly *had sex with anyone other than my husband. He was my everything. No other men even existed. But... I had to tell him something. What could I possibly say to let him know he was no longer the only person I'd been with, without telling him I'd been raped, which would have either gotten him hurt or put away for the rest of his life? So I lied and told him I'd been drunk and slept with someone.*

"I guess I was hoping he'd forgive me and we could move

on from it. Part of me thought maybe our love for each other would be enough to keep him from leaving, that we could get through anything. But knowing it was his one deal-breaker, it wasn't that shocking when he finally spoke the last words I ever heard him say to me. 'I'll have the divorce papers sent to you.'"

Every word she says rings true. As she explains her train of thought from all those years ago, I know in my heart everything is exactly right. I *knew* she would've never cheated on me. It's why I asked her to marry me in the first place. I *knew* I was the center of her universe, her every thought orbiting around me. And it dawns on me. *This*. This is where my decade-long obsession with following her must've birthed from. My stalkerish compulsion to always have my eye on her, to always know she's safe, to know her every move. It's because I knew, gut deep, I'd made a mistake. Somewhere deep inside me, I knew jumping the gun and sending her those divorce papers was... fuck, it was *wrong*. And because I'm a dumb fuck, instead of admitting it and working things out with her, I followed her around this long like a goddamn psychopath. I snort at my decisions, my mistakes, so pissed off with the old me I could knock myself the fuck out. My actions had been my way of dealing with the guilt of never giving her a chance, after she had put all her trust in me. She'd trusted me to keep her safe, yet I'd dropped her like a hot rock.

I jump in my seat as a hand squeezes my shoulder. I glance up from my misery into the face of Doc, who has nothing but sympathy in his eyes. It's a look I normally detest from anyone, but right now, admittedly, I need it.

"You couldn't have known, Corb," he tells me, his voice low.

"I did know, Doc. Something in me knew. It has to be why...."
I shake my head, unable to finish, but he does it for me.

"It's why you've always watched her. It's why you came back, took the job I offered you, and moved in right across the street from her. This is why you could never let her go," he says, though it's more to himself as his eyes look through me, putting all the pieces together in his mind. After a moment, he focuses his gaze again. "So what now?"

My face hardens. "Now, we find that motherfucker."

TRUTH revealed

RUTH revealed

TRUTH revealed

TH revealed

revealed

Ten

Vi

FOR THE FIRST TIME SINCE I started these sessions, I sit calmly in my spot on Dr. Walker's sofa. As tough as it was to reveal all, now that I have, it's like a huge weight has been lifted off my shoulders. It makes me almost regret not doing it sooner, if not with my first therapist, then with one soon after she retired. But something tells me it probably wouldn't have had quite the same effect as it did with him. I don't know of another therapist who would have spanked me out of a panic attack.

"All right, Vivian. Today is your last required session with me, but know that you are welcome to continue coming if you see fit to do so. I have quite a few people from the club who continue their weekly appointments with me," he assures, and I think I might just take him up on his offer. "I've already sent Seven my approval letter for your membership request. So I'd like to take today as an opportunity to discuss my findings, if you'd like my professional opinion?"

"Of course," I state, adjusting in my seat. I pull my leg up beneath me to get comfortable and settle in to hear what he has to say.

"First off, I'd like to reassure you that you are not alone. There are thousands of cases where survivors of a sexual assault end up participating in BDSM," he informs, and it surprises the hell out of me.

"Really? I mean, you'd think that someone who has..." I clear my throat, still unused to saying the words aloud. "...been raped would want to stay far away from sex involving... ya know, the stuff that goes on in that kind of relationship." My face turns hot. "The spanking, the tying up. I always thought that would make it worse for someone who had been put through what... what I went through."

"Quite the contrary. So many survivors claim BDSM is healing for them. And yes, at first glance, one would think all that would be a trigger for the survivor, as opposed to being therapeutic. But just think about it. BDSM is a power game. In the books you write, who actually has the power?" he asks, a small smile on his lips.

I think for a moment, visualizing my characters, and realization hits. "The submissive. They can end a scene by just saying their safe word."

Dr. Walker nods approvingly. "Exactly. They are the ones *allowing* it to happen at all. Therefore, they hold all the power. Now, that's not to say a survivor can't find the role as a Dominant just as therapeutic. *You* might not find it appealing, but I'm sure you can imagine how empowering it would feel to be the one in control of a scene."

"Oh, for sure. I guess that's why I find it so surprising that I still want someone else to have control over me. I just don't have the desire to ever dominate anyone. I thought something was wrong with me that I have these... needs, especially since my control was taken from me against my will," I confess.

"There is absolutely nothing wrong with you, Vivian. Your desire to give up control comes from wanting to give it freely, to be the one to hand it over instead of it being stolen from you." As he says the words, it all becomes so clear in my mind. It all makes so much sense. He goes into further detail, and I have a feeling it's because he knows I crave information.

"When someone who has been sexually assaulted takes on the submissive role in a partnership, on the surface, one could argue they're recreating the abusive experience by having the power taken from them and being subjected to the pain, the humiliation, the violence of the act, which could obviously expose them to PTSD. But, in a real BDSM relationship, the sub, as we stated before, has the power. They're the one who creates the rules beforehand, what they give the Dom permission to do, how far they want them to go, and, just like you said, when to use their safe word to bring everything to an immediate halt."

I absorb everything he says like a sponge, hanging on his every word. Seeing my utter fascination, he continues.

"In a proper BDSM relationship, there is established trust and understanding between the Dom and sub. So in your case, as the sub, you are then able to *be* submissive, but in a situation where you remain safe and in control of what does or doesn't happen to you. So you, as a survivor of sexual violence, having this type of control in a scene can theoretically be empowering. Therefore, it can be healing, because you would basically be rewriting the story of what happened to you a decade ago. On the other hand, other survivors take on the Dominant role as a way of feeling they are the one who is in control, because they are the one doling out the sadism. Use that information for your next book." He smiles, and it's infectious.

A few weeks ago, you couldn't have paid me to believe I'd be smiling during a therapy session, after having told a doctor I'd been raped. But here I am.

"I... I have something else I need to talk about, if that's okay?" I ask. I had weighed not bringing this part up, but having confessed everything else to Dr. Walker, I figure it can't hurt.

"Certainly," he prompts, gesturing with his pen before grabbing his notepad from his side table.

"I haven't..." I shift on the couch cushion, suddenly embarrassed by what I'm about to say. I take a deep breath, close my eyes, and decide to just blurt it out. "I haven't had sex since that night. I've been in relationships, and when it would finally come time to be intimate, as soon as they'd put their hands on me, I'd freak the fuck out, leave, and fall off the face of the planet. Never talk to the person ever again."

I see a flash of surprise cross his face before he hides it behind his professional expression. He writes something down as he speaks. "You haven't had intercourse in ten years?" he confirms.

"Correct," I whisper, and my tone draws his eyes back to me.

"Vivian, there is nothing to be embarrassed or ashamed about. From what you've told me, and from the many, *many* cases I've studied, the inability to be intimate with someone after having been raped is completely normal. Particularly from what you divulged about your past. You waited until you were eighteen to ever become sexually active in the first place. In this day and age, that's pretty mature, especially with hormones running rampant, and girls going through puberty at such early ages. You married the man who you gave your virginity to. He was the only person you were ever intimate with." He pauses, looking me in the eyes seriously. "Now, do you understand what I just said? He was the *only* person you were *ever intimate* with. Meaning, you were never *intimate* with Alan. What he did to you is not being intimate. The word itself can be defined as 'private and personal.' Something you do willingly and freely. You only did that with Corbin. And from your telling of your past, it had been a big deal, a huge decision on your part. Your virginity meant something to you. You gave it to the one and only person you ever trusted, and had thought you were going to spend the rest of your life with him, only being intimate with him during your lifetime. So no, it's not something you should be ashamed of."

I nod vigorously. "Okay, thanks, Dr. Walker. Enough about that. Can you get back to the BDSM stuff?" I laugh nervously, uncomfortable thinking about Corbin and him being the only person I ever trusted. How sad is it I've never been able to trust anyone since, even ten years later?

"I can see that's a prickly subject, one I'd like to revisit during a later session, if you choose to return. But yes, since you're here right now as part of your club membership initiation, I'll get back to the BDSM stuff, as you put it." He gives me a look that says he's a little disappointed I don't want to continue where he wanted the conversation to go, but does as I requested anyway.

"In our first session, we touched on what BDSM is about. Sadism and masochism, which you have a lot of knowledge about because of the genre of your books. Needless to say, many survivors can find it difficult to engage in anything that results in sexual pleasure. They may feel guilty for getting aroused, thinking it's in some way wrong to feel in any way sensual. Others, unfortunately, find getting aroused is a trigger. They have flashbacks, memories of their assault. And then there are others who just can't become aroused at all and avoid sex. Do you have anything to say about this subject?" he asks in his therapist voice.

I think for a moment before answering. "I think I may be a mix. I can get aroused. I do. I mean, my career is based on arousing people with my words. I get turned on during my research. I..." I can't believe I say this out loud, but just go with it. "I masturbate. But I do avoid sex with other people. There have been a couple of times when I thought I wanted to become intimate with someone I was in a relationship with, but when it came time to actually do it, nothing. Sometimes, there was absolutely no sexual desire, but *every* time, it was an overwhelming sense of... not fear, and not quite guilt, but just a sense of it being... wrong. Like I was in a situation I was not supposed to be in. I would get this feeling of being in a place I shouldn't be and I just needed to leave right then. Like my flight instinct was going off."

He nods, writing something down, then asks, "Were these D/s relationships, or vanilla, meaning normal, non-BDSM relationships?"

"Vanilla. I've never been in a D/s relationship before. I mean, not where it was talked about," I reply.

"Can you expand on that?" he requests.

"Well... for some reason, I feel like my relationship with Corbin was slightly D/s. We never talked about it, but just... the way it felt was like he was definitely dominant, and I'm naturally submissive. It worked for us. Beautifully. I loved the way he took control, not only in the bedroom, but how he took care of me. Always protected me. And I doted on him. It gave me actual physical pleasure to please him. It was practically orgasmic when I could make that man smile. You see, he was very serious. Very reserved and... broody, I guess? So when I could make Corbin smile, and even laugh..." I shake my head, remembering Corbin's perfect smile, and the tone of his wonderful laugh. "...it was a feeling of complete euphoria. I didn't know what dominance and submission were until I read about it in a romance novel, and as I was reading it, it struck me as so familiar, because it's like I was reading the same feelings I got when I was with Corbin. And I guess that's where my obsession with BDSM came from, why I started reading everything I could get my hands on about it, and eventually, why I started writing down my own fantasies."

He nods. "Very good, Vivian. A lot of people aren't so cognizant of when they are being controlled. Whether they want to be or not." I smile, sitting up a little straighter and glowing under his praise. "In the bedroom with Corbin, did he ever incorporate pain? Maybe not the sort of pain you'd associate with BDSM, like with tools and equipment, but—"

"Oh, for sure," I interrupt, knowing what he means. "It wasn't an every time sort of thing, but he definitely loved testing my tolerance. Whether it be nipple-play, or how roughly he took me. But he was always so careful. His concentration during those times... it's like he was zeroed in on what I was feeling, not caring one bit about his own pleasure. He always brought me to that perfect line, where any further and I would have tapped out, but he never once took me past there. So perfect...." My face flushes as I realize my heated rambling. I glance at Dr. Walker, seeing he's watching me closely, and it makes me fidget. But he puts me out of my misery by going back to the facts.

"Some survivors who get into BDSM say they have found the use of pain to help them experience sexual pleasure that is non-triggering. As I'm sure you're aware, there is a very strong link between pleasure and pain. Pain releases endorphins and adrenaline, and when combined, it stimulates the body and creates a sense of euphoria. When a Dom uses pain alongside sexual stimulation, many survivors claim that the pleasurable feelings that follow the pain, and then the pleasurable feelings being associated with sex, has basically... reprogrammed their brain into remembering that sex is supposed to be a gratifying experience.

"Others have stated that pain within their trusting D/s relationship can help them remain focused on the present without being triggered. They don't experience flashbacks or negative memories associated with sex, because the pain keeps them grounded, allowing them to stay in the here and now. So those people who had once reported sensuality feeling wrong because they associated it with their rape, they are now able to experience arousal without any of the negative connotations to that sensation, thanks to the pain," he explains.

"Fascinating," I breathe.

"But, on the other hand, unfortunately there are some survivors who state that they use physical pain to punish themselves for feeling aroused. Obviously, using pain in this way is unlikely to be healing, and can result in traumatizing the survivor even more after their original assault. Do you have anything to say about this?" he prompts.

"Me? Hell no. I don't self-harm. I mean, I'm sure it's not good for me that I stay locked away with no friends or human interaction, but I'm not into cutting or anything. Plus, I'm here to change that part. I figure if I spend all this money to join the club, I'll be able to force myself to use my membership. Waste not, and all that," I reply, and he smiles gently.

"Very good. There are two things left I want to talk about. The first, I'm not sure applies to you, but I know you'd like to hear it as research for your book. You seem like a gentle soul, Vivian. You're timid and sweet natured. As I've stated many times, a *natural* submissive. It's just part of your personality, who you are. But there are some people who find that expressing anger can be healing. Now, your assault was a one-time experience. So, like I said, this part might not apply to you as much. There are some survivors who were in abusive relationships. For whatever reason, they stayed with the person who would assault them over and over again. Most of these people learn to switch off their emotions during the situations as a way to protect their minds. And the one emotion they suppress the most, because it's the most likely to get them hurt if they show it toward their abusive partner, is anger. To put it into perspective, what happened when you tried to fight Alan off?" he asks gently.

"He fought harder. He overpowered me. It pissed him off more that I wasn't just lying there and taking it, so he got... rougher," I state.

"Yes. So therefore, these victims, after being assaulted over and over again, they learn not to fight anymore. They learn to just lie there and take it, as you said. So, once they escape the relationship and get into BDSM, you can imagine what a relief it would be to be allowed to express all that anger they had trained themselves to swallow back," he says, and I nod.

"Most definitely. But, I'm not sure what that has to do with BDSM," I confess.

"A lot of survivors have reported feeling regretful, because they feel like they gave up, didn't fight hard enough, or because they didn't show how angry they were over being violated. Even though it wasn't safe for them to do so. There is a scene that a Dom and sub in a proper BDSM relationship can act out that is very therapeutic for a submissive who has had to suppress anger. The sub finds themselves in a situation where they are being dominated, just like during their abuse, but this time, their Dom will allow them to express their anger at what is happening to them. This releases some of that anger they've had bottled up for so long, healing them in ways that never would've happened had they not gotten into BDSM," Dr. Walker explains almost giddily.

"That's a beautiful thing right there. I can totally see how it all works. But... I mean... is there something wrong with me that I don't feel angry over what happened? I feel more... sad about it. Sad that it made me lose my husband. Sad that Alan did that to me, when I had only been trying to make sure he would be okay after drinking."

"Vivian, I think you *are* angry about it, but you are so... *good* that you don't even recognize the emotion. Do you feel like you were taken advantage of?" he prompts.

No hesitation. "Yes."

"You were happily married to the love of your life. Are you angry you felt you had to lie to protect him, because this asshole forced himself on you?"

"I mean... it was my choice to lie." I shrug.

"Vivian. He was your soul mate, you called him. And you've had to spend the last ten years without him, since this awful thing happened to you. How does that make you feel?"

"Sad. I'm sad I had to give him up," I say, feeling confused, because that adjective just doesn't fit right with what I'm experiencing.

"No, Vivian. What do you feel toward Alan? He took your husband away. You were living your happily ever after, and he took it away from you. What. Do. You. Feel?"

I search for the emotion inside me, never having been able to put my finger on it before, but with Dr. Walker trying to nudge me in the right direction, my sites finally lock on it, and as a tear trickles out of the corner of my eye, I breathe, "Pissed off, Doc. I feel pissed off. But I don't know what to do with that."

"Very good, Vivian. And that's what we're here for. We will teach you what to do with that, so you can begin to heal. The scene I was telling you about, where the sub is able to express their anger, it can feel almost like rewriting the script of your past and help you to reestablish control. This scene only works though when the survivor is allowed to express their anger in a situation where they deem it permissible and understandable. Also, it cannot be done alone. There are some power plays done when the D and s are not together. He may tell her to do something over the phone while he's at work, and then send proof through a picture, or what have you. But for this to work, the Dom should be present, ensuring there is someone who can bear witness to the survivor's anger so that it is no longer hidden from everyone. It can help them to break the silence many individuals have found themselves trapped in. That, Vivian, applies to you. The opportunity to release anger can be a very cathartic and fulfilling experience, and can free you to deal with some of the other issues the abuse left you with," he tells me, pointing at me with his pen before bringing it to rest against his full lips.

I fidget, uncomfortable with the idea of expressing anger. I've always been a quiet person. I don't like drawing attention to myself. And letting anger out sounds... loud. "I think that's something I'd have to build myself up to," I say, and it pulls a smile out of him.

"Most definitely. But just know, if it happens at the club, you would not be judged. No one would even blink. The scene has been acted out many times. It's actually very emotional and beautiful to watch. When it's over, the sub is so peaceful it can bring a tear to the eye of even the most hardened of Dominants," he says, as if from experience.

"I can imagine." I smile.

"Okay, we have about ten minutes left, Vivian. The last thing I'd like to talk to you about today, which we can expand on if you come back, is the establishment of trust. This, I believe, is your biggest issue," he states, and I nod.

"For sure," I agree, settling in for the information I'm hoping he's about to lay out for me. He doesn't disappoint.

"Needless to say, for you and most survivors, your sense of trust has been demolished. With anyone, not just a sexual partner. But in intimate relationships, you struggle with establishing trust and a sense of safety. A proper BDSM relationship is built on trust. You might know the mantra of our community, 'Safe, Sane, and Consensual.' So when a survivor enters a D/s relationship, where the concept of that mantra is highly respected, it can be a very positive, healing experience. In a safe and loving BDSM relationship, the partners talk about the rules regarding their sexual play in a way that many people in non-BDSM relationships do *not*. Think about it. In your relationship with Corbin, were you verbal about the things you did and did not like in the bedroom?" he asks.

"Yes. He was always very verbal during our lovemaking. He made sure when we tried something new to go slow and test my tolerance. He would stop to ask me if something felt good before continuing and taking it further," I reply, my tummy filling with butterflies at the memories.

"Now, since he's the only experience you have with consensual sex, think about the non-BDSM books you've read. Do those partners do a lot of talking during the sex scenes? Does the hero completely make sure that the heroine is okay with something before he does it?" he prompts.

"No, not really. They just go for it and hope for the best, I guess." I laugh.

"Exactly. So, in a D/s relationship, the sub has complete control over what happens, and their Dom knows what is off limits. In a proper and loving BDSM partnership, the sub can be assured that their Dom will stick to the rules, and they can let go and trust them. Survivors can find it therapeutic to be involved in a relationship that has such strict rules, and as long as these guidelines are followed to a T, it can lead to an increased sense of trust between partners. It can also create a sense of trust in themselves and with the world around them, allowing the sub to finally come out of their shell and establish friendships they might not have had before." He places his notepad and pen on his side table, then leans forward to rest his elbows on his knees, clasping his hands together.

"Now that... *that* I look forward to. When the hell do I do that part?" I giggle.

"Well, the next step in your initiation is getting with your sponsor to establish your guidelines. So, guess what?" He grins.

"What?" My eyes widen.

"As early as tonight is when the hell you do that part." He winks, and my heart thuds in my chest.

"Holy shit," I whisper.

"Yep." He stands and holds out his hand for me to shake.

With no hesitation this time, I place my hand in his, gaining comfort as it wraps around my much smaller one before he releases me and gestures toward the door. I really like Dr. Walker. I feel like I can talk to him about absolutely anything without judgment, and I plan on coming back for weekly sessions. Now, that may possibly change if I ever run into him at Club Alias. I don't know how I'd feel about seeing my therapist acting out a BDSM scene, and then turning around and seeing him with his shrink hat back in place. Or vice versa. I have no idea if it would be weird to see him in this setting after he sees me naked. But I guess I'll soon find out.

Eleven

Corbin

"**I** HAVEN'T…" HER SEXY LITTLE BODY adjusts in her seat, and I can see clear as day how embarrassed she is about her next statement. It's one I've replayed countless times just to hear the words leave her perfect lips. *"I haven't had sex since that night. I've been in relationships, and when it would finally come time to be intimate, as soon as they'd put their hands on me, I'd freak the fuck out, leave, and fall off the face of the planet. Never talk to the person ever again."*

"You haven't had intercourse in ten years?" Doc asks, his normally stoic and straight face faltering for a fraction of a second. I'd nearly choked the first time I watched the footage.

"Correct," my Vivian confirms, and I'm so overwhelmed with the swirling emotions inside me that it makes me feel almost faint.

But the one thing I *can* focus on—Alan. When I murder him, I'll go back to being the only person on the planet who has ever been inside Vi.

I pick up my phone and dial Seth.

"What's up?" he answers after the second ring.

"I have a job," I state, and a wicked grin spreads across my face.

As ALWAYS, I FEEL her presence like a physical thing. It's like as soon as we get within a certain distance of each other, my body knows we're breathing the same air. I see her lithe form come up the stairs at the front of the club from my perch on the second floor by the office entrance, and she stands there, looking around the circular room like she has no idea where to go. Or maybe she's trying to decide if she's going to stay or run. I gave her specific instructions to meet me, or "Seven," at the third reserved booth to her left.

I breathe a sigh of relief as she moves, making her way to our table, and that's when I head down the stairs. I tell myself to slow down, take my time. *Don't be too eager to get to her. She's supposed to be just another sub to you.* I approach the booth just as she's pulling her bag from across her shoulder, setting it beside her on the cushioned bench. She jumps a little when she looks up and sees me.

"H-hey, Seven," she stutters shyly, pushing her hair behind her ear, her cheeks a pretty shade of pink.

"Good evening, V," I tell her, remembering to use the

nickname Seth calls her. "Are you ready for your first lesson in submission?"

"Yes and no," she answers nervously but honestly, and I smile behind my mask. "I don't really know what to expect."

I take a seat across from her, placing my elbows on the table and gripping my hands loosely together. "This will be way easier than it usually is for me. With your knowledge of BDSM from your research for your books, you actually do know what to expect. You will just be experiencing it yourself for the first time."

She fidgets in her seat. "Seven, I should warn you. I'm not used to people touch—"

"I'm well aware of your aversion to other people touching you. I know your history. Your issues. I know you are a survivor of sexual assault. But you're strong. You've made it this long without any help, without any way of healing from your experience. *You* can handle this." I put strength into my words, shooting them across the table to try to build her confidence in herself. In those words, I'm speaking to her as Corbin. Conveying I know everything. I know she lied to protect me. Now it's time for me to take care of her. "We've been friends for over a year now. Somewhere inside you, you know you can trust me."

She nods. "I do."

"Good." I stand from the booth and hold out my hand to her. "Shall we?"

She looks at my hand and then does something that makes my heart pang. She closes her eyes, takes a deep breath, lets it out, takes one more lungful... and dynos. Her tiny hand slips into mine as she opens those beautiful green eyes, looking up to the slits in my hood, even though I know she can't see mine clearly.

She reaches behind her with her free hand and grabs her bag before standing, and I lace my fingers through hers.

"Very good, my sweet," I murmur, pulling her closer to me. I lift my other hand to push a strand of hair back that has fallen on her face, and she blushes, sucking in a breath of air. "You're already doing so well." She swallows and nods, and I make a mental note to be very verbal in my praise. She'll need the reassurance to get past her hatred of being touched. It makes me hate her rapist even more. My baby girl, unable to stand the feel of anyone's hands on her for a decade. Not even the innocence of someone hugging her, or the friendly gesture of someone squeezing her shoulder for a job well done. But at the same time, for selfish reasons, it makes me happy no one else has been able to get their hands on Vi. I just hate that it makes her feel so uncomfortable when someone unknowingly puts her through it.

"We have a private room tonight. There's a curtain built into the wall, so during your training, if you're more comfortable not having an audience, we can have privacy," I tell her, as I lead her around the row of booths and to the walkway between them and the circle of playrooms.

"That's a relief," she whispers, and I can't help but smile. She always was self-conscious of her body. The only time she never minded eyes on her was when she was up on a rock wall. My goal is to build her confidence to where she will enjoy playing out scenes, her beauty on display for the club to see, as sure of herself as she used to be while she was climbing. Nothing would be hotter to me than that. I would love to show off my gorgeous Vi, give everyone a glimpse of what only I can have. Because although I want every eye in the club on me taking her, I will always be the only one who's ever inside her.

I lead her into the very last playroom, reaching out to turn the dial on the wall, bringing the light up to a level to see clearly, brighter than in the dance floor area, but still dim enough that she'll be relaxed. She glances around the room, taking in all the equipment, the padded table, the desk over to the side, while I push a button by the light dial that closes the floor-to-ceiling black curtain that will seclude us from the rest of the club.

I cross my arms over my chest, feet shoulder-width apart as I watch her circle the room. Every once in a while, she reaches out her delicate hand to gently stroke the leather tail of a flogger hanging on the wall, or the cold steel of a shackle lined in padded fur until she finally reaches me once again, her face heating when she realizes I'd been observing her.

"I'm sorry. I... you're going to have to tell me what to do. I don't really know how this all starts," she tells me quietly.

"If this was one of your books, what would happen next?" I ask, wanting to make her talk to me, to loosen her up.

She bites her lip for a moment, her eyes glancing to the side before she brings them back to me. "Well, the hero would give her instructions on what to call him, rules to follow for him, since every Dom is different. Some want their sub to greet them on their knees, while others have them strip naked before they even enter the room. Since this is training and not an actual scene, I'm not really sure."

I nod, uncrossing my arms and taking a step toward her. Her head tilts back slightly, but she doesn't take a step back like I can tell she wants to. "Normally, with a sub, I have to start from scratch. Teach them all about the tools of the trade. Make them learn a whole new vocabulary. But you know all those things already. We have the ability to start with actual demonstrations.

Yet that requires me to touch you, V." I step up to her, my body a hairbreadth away from hers, and I lean down to whisper into her ear. "Will you let me touch you?"

I smirk behind my mask as I see her shiver, the tiny hairs on her arms standing on end.

After a moment, her expression going from a moment of panic to consciously searching for inner strength, I see her decision as it crosses her face. "Yes."

"Very good, V," I murmur, and then take a step back. "Place all your things in the trunk, there." I point to the black footlocker next to the door. "For now, I want you to take off only what you're comfortable with. Eventually, I will you give you a list of acceptable items to wear in my playroom."

She glances at the footlocker, seems to mull over what I've told her to do, and then steps toward it. I move away, and when the backs of my legs hit the leather chair against the wall, I lower myself into it, giving her all the space I'm willing to give.

She opens the trunk and places her bag inside, and then unzips her hoodie, letting it drop on top of her bag. She places one hand on the wall for balance as she unlaces one maroon Converse and then the other before toeing them off, setting them into the footlocker along with her socks. She straightens then glances over at me, obviously nervous as she decides how much to strip. My heart pounds in my chest as I wait for her to continue, if she will. And my dick instantly hardens as she reaches for the waistband of her leggings. She pulls them down her long legs, catching her balance on the wall once again to yank the tight, stretchy fabric over each foot, leaving her standing in her black tank top and white boy-short panties. Placing them into the trunk, her hand grips the lid for a moment as she seems to process something in her mind. Finally, she lowers it, closing the footlocker.

She turns to me, a look of regret on her face. "I… I think that's as far as I can go right now, Seven," she murmurs, looking at the floor.

Immediately, I'm within reach, pulling her face up by her chin to meet my hidden eyes. "Sir. From here on out, when you are in this club, you call me Sir. Understand?" I instruct, unable to stand her calling me by Seth's Dom name any longer. Everyone else has been informed not to address me by any name until I say otherwise. I passed it off as a Dominant's command in an e-mail to all employees and members, when really I didn't want some dumbass outing me in front of Vi.

"Yes, Sir," she breathes, her eyes becoming hooded, and my cock twitches behind my zipper. Suddenly, a flashback of the day I met her fills my mind. Glover calling me sir, which confused Vi, who hadn't been around military men before.

"Sir?" she had asked, looking between the two of us, and my hand had tightened around hers after shaking it as I introduced myself. The respectful title coming from her sweet lips had instantly made flashes of a moment exactly like the one we find ourselves in now float through my head, as if it were a glimpse into the future.

"If this is as undressed as you are comfortable with, we can continue. Next time, I will require one less item of clothing. Understood?"

"Yes, Sir," she agrees and swallows, and I drop my hand, but not before tracing the line of her feminine jaw, causing her nipples to harden behind her tank top.

"Tonight, my goal is to get you acclimated to my touch. Dr.

Walker told me he explained a couple of ways we can do that without setting off any triggers."

"Um... yes, he explained about pain, but I... I don't know if I'm ready for all that yet," she confesses. "I believe, if you don't mind going slow, I trust in our friendship enough to stand... I mean... shit." She shakes her head.

"What it is, b—my sweet?" I catch myself from calling her baby girl, the endearment I always used to call her.

"I don't want you to think that your touch is in any way repulsive. I promise it's not you. I—"

"V, I'm well aware my touch is not repulsive. And I know someone being physical with you in any way sets off bad feelings in you. Thank you for your trust. I will go slow with you. It is the job of a Dom to have heightened awareness of their sub's feelings. I've been doing this for many, many years, and I will be able to tell just how far to take you and at what speed," I assure her, even though I have mixed feelings about this conversation. On the one hand, I feel the sting of guilt abusing her trust, since she believes I'm Seven, her friend she's been talking to for a year now, learning everything about BDSM from him. But on the other, I'm jealous as fuck of the trust she's given him. But I've come too far to stop now, and there's no way in hell I'm gonna back down and let some other fucker touch what's mine.

"Thank you, Sir," she whispers, and then bites her full bottom lip.

"You're welcome. Now..." I turn and circle around the padded black leather table in the middle of the room. It looks like a massage table without the face cradle. "I want you to lie down. You choose whether you'd like to be face up or face down. Mind you, you're getting to make a lot of choices during this first training session that you won't be getting later. Tonight's all about getting to know each other's touch."

She nods and comes to stand across from me, the table between us. After a moment, she hikes up one creamy thigh, placing it on the dark, smooth surface before pulling herself all the way up, turning onto her stomach and lying down. This doesn't surprise me. Face up on my table makes one feel very vulnerable and exposed. It's a person's natural instinct to protect their vital organs, covering their torso. But this gives me a perfect view of her shapely ass, even if it's hidden behind the white fabric of her underwear.

"With you face down, would you feel comfortable with me taking your shirt off? I need to expose more skin in order for what I have planned to work."

She bites her lip, and then asks, "Can I keep my bra on?" I quirk my brow, even though she can't see it, but she corrects herself all the same. "Sir?" she adds quickly.

"Yes, but I'll need to unhook it." She nods, sitting up and reaching for the hem of her tank. "No," I growl, and she halts immediately. "I did not instruct you to take off your shirt. Remember, you are only to do as you are told unless I leave the decision up to you. Understand?"

"Yes, Sir," she murmurs, visibly shaken at being scolded. She lies back down, and I come around to the head of the table, gently stroking her hair to ease her worry. And to my surprise, instead of tensing as I expected, she relaxes immediately. She always loved it when I played with her hair after I made love to her.

I reach down her body with both hands and take hold of the bottom of her shirt. Slowly, and making sure to touch as much of the soft skin of her sides as possible, I drag the tank up and off of her. But it's not the view of all that beautiful creamy skin that brings my cock to full mast.

It's her giggle.

She fucking giggled. It's a sound I haven't heard in ten years. God, I used to love that sweet, innocent, feminine sound. I used to tickle her just so I could listen to it. And there it was.

She must be worried that I've completely halted all movement, thinking she's done something wrong, because she apologizes. "I'm sorry, Sir. I should've warned you, but I actually forgot how ticklish I am," she says sadly.

"No need to be sorry, my sweet," I tell her gently, stroking her hair again before moving to place her shirt inside the trunk. Then I go over to the dark-stained wooden cabinet in the corner of the room, opening up one of the doors and grabbing the two things I'll need for tonight before coming back to her side, pulling the small rolling table with me from its spot against the back wall. I place the two items on it and then face my girl once again. "All right, V. It's time to begin. Close your eyes," I command, and when she does, I take her wrists from where they were up by her face and gently unfold her arms so they are now relaxed by her sides, her palms facing the ceiling.

To keep her from jumping, I keep contact with her skin at all times so she can follow my touch instead of wondering where it will land next. I glide my fingertips up her thin arms then my hands meet in the middle of her back, where I unhook her light-gray bra with ease, tucking the sides down between her biceps and her breasts. Now I have the perfect blank canvas of her back to work on as I move her long dark hair out of the way.

"First, I will start with my hands. And then I have a simple but very effective tool I'd like to introduce you to. So try to relax and become familiar with my touch," I say, and I smile as I see her ass muscles flex before she forces herself to melt into the table.

"Yes, Sir," she mumbles, keeping her eyes closed.

I grab the bottle of massage oil, and pour some into my palm. I rub my hands together, warming the oil, and then ever so gently place them on her back, my fingers spreading wide. She gasps but then catches herself, her eyebrows pinching together for a moment before her face softens, a breathy moan leaving her plump lips as I push my palms upward along her spine.

"That's it, my sweet. I want to hear your pleasure," I tell her softly, grinding my cock against the cushioned side of the table. Jesus fuck. I'm more turned on just from touching her back and listening to her quiet moans than I have been in a decade.

Teach her, Corbin. You're supposed to be teaching her. Helping her heal. Not perving on her and about to come on her goddamn back!

Inhaling a breath to center myself, I then instruct, "We're going to play a game. The grown-up version of Red Light, Green Light. Whenever I say 'Color,' you are to tell me Green if you are completely okay, Yellow if I need to back off or slow down, or Red if you need me to stop. I'll ask you this throughout the night, but you can always tell me Yellow or Red if you need to at any time. Understand?"

"Yes, Sir," she breathes, and her hips unconsciously flex against the table. I close my eyes and pray for strength, feeling weaker around this tiny woman than I've ever felt against the deadliest of enemies.

I take my time, kneading her muscles, stroking beneath her

shoulder blades, squeezing the base of her neck, and then move lower, massaging around the dimples at her lower back. "Color?" I question.

"Green, Sir," she murmurs, and I grin behind my hood. Her research for her novels taught her well. Most new submissives would have forgotten to add Sir when responding. But not my Vi.

"Such a good girl," I tell her quietly, and she melts beneath my praise. Keeping contact with her flesh, I drag my fingertips over her ass, down her legs to her ankles. Knowing she's ticklish and not wanting to disturb her from her relaxed state, I purposely avoid her feet, remembering that was her most ticklish spot. She once told me her idea of hell would be to spend the rest of eternity having her feet tickled. I smile at the memory, and I add more massage oil to her long legs with one hand while stroking her calf with the other. I knead her small limbs, noticing her legs are thinner than they used to be, not as ripped with muscle since she stopped rock climbing. As I work my way up her thighs, my eyes go higher, seeing her hips are wider than they once were. She has a woman's body now, not the one of the teenager I was once married to. As stalkerish as I was, keeping my eye on her for all these years, I never allowed myself to see her naked. If I saw through her window she was about to undress, I always turned away, never wanting to violate her in that way.

So now, up close, with her lying beneath my palms in only her panties, I take in the flare of her hips. She's still thin, but her sides, and I'm sure her stomach, are now softer than they were before. It makes me wonder what her breasts look like now. She always wears hoodies or shirts that keep her covered. Even the tank she wore had a high neck. I've never once seen her in anything low-cut. Are they small like they used to be? Not even a handful? The perfect size to pull into my mouth, making her scream out in pleasure as I pinch her other nipple between my fingers? Or has she developed more since I last saw her naked?

"Yellow, Sir," she whimpers, pulling me out of my trance, and I realize my hands had tightened forcefully around the upper part of her inner thighs. I immediately loosen my grip but don't move away, so close to the treasure between her legs.

"Good girl, V. I'm proud of you for speaking up. Never be afraid to tell me when you are uncomfortable," I praise, and feel her legs loosen and see her ass muscles unflex. "Was it the force or the location of my hands that made you call Yellow?"

"Force, Sir. Location is... good," she murmurs, and I can't help but smile.

With that bit of information, I work my hands higher, until I reach the elastic of her boy-shorts around her thighs. Taking a chance, I keep my touch gentle as I slide them beneath the soft fabric and begin to knead her ass. At her light moan, tension leaves my shoulders, happy she didn't stop me. I spend time here, allowing her to familiarize herself with my hands on her in such an intimate place, before I finally ask, my voice low and deep, "V, would you allow me to take off your panties? You may stay facing down and can ask for a robe at any time to cover you completely if you need."

I watch the side of her face, her head turned so I can only see the left side of her beautiful profile. She pulls her bottom lip into her mouth as I continue to massage her glutes, but eventually, she nods. "Yes, Sir."

Never removing my touch from her skin, I grasp hold of her panties and swiftly slide them down her long legs, placing them on the rolling table beside us. I suck in a breath at the sight laid out before me and hope my mask hid the sound. Jesus Christ, she's more beautiful than ever. My mouth waters at the triangle her legs make between her thighs. I want to bury my teeth in the creases beneath her cheeks, the plumpness there making my cock pulse.

I use one hand to squeeze more oil onto her ass before massaging her there. It takes every ounce of my self-control to keep myself from either coming in my pants or burying my face there. As I mold her flesh with my hands, it spreads her cheeks, and I catch glimpses of her pussy. Even in the dim lighting I can see it glisten, and I choke back a groan knowing what I'm doing to her is turning her on. My sweet Vi is finally feeling aroused at the hands of another person. She's not running away afraid at my touch as she did with everyone else. No. Not only is she allowing me to caress and knead her perfect body, it's making her feel good, soaking her core.

Suddenly, as I find a rhythm with my movements, her hips begin to tilt up with my every downward stroke. "Color?" I growl, having no control over my voice.

"Green, Sir," she breathes, her hands making tiny fists at her sides. Her nails dig into her palms, and I can tell she's holding something back. Not wanting to break her out of the trance I've got her in, I don't tell her to ask for what she wants. I know my Vi. Even after all these years, I know her tells. I know her body. She wants me to touch her intimately, so I give her what she craves.

On my next downward stroke, as she lifts her hips once again, my two thumbs drag lower until they caress the drenched lips of her pussy, and she shudders, taking in a stuttered breath. I follow my pattern again, up the cheeks, around the dimples of her lower back, and then down her center, my cock throbbing at her whimper. The next time I make my circuit, my thumb presses into her gently, and she grasps the edge of the padded table as she moans.

"Color?" I rumble, my hands moving up then stroking down, but this time, I use my thumb to circle her clit, and she cries out.

"Red!" She tries to curl in on herself, but lying on her stomach, she doesn't have room for much movement. As she begins to panic, it snaps me out of my own passion, and with swift movements, I pick her up, stride to the leather chair against the wall, and curl her into my lap as I sit down, her naked form molding against my chest as she lets out a sob.

"Shh, my sweet. I've got you," I whisper against her hair. I rub her back, the massage oil slick on her skin. As her breathing calms, I know I have to do the Dom thing and talk about what just happened, when all I really want to do is hold her like this forever. "V, I need you to tell me what just happened. Did I just trigger you? You need to help me understand so I know when not to do something."

Her face buries deeper into my chest, and if she listened, I know she'd hear my heart pounding there. I feel her shake her head. If we were just Corbin and Vi, I'd let her fall asleep in my arms, giving her rest after she'd been put through so much. But I can't. Right now, we're Dom and sub, and she has to communicate.

"V, tell me what just happened, or I *will* punish you," I demand in my Dom voice, and she stiffens.

"I... you...." She pants for breath, but nothing else comes out.

"On the count of three, V, I will be forced to spank you if you don't answer me. This is your last chance. One... two..."

"I was about to come!" she cries, and my brow furrows. "You were about to make me come, and... and...." She sobs, and the sound breaks my heart.

"And what, my sweet? What would be wrong with orgasming?" I ask.

I feel her tears soak my shirt, and I hold her tighter. "I've... I'm sorry, Sev—Sir. I just... only one man in this entire world has ever given me an orgasm. And even after all this time, even though we've been divorced for a decade, I panicked, because it felt like I was... was... ch-chea—" Her body wracks as she cries against my chest, and my heart both swells with love for this woman, and aches for the pain she's gone through. It hits me at this very moment: she's loved me all these years. While I've tried to hate her all this time, she's felt nothing but the love she's always had for me. She gave up her own happiness to protect me, and her love never faded.

"You felt like you were cheating on m— him? Corbin, your ex-husband?" I close my eyes at the thought. My sweet Vi. My beautiful, innocent baby girl. Her pain seeps into me, and all I want to do is take it away. I think about removing my mask, telling her she doesn't need to feel like she's cheating on me, because it's me who was about to make her come, but I can't. Not now. Not yet. How the fuck would I explain that? She's too fragile right now. She needs to be stronger before I drop that bomb on her.

"I-I know it sounds completely stupid," she whimpers, but I'm already shaking my head and shushing her.

"No, V. I know your story, remember? I know you gave him up for his own good. You still love him. I understand why you feel the way you do," I murmur against her ear.

She sniffles and melts against me. "Thank you, Sir. You really are the closest thing I've got to a best friend," she whispers, and I smile against her hair.

"Yeah. You're mine too, V."

After a few minutes of just holding her, when I'm starting to feel nervous things will be awkward when we come out of our embrace, she surprises me. "I'd like to continue with my lesson now. I mean... if I didn't make it weird."

"Naw, my sweet. You didn't make it weird. That's the beauty of a D/s relationship. The communication between us will be stronger than in a normal relationship. I'll give you one last choice for the night, and then starting at our next session, you will only be following orders. Understand?"

"Yes, Sir," she replies, sitting back to look up into my masked face.

"You're naked. Would you like me to carry you back to the table, or are you comfortable to walk?" I ask, and her eyes widen as if just realizing her state of undress. She looks down at herself, the cups of her bra resting on her stomach below her breasts, and that's when I finally get my first look at her. I suck in a breath.

Dear Jesus fuck.

Her once A-cup sized breasts are now more than generous handfuls, and I know for a fact they couldn't have grown that much on their own. She flushes from her scalp to her toes at my hiss and attempts to cover herself by mashing herself up against me.

"You..." What do I say? I can't exactly ask her anything about her body, seeing how she believes I'm Seth, who never saw her in person before all this. He wouldn't know that she didn't used to look like... this. "You have an amazing body, V," I rumble.

"Th-thanks, Sir. I... no one has seen me naked since...."

"Since your ex?" I finish for her, but that's not where her mind was.

"Since my assault. Since my augmentation. For a long damn time, really," she confesses.

There we go. The perfect opportunity. "Your augmentation?"

"Yes, I... it's the one thing I've bought for myself since my books became successful. I've always been self-conscious about my body. I always had extremely small breasts, and I always thought it would boost my confidence if I just bit the bullet and got a boob job. So I got one a little less than a year ago. Although I like what I see in the mirror a hell of a lot better than I did before, it still didn't do anything for my confidence around other people, and I end up just covering them up anyway." She shrugs.

How the fuck had I missed Vi getting surgery? A little less than a year ago? Was I on a job?

She answers my questions without me having to figure out a way to ask. "Luckily, it didn't hurt nearly has bad as I thought it would. I went in one morning, was under anesthesia for a total of forty-five minutes, and then left the office as soon as I came out of it. Recovery was forty-eight hours, which I spent at my parents' house. Easy peezy."

"I'm sure you were just as beautiful the way you were before, but..." I nod. "...you're fucking gorgeous, V."

A smile tugs at her perfect lips. "Thank you, Sir."

I stare into those mesmerizing green eyes of hers while she takes in my hood. She tilts her head and lifts her hand, placing it against the leather covering my cheek, and my heart thuds. I used to love when she'd look at me like this, her fingers running along the stubble at my jaw.

"What do you look like under there?" she breathes, and it's more like she's speaking her internal thought aloud without realizing it.

I don't want to lie to her. So instead of replying, I stand, lifting her into my arms, and carry her to the padded table. Without being ordered, she returns to her position on her stomach, and I let it slide since I had previously given her the choice.

As I reach for the instrument I plan to use next, she giggles, and my head snaps to her, but her eyes are closed. "What's funny, V?"

"Sorry. Nothing, Sir. I just realized... you held me. My body was pressed up against yours, naked no less, and I didn't run. I... I haven't not run in a long time is all," she tells me quietly, and my chest swells. God, she still has the ability to warm my perpetually cold heart like no other woman before or since her, and I feel the part of me I once thought completely dead starting to stir inside me, waking from its eternal sleep.

But I have to stay in character. If I were Seven, what would I say to that?

"Yeah, the ladies can't resist me," I say in a cocky tone, and she scoffs before letting out another one of her giggles, making me smile. "All right, V. There's one last thing I wanted to introduce you to tonight. Has your research led you to a Wartenberg wheel?"

"Yes, Sir. Usually made of stainless steel, it's a circle of evenly spaced pins with a handle that allows you to roll it across the skin. It was initially designed to test nerve sensitivity, to see if someone still had feeling in a place on their body," she explains.

"Very good. Have you ever felt one before?" I ask, rolling it against the palm of my hand, enjoying the prickly sensation.

"No, I haven't, Sir," she replies.

"Okay, well, you're about to."

"Yes, Sir," she breathes, and I smile, because I can tell she's actually excited about the prospect of experiencing it for the first time.

As not to startle her, I warn her, "You'll feel my hand on your ankle." At her nod, I wrap my palm around her tiny ankle. "And now we begin." I place the wheel on her flesh in the space between my thumb and forefinger, and without applying much pressure, I begin to slowly roll it up her calf, watching the goose bumps rise on her skin.

"Oh," she moans, and I grin behind my mask.

"Color?" I ask, even though I already know her reaction was a good one.

"Green, Sir," she replies. "Very, *very* super green."

Twelve

Vi

THE NEXT MORNING, I WAKE UP smiling. It's a foreign feeling. Normally, when my alarm goes off, it's a battle with the snooze button, depending on how late I stayed up writing. But not today. After leaving the club last night, having made plans with Seven to come again tonight for another training session, I immediately came home, grabbed my vibrator out of my nightstand drawer, and took care of myself. My orgasm hit me within seconds.

Seven used the Wartenberg wheel on me for a few minutes, until I was a writhing mess on his table, and when I started getting that tingling feeling between my thighs and called Yellow, he stopped, not wanting me to get to Red with another panic attack. And then I got to experience aftercare for the first time in my life. It had always been one of my favorite moments in my books to write, when a Dom takes care of his sub after they're done with a scene, bring her down from her high gently before she has to face reality once more. I was so unbelievably comfortable in Seven's hands. I didn't shy away from his touch. It could only be because I'd known him for a year, getting to know him through our messages and his videos of BDSM demonstrations.

During our aftercare, we talked about everything we'd done last night, including my little episode when he almost made me come. I was still embarrassed that it made me feel like I was cheating on Corbin in some way, if another man made me orgasm. I mean, what sense does that make? We've been divorced for ten fucking years. I haven't spoken to him in that long. I had tried to find him in moments of weakness, checking to see if he had a Facebook profile, or Instagram, Twitter... but I always came up short in my search. It's like he had completely fallen off the planet. I had no idea if he was even still alive. What if I lived with this silly feeling of being unfaithful to him... and he wasn't even among the living anymore? I mean, you search for anyone in the whole world, and they will at least come up in some sort of Google results. But not Corbin. Not a LinkedIn, nor a Tumblr. No obituary either, though. It's like he had never even existed at all.

I had voiced all this to Seven, confessing how I have looked for Corbin. He asked me what I would've done if I had found him. Would I have told him the truth of what happened all those years ago? I don't think I would. I just wanted to see if he was alive, if he was happy. If he had found someone else.

Moving away from that subject when he saw it made me sad, he had a suggestion. In order to further my induction into BDSM, I would need to get over the whole orgasm-makes-me-feel-like-I'm-cheating-on-my-ex-and-sends-me-into-panic-mode thing.

Seriously. If just a little massage on day one makes me feel like I'll combust, how the hell would I be able to handle it when we moved on with my lessons? So his suggestion was... pretend he's Corbin.

At first, I scoffed at him. How fucked up would I be to imagine Seven was my ex-husband in order not to feel guilty about Seven making me orgasm? My head spins just trying to keep that straight in my mind. I mean, I already need therapy. But as I thought about it, and he continued to tell me he didn't mind, that it wouldn't hurt his feelings whatsoever, I began to realize it wasn't such a bad idea. He wears a mask. I have no idea what Seven looks like anyway. So in my mind's eye, would it really be so bad to pretend it's Corbin dominating me? And if I imagine it's Corbin, would I be able to get past the awful feeling I got as my climax so easily built while Seven's hands were on me? And it wouldn't have to be forever. Just until I got used to another man making me come. Then I could stop imagining it's Corbin's perfect face behind that black hood. It would be the same as what Dr. Walker told me, with the "expression of anger" scene. I could rewrite my script until the past was erased—or at least until it didn't hurt anymore.

But for the rest of the day, I have a word count to hit. And thanks to Seven, I'm feeling remarkably inspired.

Corbin

I STARE AT MY computer screen, where the image of me holding Vi in my arms in the leather chair against the wall of the playroom has been paused for the last fifteen minutes. Members, including Vi—who signed all the contracts and paid her membership fees yesterday—are aware there are security cameras in all playrooms for their protection. As sexy as it is watching her on my table, as my hands trail all over her body, especially when she was just... about... to come, it's this image I love the most. Vi curled up in my lap, her beautiful naked body pressed trustingly against my entirely black form. She looks so small, fragile, and I look like an ominous shadow, wrapped around her protectively. It's not lost on me that it's the personification of what I've been to her the past ten years—a shadow, protecting her from afar.

Maybe I wouldn't have done it for so long and so obsessively if I hadn't kept her from being mugged in the first month I started following her. Shit, she has no idea a guy was even trailing her. He had spotted her at the grocery store, and I kept my eyes on him as he slinked around the aisles, staying out of her sight. After she'd paid for her two plastic bags of groceries, she started her trek home two blocks away, completely oblivious she had a tail.

I don't like to think about what could have happened to my sweet Vivian had I not stopped him from following her inside her apartment building. But hopefully the fucker thinks twice before pulling that shit again, after he woke up naked and beaten to a pulp a couple of alleys away. And yeah, he did wake up. I could tell by all the transactions on his bank account and the e-mails he sent out, which I accessed through his personal information on his driver's license and his social security card he had in his wallet. He's now in our "Fuck up one more time and your ass is ours" database.

My phone rings, and I glance at the screen. "Fucking finally," I grumble, and then answer the call. "Give me good news, Seth."

"Unfortunately, I can't, bro. This Alan Fischer dude just fell off the fucking planet. I was able to find his lease agreement for the apartment he used to share with V's friend Sierra, but after he moved out, absolutely naddah," he tells me.

"Fuck!" I growl. "Nothing? No social media, no bank transactions...? He was in college with Vi. There's nothing from his transcripts there?"

"Corb, I've been doing this even longer than you, remember? I know all the avenues to look. There's nothing. It's like he's one of us or some shit. Completely wiped clean."

I sit back in my office chair and rub my hand over my shaved head, letting out a frustrated groan. "Wait... I have an idea."

"Hit me."

"Later. Turns out, Vi played FBI agent and tried to find me a while back. From the sound of it, she was pretty damn crafty about it. Searched all sorts of different sites and shit that most people wouldn't have even thought of. I wonder if she was curious enough to try to look up Fischer," I say, as I start tapping on my keyboard, logging in to Vi's computer. I go into her browser history and search for the name Alan. "Bingo."

"What is it?" Seth asks excitedly.

"Putting you on speaker," I say, pushing the button for it and setting my phone on my desk so I can use both hands. After a few minutes of looking around her computer, I find a file. "Motherfucker."

"What? Dude! The suspense is killing me. Quit playing," he whines.

"Is it odd that I find Vi's search skills fucking hot as hell?" I question.

"Corb, I swear to God...."

"All right, all right. Looks like Alan Fischer legally changed his name to Kevin Valdaperez when he turned into some D-list movie director in Austin, Texas. Oh, look. How cute. He even has his own IMDB page." I flip through the pictures on the website, screenshots of his low-budget horror flick mixed in with images of the motherfucking rapist himself on the red carpet, some coked-out skank on his arm while he grins into the camera. "Jesus fuck," I breathe. "You ever look into someone's eyes and just know they're fucking evil?"

"Every time I take a job, bro," he confirms.

"I mean, I've seen some pretty malevolent-looking people in our line of work... but this guy...." I send Seth the picture of Alan on my screen and wait for him to open it.

"Dude."

"Yeah."

"He looks like he doesn't have a soul. Like, not even fucking around," Seth says, his voice conveying the same creeped-out feeling I have the longer I look into Alan's almost-black eyes. They're so wide you can see the whites all the way around his irises, looking almost wild as he... I guess you would call that a smile? "I mean, we ain't no punk-ass bitches, Corb. But that dude is fucking creepy."

"Yeah. And that's the motherfucker who raped my wife," I murmur, as a mix of sadness, anger, and full-on determination fills me. "His ass is mine."

Thirteen

Vi

"HOP RIGHT UP HERE, MY SWEET," Seven tells me, patting his hand in the center of the padded leather table in the playroom.

"Yes, Sir." I climb atop the soft surface and sit Indian-style, waiting for my next instruction.

"As adorable as you are sitting like that, I prefer a more classic submissive position when greeted. First, sit up on your knees," he commands, holding his hand out for me to grasp for balance as I do what he said. As I place my fingers into his palm, an electric current shoots up my arm and down into my gut, setting off the butterflies that had taken up residence there whenever I started coming to Club Alias. "Good girl. Now, flatten the tops of your feet against the table then sit back on your heels. It'll feel awkward at first, but you can adjust your knees and feet until it feels more comfortable, and then it'll become second nature. A little discomfort is actually a good thing though, because it'll heighten your awareness. Too relaxed, and you could get sloppy, forgetting your job as a submissive."

I nod, adjusting myself until I'm resting on my heels. I'm pretty comfortable now, but I can tell that sitting in this position too long would make my joints ache.

"A lot of Doms prefer for their submissive to avoid eye contact. I'm normally one of them, but in your case, I actually enjoy looking into your eyes," he confesses, stroking a fingertip along my jawline and making me shiver. "Eye contact is usually seen as a challenge, but with you, I'm well aware of your submissive nature and your love of absorbing information. I can see those things in your eyes. So I will not require you to look away from me."

A small smile tugs at my lips at his sweet admission. "I have a question, Sir."

He nods. "Go on."

"Sometimes, I find myself overwhelmed, and I do look away without doing it consciously." I don't know how to pose what I'm trying to ask as a question, but thankfully he knows what I'm getting at.

"You will not be punished for looking away unless I've given you a specific order not to. With me as your Dom, your job as submissive is foolproof. Follow my demands, and you'll have nothing to worry about," he assures, and I sigh in relief.

He walks over to the rolling table on the other side of where I perch and picks up a piece of paper before returning to face me. "This is a list of the acceptable items of clothing allowed in my playroom. When we meet next, I expect you to be wearing something off of this list, and you are to greet me here, in this position."

"Yes, Sir," I agree, watching as he walks over to the footlocker by the door, opens the lid, and places the paper inside with my belongings. I had stripped down to my bra and boy-shorts when we first got here tonight, remembering his requirement to shed one more item of clothing than the first training lesson. Instead of returning to me, I follow his movement as he walks to the back wall, selecting three different items off of their hooks, and I gulp. I face forward again, my heart pounding as I stare at my clenched hands on my thighs.

"Have you ever felt a flogger before, V?" he asks, as I see him place the three toys on the table next to my legs.

"N-no, Sir," I reply, annoyed with my anxiety.

"You've written about them in your novels, correct?"

"Yes, Sir. But only by using research off the internet and the demonstration videos you sent me."

"What I have here are three different kinds of floggers. There are countless variations when it comes to shapes, sizes, and textures. There's a wide range of sensations they are capable of, from soft and gentle, feeling almost like a tickle or a massage, to hard and stinging. What really makes the difference in how a flogger feels are the number of tails it has, the width of the tails, and what they are made of," he explains, and picks up one of the toys in question, handing it to me. "This one is made of deerskin. Notice how soft and wide the tails are. No matter how heavy-handed I become with this one, it would not be painful at all."

I run my fingers through the soft material, trying to imagine what it would feel like on other parts of my body, before handing it back to him. He sets it down and picks up another.

"This one is made of suede. The tails are slightly narrower but longer than the first one, and it also has a lot more strips of material. This would give you more of a thumping sensation, much stronger than the deerskin. Still pretty painless though."

He places it in my hand, and I can feel the weight difference from the first. I slap it against my palm a couple of times, enjoying the way it thuds as opposed to stings. Seeing him pick up the last one, I trade him floggers, my lips turning downward slightly at the feel of this new one.

"This one is made of leather. The tails are narrow and few in number. Several are braided, and a couple have knots tied at the ends. This would produce a very intense sensation, since the flogger itself would have more bite to it. Even with a gentle hand, this one would definitely be felt," he informs darkly, his voice dropping low and sexy. Obviously, this one is his favorite. I think I know what's coming next. This is my lesson for the night. I think he's going to give me a choice of which one I'd like to try, but oh how wrong I actually am. "Tonight, I'll be using all three."

My eyes widen, and my heart thuds just thinking about him using the third one on me. But as he leans down near my ear, his proximity makes my core clench.

"No need to worry, my sweet. By the time I reach the leather, you'll be begging for it. The other two are nothing but a tease," he whispers, and my nipples pebble as his breath tickles over the sensitive skin of my neck. He leans away, takes a step back, and crosses his massive arms across his chest. "Now, hop that sexy ass off my table and bend over."

"Um..." I sit up straighter and look around the table. "Just like...."

At my confusion, he holds his hand out to me once again

and helps me down off the table, but instead of letting me go, I squeak as, in one smooth movement, he spins me to face the black leather surface and bends me over with a firm hand against my back, between my shoulder blades. My arms come up instinctively to catch myself as my front lands on the padded table, and my breath catches as Seven presses himself against the backs of my thighs. I feel the rough material of his black pants against the delicate flesh there, and then register the bulging erection nudging between my cheeks. If it weren't for his pants and my boy-shorts, it would take zero effort for him to slip inside me.

"Color?" he growls, his calloused hands running down my back and over my hips to grip my ass, spreading me open as he squeezes, making me whimper as he swivels his hips.

Realizing I have no fear in this moment, only a bit of nerves from being surprised by his sure touch, I clear my throat so I can give him a steady-voiced, "Green, Sir." Gone is the Dom from yesterday, who handled me as if I were made of glass. He had warned me. He made it perfectly clear that after last night, he would treat me the way a sub would normally be treated. He gave me the opportunity to ease into this, allowing me to become comfortable with his touch. And for that, I'm grateful, because being manhandled in this way has my pussy throbbing in a way I haven't felt in a long-ass time.

Suddenly, the cool air hits my skin as he steps away, leaving me wanting more of his closeness. But instead of mourning the loss, I take in this unfamiliar but welcome feeling of missing his touch. I *want* to be touched. Well... by him at least.

I listen to his movements, and after what seems like forever, I feel him strapping something to my wrists from the other side of the table. I lift my head to see what he's doing, and find my arms encased in bulky leather cuffs, their buckles looking strong and ominous above my dainty hands. Yet, the shackles themselves are soft and squishy, so they don't hurt the bones in my wrists as he takes the chain between them and hooks it to a carabiner attached to the side of the table.

"Some people's natural reaction to being spanked, flogged, whipped, or what have you is to reach back and try to cover themselves with their hands. This could end up in an injury, and since I want to take care of my sweet little sub..." He cups my lifted chin in his hand and swipes his thumb over my bottom lip, leaning down to my eye level, even though I can't see his behind the shadow of his mask. "I'm just taking precaution. With your hands strapped, I won't have to worry about you trying to block me."

I feel like I need to respond, so I say the only thing that comes to mind. "Thank you, Sir." His grip on my chin tightens for a moment before he gently lets me go.

"Such a good girl," he murmurs, so low that I'm not sure he meant for me to hear it. Either way, it has me melting into the table, a sense of fulfillment overwhelming me at pleasing him. "And our scene begins," he tells me moments later, and I close my eyes, bracing myself for the stinging feel of a smack against my ass.

Instead, I feel the gentle touch of Seven's fingers tracing along the line of my panties before he swiftly removes them. The material pools at my feet, but I don't step out of them, since he didn't instruct me to do so. I feel my heart pounding between my spine and the padded table, feeling exposed yet desired as he glides his fingertips up my inner thigh.

"Color?" he rumbles behind his mask.

"Yellow, Sir," I reply, fighting back the urge to clench my legs together to keep him from going any higher. I'm scared I'm going to panic again if I get close to orgasming. But I'm enjoying the tickling sensation along my thigh, so I don't call Red.

"Remember what we talked about, V. As your Dom, I give you permission to imagine whatever you need to get you through the scene." I feel soft fabric against my side, along with an inferno of body heat, and when I open my eyes, I see he has bent over next to me on the table to speak directly to me, ensuring I'm absorbing his words. He braces himself on his elbow while trailing the fingers of his other hand up and down my spine soothingly while he speaks. "Our goal for the night is to allow you to enjoy your first orgasm with another person in many years. Tonight, I *will* make you come. But I'm depending on you to allow yourself to let go and experience it as the gift it is. If it's your ex-husband you have to hold in your mind to get you there, then by all means, do it. Again, I promise you won't hurt my feelings. This is all about you, my sweet."

I can't imagine a better or more selfless Dom to be paired with. I can't see any other person not only being okay with someone picturing them as somebody else while being intimate, but encouraging it, just so they could experience an orgasm without feeling guilt. I'm so lucky to have found Seven, and the realization only makes me want to please him more.

I look into the slits of his hooded leather mask and try to convey with just two words that I'm ready for what he has planned for me tonight. "Green, Sir."

He nods then stands. Seeing him take one of the floggers into his hand, I close my eyes again, this time picturing Corbin's handsome features in my mind. With the image in place, the rest of the world disappears. I can hear Seven speaking behind me, but I brush the words off and focus solely on keeping my love's face perfectly clear.

As the first stroke of the soft tails of the flogger brushes against my bare ass, it brings me to the here and now just long enough to be cognizant of my Dom asking me "Color?"

"Green, Sir," I breathe, and then allow myself to submerse in Corbin's image once again.

Soon, the strokes come one behind another without him pausing to ask. I'm aware of the entrancing noise the flogger makes as it whooshes through the air before caressing my flesh, but what takes up more of my consciousness is the fact my pussy is throbbing in want.

My thighs rub together, trying to soothe the ache between them the longer the tails tease me. Across my ass, up and down the backs of my thighs, and then stroking across my lower lips, I part my legs to get closer to the flogger's teasing touch. Suddenly, an image fills my mind of Corbin standing behind me, being the one wielding my new favorite toy, and I moan wantonly. I roll up onto my tiptoes, trying to expose more of myself to him, but suddenly, everything stops, and my brow furrows as his image wanes.

"Moving on to the suede, my sweet."

With my eyes closed and my ex's face in the center of my mind, I get the eeriest sensation as Seven's voice transforms into Corbin's. It's been ten years since I've heard his deep, sexy timbre, but it's like thinking of him so intently made me conjure everything about him, right down to his voice. It sends a chill up my spine just as the first stroke of the suede flogger hits my skin.

I can feel the difference between this and the first one. Still painless, just as he'd promised, there's just more weight behind it, and it covers more area of my body, since the tails are much longer.

Again, as he finds a rhythm with the flogger, moving up in speed until the tails are spinning through the air in a continuous loop, I feel myself pressing into the sensation, lifting up onto my toes once more to encourage him to focus on my core. With Corbin's mesmerizing dark eyes at the center of my mind's eye, if he would just slap the tails a few times in a row against my pussy, I have no doubt I would come in a heartbeat.

But he evades what I so blatantly want, and I whimper as my hips grind against the table of their own accord. My hands tug at their chains, trying to break free so I can reach down between my legs to give myself some relief, but I have no such luck. Finally, when I'm a writhing mess atop his table, just like I was under his Wartenberg wheel, I can't take anymore.

"Please, Sir," I sob, squeezing my thighs together.

"Color?" he asks, slowing his strokes.

"I... I don't...." I wiggle in my bonds, unable to control my fidgeting. "Green, but Yellow, Sir."

"I need a clearer answer than that, my sweet," he tells me, and delivers a direct hit right to my clit.

"Oh!" I cry, but it trails off into a moan as the delicious sensation tingles throughout my entire body.

"Color, V," he demands.

"Green, Sir. Holy fuck, Green. I just need... more. Please," I whimper, and that's when all movement stops.

Suddenly, I feel him press himself to my backside before he bends over me, covering me with his rock-hard body. His erection nudges against my pulsing core, and my hips unconsciously lift to fit myself more snugly against it. He moves my hair out of my face, where it had fallen during my thrashing, exposing my ear and neck to his breath, as he whispers, "I told you you'd beg for it."

I open my eyes just long enough to see him reach out for the leather flogger before I clamp them shut once again, not wanting to lose too much focus. With Corbin's perfect body in my mind, his tan skin covered in tattoos over sinfully hard muscles playing across the backs of my eyelids, the first stinging stroke of the last flogger makes me shudder against the padded table.

The new bit of pain along with the pleasure tries to center me in the here and now, just as Dr. Walker had told me, so I have to focus more intently on keeping Corbin in my head as the next blow slaps across my ass. I hiss in a breath, provoking "Color?" from my Dom, and after I sob a desperate "Green, Sir," he continues.

I can feel each individual knot along with every braid of the leather flogger's tails as he takes stroke after stroke against my flesh. My ass cheeks and the backs of my thighs have now gone mostly numb, bringing my pussy into complete focus, every nerve ending inside my clit begging for release.

I can feel wetness starting to drip down the inside of my legs, so aroused from my Dom's teasing torture. I'm so built up, dying for relief, that I can no longer even move. No more fidgeting, no more writhing. I've melted into the table, trying to center all my consciousness between my legs, praying that I can just spontaneously come without having to be touched there.

But alas, it doesn't happen, and as I give up the notion, submitting to the idea that this will forever be the state I'm left in, a new sensation blankets me. I feel like I'm floating, yet drowning at the same time. It's not a scary feeling though. It's actually quite relieving, much better than the aggravation of wanting to orgasm but having no way to reach it. My love's perfect face fills my mind once again, and his lips become the center of attention. Just as I'm about to picture kissing those delicious lips, they begin to move, and I hear his voice in my ear.

"Ahh, there it is, my sweet. Now, relax... and enjoy."

Suddenly, I feel a finger begin circling my clit as two more fill my pussy. I can hear how wet I am as my Dom strokes in and out of me before massaging expertly against that special spot inside me. And with a few more circles against my exposed nub, my inner muscles clamp down on his fingers as I scream my release.

The relief is so overwhelming that tears fill my eyes then spill over. I moan, my entire body shuddering as he halts his movement but stays inside me, allowing me to feel my pussy milking his fingers.

"That's my girl," he murmurs against the back of my shoulder, and I'm still so saturated in my fantasy that his voice still sounds like Corbin's. It's not until he slides slowly out of me that I open my eyes and let myself become aware of my surroundings once again.

TRUTH *revealed*

TRUTH *revealed*

TRUTH *revealed*

TH *revealed*

TRUTH *revealed*

Fourteen

Corbin

K EVIN VALDAPEREZ, born Alan Fischer. Divorced. One child.
The mother has full-custody and a restraining order
against Daddy Dearest. In and out of rehab too many
times to count. Looking at records, he entered a treatment facility
not long after my divorce from Vi. Reason: cocaine and alcohol.

Thinking back to Vi's recollection of her assault, she kept
referring to the way he was "so strong" and "stronger than he
should've been." She thought it was the alcohol that had given
him super strength. Negative. Alcohol would've made him
sloppy. She had said she waited for what felt like forever for him
to go to sleep, but he kept fidgeting. Alcohol would've made him
pass out. It was the cocaine. But my sweet, innocent Vi had never
been around alcohol before, much less drugs, so she would've
had no idea Alan was in fact coked out.

He left rehab that first time with what seemed like a new outlook on life. Changed his minor in theater arts to his major before moving to Texas. The next couple of years were a blur of him trying to make it big as an actor, getting back into drugs, when apparently he gave up being in front of the camera and decided to write his own shit. A horror flick called *The Maniacal Asylum 5*. I tried reading the summary, but it was so twisted and obviously birthed from being on many drugs at the same time that I gave up.

The movie made it all the way through the filming and releasing process. The pictures I'd found of him had been at an independent film festival in Austin. You can't even find that shitty excuse for a movie on video. It's uploaded on the internet for the world to see... if anyone cared to.

Nowadays, ole Alan moved back to the east coast. This wasn't in Vi's file on him. She mustn't have looked into him in a while, because he now teaches acting classes in Wilmington, because, ya know, those who can't do, teach. His Facebook profile shows all sorts of photos of his house, a beautiful, expansive mansion just outside the city limits. Really, though, he must've either broken in or taken selfies during an open house, because he actually lives in a decrepit apartment near the university. The thought of the motherfucker being anywhere near college-aged girls, the age Vi was when he raped her, makes my hackles rise even higher. His only saving grace is there is absolutely nothing on his record for being a sexual predator. But then again, Vi never turned him in either.

So many rapists get away with what they do to their victims. In Vi's case, Alan was handed the perfect victim, a person he more than likely knew hated being the center of attention and would never want to draw eyes to herself. So he knew when he attacked her that he would probably get away with it.

I can only imagine how torturous it was for Vi after that. She and Alan shared a class together at their college, used to study together at his and Sierra's apartment. She had to see that motherfucker every day at school, and any time she wanted to hang out with her girlfriend at their place. Doc hadn't had time to touch on that part, so God only knows what she went through having to share space with her rapist during her day-to-day life.

And I had divorced her.

No questions asked. No thinking it through. No trying to work it out. I had sent her the divorce papers and never spoken to her again, leaving her alone to deal with everything on her own.

Sure, I had thought she cheated on me. But so what? It's been proven time and time again that if a couple goes through counseling and works through infidelity, they have a higher likelihood of staying together, happily married, than the ones who never went through it in the first place. They are the couples who worked hard on their marriage, the ones who fought for each other. And I did none of that. I had chucked up deuces and said I'm out, while Vi was left to deal with being assaulted, no one to turn to because her person, as she used to call me, had divorced her at the drop of a hat.

I feel like a piece of shit. And I don't know if I'll ever be able to make it up to her, but God knows I'm going to right the wrongs done *to* her, and I won't rest until that fucking cocksucker is no longer breathing.

IT'S BEEN A few days since Vi's and my last training session, since I made her come for the first time in a decade. Her first orgasm with another person in as many years. And she had come to my face. She had finally reached that peak, climaxing thinking about me, Corbin, not to who she thought was Seven. I had sensed torn pieces inside her stitching back together, and it was a heady feeling, knowing I was helping her heal. It makes me want to repair more of the broken parts of her psyche. The only way to move forward and do that is to take Doc's advice and allow Vi to express her anger. I've never done that scene before, but I have witnessed it, and I want to do that for her. It will be emotional, for her of course, but even for me, someone who has been emotionless for ten long years. But I have to be strong for her. I have to grin and bear it, the same way I do when I want to just hold her, but talk it out with her like I know I should.

I pull up the messenger for my fake Seven Facebook profile, clicking on her name.

> Me: Afternoon, my sweet.

> VB Lowe: Hello, Sir. ☺
> Me: I will give you a day to prepare yourself. But tomorrow night, we will be doing your anger expression scene. Normally, it's done with witnesses, but under your special circumstances, I will allow it to be done behind the curtain.

There's a pause on her end, but soon, the three dots start dancing in our chat window.

> VB Lowe: Yes, Sir.

I breathe a sigh of relief.

> Me: Good girl. Choose something from the list of acceptable attire I gave you the other night. Be at the club at 10:00 p.m. and meet me in position at the table in our playroom. You are allowed one glass of wine from the bar.
> VB Lowe: Yes, Sir.

An idea strikes me, and I grin.

Me: How long are your chapters normally?

VB Lowe: Um... usually around 3k words. Unless it's a love scene. Those run a little longer.

Me: Between now and tomorrow at 7pm, write me a love scene involving two sex toys. 6k minimum. Send me the file here by that time. If you fulfill my demand, you will be rewarded. If you don't meet your deadline, there will be consequences.

I hit Send and sit back in my chair, smirking to myself as I watch her respond. The three dots dance on the screen for a while, but when her reply comes through, it's short. Which tells me her original response was much longer before she deleted it and sent something else.

VB Lowe: Yes, Sir.

This could be mutually beneficial. I've seen the way Vi stresses about meeting her writing deadlines. She has no one to push her, encourage her, except for readers demanding the next book in her series. I can only imagine that sort of pressure without support and the right kind of inspiration could cause writer's block, the author's equivalent of performance anxiety. So maybe with the prospect of a reward for busting out a couple of chapters for her book will be inspiration enough to push her along. Or at least the thought of being punished for not following my command will be incentive to force her mind to focus and get it done. It will benefit me in return, because nothing fucking turns me on more than knowing my Vi will be spending the next twenty-three hours pushing herself to follow my orders.

TRUTH *revealed*

RUTH *revealed*

TRUTH *revealed*

TH *revealed*

TRUTH *revealed*

Fifteen

Vi

I SET UPON MY KEYBOARD LIKE a woman possessed. The words flow from my fingers as if my hands have been taken over by the characters themselves, using me as their vessel to tell their story. By the time 6:45 p.m. rolls around, I've blown Seven's six-thousand-word requirement out of the water. I open our chat window and attach the file.

Me: Here you go, Sir. It's a good thing you gave me a minimum word count as opposed to a max, because I don't think I could've stopped if I tried. *laughing emoji*

I see the green circle show up by his name as he signs on, and I smile, feeling proud. It's a new emotion for me. I mean, I've felt pretty good about myself since I started writing. The first time I typed The End, I couldn't believe I had actually written an entire book. Now, seven books later, that feeling never goes away each time I type those two little words, and my readership grows with each title I release. Who wouldn't feel good about being successful at what you do as your career of choice? But right now, as I wait for his response, I anticipate his praise with more excitement than I ever have waiting to see how people react to a new story I put out. He doesn't disappoint.

> Seven: 13,732 words. V, you're amazing. I'm so very proud of you, my sweet.
> Me: Thank you, Sir. *blushing emoji*
> Seven: Are you ready for tonight?
> Me: Ready as I'll ever be, I suppose.
> Seven: All right. While I read this, I want you to go relax. Take a hot bath for the next hour and prepare yourself for me.

My jaw drops and I sit back in my computer chair. Holy shit. He's...

> Me: You're going to read it, Sir?
> Seven: Of course I'm going to read it, V. 1- How would I know if you followed instructions and wrote a sex scene involving two toys? And 2- You obviously worked your sexy little ass off for the last day on this. What kind of Dom would I be if I didn't show my sub the respect of appreciating all that hard work she did to fulfill my command?
> Me: I suppose not a very good one, Sir. LOL!
> Seven: Exactly. Did you sleep at all, or did you pull an all-nighter to more than double what I asked for?
> Me: I slept a few hours early this morning, Sir.
> Seven: All right. You have three hours before we meet. Relax in the tub as instructed, but then I want you to take a nap before you come. Trust me, you'll need to rest up for what we will be doing tonight.

I go to type "I'll try," but I know that would never fly with Seven. I'll more than likely never be able to fall asleep. The anticipation of tonight will probably not allow it. So I just send him a "Yes, Sir" hoping I'm not lying, before I sign off.

I spend the next hour in my claw-footed tub, soaking in my Beautiful Day scented bubble bath from Bath and Body Works. I take my time preparing myself for my Dom, shaving my underarms, legs, and bikini, and when the timer goes off that I set on my phone, I let out my bath water and stand up to take a shower. I lather up with my loofa using the same scented body wash, and then shampoo and condition my hair.

I dry off quickly then blow-dry my hair before slipping between my sheets to try to fall asleep. I set my alarm for 9:30 p.m. Just enough time to get dressed and make it to the club for our appointment.

As I lie here, it hits me full-force. I will be having sex tonight for the first time in ten years. Seven and I will be acting out a scene in which I will be forced to express all the anger I've bottled up inside me for so long. I've done research on this scene several times since Dr. Walker told me about it. I chatted with Seven about my findings as well. In order for it to work, I will have to imagine him as Alan. Instead of having to recollect everything from that horrible night, I encouraged Seven to re-watch the video of my session with Dr. Walker, in which I went into great detail about what he had done to me. This way, he can act out what happened as closely as possible.

It's one thing to pretend Seven is Corbin, giving me the ability to orgasm without the guilty feeling of somehow being unfaithful to my ex. But it's another thing entirely to imagine him as my rapist. Won't that make me afraid of Seven if I picture him as someone who hurt me? Will it destroy the trust I've established with him? I've been assured it won't by both him and Dr. Walker, and by all the websites I've read. Because, during the scene, I will win the battle against my attacker, and because of the aftercare when it's complete, they tell me I will feel nothing but relief afterward.

It still worries me though. I really like Seven, and I hate the thought of anything causing me to feel differently toward him. He's my closest friend. I don't have romantic feelings toward him, although I'm obviously sexually attracted to him. That's a whole new set of feelings for me too. Before all this, I'd never willingly done anything physical with someone I didn't love.

Maybe that's another small reason I was never able to be intimate with the guys I dated. I never loved any of them either. But with Seven, I'm somehow able to separate the sex and my heart. Possibly because I'm using the training as a form of therapy. As long as I look at it as a way of healing, my mind doesn't worry about the emotions involved. Plus, I've read all sorts of stories where a sub's Dom isn't necessarily her partner in life, both in romance novels and real-life memoirs. They fulfill a part of themselves that their significant other doesn't. I personally would never be able to have a Dom separate from someone I was dating or married to. But since I'm single, I find no problem in having one that's in no other part of my life.

Without even realizing I dozed off, my alarm is suddenly blaring from my phone, and I stretch my limbs as I reach for it on my nightstand. At least I know I didn't lie to Seven when I told him I would take a nap. I have no idea how long I was actually unconscious for, but he never specified how long I had to sleep when he made the command.

I stand from my bed and walk out into my living room to the new bag of lingerie I threw on my couch after I got home from the mall yesterday. I'd spent a small fortune at Victoria's Secret buying everything on Seven's list of acceptable items, as opposed to picking and choosing. I don't go shopping often, so I figured I might as well get everything in one fell swoop.

If I actually took the time to make a decision over what to

wear tonight, I'd give myself an anxiety attack. So instead, I just reach in with my eyes closed and pull out the first thing I grasp. Unfolding it, I see I grabbed the burgundy lace panties I'd purchased, so I look in the bag long enough to find the matching bra before heading back into my room. I slip on the lingerie, lifting my breasts inside the cups, and turn toward my full-length mirror on the back of my bathroom door.

"This is as good as it's gonna get," I murmur, something I've always said to my image when I try in any way to look decent for public consumption. I pull my comfy black T-shirt dress over my head, and then my ever-present hoodie, and slip on my fuchsia ballet flats. Checking my phone and seeing it's 9:45 p.m., I grab my bag, throw it over my shoulder, and head out the door.

TRUTH *revealed*

RUTH *revealed*

TRUTH *revealed*

TH *revealed*

revealed

Sixteen

Corbin

I JUST FINISHED MOVING A second padded leather table into the playroom, butting it up against the one always there, before locking the legs together with zip ties to keep them in place, when I get that familiar feeling in my gut. Vi must've just arrived. I glance at my watch. 9:57 p.m. Such a good girl. She must've decided against the glass of wine I'd approved, because if she is anything, my girl is punctual. It's against her very nature to be late, especially having been given an order to be in place at a specific time.

I slip out of the room and into the shadows just in time to see her coming up the walk space between the booths and the playrooms, and then watch her disappear into our room. I sidestep along the darkness of the booths in order to observe her. She immediately goes over to the footlocker and strips quickly out of her hoodie, dropping it and her bag into the trunk. She toes off her dainty little shoes, so completely opposite of the sky-high stripper heels all the other women in the club choose to wear, and it makes me smile. My sweet Vi, still so innocent.

Yet as she grasps hold of the bottom of her dress, which reminds me of a long black T-shirt, what she reveals beneath it as she pulls it over her head is anything but innocent. My eyes land on the dark red lace panties first before moving up to the matching bra that does little to conceal her delicious and voluptuous breasts. Jesus fuck. The Vi I was married to was irresistible. But this Vi... this Vi has the ability to bring me to my knees. And it has nothing to do with the size of her breasts. It's the way she holds herself now, without even comprehending it. She has more confidence in the way she looks than she realizes. No longer the shy girl who slouched and tried to hide herself, she stands up straight, shoulders back, the sway of her back making a beautiful silhouette against the dim lighting of the playroom.

She drops her dress into the footlocker before shutting the lid, and then walks briskly to the other side of the doorway, reaching for the button on the wall. She turns, her long, shiny, dark hair swinging out from her body, to hurry over to the padded tables, and I see her climbing up into position before the curtain closes.

I glance at my watch once more. Ten on the dot. My cock is already pulsing from the way she carries out my orders to a T. So fucking perfect. Always was, and always will be.

Taking a deep breath and letting it out, I reach up to feel that my mask is in place before heading inside the playroom.

She waits for me in the center of the table on her knees, her ass resting back on her ankles and her hands relaxed in her lap exactly the way I instructed her. A small smile lifts her lips as I enter, and her obvious happiness at seeing me makes my chest expand. She seems a lot calmer than I anticipated for this night. I'm not sensing the anxiety or trepidation over what's to come that I expected she'd be feeling.

"Good evening, my sweet," I say low, coming up to her. With her on her knees on the table, she's exactly my height, putting us face-to-face.

"Good evening, Sir," she replies, her voice coy.

"How are you feeling? Are you nervous?" I ask, reaching up to tuck her hair behind her ear. Her head unconsciously leans in to my touch, making my heart thud behind my ribs.

She bites her full bottom lip before she responds. "A little, Sir. More about what's expected of me, as opposed to the actual... having sex part." Her face flushes.

"Expected of you?" I prompt.

"Yes, Sir. Dr. Walker said for this to work, I will have to fight against you. I will have to show my anger. If you haven't noticed, I'm not a confrontational kinda girl. I don't get loud. I—"

"Shh, shhh." I cup her soft cheek in my palm, seeing she's working herself up. "Just do what feels natural to you, okay? I can assure you, if you allow yourself to be in the moment, putting yourself in the headspace of that night, you will have no problem showing me your anger. You're stronger than you think, my sweet."

She nods, closing her eyes.

"The only thing I'm going to do first is, since it's been so long since you've had intercourse, I need to get you ready. As painful as your experience was that we are going to reenact, I don't want to actually hurt you. That would go against everything we're trying to do here. So... V, lie on your back. Hands above your head," I order, and without hesitation, she moves into place.

Fucking buffet, I think, as she stretches out before me. It takes every bit of my self-control not to pounce on her, devouring every inch of her succulent, creamy skin. But tonight isn't about me. Not in the slightest. Tonight is about taking care of my baby girl.

I move to the foot of the table, and grasp her ankles, sliding her feet toward me to stretch her legs out straight. She doesn't even flinch, and I love that I can touch her now without her cringing away. I walk over to the back wall, grabbing an item I need before moving to the head of the table. Her eyes peer up at me, so trusting, and even though she can't see it behind my mask, I smile down at her. God, I love this woman. I'd do anything for her. This will be one of the hardest things I've ever had to do, putting her through something so emotionally horrendous, but knowing it will help her heal, I suck it up. I can do this for her. I can help fix her broken pieces to make her whole again, giving her back what she lost of herself—no, what was taken from her against her will.

I stretch the blindfold out between my hands above her face and see her eyes move from my mask to the scrap of black velvet. A smile spreads across her face. "You really did read my story," she breathes. "So that means...."

"I found the two items you chose for your story highly entertaining, and I thought I'd let you experience them, since you so eloquently wrote about them all day." I tie the blindfold in place just as the look of apprehension crosses her beautiful face when it dawns on her what the second item she wrote about was. "I can only assume you've never experienced it before, seeing how there's no way the heroine in your story would've lasted so long against the toy's power." I lean down to whisper in her ear, "Either that, or her Dom is a wicked sadist, forcing her to try to control her orgasms while using *that* device." I smirk as goose bumps rise across her flesh.

"N-no, Sir. I've never tried it before," she confirms, and I nod to myself as I move to the cabinet to grab the toy in question. Every item used during any scene is thoroughly sanitized before it's put back in its place. And with our strict rules about being medically tested, I know we have nothing to worry about when it comes to using the items in the playrooms.

I unravel the cord as I walk to the foot of the padded table, where Vi lies fidgeting, visibly trying to relax as she exhales through pursed lips. I plug the cord into the outlet set into the floor at the foot of the table then set the long, bulky white device next to Vi's leg. With her blindfolded, I'll be able to use my lips on her, something I've been dying to do since this all began.

I roll my mask up to my nose from the neck, keeping it on just in case I have to cover my face in a hurry, and warn, "You'll feel my hands on your ankles, my sweet." I see her swallow and nod. "Remember your colors."

"Yes, Sir," she breathes, as I place my hands at her ankles, on the outside of her long, perfectly smooth legs.

Slowly, I glide upward, enjoying the way she unconsciously arches her back slightly, wanting closer to my touch. When my hands reach the lace of her panties, I tease her, sliding my fingers along the inside of the elastic. Her knees part before she forces them back together, and my cock pulses at the instinctive response.

"Relax, V. This is all about getting you ready, making you feel good. You know I won't hurt you," I say, my voice low. With my hood up, I need to take care disguising my voice. After ten years, I'm not sure if she'd recognize it or not, but I'm taking no chances. "Become conscious of your entire body. Start with your toes. Feel the air between them as you stretch them out, and then relax them. Then your feet. Let them become heavy. Feel them sink into the padding. Now up your long, beautiful legs." I watch the muscles in her thighs flex before they go limp. "Release the tension in your perfect ass. Let it flatten against the table beneath you. Up your back, and to your shoulders. Relax, my sweet. No biting that plump lip. Let it go. No creases between those eyebrows. I want you to melt into my table."

When she does what I've instructed, that's when I grasp her panties with both hands and slide them down her legs and off, leaving her pussy bare and exposed. Her knees jerk together once before she forces herself to relax again, but as I wrap my hands around the backs of them and slide her whole body toward me, she lets out a squeak.

Her nervousness makes me leery of her taking off her blindfold, so I leave her long enough to grab padded cuffs from the back wall. "V, I'm going to attach your hands to the table. This will only be during our warm-up. I promise I will take them off before our scene begins. Color?"

She bites her lip, mulling over what I've said, before she nods once. "Green, Sir."

"Good girl," I whisper, wrapping each soft leather, fur-lined cuff around her wrists before pulling her arms out straight to attach the center of the chain to the carabiner at the head of the table. Keeping contact with her flesh, I trail my hand along the length of her body as I make my way back to the foot of the table. Her toes grip against the padded leather top, her knees pointing to the ceiling, and when I reach them, I take one in each hand and gently spread her legs open.

She exhales a long breath, making herself relax as I ordered, showing more control than I feel like I have at this moment. All I want to do is set upon her like a starving wolf who was just thrown a succulent steak. But I know I can't. I have to go slowly. All the building aggression I feel to take what is mine will have its time to be let out whenever we start our scene.

"You'll feel my lips on the inside of your left knee, my sweet," I breathe against her flesh, before I inhale her delicious scent. Her soft whimper has me glancing down as my lips press to her skin, and I see her clench at the contact. Vi never could resist when I'd worship her this way, trailing kisses all the way up her inner thighs, my scruff scratching at her tender flesh as I make my way to her bare pussy.

"Breathe, V," I order, right before my tongue swipes up her center.

She gasps, her knees falling wide as I stroke gently at her clit, and her taste consumes me. Jesus fuck, how I've missed this, the way she smells, how wet she gets for me, her uncontrollable response to my mouth on her most sensitive place. I eat at her until she's a writhing mess on my table, and when I know she's about to come, remembering all her body's unconscious tells, I give her permission to do so. "Come for me," I command, and suck her clit into my mouth, making her body arch as she screams out her release. She shudders against my face and then tries to get away, her heels pressing into the table as she attempts to move back toward where her hands are attached.

I grasp onto her thighs in a viselike grip, and she halts her movement, whimpering as she forces herself to follow my silent order to hold still. I suck her pussy lips into my mouth, letting go with a pop as I reach for the device at her hip.

I flip the switch to low, and the deep, loud buzzing sound fills the playroom. She tenses for a moment, so I ask her, "Color?"

"Green, Sir," she moans, as I trail the Hitachi up the inside of her right thigh.

The wand is the most powerful of all vibrators, with a cushioned bulbous head on the end that flexes as it's pressed against someone's body. Even the low setting is mightier than any battery-operated toy.

"In the scene you wrote for me, you had the Dom and sub practicing orgasm control using the Hitachi. Such a thing would be almost cruel in reality, seeing how it's normally used in the opposite way, to force a sub to come as many times as possible," I explain. "I'm going to show you just how impossible it would be."

When I reach her center, I don't give her warning, wanting her to feel what the sub in her story would've felt. I press the large white head of the vibrating device to her clit, and she sucks in a sharp breath, her body instantly folding in on itself as she curls her legs up, her wrists yanking at the cuffs, making the chain clang. The sound mixed with the buzz of the Hitachi, along with her panting cry nearly makes me come in my pants.

"Oh, God," she whimpers, her head thrashing between her outstretched arms, her brow furrowed behind her blindfold.

"Exactly, my sweet." I smirk. "Let's see just how long you can go without—"

"I'm coming!" she cries, and her whole body convulses as she grinds against the wand.

My eyebrow quirks evilly as I keep the device pressed against her. I can only imagine just how sensitive she is right now, and it's evident in the way she starts to panic, trying to get away from the powerful vibration between her legs. "Uh, uh, uh, V. You had that poor sub under her Dom's wand for almost an hour. You didn't last a full minute. Shall we try again? See if you can hold off your orgasm a little longer this time?"

I grip onto her thigh with my free hand and rotate my other wrist, swiveling the head of the wand around her soaked flesh, and she screams once again, her back arching, pressing her breasts skyward as she comes again.

"Yellow, Sir!" she calls, which surprises me.

I pull the device away from her clit but don't turn it off. "Yellow, my sweet? Very interesting. You don't want me to completely stop?"

She pants for breath, a fine sheen of sweat covering her beautifully flushed skin. "I... I don't want *you* to stop. Just the wand, Sir," she clarifies, and I close my eyes, smiling. God, I love this woman. To the depths of my fucking soul, I love her.

Knowing what must come next wipes the smile from my lips. I flip the switch, cutting off the wand, and unplug it from the floor. I wind it up and place it in the bin by the door for cleaning before walking back to the head of the table. I unhook the chain from the carabiner, unstrapping the cuffs from her wrists, tossing them to the floor. I take hold of her hands and pull her back up to the head of the table then place my elbows on either side of her head to look down into her still-blindfolded face. I press a kiss to her cheek, unable to help myself, wanting to give her comfort when we're about to do something that will be one of the hardest things she's ever had to go through.

"V, will it help you to keep your blindfold on during the

scene?" I ask gently. "You have to imagine I'm your attacker. Will it help you picture that more clearly if you keep it on?"

She shakes her head. "N-no, Sir. I think that would make it too scary. You wearing your mask should be good enough," she whispers.

I can sense her anxiety, but she's so numb from her three orgasms that it's not nearly as bad as it would've been without our warm-up. "Fair enough. Color?"

She swallows, the action clear as I brace myself above her, looking down into her perfect face, wanting to do nothing but kiss her, devour her lips with mine, make love to her mouth and fill her with every ounce of strength I have in me. I wish I could heal her in some way that wouldn't put her through so much pain, but I know there's no other way. "G-green... Sir."

I nod, placing a soft kiss on her cheek once more before I stand, pulling my mask back into place. I lift her head and untie the blindfold, taking it over to the bin by the door. When I face her, I see her eyes are staring up at the ceiling as she tries to ready herself for what's to come.

I take a breath and move back to her side. "After we get into position, the scene will begin. I will no longer be Sir. I will be Alan. You will speak to me as if I am actually him. The only thing that will end the scene is if you call Red. Understand?"

Her fists clench and unclench by her sides. "Yes, Sir."

"I attached the other table because you were in bed together when it happened. Were you on his left or right?" I ask.

"His right, Sir," she replies, and I nod.

"All right. Move over to the other table then. They're hooked together, so don't worry about them sliding apart. You're safe, V. Remember that. I'm not going to let anything happen to you.

But when the scene starts, I want you to fight. Fight me like your life depends on it. Don't worry about hurting me. I promise I can take it. The music outside the playroom is loud enough that nobody is going to hear you. It's just you and me, my sweet. No need to be embarrassed. Get as loud as your lungs allow. That's an order."

"Yes, Sir," she whispers, sitting up to slide across the padded black leather surface to the second table.

"Good girl. Now, this is your last opportunity to ask a question if you have one before we start," I warn.

She thinks for a moment, and then glances down my body. "He... he was naked, Sir. Are you...?"

I shake my head. "In order for you to picture me more clearly as him, I will stay clothed," I reply, feeling my lip twitch at her look of disappointment. I brush off my humor though, needing to keep my head in the game.

I climb up onto the table she vacated and look down at her, my heart clanging in my chest when I see her trepidation. But knowing she can call Red at any time puts me more at ease. She can stop me before I truly cause her any sort of pain. I can't show her any sort of weakness. She's depending on me to get her through this, to act my part and help her heal, so I lie back on the table. "Scene starts now."

I roll to my side, facing away from her as if I'm lying in bed. Remembering what she said about that night, I twitch occasionally. I move around like I'm trying to get comfortable enough to fall asleep. I do this for a long time, waiting until she relaxes behind me. She knows what's coming, anticipating my next move, so I have to hold off until she's not so tense.

God, what the fuck am I doing? I close my eyes, trying to

calm my own heartbeat, which is flying, adrenaline pumping through my veins, readying me for the attack as if it's real. What I'm about to do to her goes against everything inside me. I would *never* do anything to hurt my sweet Vi. And here I am, about to make her relive the single most awful thing that she's ever had to live through... something she had to survive. It just feels wrong.

But I can't back out now. The only thing pushing me forward is knowing without a doubt that this is for her own good. I've seen this scene heal assault victims with my own two eyes. I have to do this for her. After leaving her all those years ago to deal with this shit on her own, this is the very least I can do to help her fix herself.

So with that thought in mind, as I hear her breath even out behind me, I unbuckle my belt and let go of my surroundings then make my move, recalling everything she said that motherfucker did to her.

I roll on top of Vi, immediately pressing my hand over her mouth roughly. Her eyes pop open, and the look of sheer terror inside their depths almost makes me stop right off the bat.

But that's when she starts to fight. My baby girl *fights*, and seeing she's in this wholeheartedly, every ounce of trepidation I felt before leaves me, and I jump in the ring with her, only inside my heart, I'm fighting alongside her, not against her.

Her hands shoot up to my arm holding her head to the table by her mouth, and she claws at my black long-sleeved shirt. She's already naked from the waist down, but as she bucks and kicks, her screams muffled behind my hand, I would actually have to apply strength to force myself inside her. But that's not what he had done to her. Not yet.

"Why are you fighting, Vivian?" I ask evilly, the same thing she had told Dr. Walker that Alan had said. "I know you want me. I see it every day when you come over to study, the way you look at me. You fucking want me so bad." Using my other hand, I trail it down her stomach, and using her nails digging into my arm to center me in the scene, I slip two fingers inside her. Any other time, feeling her walls clamp around my hand would've been my undoing, but as she lets out a wail behind my hand, tears streaming down her face, I stay in character. I curl my fingers upward against her G-spot, massaging it and feeling her legs clamp around me, trying to shut me out.

"Stop all your fucking crying, Vivian," I growl, fluttering my fingers against the spot that will force her to come against her will. "Relax. Just let it happen. You know you want it. If you stop fighting it, I'll make it feel good." His disgusting words leave my lips, and my heart cracks in my chest as she tries to shake her head. I can feel her muscles working against my palm, and knowing I need to let her release her emotions, I take my hand away from her mouth.

"*No!*" she screams, as I work my fingers inside her.

Any second now, she will orgasm, even as she tells her body not to. It's this betrayal that is so damaging to a rape victim's psyche. I press my hand to the center of her chest, keeping her in place, but allowing her to fight against me.

"No! Nonononononono, stop! Alan, stop! You can't do this to me!" she wails, thrashing as much as she can under my weight. Her face is red with exertion and wet from all her tears. Bile rises in the back of my throat, seeing my baby girl like this, knowing that motherfucker had witnessed her in the same way, begging him to stop, and he didn't care. He didn't care about my sweet, innocent wife, the one who had been so worried about him that she didn't want him to sleep alone in case he got sick.

I shake off the feeling, knowing I have to finish this out. We've come too far to stop now. My thumb joins in, circling her clit as I stroke along the ceiling of her pussy with the two fingers inside her, and I see all the emotions in her eyes when she realizes her body is betraying her the way it had all those years ago.

"Oh, God. Please no. Please. *Please!* Alan, you can't! I'm married. You're not my husband! You're not my Corbin. You can't do this to me!" she screams at the top of her lungs, and at the sound of my name leaving her lips, I jerk, pausing in my ministrations.

She continues to cry, but with me giving her a reprieve from her body's instinctive responses to my forced pleasure, her strength is renewed, and she begins to fight harder than ever before. She reaches up with her tiny fists and punches me in the chest over and over, and I take it. My little wife is so small and fragile her blows barely sting. But knowing she's putting every single bit of her force behind the punches, I feel each one as if it's a direct hit to my heart. I take them as my punishment for leaving her, for not reading into that last conversation hard enough before I divorced her without a second glance.

But it's when she starts to chant, as if it's the only thought left in her mind, the only thing important to her, that I feel myself begin to break. "I promised to be loyal. I promised him. I promised! I promised him I would be loyal! It's the only thing he asked, and you're going to make me break my promise!"

A tear slides down my cheek behind my hood as she thrashes beneath my hand holding her down. I know I have to finish out the scene, but fuck, this hurts so badly. My poor, sweet Vi. God.

She had to go through this. She had to live through all of this. I can't bring myself to force her to come. I don't want her to go through her body's betrayal again. I just can't. So I move forward in her recollection.

When she sees me pull my fingers out of her and begin working the button of my pants, she snaps.

"No!" she shrieks, fighting with all her strength. Whereas before she was trying to get me off of her, she now tries with all her might to get away. She reaches back behind her, grasping onto the head of the padded table to try to yank herself backward. She attempts to twist her body to pull herself, but she realizes she doesn't have the arm strength to get away.

That's when, just like in her story she told Dr. Walker, she remembers how strong her legs are. I can see the idea form in her head as clear as day right before she pulls her feet up, lodging her heels against my hips. As she tries to kick me off, all I have to do is press my weight downward in order not to budge.

God, my sweet girl never stood a chance.

"Stop!" she cries. Her voice is hoarse from all her screaming and wailing, and I can feel her sobs within me as she weakens. "Please, Alan. Please stop." Her body wracks as she weeps. "You're not Corbin," she whimpers, as I get my pants down over my hips, my cock springing free, and I realize I'm one fucked up asshole that I'm even able to get a hard-on during all of this. When she looks down and sees it, a tiny bit of her strength renews, and she tries kicking me off once again. "No! No! You can't do this, Alan!"

The name is like a slap in the face. I hate it. I hate the thought of him being in her mind as I'm this close to her, the head of my cock nudging against her entrance.

"Alan, stop! Please! I won't tell anybody! If you just stop, I won't tell anybody. I swear! Just don't do this to me! Please don't do this to me! Don't make me break my promise to Corbin. You can't be inside me! You're not Corbin. You're not Corbin!" Her fists slam against my chest as she goes wild beneath me, feeling me press against her pussy. Yet, it's only when her eyes come up to focus on the slits in my hood, and I see how tortured she is, truly in the moment when she was raped ten years ago... I can't take anymore. She can't see my eyes, even though mine are locked with hers, but it's in this second, when she wails "You're not Corbin!" one last time, screaming at the top of her lungs as she gives one final blow with all her strength, when I give in.

I reach up and rip my hood off, my dark eyes blazing down into her green ones, and sink inside the fist-tight heat of her pussy. "Yes, I am, baby girl. I'm Corbin."

Seventeen

Vi

THE ORGASM THAT RIPS THROUGH my body feels like it enters my very soul. My hands, which had been balled into fists for the last several minutes as I fought against my assailant, now clasp him to me as he seats himself inside me, unmoving. My pussy ripples around his thick length, one so familiar even though I haven't felt it in a decade. It fits me as if it was made for me, filling me up to the brim.

I can't look away from those intense chocolate eyes, the ones I've dreamed about every single night since the day I met him when I was eighteen. And even though I'm going through a mind-fuck to end all mind-fucks, all I can do is stare as I come.

Corbin leans down, bracing himself on his elbows on either side of my head, bringing him nose-to-nose with me. Even though it hurts my eyes to try to focus on him while he's this close, I still can't look away. Even as tears begin to slide down the sides of my face, I can't blink. If I blink, his image could disappear.

Seven let me imagine Corbin's face while he made me come. Have I officially gone off my rocker, truly believing the man inside me looks just like Corbin? Or does Seven really look like my ex-husband? No... surely not. He would have to be his identical twin to look so perfectly like him, an exact replica.

But... no. He... he had called me baby girl. He said...

"It's really me, Vi," he whispers, running the tip of his nose along the bridge of mine, and I whimper, unable to speak. "Breathe, baby girl," he orders, pulling out slightly to plunge back in, making me gasp.

"C-Cor—" I choke on the name. My brain just isn't catching up with what's right in front of me... what's right inside me.

"Say it, Vi. Say my name," he demands, thrusting in me once again and making my eyes roll back as I moan.

I automatically follow my Dom's orders. "Corbin." It comes out on a breath as my eyes come back to focus on his face, a face so beautiful that my memories of it don't even compare. He's so much more handsome than I remember. Or has it grown even more perfect with age? Ten years. Ten years have been good to my breathtaking ex-husband.

"I'm going to make love to you, Vi," he tells me, and I nod, even though he wasn't asking permission. "You're mine, and nobody is ever going to take you away from me ever again."

Tears pool in my eyes before they overflow, seeping over my bottom lashes to trail down my cheekbones, where he leans down to catch them with the tip of his tongue. If this is a dream, I never want it to end. If I've snapped and gone completely crazy, the scene we just enacted having finally broken me, then I never want to be fixed. I want to stay like this forever, my Corbin so perfectly clear in my mind that when I reach up and stroke his cheek with my fingertips, I can actually feel the stubble there.

He begins to move inside me, with quick outward strokes followed by slow plunges, swiveling his hips every time he meets the deepest part of me. Sliding one hand down the length of my body, he then takes hold of my left thigh and hikes it up higher around his hip, his fingers digging into my skin as he picks up his pace.

I wrap one arm around his rock-hard back, feeling the muscles working there, and my other hand stays cupping his cheek, unable to move it away for fear his face will disappear.

Yet the higher and higher he builds me up, the more and more reality sets in. Only Corbin has ever taken me to such heights. Only Corbin, the love of my life, has ever made me feel this good. And as he bends down and finally takes my lips in a life-altering kiss, my soul reaching out to lock hands with his once again after they had been wrenched apart so long ago, I know for a fact the man deep inside me is really him. I'm making love to my Corbin.

The realization snaps me out of my lust-induced stupor, and with a sob, the hand holding his cheek locks around the back of his neck as I cling to him, sinking the nails of my other hand into his back. "Corbin!" I cry into his mouth, and he swallows it as he rests his forehead against mine and nods.

His eyes close as his face twists with emotion. "It's me, baby girl," he whispers.

"It's really you." My voice comes out hoarse as he meets my stare, and then I gasp as he sets into a demanding pace. I remember this. I remember it clearly as if it were yesterday and not a decade ago. This almost pained look on his face, the concentration crease between his black brows, the smoldering look in his deep brown eyes, the sexy flare of his nostrils, the slight parting of his lips. He's determined to make me come, and he's ready to fill me up as he joins me when we jump off the cliff together.

"Oh, God!" I shout as I hold on for dear life. He pounds into me, and just when I think I will pass out from the sheer pleasure of the full-body orgasm, he growls above me then slams his lips down on mine, kissing me ferociously as he spills inside me.

I'm enveloped in everything Corbin, his physical body, his intoxicating scent, his very aura. It all surrounds me. And I never want to leave my safe cocoon.

But after a while, my hips start to ache, no longer used to having his powerful body between my thighs. As I unwrap my legs from around him, he slips his muscular arm beneath my lower back, sits up, and lifts me, sliding off the table to carry me over to the leather chair against the wall to cradle me in his lap. As he runs his fingers through my hair, I cuddle into his chest, breathing him in.

"I have so many questions," I whisper.

"I know, baby girl," is his only reply, clearly not knowing what to say, just like me.

He holds me like this for what feels like forever, until I feel like I could fall asleep in his arms. I know I should feel... something. Anger? That's what a normal person would feel having been fooled into thinking— No. I stop that train of thought, refusing to ruin the first peace I've felt in over ten years.

Suddenly, a voice fills the room, and I jump, startled out of my bliss.

"Sarge, please bring your sub to your office. It's imperative for her healing."

Corbin sighs beneath my cheek, and I glance up into his stormy eyes. "Looks like I'm in trouble and getting called to the principal's office," he murmurs, leaning down to kiss my cheek.

"Sarge?" I lift a brow, and he shakes his head. "Was that Dr. Walker?" I ask.

"The one and only," he replies, standing and carrying me over to the back wall, where he sets me on my feet before grabbing a silky black robe off a hook and wrapping it around me. I stick my arms through the sleeves and watch his hands work as he knots the belt then zips and buttons his pants.

After he refastens his belt, he takes hold of my hand and leads me out of the playroom to a set of stairs. Feeling the metal of the steps, I realize I'm still barefoot. My belongings are still in the footlocker in the playroom, but since Corbin didn't bother with it, I assume my stuff is safe until we return.

We enter through a door at the top of the staircase then he pulls me into one of four offices lining a corridor. I look around, seeing a black leather couch against one wall, and a large wooden desk at the back of the room, with a computer chair behind it and two black leather seats on the opposite side, close to where we stand. It's completely bare except for the computer monitor sitting atop it. The space is totally impersonal, no pictures or art on the walls, no color. Barren. It makes me shiver thinking of trying to work in such a cold environment.

"This is where you work?" I ask quietly.

"Only part of the time," he says, just as Dr. Walker fills the doorway. Corbin eyes him, his demeanor reflecting annoyance. "What's up, Doc?"

"Well... that certainly didn't go as planned," my therapist states, coming fully into the room, moving to one of the leather seats in front of the desk and spinning it to face the couch against the wall before taking a seat. He gestures toward the sofa, and Corbin pulls me over to it. When he plops down, he tugs on my hand, making me land in his lap.

"Kinda interrupted our aftercare, Doc," Corbin tells him, irritation clear in his tone.

"I felt it was very important to call you in here, to make sure her aftercare ran smoothly," Dr. Walker retorts.

"Wait. Did... did you see everything that happened in the playroom?" I question, my face heating with embarrassment.

"Vivian, you were made aware there were surveillance cameras in the room for safety. We"—he gestures between himself and Corbin—"went against protocol for your anger expression scene, or AES, under the agreement I would supervise, behind the scene, if you will."

"He's got jokes," I mumble up to Corbin, who smiles down at me before kissing my forehead.

"Normally, those scenes are done with witnesses, but knowing your discomfort with showing such strong emotion in front of people, we arranged for me to watch it unfold outside the room. Things can happen during an AES. A survivor can trigger. And it's important for a professional to be present in order prevent disaster from happening," he explains, and I nod.

I sigh, giving in to my understanding. "I read about that in my research, after my last session with you," I confess.

"V, I believe you might be in a state of shock right now. You just found out that your Dom, who you thought was someone else, is actually your ex-husband. Yet, here you sit, completely unemotional about the revelation," Dr. Walker tells me.

I nod again. "Oh, for sure." I giggle, sounding a little insane even to my own ears. "I don't think my brain has caught up with what's happened yet. I still kinda feel like I'm dreaming."

"That's why the next couple of hours are very important, why I called you both in here, because I don't think even Corbin will be able to deal with everything on his own. Both of your emotions are in this, and knowing how fragile your state of mind was during our therapy sessions, and me being on the receiving end of Corbin's rage when he watched those videos, I couldn't just leave you two to take on this eggshell path you're about to walk."

I look down into my lap, taking in his words. As much as I'd love to stay in this state of uncaring bliss, I know that if I were to be alone when the reality of it all hits, it might just be the final straw that cracks my mind for good. So I nod. "Okay, Dr. Walker. I... I have so many questions," I repeat what I said in the playroom, and Corbin lifts his hand to scrub at his shaved head then down over his face. It's the same move he used to make when he was stressed about work back when we were married.

"The most important thing to remember as we hash all of this out is to remain calm. Emotions will run high, but let's speak to each other with great care. Actually listen to what one another has to say. Absorb each other's responses. Think about your answers before you respond to a question. And above all, be honest. This is imperative." He speaks to both of us, leaning down to brace his elbows on his knees to get closer, conveying with his voice and eyes how critical his words are.

"Agreed," I reply, and then glance into Corbin's face. Gone

is the annoyed attitude, seriousness filling its place. It's obvious he respects his co-worker. Which brings about my first question, turning into several. "What... I don't know what's been true during all of this. Y'all are really the owners of this club, right? The therapy sessions, all of that. Those were real? All members have to do those?"

"Yes, Vivian. All of that is true. We really own this club, along with Brian Glover and Seth, who you know as Seven," Dr. Walker responds.

"So Seven is a real person," I murmur, tucking my hair behind my ear.

"Corbin, you've been quiet through all of this. I think it would be beneficial for Vivian if you were to answer her questions from here on out," he tells him, and Corbin nods.

He lifts me off his lap but sets me directly next to him, still nestled against his side, taking my hand. "Yes, Vi. Seven is a real person. You really were speaking with him all this time, until a month ago, when you stepped into our club. That's when I took over," he confesses, and I absorb that information.

I speak out loud to get everything straight in my head. "It really was Seven who helped me with all my research for my books. It was him in all the demonstration videos he sent me." I let out a nervous laugh, breathing a sigh of relief. "So at least I know I wasn't actually watching *you* do the BDSM thing to all those other girls."

"No, baby girl. That was Seth." Corbin looks from me to Dr. Walker. "Is he here, by chance?"

"Yeah." He lifts his hips off the chair to pull his cell out of his pocket, typing something into his phone. Immediately, we hear a door opening down the short hallway, and footsteps approaching quickly.

I look up as a cute guy with perfectly disheveled light brown hair fills the doorway. He's wearing the same thing as Corbin, black pants and a long-sleeved black T-shirt, the same thing he also always wore in his videos and on FaceTime. He's taller but more slender than Corbin, and his body structure matches what I saw on the computer as well. I remember thinking how much more muscular he seemed in person the first time I came to Club Alias, brushing it off as people looking different than they do on the internet. Little did I know it wasn't him at all.

"Seven?" I confirm, a small smile forming on my lips when I realize I'm meeting my real friend for the past year for the first time.

"It's me, V," he acknowledges, coming to stand in front of me and opening his arms.

I immediately stand and wrap my arms around his waist, ignoring Corbin's growl behind me as Seven squeezes me in a tight hug. Just as quickly, he lets go of me, and I sit back down, instantly being bound to Corbin's side with his viselike arm around my body. Possessive as ever.

Seven pulls the other leather chair over to sit facing us beside Dr. Walker. Surrounded by three handsome men, I'm surprised I don't feel intimidated, but all three of them are special to me in some way. Two things dawn on me at the same time, and I can't help but voice them.

"I just realized..." I look at Dr. Walker first, and then to Corbin then back to Seven. "I just hugged you."

Seven's eyes sparkle as he grins, sitting back in his chair as Corbin huffs. But it's Dr. Walker who speaks. "I noticed that too, Vivian. No hesitation. The second he opened his arms, you didn't even think about it. You allowed him to touch you without any uncertainty. That's great progress as far as your aversion to touch goes."

"Also, did I hear you correctly? Did you say the fourth person who owns the club with you is Brian Glover?" I can't hide the excitement in my voice.

"Yeah, baby girl. My old cherry," Corbin speaks up.

My hands clap together happily. "That's wonderful! I always wondered what happened to him. I've looked for him several times over the years." I turn to look into Corbin's eyes. "You too. I looked for you, and it's like y'all never even existed. But I guess you know that already, since it was actually you I was telling about that." My voice lowers.

"Awkwaaaard," Seven sings, and Dr. Walker reaches out, punching him in his arm. "Ow! What the fuck?"

"If you can't behave yourself, I'll make you leave. This is serious," he retorts.

"What? She seems fine!" Seven gestures toward me. "Here I thought she would kill us all when she found out it was actually Corbin pretending to be me after he followed her around all these years. But look at her."

Corbin and Dr. Walker both suck in a breath as their eyes come to me, and my heart thuds in my chest at both their attention and what Seven said as my mouth falls open. "Followed me? For years?" I whimper.

"You loudmouth motherfucker," Corbin seethes, and before I know what's happening, he lunges off the couch toward Seven, only to run into the giant brick wall that is my therapist.

"Remember what I said, Corb. Control your emotions," Dr.

Walker says firmly, and I see Corbin's fists clench and unclench at his sides before he slowly lowers himself back in his seat next to me.

"Sorry, bro." Seven has the decency to look ashamed at his slip.

"Let's get back on track. Everyone, take a deep breath and let it out." After we do as Dr. Walker instructs, he continues, "Vivian, ask your questions. What is important to you to learn first? And then we will all help fill in the blanks of what you don't know to ask."

I nod, sitting back against the couch cushion, the side of my leg still pressed against Corbin's, but enough space between the rest of our bodies for me to think straight.

"What does he mean you followed me all these years?" I question quietly, not looking over at him.

Corbin scrubs down his face once more before sitting up straighter, turning to face me more in his seat. He takes a breath, and that's when I finally look up to meet his eyes. There's so much pain there it hurts my chest, and instinctively I reach out to take his hand.

"To answer that, I have to back up a few years," he starts, and I nod. "After that phone call... the last time I ever spoke to you, I sent you those divorce papers, but something in me couldn't let you go. It wasn't until your therapy sessions when I learned the truth about what happened to you, that I realized why."

It's not until this very second that I become completely aware of the fact that Corbin would have seen all the footage of my sessions with Dr. Walker. "You... you know everything?" My voice catches in my throat and I have to swallow past the lump there as I try to fight off my urge to burst into tears.

"I know everything, baby girl. I know you never cheated on me. I know you lied to protect me, to keep me from going after that motherfucker and ending up in jail. And after I learned all of this, I couldn't even be mad that you lied to me. Because you were exactly right. I would have gunned him down, uncaring what happened to me after I slaughtered him." He reaches out and tucks my hair behind my ear, and I lean in to his touch.

"Let's return to her original question," Dr. Walker inserts gently. "Continue from after your divorce."

"Right." Corbin clears his throat again. "I stayed in the army for a few more years, but always kept my eye on you as much as I could. Just making sure you were okay. But then I got deployed again, and I was shot—"

I gasp sharply, my hand coming up to cover my mouth as a tear finally spills from my eye. "You were shot?" I cry behind my hand, searching his face, which seems unaffected by something that has me distraught inside.

"Yeah, babe. No big deal. I was actually shot twice and stabbed once. But I'm all good. I got to keep one of the bullets, though. I set off metal detectors every time." He smiles, trying to lighten my worry, but I only shake my head, slinging a couple more tears free. Seeing my distress isn't going away with his joking words, he pulls my hand away from my mouth, holding all four of our clasped hands to his chest as he speaks firmly. "Baby, I'm fine. I promise. What we just did in the playroom, did that feel like I wasn't all right?"

My face flames thinking about our lovemaking, heating even further when I realize it had been witnessed by Dr. Walker as well. Instead of following up on that, I get us back on track. "What happened after you were hurt?"

"Well, they gave me a couple awards and sent me on my way with a slap on the ass. Kicked me out with an honorable discharge. That's when this guy approached me," he explains, hiking his thumb over at Dr. Walker.

"He wanted you to run the club with him?" I ask, glancing over at the therapist, who cocks his eyebrow at Corbin, who goes silent. "What? What is it?" When he still doesn't answer, my eyes find Dr. Walker's once more.

He looks between Corbin and me for a moment before leaning forward to brace his elbows on his knees once again. "All right. In my professional opinion, full disclosure in this session is imperative to reestablishing trust. I don't think it's even hit Vivian yet that you're sitting here with her, Corb. You being the center of her thoughts all these years, it probably still feels to her like she somehow conjured you. Especially having learned you're here while she was so deep into her AES. She was already imagining you were someone else, reenacting the most traumatizing experience of her life. And then in the middle of that, you revealed that not only was she not with her rapist, and not even who she thought was her Dom, Seven, who would have had a stranger's face, but *you. Corbin*, the person you had encouraged her to imagine during her training sessions so she could orgasm without guilt. Can you possibly conceive the mindfuck she is going through right now?"

"You didn't see the fucking terror in her eyes," Corbin growls, his hand tightening around mine. "You didn't feel what I felt when she looked up at me and was genuinely afraid of me. You have no idea what I just went through when she glanced down at my cock between us—a part of me I've only ever used to show her how much I fucking love her—and panicked because she was so goddamn terrified of what it would do to her."

I look at him through tear-filled eyes. This man... he must still feel for me what I've always felt for him. If he didn't, my fear wouldn't affect him this much. I brace myself for a verbal battle between the two men, but being the amazing therapist he is, Dr. Walker brushes off Corbin's defensiveness.

"That's very good, Corb. That was more emotion from you than we ever got in our sessions," he says in a way that doesn't sound patronizing at all, but encouraging. "You're right. I didn't see what you saw when you were face-to-face with her. I didn't feel what you felt. Please, make me understand. What did you feel?"

My eyes move to Corbin, who's into Dr. Walker's, seeming to be having an internal battle. If he's anything like he used to be, there's no way he would talk about his feelings with another man. He always had to be the strong one, the rock all his soldiers could lean on. Plus, we were so happy together I don't think he ever really needed anyone to confide in. But I'm pleasantly surprised once again as he lets down his stone wall and starts talking.

His voice is quiet but intense. "I was always her protector. She was such a small, fragile little thing. I used to compare her to a skittish kitten. But when she finally opened up to me, it's like my strength finally gave her claws. Over the two years we were married, my baby girl grew into one hell of a woman. You wouldn't even recognize the Vi *you* know as the person I introduced as my wife back in the day. And when I found out what really happened to her, it all finally made sense why she had not only reverted to the fragile girl I first met in that rock gym, but fallen so much farther than that. I was *always* her protector," he repeats on a whisper, looking over at me for a moment before returning his eyes to Dr. Walker. "That's why I followed her. I kept my distance... to protect myself, I guess, since what she'd told me during that phone call had been the most painful thing I'd ever felt in my goddamn life. But I still felt compelled to watch over her."

Dr. Walker nods and looks over at me. "Vivian, do you have anything to say about the fact Corbin kept his eye on you for the past ten years?"

I think about that isolated revelation for a moment, pushing aside everything else so I can focus on how I feel about it. "I... hmm...." I try to form a complete sentence, but it comes out stunted. I bite the inside of my cheek, feeling kind of embarrassed by the way I truly feel.

"You'll get no judgment from us, V. Remember you're safe here. All of us care about you, doll face," Seven speaks up, and I can't help but smile. I always did love his easygoing personality in his messages and videos.

"Well, I don't feel like my reaction to that part is... normal," I confess.

"Normalcy doesn't matter, Vivian. Just be honest," Dr. Walker encourages, and I take a breath, nodding.

"To be honest, I find him... essentially stalking me for the past decade kinda... hot as fuck?" My face heats. I'm used to writing my naughty thoughts while hiding behind a pen name. I've never really voiced them aloud before.

Dr. Walker gives me a small smile while Seven laughs boisterously. I glance over at Corbin, who looks like he's fighting his own grin while biting his lip. The gleam in his eye tells me he likes my honest answer.

I turn to Seven with a grin and point at him. "You! Stop laughing at me. You of all people should know I'd find that shit sexy. You read *Her Master's Revenge.*"

He holds his hands up in surrender but still chuckles. "Like I said, no judgment here. And true fucking story. That book was hot," he says, and he looks over at Corbin, who has confusion written all over his face. "Don't look at me like that. Yeah, I read it. One, I fed her all the BDSM stuff that went into it, so I wanted to see what she wrote. And two, it's like porn, bro, only you get to use your imagination and make the people look the way you want them to. Hot as fuck, dude."

"I was more confused over the fact you know how to read," Corbin jabs, and we all laugh, the tension in the air lessening a bit. He turns to me, his brow furrowed. "What was that book about?"

"Well, the hero meets the heroine one day, and it turns out she's a professional thief. He thinks she's agreed to a date with him, only for her to turn around and rob him blind. I won't go into much detail and spoil it, in case you want to read it some day. But anyway, it's called *Her Master's Revenge* because he finds her after she disappears, and he stalks her for a long-ass time, just waiting for the opportune moment to seek his revenge. It's an enemies-to-lovers BDSM romance. My first one to hit best seller," I tell him proudly, and I realize I want to fill Corbin in on all I've accomplished as an author. It's the one thing I feel confident in, the same way I used to feel about rock climbing back in the day.

But I'll save that for another time. It's starting to hit me that's it really Corbin, my Corbin, sitting right next to me. In the flesh. Looking at me with those chocolate brown eyes I've dreamed about every night for as long as I can remember. And they're boring into me with the same look of unequivocal love they used to—not the look of hatred I always feared I would see if I ever saw him again, knowing he believed I cheated on him.

My smile fades as it all sinks in, and I feel my breath stutter in my chest. My eyes cut to my therapist then back to Corbin as my chin trembles, and right as a sob burst from between my lips, I vaguely hear Dr. Walker say, "Here it is, Corb—" as my love effortlessly lifts me into his lap and wraps me in his powerful embrace.

That's when I fucking lose it.

TRUTH *revealed*

RUTH *revealed*

TRUTH *revealed*

TH *revealed*

TRUTH *revealed*

Eighteen

Corbin

I CLOSE MY EYES AND TRY TO ABSORB all her emotions as Vi's body shakes against mine, hearing Doc's instructions through her cries. "She's not having a panic attack like in our session, so don't snap her out of it like I did. She needs to let it out. It's finally hit her."

My face twists with pain, hating my Vi is having to go through so much to heal. I nod, my chin resting on the top of her head as she weeps, letting Doc know I heard him. As much as I hate it when she cries, I know he's right. She needs to be allowed to let everything out that she's had bottled up for so long. And that's when she begins to mindlessly speak through her gut-wrenching sobs.

"It wasn't my fault, Corbin. I tried to stay loyal. It was the only thing you ever asked of me, and I failed. But it wasn't my fault.

I tried to fight, but I was too weak." She gasps for breath, and when I start to shush her, I see Doc shake his head vigorously.

He whispers, "She's telling you everything she always wanted you to know. Even if she had found you during her search, she wouldn't have been able to tell you this, because she would have still wanted to keep you safe. But you know everything now. Let her have this."

I bob my head then place my stubbled cheek to the top of her hair, holding her tight against me.

"I'm sorry I lied. I promised I would never be dishonest with you, but I lied to keep you from going after him. He was *so strong*. What if he had hurt you? Or if you killed him, I couldn't live with myself if you went to jail because of what happened to me. I had to lie." The longer she purges all her thoughts, the quieter her crying becomes and she begins speaking clearly, her voice growing stronger and stronger. "I lied because I loved you so much. And I still do. Not a single bit of my love for you has ever faded. I tried moving on, finding someone else, but I just couldn't. I couldn't even let them touch me. Because they weren't you. And I've always belonged to you."

If I didn't already know Doc was badass at what he does, this right here would have confirmed it for me. I can almost feel Vi's broken pieces fitting back together as she gets to tell me everything she's longed for me to know. Her side of the story. Not wanting to fuck up her progress, I glance up at Doc with a questioning look on my face. He nods, letting me know it's a good time for me to respond to her outpouring.

"Look at me, baby girl," I murmur against her hair, but when she doesn't move, I use my Dom voice. "Vi, look at me." She immediately lifts her chin to meet my eyes. "First of all, none of it was your fault. You stayed loyal to me. You never broke your promise. Understand?"

"Yes, Sir," she replies, automatically reverting to her submissive persona.

"Second, I forgive you for lying. I understand and agree with why you did it, so no more feeling guilty about that. Just don't let it happen again," I demand, and she nods.

"I promise, Sir."

"Finally, I know you tried moving on. I saw it while I watched over you. And although I had thought you slept with the men you dated before ending things with them, I learned in your therapy session that you never did. But even if you had, you would still belong to me. I don't give a fuck I'm not the only one who's ever been inside you. Because I'm the only one who has ever owned your heart."

I watch as Vi's chin trembles before she buries her face in my chest. I run my fingers through her hair as she sniffles, her tears soaking through my shirt. And when she finally gets ahold of herself and meets my eyes once again, hers sparkle with happiness through her tears as she gives me the most beautiful smile, one I haven't seen on her face since we were married.

I cup her cheek in my hand and lower my lips to hers, hearing her whimper before she melts into our kiss. It's like the weight of the world has just lifted off her shoulders, and she can finally relax for the first time in ages.

Our passion escalates, my hand tangling in the back of her hair to tilt her so I can deepen the kiss. When I hear a throat clearing, I open my eyes to find Vi's still closed. With one more gentle peck to her lips, I pull back to look up at the other two people in the room.

"I know we're all a bunch of voyeurs, but maybe you two could hold off on molesting each other until we finish talking?" Seth says, a smirk on his stupid mug.

Vi's face turns red as her eyes widen, and she turns to face him. "My bad," she says, wiggling out of my arms to sit propped next to me.

"Shall we return to Vivian's question before we went off on this tangent?" Dr. Walker suggests. "She wanted to know what happened to you after you got out of the military. Seeing how it looks like she's here to stay, Corbin, why don't you pick up from there?"

"Do I have your permission for full disclosure?" I ask my friends. If I tell Vi everything, the two of them would have to put their trust in her as well. We've never allowed anyone else into our circle before, keeping what we do outside the club a secret.

Doc and Seth look at each other a moment, holding a silent conversation between the two of them, before they face us once again, both nodding their approval.

"And Brian always adored her, so I'm sure he won't care. I'd message him to ask permission, but he's on a job," I add, and they both agree.

"On a job?" Vi prompts, her brow furrowing.

I take a deep breath, trying to figure out where to begin. "Okay, so the day I got my exit papers from the army, Doc contacted me. He had followed my military career, impressed by all my accomplishment. My Ranger tab, winning the marksmen comp, etc. And he offered me a job. We own the place next door as well."

"Oh, the security place? That's cool. What do y'all do, like, protect famous people who come to town or something? Are you a younger, hotter version of Liam Neeson?" She grins at me, wiggling her eyebrows above her red and puffy eyes. I know she's still struggling, but I can see her easing into the Vi I remember her being. My beautiful wife who has no idea just how strong she is.

I can't help but chuckle. "Not exactly. Yes, we're available as hired security, but our main job... well... it's...." I don't know how to tell her without her freaking out. I mean, learning someone kills people for a paycheck... a person probably wouldn't respond too well to that. Right?

I look up to the guys for help.

"You know what a mercenary is, doll face?" Seven interjects, seeming all too happy to spill the beans.

"What, like Blackwater?" she asks.

"Sort of. That was a private military company that was eventually bought by a group of private investors. They're on a much bigger scale than what we are," he explains.

"What you do... which is what?"

"Well...." I try again, but anything I start to say just sounds... bad.

"We kill people for money," Seth says, and it takes everything in me not to jump up and punch him in the throat as Vi jerks in response. "Bad people, doll face. Very, *very* bad people. Motherfuckers who deserve it but get away with the terrible shit they do because they're rich or there was a technicality that helped them escape prosecution."

She mulls this over for a moment then looks up at me. "So you're like... vigilantes. Y'all are basically Arrow?"

"I knew I liked you," Seth says, and I frown, a growl starting deep in my chest. "Calm your tits, bro. I know she's your girl. But

I won't hold that against her. She just compared us to a comic book superhero, which makes her cool as fuck."

She smiles at that, and seeing that look on her face stops my over-protectiveness. At least for now.

"So, what? You guys find out about these 'very, *very* bad people' in the news and then go after them and make them sleep with the fishes?" she asks jokingly.

"Not exactly," I reply. "For example, do you recognize the name Brock Williams?"

"The swimmer guy? Yeah. I don't watch the news, but that asshole's trial was plastered all over Faceb— Wait... didn't I see something about him drowning recently? Evidence showed the idiot ran right into the pool's wall while he was swimming alone. I might have done a happy dance and yelled 'Karma!' at my computer screen." She looks between the three of us. "That was y'all?" she asks, surprised.

"Guilty!" Seth confirms, pointing at me.

Her eyes lock on mine, and I hold my breath. What will she think of me? Will she be disgusted by what I do for a living? Will she want no part of me, now that she knows I kill people for money?

"Bra-fucking-vo. That guy was a freaking douchenozzle!" While a snort leaves Seth, I'm frozen in place, my heart kick-starting and lightness filling my chest. She carries on, oblivious to the rush of love I have racing through me. "Everyone knew he killed her. And then to turn around and basically call her a whore when he got out of his short little sentence? Even I was fantasizing about offing his ass," she confesses.

I shake my head in wonder. "I fucking love you, woman," I tell her through a sigh of relief. Her face changes, a flash of emotion crossing her beautiful features.

"I love you too," she says, her voice conveying how deeply. I see her curiosity move across her face like a digital billboard before she asks, "So how does it work? How do you decide who to go after?"

"They're paid jobs, baby girl," I reply. "We get contacted by someone, in this case her father, and they pay us to get the job done. We're very particular about what we take on. We don't do bullshit like cheating spouses or other people who don't deserve it. It's strictly cases such as that one, where he only avoided his punishment because his daddy was rich and could hire a team of the sleaziest lawyers."

"Fascinating," she breathes, and I can see it clear as day she's tucking all of this away in her author brain for future use.

"Am I going to have to proof all your books before you publish to make sure you don't out us?" I cock my brow.

She looks hurt. "I would never do that."

I nod, kissing her forehead. "I know, babe. Only joking. But I'll still be reading your books from here on out. That scene you wrote me was fucking sexy. It'll be some sort of... intellectual foreplay." I grin, and she smiles.

"Well, now all that's out in the open, if you guys don't need anything else from me, I've got a date with a redheaded sub and a St. Andrew's Cross," Seth says, standing from his chair.

"It was nice to finally meet you in person, Seven," Vi tells him. "Or do I call you Seth? I'm not really sure what the rules are."

He points to himself. "Seven inside the walls of the club, Seth outside, if we ever have the pleasure of getting to hang." He points over to Doc. "Doc inside, Dr. Walker out... or Neil, but nobody ever calls him that." He gestures to me, and I cock a brow. "Sarge inside... or your future baby daddy on the outside," he tells her, humping the air and pretending to smack someone's ass, making her laugh. The sound is melodic and natural, and just one more thing that's so fucking perfect about her. I shake my head at Seth but grin, not hating the idea of someday putting my baby inside Vi.

"And what about Brian?" she asks, and I can tell she's anxious to see her old friend.

"Brian is known as Knight inside Club Alias," Doc answers, and I smirk when she bursts into a fit of giggles.

"Knight? Really? Brian Glover goes by Knight... and people take him seriously?" she questions, turning amazed eyes on me.

"I think you'll be surprised what ten years have done for the awkward baby giraffe we used to climb with, baby girl. And the nickname came from that trip we took to the Renaissance Festival in Raleigh that time, when he first started collecting swords. Kinda stuck with him," I explain.

She smiles broadly. "That was so much fun. I still have the ring you got me from one of the tents, and the necklace that has my name written on a grain of rice," she confesses, and whatever ice that might've still been clinging to my heart completely melts away.

Seth heads for the door, throwing a peace sign over his shoulder. "Deuces!" he calls, and disappears into the hallway.

"Vivian, do you have any questions? You're taking everything so well. I just want to make sure the worst of your shock is over," Doc prompts. I hold my breath. This really has gone better than I imagined.

"I guess...." She pauses, glancing at me before her eyes fall to where her hands nervously toy with the belt of the black robe she's wrapped in. "What will this mean for us? Like, I mean...." She sighs, tilting her head back to search the ceiling for what she wants to ask. "First and foremost, us, Corbin and Vi. Do we just pick up where we left off, like we didn't just spend the last ten years apart? And then secondly...." Her face pinkens, piquing my curiosity.

"What is it, baby?" I encourage.

"Well, what will it mean for us, me and my Sir?" she finishes shyly.

All the tension leaves my body when I realize she's worried about our relationship as Dom and sub. I fight the smile that tries to spread across my face, not wanting her to think I'm laughing at her concern. "If it's up to me, nothing changes as far as that's concerned, baby girl. I want nothing more than to continue with your training." She still looks worried though, and my brow furrows as she bites her lip.

"What else do you want to ask, Vivian?" Doc prompts, and I silently thank him.

"You... you own this club. You're a Dom here." She turns to stare seriously into my eyes. "I really don't want to know what's gone on with you here. I'd like to live in a fantasy bubble where you never touched another woman in the decade we lost. I know that's not true, and I know we're supposed to be completely honest with each other from here on out, but I'd like you to just... I don't want to know, okay?"

"Are you sure that's what you want?" Doc asks, a look of concern crossing his face.

"As far as that part of his life, I'm gonna go with what I don't know can't hurt me. I know myself. I'm a jealous person by nature. And in this case, curiosity will never get the best of me. I just really, *really* don't want to know," she implores.

"I can make that happen, Vi. If that's what you want, I can contact every member and make them sign another nondisclosure agreement making them agree to never speak to you of anything that's happened in this club," I reply seriously.

"I don't think all that's necessary. Just... keep your past as a Dom to yourself. The other subs, I mean. Not what you've learned."

Her coy smile is infectious. "I can do that, baby girl. And to answer your first question, you're mine. I let you go once, and you can bet your sexy little ass that'll *never* happen again."

Nineteen

Three weeks later...

LOOKING BACK AT THE PAST FEW weeks, I picture myself as a
character in one of my books. I visualize every detail, right
down to the clothes I was wearing on each day and the
food I consumed when I remembered to eat between writing,
therapy sessions, my training at the club, and the blissful time
I've spent with Corbin.

If my life were one of my stories, what would people say?
What would the reviews be if I looked on Amazon?

Those beautiful souls who believe in fairy tales, they'd be my
five-star reviewers. The ones who enjoy a good instalove story,
who look past the heartbreak they've experienced in their own
lives and can still appreciate that, for other people, love at first
sight and second chances really do exist.

But on the other end of the spectrum, I can see readers of my life story saying things like "too far from reality" or "heroine too weak" or "no one would ever forgive so easily." Little would they know that it is *my* reality. It doesn't make me weak; it just means I knew from the second I met Corbin when I was just a girl at eighteen years old that I was put on this earth to be with him. And I *did* forgive that easily.

I lost ten years with my soul mate. Why hold on to a grudge and waste more of our precious time in this world when we could just let go of everything from the past and enjoy our present and our future?

But thankfully over the past year of my writing career, I've trained myself not to dwell on people's reviews of my stories.

We've spent every spare minute of the last three weeks together catching up, making up for lost time. It became a game of sorts. I tell him something, and it's either new information or he tells me in that sexy deep voice of his "I know." If it's something he already knew about me, he then tells me where he was when he watched me. Sneaky fucker. So most of it's been more of him telling me what's been up with him over the past decade—minus anything dealing with the club.

The only thing that hurt my heart a little was the fact he lived right across the street from me for so long. He was right *there*. Within reach. All those times I had searched for him on the internet, sitting at my desk in front of the window in my bedroom, all I had to do was look out at the complex across the street, and there he would've been. When he saw my heartbreak over this, he tried to make me feel better by taking me to his condo, where he stood me in front of his window, showing me I never would've spotted him. Placing the binoculars to my eyes, I got to see his view of where I sat every day, working on my novels. Watching over me like some sort of fallen guardian angel.

With my lease ending in just over two months, we decided I should move in with him, since he owns his condo and mine is just a rental. I've been on deadline for my latest novel, so packing and transferring all my stuff has been slow going, although we've still spent every single night together, sleeping in each other's arms.

I've tried to get him to tell me stories of his mercenary missions, but he tends to change the subject. I get the feeling he wants to protect me from that side of his job. I've told him it doesn't bother me. I mean, I used to be a military wife. I knew and fell in love with him when he was a sniper in the army. I was aware of what he did overseas. So why would I feel any differently about him doing basically the same job here in the States? I don't really understand politics, and never really got why we are at war with people in other countries, so at least now I could comprehend why he would be killing the people on his list. The ones he *has* opened up about have been nothing but deserving of the justice he doles out.

But then he puts his hands and lips on me and I think of nothing else.

If I thought our sex life was amazing when we were married, it didn't hold a candle to our intimate moments now. My submissive training has been nothing short of magical. Corbin in his role as my Dominant fulfills a need inside both of us that makes our time outside the club feel even more loving. We don't use BDSM every time we have sex. We make love with a passion that can't even be described. But when we do act out a D/s scene... the sex and the aftercare leave me feeling more desired and at peace than I've ever felt. I walk out of the club feeling like a fucking queen, while our lovemaking at home makes me feel like a goddess, Corbin always taking the time to worship me in a way I know only he can.

It's with these thoughts in mind that I finish up the last love scene in the book I'm about to have to send to my editor, Bex, next week. All I have left is the grand finale and their happily-ever-after epilogue, and then I'm taking a month-long break from writing so I can pack the rest of my stuff up to move it into Corbin's place, and then enjoy just being... his.

Corbin ordered me to write at my apartment the past couple of days so I could concentrate and work in peace, because he had another job come in. He said with the constant phone calls between him and the other guys plus all the research and verbal brainstorming, it would keep me from meeting my deadline. Which, according to him, would result in me not only being yelled at by Bex, but a punishment from him as well. As much as I enjoy my "punishments" from him, I'd much rather avoid the wrath of my saucy British editor.

I close my laptop for the day, slipping it into the padded compartment of my Vera Bradley tech backpack before rolling my charging cord up and putting it into the other pocket. I thread my arms through the straps, grab my keys and phone, and head out of my apartment, locking the door behind me. I cross the street, type in the security code that opens the front door to Corbin's complex, and ride the elevator up to the condo I will be calling "ours" next week.

When I use my key, entering the foyer that spills into the huge, mostly empty living room, I automatically sense that Corbin isn't home. I drop my bag on his one recliner, turning to head for the bathroom. I've been commanded to take a hot bath after every writing session. He told me it always killed him watching me through my window, trying to pop my back on my desk chair after hunching over my laptop for hours. He gives me a backrub every night at bedtime. It usually turns into a sensual massage that leads to even more pleasurable activities.

As I cross the room, passing by his massive desk, one that looks similar to the one in his office at the club, I notice a folder that's fallen between it and the filing cabinet next to it. The manila folder sticks out against the dark hardwood flooring on this side of the desk, but wouldn't have been seen from the rolling chair on the opposite side. Hoping it's nothing Corbin would be missing right now, I shimmy it up the crack, pulling my cell out of my pocket to call him to see if he wants me to take it to him wherever he's working. Most of the time, they meet at their security office next to the club, but sometimes they choose one of the guys' places to convene.

I carry the folder into the bedroom and notice a piece of paper in the middle of the bed.

Vi,
I will be home in the morning. Wrapping up the job tonight. Take your bath and get some rest. I have a scene planned for tomorrow evening, and you'll need your strength.
Love,
C

A chill goes up my spine and I grin. I can only imagine that "wrapping up a job" would be quite the adrenaline rush. Plus, the sense of mortality would definitely make a person want to do something to make them feel alive. I can't wait to see what he has planned.

Remembering the guys didn't bother Brian while he was on his job, I decide not to message Corbin, just in case he's already in a situation where he shouldn't be distracted. Instead, I pick up the folder with full intentions of taking it back to his desk... but curiosity gets the better of me.

Everyone knows that saying "curiosity killed the cat." But never have I fully understood the meaning behind it until this very moment. A proverb used to warn people against sticking their nose where it shouldn't be. I shouldn't have opened that file. I know this, as I stare into the cold, soulless eyes of my rapist.

My legs give out from under me and my ass lands on the end of the bed, the folder hitting the floor as its contents spill out. There are countless photos, past and I guess present, of Alan in various situations. The one of him on the red carpet with one of the actresses from his film, a couple of pictures of him that come up in a Google search, and then also some taken out in public, the kind you see in movies, snapped with a long-lens camera by a PI, the subject unaware while they're buying coffee, shopping, or getting into a car.

I slide off the edge of the bed and crouch over the file, reaching for some papers and seeing they're notes Corbin has made. Everything I'd had in a folder on my computer is here, with the addition of the past two years I haven't followed up. The last I knew, Alan lived in Austin while he did his director thing. According to the paper in my hand, he no longer lives half a country away, a safe enough distance that allowed my mind to stop worrying he would ever come after me. No, this says he lives only an hour and a half away in Wilmington, where he teaches theater arts at the university there.

So close, within a short driving distance. Working every day around girls the age I was when he'd assaulted me. I never turned him in. I was too afraid, too ashamed. And now, because I didn't tell anyone what he'd done to me, no one knew not to hire him for a job that put him in a position of authority around young women. No one knew he was a rapist. God only knows if I was the only one he did that to, or if there are more of his victims out there like me, who never said anything either.

Or maybe he had struck again, but instead of going to the police, the survivor hired Imperium Security to get the job done. But that would mean Alan had gone beyond assaulting his victim this time. As horrible and traumatizing a crime raping someone is, it doesn't equal taking the attacker's life.

So I start searching through the papers, looking for any indication of who could've hired Corbin. A check stub for the job, the name of Alan's victim, anything, but there is absolutely nothing here. What I do find, though, is a complete manuscript of my session with Dr. Walker, when I had gone into detail of what happened to me, along with a log of Alan's movements over the past several weeks. And that's when I see the Post-It note stuck to the very back of the folder.

March 28
8pm

"Oh no," I breathe. "No, baby. Nononono...," I chant as I scramble for my phone, and when I light it up, I see it's 6:52 p.m., today's date, March 28, scrolled beneath the time like an omen. Finding Corbin in my Recent Calls log, I press Send. "Pick up, pick up, pick up," I beg, letting out a frustrated cry when it goes to voice mail. "Corbin, baby, I know what you're doing. Please, you have to stop. Don't do this."

I hop up off the floor with the papers tracking Alan's routine gripped in my hand. Grabbing my purse from the chair by the bedroom door, I then toss my phone inside before hurrying to Corbin's recliner to scoop up my keys. I barely take the time to lock the door behind me before I run full speed toward the elevator.

I hit the button over and over, knowing damn well it won't make the elevator move any faster, but if I don't do something to expend some of this anxiety, I will have a full-on panic attack. When the doors ding open, I jump inside and hit the button for the parking garage.

I run to my car, thanking the gods the door unlocks automatically as I get near it with my keys, plop down into the driver seat, slam my foot down on the brake, and push the ignition button. I back out of the parking spot like a fucking stunt driver, hardly glancing in my mirror to see if anyone is behind me. Wilmington is an hour and a half away. I'll never make it in time with just a little over an hour to get there to stop Corbin.

I make it to the highway without passing any cops, but as soon as I see the exit that will put me on the clear shot to the outer banks city I'm heading to, my foot presses on the gas, the needle shooting up well past the speed limit. Using the buttons on my steering wheel, I try calling Corbin again, but it goes straight to voice mail without even ringing this time over the Bluetooth speakers. I don't leave a message knowing he's turned his phone off, which means he's probably already in place—wherever he plans to murder Alan.

I reach over and grab the paper off my passenger seat. It's so obsessively organized that I find Alan's Tuesday activities quickly.

Tuesday
A.M.
7:00- Morning run/workout at campus gym
9:00 – 10:50- Class 1
11:00- Lunch, normally on campus
P.M.
12:10 – 2:00- Class 2
2:00 – 5:00- Office hours, Room 262, same hallway as classroom
5:00 – 6:00- Dinner, Denny's on Ocean Ave.
6:00 – 8:00- Teaches private acting class in local theater next door to Denny's
8:00- Returns home, 342 Magnolia St. Apt. 2C

Glancing at the time on the dashboard, I see it's now 7:22 p.m. Trying my best not to swerve, I type in his home address, seeing how that's where he should be at the time Corbin wrote on the Post-It note in the folder. When Siri is done calculating, it tells me I should arrive at 8:27 p.m.

"Fuck!" I yell, slamming my hand down on the steering wheel. I should give up. I should stop racing down this highway at breakneck speeds, turn around, and wait for Corbin to return home in the morning. There's no use.

But it's the memory of why I lied to him ten years ago that keeps me moving toward my destination. Alan had been so strong, completely immovable when he attacked me. He wasn't some little pipsqueak who got lucky in his mission to overpower me. No. He was a pretty big guy. Not as muscular as Corbin by any stretch of the imagination, but taller and had mass to him.

If I were to go back to wait for my love to return, and then him never show up because Alan hurt him, I would never be able to live with myself.

I *have* to get to him.

Twenty

Corbin

I GLANCE AT MY WATCH. 7:58 P.M. From my car in the Denny's parking lot, I have the perfect view of the front door to the local theater where Alan is finishing up tonight's acting class.

I've fantasized about this moment over and over since the very second the truth was revealed. So many ways I could make him pay, but the result was always the same. It would cost Alan his life for what he did to my wife.

I know our code, a life for a life. But what he'd done to Vi... he had ruined hers that night, making her live with what happened for the past ten years, so what the fuck is the difference? And no matter how much healing she does, no matter how happy we will be from now until the day she dies, we'll never get that time back, and she'll still have to carry around the memory of her assault. I'll spend the rest of my days on this earth trying to make her forget, but it will always be there. Even if she goes a long time without ever thinking about it, something could always trigger the memory. A stranger in passing who looks like Alan. A waft of whatever cologne he was wearing that night as we walk through a department store. Fuck, who knows? The tiniest, most inconsequential thing could pull it back out. It'll never fully disappear.

And it's with these thoughts in mind that when I watch the cocksucker himself exit the building and get into his Ford Focus that's seen better days, I follow him. I keep enough distance that the wannabe actor will never suspect he's playing the part of prey to my predator.

A short time later, he pulls into the parking lot of his rundown apartment complex and I keep driving, turning into the parking lot on the opposite side of the building. I cut the engine and hop out, grabbing my backpack full of tricks out of the back seat before I close the door quietly. I still haven't decided which tool I'll use to make him suffer. Or maybe I'll take the time to use them all. With only an hour and a half drive home and Vi not expecting me to get back until tomorrow, I've got all night to play this game.

With Brian's help, who kept surveillance on Alan after the job he finished up three weeks ago, I know exactly what he does every night of the week, right down to when he likes to take a shit. No friends to speak of, no family in this state, the only people to miss him will be the students and staff at the university, and even they won't know something's happened to him for almost two days, since he doesn't teach another class until Thursday afternoon.

I check my watch again as I climb the stairs leading to his apartment, passing no one on the way up, and I see it's 8:11.

Knowing that he always drops his shit at the door and heads straight into his bathroom to shower every single night like clockwork, entrance will be a breeze.

I stand in front of his door and pull off my backpack long enough to grab the black leather mask and matching gloves inside, tugging them on. How poetic to kill the motherfucker while wearing the very same hood I wore while I acted the part of him during Vi's anger expression scene. It was this mask she stared up at as she healed herself with her screams. And it's this mask that will be the last vision Alan will ever see, burned into his mind for all eternity as he's finally dragged through the gates of hell.

I pick the lock as easily as I would open his front door with a key, entering the dank apartment and shutting it behind me silently. I hear the water running behind the wall immediately to my right, and I set my backpack down next to the bathroom door. I close my eyes for a moment, bracing my hands against the doorframe, shifting through the Rolodex of ways to make him pay.

A sinister grin spreads across my face behind my mask, deciding exactly how to begin. I'll have to be careful at first; with him in the shower, I don't want to risk him slipping and smashing his head open. No. That would be entirely too quick a death for someone deserving of torture.

I hurry to his tiny kitchen, pulling open drawers almost noiselessly as I search for the one thing I'll need. Bingo. I slide it into my pocket and make my way back. I bend down and unzip the front pocket of my bag, pulling out the preloaded syringe full of street-grade fentanyl, one of the many drugs Alan went to rehab for. I uncap the needle, holding it up and pressing the plunger just enough that a tiny bit of the liquid comes out, making sure there's no air in the tube. Then, taking a step back in the narrow entryway, I lean my back up against the wall directly in front of the bathroom door and wait.

I can only imagine the shock Alan will feel as he opens the door, completely unsuspecting, and sees me standing here, entirely dressed in black, my leather hood in place. I'm sure I look like a fucking executioner, or maybe Death himself.

The water shuts off, and I hear the rings holding the shower curtain screech across the metal rail. I stand up straight, syringe gripped in my hand with my thumb on the plunger, hearing shuffling, as if he's drying off with a towel. I glance at my watch one last time—8:22 p.m.—before covering it with my black sleeve.

Finally, I hear the doorknob jiggle, and every muscle in my body tenses, a panther ready to pounce. The door opens, and all the steam from the shower billows out, revealing Alan with a red towel wrapped around his waist. When his eyes discover my still form right in front of him, it's a look of confusion that crosses his face first, as if he's trying to figure out if he's just seeing things. But as I raise the needle in my black-gloved hand, I finally get the reaction I was waiting for. Pure unadulterated terror fills his black, soulless eyes.

Before he can even take a breath, my hand shoots out with flawless precision, jabbing the needle and depressing the plunger in the inner crease of his elbow, his arm stretched out in invitation with his hand still on the doorknob. Even though my emotions are in this job, the kill completely personal, my head is clear. I still have to make this look self-inflicted. Alan being a former druggie just makes it so beautifully easy.

"Fuck!" he yelps, jerking his arm away, but it's too late. He stumbles backward, his ass landing on the sink behind him as his towel comes loose, toiletries and his glass bottles of cologne falling to the tile floor beneath his feet. They shatter, setting off an explosion of sickly strong scents—so potent I can smell it through the leather of my hood.

"Evenin', Al." My voice is almost maniacal, and his eyes widen as I step closer.

"Who are you? W-what do you want?" he stutters, not quite slurring. The drug affects his body first, making everything warm, lax, and heavy feeling. I chose it because it wouldn't totally knock him out with this size dose. I want him conscious for everything I do to him. Just like Vi was.

"I'm the man whose wife you raped, and I'm here to make you pay," I answer conversationally, and his head jerks back, clanging against the glass mirror behind him. "Careful now, bud. No knocking yourself out."

"I-I... I didn't rape her, man. She came to my office begging for it. She flirts with me every day in class," he rushes out, his body slowly melting into the bowl of the sink.

I smirk behind my mask. So the motherfucker had done this to more than just my sweet Vi. Makes this even sweeter. "Hmm... this sounds so familiar. 'Stop fighting it,' you told her. 'I know you want me. I see it every day.'" I take another step into the bathroom, and the fucking pussy immediately bursts into tears. "'Stop all your fucking crying, *Vivian*. Relax. Just let it happen. You know you want it.'"

The color drains from his face, realizing exactly who I'm here to avenge. "I... I—"

"Raped my wife, when all she wanted to do was make sure you were safe?" I tilt my head, reaching into my jeans to pull out the steak knife I grabbed from his kitchen. I watch the panic fill his eyes. I see the struggle on his face, his mind telling his body to get up and fight, or at least run, but all he can do is jerk his limbs a bit.

I take one last step toward him, raising the knife. "'If you just stop fighting it, I'll make it feel good.'" With that final disgusting line he'd said to my baby girl, my fist plunges downward, stabbing directly into the root of his pathetic excuse for a cock.

His face turns ghost white as he sucks in a breath to scream, but my gloved hand clamps across his mouth right as he releases his girlish shriek, smashing his head against the mirror as he had done to Vi in his bed. I twist the knife still in my grip, watching the blood vessels in his eyes burst as he continues to scream against my hand. I look down, admiring how the blood gushes from the hole in his dick, turning the red towel beneath him a darker shade of crimson. Right as I'm about to lift my knife to stab him again, I hear a voice behind me.

"Baby, stop."

I look up into the mirror, seeing Vi in its reflection. Is she an apparition? Is she the angelic half of my conscience, telling me I shouldn't break our code? She can't really be here. How would she have known?

"Corbin." She takes a step closer, and I feel her hand come to rest in the middle of my back. That's when I know she's real. "You can't do this, baby. You have to stop."

She goes to take a step to see around me, but I halt her movement. My body would be blocking her view of the butchery that lies before me. "Don't move," I order in my Dom voice, and she instantly stills, her fingers flexing between my shoulder blades. "You can't see this, baby girl. You need to get out of here.

Now." I watch her face in the mirror. Everything in her is telling her to follow my demand, yet she struggles against it. I see her take a deep breath, letting it out slowly. "Don't do it, Vi," I growl, knowing full well she's mustering her courage, the exact same way she would years ago when she rock climbed. I know after she takes that next breath, she's going to dyno, leaping into this with her whole heart.

Her chest expands as she closes her eyes, and then she takes one giant step sideways to the right. I watch her beautiful green eyes open in the reflection, meeting the slits in my leather hood, before they lower to the massacre beneath my hand.

She gasps, her hand coming up to cover her mouth, and her eyes raise to look into the ones of her rapist. He's stopped his screaming, only having the energy to whimper behind my leather glove, tears pouring from his eyes and dripping down over my glove. As his blood drains, his body wilts, and probably the only reason he's still conscious is because the drug I gave him elevated his pain tolerance.

Vi swallows, meeting my stare in the mirror once again. "You... you cut it off?" she whispers.

"Not yet," I answer, my voice steady.

"Baby, you can't kill him. If you do, it will have all been for nothing. All that time I gave up with you, the lie I told to keep you from killing him, to keep you out of jail, it would have been for *nothing*. You don't kill people who haven't taken a life," she tells me, her voice low but steady.

"He took *our* life, Vi. The second he attacked you, he stole our perfect life together," I murmur, my hand holding the knife twisting once more.

"But I've got you back now. He's not worth it, Corbin. Don't do this," she begs, but it's too late for me to just let him go.

"I can't, baby girl. He knows who we are," I say, and Alan tries to shake his head beneath my grip. He mumbles something, his eyes crossing a moment before they focus on mine again.

"Let him speak," Vi tells me, and wanting to give her whatever she needs for closure, I remove my hand, keeping it raised in case he tries to scream for help.

"I won't tell anyone," he slurs. "I swear, I won't tell anyone."

I shake my head. "And how exactly would you explain your tiny dick being fileted, motherfucker?" I growl, dragging the serrated edge of the knife up and down a couple of times, testing just how easy it would be to split it down the middle. I tilt it at an angle, slicing up the center of his balls. But he barely even registers my movement, his body in shock along with the help of the drug. "Say by some miracle you make it to a hospital. What the fuck could you say that would explain *this*?" I grip the hair at the top of his head and yank his face downward, forcing him to look at the minced meat between his legs that used to be his cock.

He cries harder at the sight, shutting his eyes as he sobs. "I... I don't know. Please. Just... don't kill me," he begs.

"Attempted suicide," Vi says over my shoulder, and I meet her eyes in the mirror. I allow Alan to lift his head. "You were attempting suicide. What did you give him, Corbin?"

"Fentanyl," I reply.

"I'm not sure what that is," she confesses, but I see her author brain starting to work up a story.

"O-one of the drugs... I used to do," Alan slurs.

"Yeah, but not the one you were on when you forced yourself

on my wife," I growl, wondering why I'm even having this conversation as my hand twists the knife once again.

"Baby, stop!" Vi shouts, and I immediately halt my movement. "You were attempting suicide. You took the drugs, and being the failed aspiring actor you are, if you couldn't be famous in life, you wanted to be immortalized with your death. You cut your own... penis," she says, flapping her hand in the direction of his annihilated organ, "as some... artistic bullshit."

Alan nods at the same time I shake my head. "No. There's no way. We can't trust him not to tell the police who we are, that I did this."

"I'll do anything, man. I swear I won't tell anyone!" Alan pleads, and something in those soulless eyes of his almost makes me believe him.

"Look, Corbin. We got our revenge. He'll never be able to hurt another woman ever again. He'll never be able to have sex for the rest of his life, even if he *could* find a person who would say yes. Let him go, baby," she whispers, wrapping her tiny hand around my bicep.

I close my eyes, trying to clear my head and think this through. I can't risk the cocksucker ratting us out. But I can't do something Vivian is begging me not to do.

"Please. You promised. We swore no more secrets and lies. But you kept this from me. You told me you had another job come in. You made me believe it was something else. A lie by omission is still a lie," she says, and a wave of guilt crashes over me. "But I will forgive you if let him go."

The three of us fall silent, the room seeming to hold its breath as everyone waits for me to make my decision. With one last glance into Vivian's eyes, even though it goes against everything inside me, I nod.

"Thank you," Alan sobs, making my eye twitch.

"Listen, you sick fucking excuse for a human being. I'll agree to leave here with you still alive, but I swear to Christ, if you do not follow exactly what I'm about to tell you, there's an entire team of people who will hunt you down and finish what I started. And they will have strict orders to make it as slow and painful as humanly possible. Do you understand?" I growl.

"Y-yes," he whispers, fear evident in his face as his chin trembles.

"You were attempting suicide, everything Vi said. Going out with a fucking bang so people would talk about your dumb ass for years to come. But here's the kicker, and I *will* know if you say it or not. You confess to the police that the reason you were castrating yourself is because you were ashamed. You couldn't deal with the guilt of raping the women you assaulted over the years. You will not name names. You will not drag them into your fucking bullshit. You confess, and we're square. We'll never hear from each other again," I offer, and then I wait for his response.

When he finally nods, I take his hand limp at his hip and wrap it around the handle of the steak knife still skewering his cock. I stand up and look over to Vi. "Baby girl, time to use your author skills. Go type out our good friend Alan here a suicide note. His computer is in the living room."

She nods and turns to do what I ordered, but stops to eye me carefully. "Promise you won't kill him while I'm gone?"

I can't help but grin at her. "I promise, baby girl. Oh, grab a set of gloves out of my backpack in the hallway. Leave no evidence."

"Yes, Sir," she replies with a small smile on her lips, and if I didn't have an eyeful of fileted dick in front of me, the suggestive look in her eyes would've given me a hard-on.

A few minutes later, Vi returns with a sheet of paper. I look over her words, reading the note that says everything we discussed, and shove it beneath Alan as if he placed it there before hopping up on the sink to kill himself. With the drugs in his system, it could be explained that they made him do crazy shit.

"One last thing," I add, looking to Vi. "Baby, would you mind? My hands are all bloody and your gloves are still clean." She glances at me questioningly. "In my backpack, there's a kit inside the front pocket. Grab it for me please, and then go get me a spoon out of his kitchen."

"Okay," she drawls, doing as I asked.

When she comes back, I tell her, "Place the spoon on the vanity next to him and open the kit. Take out the lighter, the little envelope, and the empty syringe, and set it next to spoon, and then grab that syringe on the floor there and put it up there too." I watch her carry out my instructions, her brow furrowed in confusion. "Good girl. Grab his cell phone there on the back of the toilet and put it on the opposite side of his body to the black tar heroin we just offered him as a party favor."

"Corb—"

"Uh, uh, uh, baby girl. I'm keeping my promise. I'm not going to kill him. And even better, I'm giving him a choice." I turn to Alan one last time. "Option A: Do what we discussed. Use your cell to call 911, and then live out your days in jail as a eunuch. Option B: There's enough of one of your old favorites in that envelope to put you out of all our misery. The choice is yours, just make it quick if you go with A. You'll bleed out pretty soon."

I turn to Vi. "Hmm, I guess there's an Option C," I joke, pulling off my gloves, turning them inside out to keep the blood from dripping.

I bend down outside the door to grab a baggie from inside my backpack, dropping the gloves inside before zipping it up. I yank off my hood, turning it inside out as well. I'll be burning all of this, the gloves, the clothes I'm wearing. Even the hood. And with it, we'll be setting fire to the memory of what Alan did to my wife, hoping to turn it to ash that will blow away, never to return. "Turn the knob for me, baby girl. It's time to go," I tell her, and she moves around me to the door. I lace my arms through the straps of my backpack and take one last glance at Alan's pathetic form on top of his sink.

And I sigh in relief as I see him reach for the spoon.

Epilogue

Vi

One month later...

"OH GOD!" I SCREAM AS CORBIN pounds into me from behind, making me come for the fourth time tonight. I'm blindfolded, strapped to a spanking horse—similar to a sawhorse that's been padded and wrapped in leather—our combined juices dripping down my legs as they tremble. If it weren't for the bench beneath me, I would've collapsed a half hour ago.

Finally, he roars behind me, emptying himself into me before covering my back with his muscular chest, kissing my neck.

Suddenly, with him still inside me, I feel something cool link around my throat. My hands are tied, so I can't reach up to feel what it is. He pulls out of me gently, and then his hands are at my ankles, unlocking them from the spanking horse. He comes around to my head and unties my wrists from the front of the bench before wrapping a robe around me, its familiar silky texture draping over my skin.

He scoops me up in his arms, carrying me over to our aftercare chair, and once I'm cradled there against his chest, he finally removes the blindfold. I blink, trying to make my eyes adjust after being in the pitch-black for over an hour while he brought my body to heights I've never reached before.

My hands find the jewelry at my throat, and I feel it until I reach a tiny lock, and tears fill my eyes. "You collared me?" I breathe, staring into those mesmerizing chocolate eyes I'll get to look into for the rest of my life.

"I did, and if you'll let me..." He reaches behind me and grabs something off the table that sits beside the leather chair. "Vi, will you marry me... again?" He smiles, opening the box showcasing the most beautiful ring I've ever seen. "I know I made a big deal out of our engagement the first time, but this time... I just wanted it to be us and—"

"Yes!" I cry, wrapping my arms around his neck, pulling him close to kiss him fiercely. When I finally let him go, he gives me the smile that never fails to make me melt.

"I love you, baby girl," he tells me, and I can see he means it with every fiber of his being.

"I love you too, Sir," I reply impishly, giggling when he tickles my side. When his hands settle around me once again, I nuzzle my forehead into his neck, looking down at the gorgeous ring on my finger. "I wonder what people would think if I wrote our story, published it as one of my books."

He chuckles, kissing the top of my head. "Do it. It's not like anyone would figure out it was based on a true story. Looking back at the last thirteen years, who could make this shit up?"

I smile, tilting my head back to look up into his perfect face. "Very true. And I know at least my VB Lowe's Lovelies would love it," I say, talking about my reader group on Facebook.

"Why is that?" he prompts, kissing the tip of my nose.

"Because... it would have hot sex and a happily ever after. As long as I give them that, they're happy girls." I smile.

"What about you?" he asks, tracing my jawline and sending chills throughout my body.

"Hmm?" I close my eyes, leaning in to his touch.

"Is that all I need to make you happy? Hot sex and a happily ever after?" he clarifies, leaning forward to kiss up the column of my neck.

"As long as that happily ever after includes spending the rest of my life with you, then that's exactly right," I breathe, as he trails his fingers down my sternum then moves to cup my breast.

"Confession time?" he whispers when he reaches my ear, and I blink my eyes open, knowing he only says that when he's about to tell me something important.

"Yeah, baby?"

"That's all I need too, but I want that happily ever after to include one more thing, maybe two. Three max," he says, and my brow furrows in confusion. "But the first one has to be a boy. That's an order."

As I realize the meaning behind his words, my eyes immediately fill back up with tears, but my face splits in a smile so wide it almost hurts.

"Yes, Sir."

The End

TRUTH *revealed*

TRUTH *revealed*

TRUTH *revealed*

revealed

revealed

Acknowledgements

I was on lots of pain meds after my surgery when I wrote the acknowledgements for book 1, Before the Lie, and I left out two very important people. Stacia, thank you for all the help you've given me since my very first book. You can catch a continuity issue like no other, and I love you for it! That goes for this book too! And John White, thank you for helping me remember all of our climbing lingo. It had been fourteen years since I'd been on a wall, and you not only jogged all those awesome memories, but had me dying laughing with all your jokes. You're a punny guy! ;-)

My sisterwife, Sierra, although I couldn't swing your character coming back from Hawaii to be the one to off Alan, thank you for being there for me 24/7 and for our hours-long FaceTime calls. I live for those and our bathtub snaps, even though our tub addiction will one day get us killed. #ourpoortoes #deathbybubblebath

Laura, now that I have you not five minutes away, I'll never be able to survive without you again. I hope Logan knows I only set y'all up so I could have you closer. (Just kidding, Logie. Love you!) Our brainstorm at Dunn Bros saved this book. Sorry (not sorry) I made you cry. A lot.

Crystal Burnette and JM Walker, who knew a duet with such a dark and ugly undertone could spark such bright and beautiful friendships? I'm so happy to have grown so close to the two of you through writing and sharing this story with y'all. I couldn't have gotten through Chapter 16 without you.

Jo Webb, my favorite Brit. Your encouragement and enthusiasm over Corbin and Vi's tale is unmatched. You're irreplaceable.

Aurora Rose Reynolds, I stole your hubby's name for my favorite character in this story, Dr. Neil Walker. When I thought, "I need a dude's name, a strong yet caring man who would do anything to help those he cares about," I automatically thought of y'all. My favorite couple in all the land. Thank you for your unwavering support. Love you!

My Hot Tree babes, Becky, Franci (my PA Extraordinaire), Barb, Rebecca, Mandy, and Tina. I cannot WAIT until Atlanta, when I'll have almost all of my favorite girls in one place for one giant group tackle hug of epic proportions! Thank you for all your hard work on my duet!

Cassy Roop and Golden Czermak, thanks again for being my dream team! And Matthew Hosea, for being the face of one of my favorite voices in my head, Corbin.

Thank you, Shannon Rutherford, for your brilliant nurse brain. That ending was so important to me to get right, and I couldn't have done it without your help!

KD-Rob's Mob, thank you to every single one of y'all for cheering me on. I hope this was worth the wait!

Last but not least, my wonderful hubby and our sweet girls. Thank you for letting me write. It's a dream come true.

I've truly gotten my happily ever after.

Made in United States
North Haven, CT
06 September 2022

23710370R00226